Cira lay asleep in the shadow of the granite. Then she awoke all at once, like a cat, and looked up to see a man sitting on a dust-colored horse watching her.

Lee did not ask any questions or seek any answers or say anything at all. He simply reached out to her. She took his hands as he lifted her up in front of him. This movement and the swell of the saddle made Cira slide back against Lee. She felt the heat of his body through her dress, felt his thighs against hers and his arms holding her. She watched his sun-browned fingers tighten on the reins, guiding the tall horse.

"I wanted to be on a mountaintop with only sky around me," she murmured, as much to herself as to him.

"Yes," he said, lips touching her neck. "I'll take you there. . . ."

GOLDEN EMPIRE

A. E. Maxwell

FAWCETT GOLD MEDAL • NEW YORK

GOLDEN EMPIRE

© 1979 A. E. Maxwell

Published by Fawcett Gold Medal Books, a unit of CBS Publications, the Consumer Publishing Division of CBS Inc.

First Fawcett Gold Medal printing: October 1979

ISBN: 0-449-14267-1

Printed in the United States of America

10 9 8 7 6 5 4 3 2 1

GOLDEN EMPIRE

1887

The dry Santa Ana wind swept between the shoulders of the San Moreno mountains and gusted down foothills cured gold by long days of California sun. The wind blew across the broad coastal plain with hot impatience until it plunged into narrow canyons leading from plain to sea. There in the canyons' shadowed places, the wind spent itself. When it finally emerged the wind was no more than a sigh breathed over the waters of Blue Lagoon.

The lagoon was as spectacular as its name was prosaic; it was as though the unknown Yankees who first saw it were so overwhelmed that they could only describe by understatement. The instant that the green combers surged between the tips of Blue Lagoon's crescent beach, the waves' color changed to vivid blue. The change was total, almost shocking. Sailors knew that the transformation was caused by a dramatic change in the ocean floor, but most people preferred to explain the sudden shift of color by citing an Indian legend that told of a god who made too much sky. The god could neither use the last, flawless piece nor could he bear to throw it away. So he fitted the dazzling fragment of sky between the arms of a deep crescent beach that came to be known as Blue Lagoon.

The god's thoughtfulness was remembered long after his name was forgotten. In a land where natural beauty was commonplace, Blue Lagoon became a mecca for ragged painters and wealthy pleasure seekers. By 1890, Blue Lagoon was known as "the finest resort in the Californias, Spanish or Yankee." A Parisian with the business instincts of an Arab trader had built a nineteen-room luxury hotel near the southern tip of the sandy crescent. The hotel was angular and dark, the very latest in Victorian architecture; surprising peaks and cupolas overlooked the pale honey beach where foam hissed shoreward from spent blue waves. Above the reach of even spring tides, a long boardwalk fronted the new hotel. There, protected from sand and salt spray, fashionable ladies swayed in long dresses and lace gloves, their fragile kid shoes daringly revealed by random surges of wind.

Crowded behind the hotel like butterflies sunning their wings, a dozen tents held the overflow of those guests too adventurous or too impatient to wait for a room. Their fanciful Arabian shelters fanned up to the edge of a clear creek that divided the small triangle of hotel land from the rest of the beach. Though the creek was rarely more than two feet wide and two inches deep, only one tent had abandoned the crowded field for the inviting sands on the other side.

Leander Champion Buckles III slouched in the saddle one leg hooked around a saddlehorn whose leather had worn through to the wooden frame. Lee eyed the flapping tent with growing anger. Everything from Blue Lagoon to the San Moreno mountains was part of the Buckles Ranch—everything but the tiny wedge of land beneath Cartier's hotel. There was nothing Lee could do about the wedge, but the stray tent was another matter.

Lee straightened and spoke softly to his horse. The big chestnut spun, pawing nervously, upset by the snapping pennants hung from every one of the tent's guyropes. Lee's long legs closed around the fractious horse. The chestnut leaped forward, scattering sand and screaming seagulls into the morning sun. In one continuous motion,

Lee bent, yanked a guyrope free and wrapped it around the saddlehorn. He turned the chestnut and kicked it into a plunging run toward the water.

The guyrope sang taut. The gaudy tent collapsed across the sand like a torn balloon. Muffled screams and startlingly clear oaths told Lee that the tent was occupied. He laughed and urged his horse on as it dragged the deflated tent down to the surf. A man fought free of the canvas, swearing and spitting sand. Behind him crawled a woman whose words spoke eloquently of French gutters. Lee freed the guyrope from his saddlehorn and turned to face the enraged pair.

"If you're half as thorough as your swearing," said Lee in French to the disheveled woman, "his money might not have been wasted."

Startled by the roughly dressed rider who spoke perfect French, the woman closed her roughed mouth and looked Lee over in open appraisal.

"Who are you?"

Her voice had once been husky, but was now hoarse with too much whiskey and too many men. Lee looked at the flesh overflowing her silk wrapper and his amusement faded. Like the gaudy tent, the French slut violated the clean curves of Blue Lagoon. He turned toward the man whose swearing had stopped the moment he had measured Lee's size.

"You're on Buckles land."

"But Cartier told me—"

"Cartier is a liar and a whoremaster," Lee said matter-of-factly as he reined the dancing chestnut around.

Without another word or glance, Lee kicked his horse into a gallop. A cloud of seagulls lifted off the beach, screaming their ire at being disturbed. The gulls were still wheeling and calling shrilly when Lee's horse switched directions, heading for the trail that wound between creek and canyon.

Cira Pico McCartney measured the pace of the horse and its angry rider. Impulsively, she slipped into the thick brush that grew along the creek. She crouched, concealing

9

her slender outline behind a screen of greasewood. She pressed her hands against her lips, smothering her laughter at the memory of the barely dressed couple sputtering out of their collapsed tent.

But that memory fled when the chestnut plunged to a stiff-legged halt not thirty feet from her. She regretted the impulse that had sent her into hiding, yet it was too late to come out now. She waited, as still as a fox, while Lee's eyes raked the underbrush. The intensity of his stare frightened her. For an instant it seemed that their eyes met; though she knew he could not see her behind the brush, she felt a sudden breathlessness. She wanted to run, but could not make her body obey. Fear and pride and an emotion she could not name flushed her cheeks and made her eyes shine like jet.

Just as Cira forced his legs to straighten, the chestnut reared and lunged into a gallop that was too fast for the twisting, brushy trail. Lee did not look back, but his amused smile was burned into Cira's memory, as was the animal grace that made him a part of his big horse.

Cira stalked out of her hiding place, yanking twigs and pungent leaves out of her hair and thinking words that would have appalled her pious mother. Cira was thoroughly humiliated to know that she had hidden from a man who would not recognize her if he had ridden right over her, a man who owned land that had belonged to her ancestors. No Pico should ever hide from a gringo, no matter how unnerving that gringo was.

With a lithe movement of hips and shoulders, Cira straightened the embroidered peasant blouse and rose-colored skirt that she had borrowed from her cousin Yolanda. The adventure that she and her cousin had been planning for the last ten days was beginning badly.

Cira stared down the narrow trail where the sound of the horse's passage was fading. She strained forward, trying to catch the last urgent hoofbeats and remembering how Lee Buckles had looked as he controlled the huge, half-wild horse. The memory was so vivid that for an instant she felt as though she were crouched again in the brush, stalked by a man's searching gray eyes.

Cira turned and ran toward the hotel, fighting the impulse to look over her shoulder. Her feet raced soundlessly between the colorful mounds of tents and up to the hotel's wide front porch. She stood there for a moment, catching her breath and remembering Yolanda's advice.

"Señor Harry is easy to work for, as long as you act stupid and don't mind being pinched."

With an inner trembling Cira would never admit, she smoothed her tousled black hair and opened the heavy door. The inset of stained-glass window glowed like jewels in the sunlight as she closed the door very quietly behind her.

"Hey, you!"

Cira kept walking quickly, afraid to look into the gloom where the voice had come from. She did not think anyone at the hotel would recognize her in a role of serving girl, but wanted to make sure by giving as few people as possible a good look at her face.

"Hey, Mex!"

A hand that was both soft and strong clamped on her shoulder spinning her around. She let her hair fall into her face and stood round-shouldered to conceal the lines of her figure.

"What in hell you think you're doing?" demanded the desk clerk. "This hotel is for whites only—unless you're one of Cartier's whores."

Cira kept her eyes on the floor, hiding the sudden anger that darkened them.

"No, señor," she said, slurring her voice with a thick accent. "Yolanda she is sick. I come for her."

"Yolanda? Who in—oh, she's the Mex that works in the kitchen." His hand shifted from her shoulder to her chin, forcing her face up. "Kinda young, aren't you, Mex?"

"I have seventeen years," said Cira, looking away in spite of the pressure on her chin.

His hand tightened, twisting and pulling her into a shaft of sunlight from the bay windows. The gray-haired desk clerk whistled silently as light poured over Cira's face and breasts and hips.

"You have more than that." His fingers freed her chin and patted her shoulder awkwardly. "Watch out for the men, Mex," he said, then added under his breath, "and I hope to God you aren't as innocent as you look."

Cira stared at him, afraid to move and afraid to stay.

"Kitchen's through there," he said, jerking his thumb over his shoulder. "Next time, use the back door."

Cira ducked around him and fled toward the kitchen. Only her stubborn craving for adventure kept her from running back to her ordered life and a house filled with the subtle crackle of starched black dresses. There she would be hidden from strangers' eyes and strangers' hands, safe in her room that was much like the convent her father had refused to send her to.

Cira straightened and slowed to a decorous walk. She was not a child to run home at her first fright. She would not spend her life locked in a barren room, listening to her mother weep and pray for the future of her too-beautiful daughter. Cira was seventeen, an age when most of her friends were married and many had children of their own. Her cousin Yolanda was barely fifteen, yet already she was stealing off to meet her *novio*. Cira would not spoil Yolanda's secret by running away and leaving her cousin's job undone.

As Cira walked into the kitchen, she wondered what Yolanda felt in her *novio*'s arms. She sighed as she pumped water into a heavy bucket. Mateo, the only man she was ever allowed to speak to, was twice her age and too proper to even touch her hand. She tried to imagine what it would be like to be in Mateo's arms while he whispered breathless promises against her hair. But the picture of Mateo's grave face kept dissolving into the memory of Lee Buckles riding a half-wild horse. She scrubbed and peeled vegetables until her hands were sore with the unaccustomed work, but no matter how much

12

she tried to think of another man—any man—Lee Buckles rode through her inexperienced longings.

In a suite two floors above the kitchen, Roger Heer gave the parlor a final check. The windows were open precisely three fingers' width and the fire in the marble-framed fireplace held three logs of equal length that gave heat without smoke. Seating was arranged so that only the big cherry leather armchair commanded an unhindered view of Blue Lagoon, the fireplace and every other chair in the room. Cigars, matches, ashtrays, ice, whiskey and cut crystal glasses were lined up as precisely as soldiers on review.

Franklin J. Kaiser walked out of the bedroom, shot his immaculate cuffs and lowered himself into the red leather chair. Without looking, he extended his left hand a few inches to the tabletop and picked up a large cigar. Though matches were at his fingertips, Kaiser ignored them; Heer had a match lit before Kaiser's fingers touched the supple outer leaf of the cigar. Kaiser puffed on the Havana as he squinted against the light shimmering off Blue Lagoon.

"How long have they been waiting?" said Kaiser, easing his aching knee unobtrusively.

Heer's solid gold pocket watch snapped open. Though his blue eyes never left the elegant watch face, he missed not one bit of the white-haired man's discomfort. Arthritis was gnawing away at Franklin Kaiser's body. Soon pain and age would begin to dull his uncomfortably shrewd mind; and then it would be Roger Heer's turn.

"Forty-three minutes, sir."

He returned the watch to its tiny pocket with a deftness that belied his stubby fingers. His quick hands were always unexpected, a fact that Heer found profitable when playing cards.

Kaiser blew out a cone of dense smoke. "Show the good townsmen in, Roger."

Heer made a gesture that was between a deep nod and a shallow bow, and left the room. Within minutes he was

13

back, followed by the five directors of the South County Improvement League. The introductions were brief; everyone already knew Kaiser by reputation, and there was only one man whom Kaiser wished to meet.

"Where is Lee Buckles?" said Kaiser between puffs on his cigar.

Jackson Moore, the thick-wristed son of Kansas Jayhawks, moved uncomfortably within the confines of his black broadcloth jacket.

"He was on the beach earlier," said Moore in his oddly flat voice. "Threw off some hotel guests."

Roger Heer smiled without moving his lips. He knew just which guests Moore was referring to; Heer had evicted them from this suite only yesterday, when Kaiser arrived. They had complained to Cartier, but as Cartier's money came from Kaiser's railroad accounts, the couple's complaints were met with smiling apologies and the firm offer of Cartier's best tent.

Kaiser grunted. "Buckles is good at that. He's been throwing my men off his property for quite a while, now." His fingers closed around the faceted neck of a whiskey decanter. In spite of the telltale thickness of his knuckles, Kaiser held the heavy decanter with apparent ease. He lifted it, then set it down without a jar. "I know it's early, gentlemen—but good whiskey, like a beautiful lady, should never be kept waiting."

The men murmured appreciatively and easily threw off any inhibitions about drinking before lunch. As they sipped and smoked and talked, jackets were unbuttoned and ties tugged a bit loose. Soon, everyone but Heer sat in congenial shirtsleeves with neckties doffed, discussing the immensely profitable future of the broad, nearly virgin stretch of land that separated the booming city of Los Angeles from the booming port of San Diego. Kaiser, as was his habit, said little. He sat behind a fragrant veil of tobacco smoke, smiling a smile that was no deeper than his lips, listening to the empire dreams of men whose ambitions surpassed their talents by the same factor that their waists surpassed their hat sizes.

14

Despite the fact that Kaiser could buy and sell any one of the five townsmen without straying beyond the petty cash drawer, he listened with no outward sign of boredom. He had realized long ago that if you tell people what they want to hear, they will give you everything they have; and if you listen well, people will tell you what they want to hear.

"Yessir, Mr. Kaiser," said James Harkness, the owner of a new two-story general store that was the biggest in the county. "You just give us a railroad line down through here and we'll build us a city—a county—hell, a whole section of state that will be—why it'll be the garden spot of the whole damn country! All we need is people to work and buy things and have babies."

"Amen," said Moore, gulping a shot of Kaiser's fine sipping whiskey. "Cut the Buckles Ranch in two with your railroad and our towns will have room to grow into real cities. And we'll grow with them!"

"Hear! Hear!" called several voices.

Upraised crystal glasses splintered sunlight into rich colors. Kaiser's smile stretched to include each man; when he spoke, his voice was husky with their dreams.

"This," said Kaiser, gesturing with his long cigar toward the French windows where crisp sea air stirred lace curtains, "is the most beautiful place I've ever seen. And I've seen nearly everything the world can offer. Someday this area will be the cornerstone of a civilization as advanced as Greece or Rome. A civilization that will be built by men such as yourselves. Yes, gentlemen, you're sitting in the center of the new Athens!"

The men applauded spontaneously, each one suddenly feeling as though he were at the threshold of greatness. That ability to generate visions was Kaiser's gift; it had made him one of the wealthiest men in America.

"Of course," said Kaiser, "there is still the problem of young Mr. Buckles. The government has . . . recovered . . . many of the Spanish Land Grants. Unfortunately, Buckles Ranch was not among those broken up and resold to deserving people. Almost 200,000 acres—"

"Right through the goddamn middle of the goddamn county!" interrupted Moore, nearly knocking a decanter off the table with an angry sweep of his hand.

"Allow me," murmured Heer, rescuing the decanter and filling Moore's glass with a generous measure of the potent amber whiskey.

Kaiser watched while Heer replenished other glasses. The room was too quiet; he sensed that for the others, the room had suddenly become filled with the looming presence of Leander C. Buckles.

"Roger."

Heer straightened at the sound of Kaiser's soft voice.

"Sir?"

"When did Buckles say he would be here?"

"I told him to be here before ten."

"Was that," said Kaiser, "before or after Buckles threw you off his ranch?"

Heer's face became expressionless, though his skin was tight with anger.

"After, sir."

"You really ought to be more polite when you're on private property," said Kaiser, smiling to the other men in the room. "After all, it doesn't matter if Buckles insulted your mother . . . you never met the woman yourself." Kaiser puffed on his cigar reflectively. "But you're still very young, Roger. Like Buckles. You'll both learn. Professor Kaiser will teach you." He chuckled and waved the cigar at the nearly empty ice buckets. "More ice, Roger. I rather think we'll have a long wait for our little school boy."

Kaiser's indulgent tones suggested an image of Lee Buckles in knickers, making faces at his superiors. The men laughed and leaned closer to Kaiser, basking in the voice that transformed their fear into laughter and their dreams into a reality more potent than Irish whiskey.

Roger Heer closed the door behind him and strode down the gold brocaded hallway. Beneath his feet was a thick blue and gold Persian rug, but its glowing colors and intricate design made no impact on Heer's senses. He was

16

caught up in the humiliation of the moment when Lee Buckles's hands had picked him up and dumped him into his rented buggy as though he had no more significance than a bag of corn. Kaiser's reference to that moment annoyed Heer, but did little more; Kaiser paid well for Heer to keep his emotions and Kaiser's secrets to himself. But Buckles had paid nothing. Yet.

The hotel had no formal bar. Beer and whiskey were dispensed from an anteroom just off of the kitchen. Usually Harry filled the guests' requirements, but Harry was upstairs soothing a patron who swore he had been poisoned. He had not, but the badly hungover guest took a great deal of convincing.

When Heer shouldered through the anteroom's swinging doors, only Cira was in the kitchen. Her face was flushed from the heat of the big wood stove and from anger at Harry's intimate pinches. So far, her great adventure had been nothing more than drudgery and humiliation.

"Ice," said Heer, banging the tin pails on the wooden counter.

Cira glanced up at him, then back at the roast she was slicing. She was almost through with it. She did not want to leave it, wash her raw hands with lye soap and then have to come back to the greasy roast.

"Now."

Cira sliced more quickly, sawing through the cold meat with more determination than skill.

"Don't you savvy English?" said Heer, raising his voice as though she would understand if the words were loud enough. "Ice. Now. For Mr. Kaiser. Savvy, Mex?"

Cira slapped the knife down and wiped her hands on her apron.

"If your Mr. Kaiser is in so great a hurry," said Cira, "he should be told not to send a rude errand boy."

Surprised by her lack of accent as much as by her tart words, Heer really looked at Cira for the first time. The reply he had planned was forgotten when he realized that he was standing close to as beautiful a woman as he had seen. Wordlessly he admired her tawny skin and black hair twisted into coils on top of her head. Her eyes were dark, almost black, but had surprising flecks of gold. Whatever her bloodlines were, she was not solely Mexican. But she was enough Mexican that no one would care if a man took her up to his room.

Heer continued to stare at her, his blue eyes sweeping her from hair to hemline. He had never seen such eyes or lips on any Mexican girl. And the rest of her was not girlish. She had the body and bearing of a proud woman, with high breasts and a narrow waist that invited a man's hands.

Heer leaned over the counter toward her. With a skill that she was rapidly learning, Cira defeated him. He had to move sharply to avoid the swinging pails as she snatched them off the counter. He stood back, measuring her as carefully as a miner measures a claim. She was a rare discovery; a beauty who was too young or inexperienced or both to realize her impact on men. Kaiser would be delighted with her, and Kaiser always expressed his delight generously.

When Cira returned from the ice cellar, Heer was waiting well back from the counter with his hands in his pockets.

"Thank you," he said as she approached.

Cira eyed him dubiously, but had no choice except to put the tin pails of ice up onto the counter. To her relief, he made no move toward her, though his blue eyes never left her body.

"I'm sorry I was rude," said Heer, smiling professionally. "I was angry about something else."

Cira shrugged and went back to the roast.

"Just looking makes me hungry," Heer said. "Do you suppose you could bring about a dozen sandwiches to Mr. Kaiser's room?" He smiled again. "There are some hungry men upstairs. And hungry men tip well."

Cira leaned on the knife, slicing through the tough roast. She felt his eyes on her back and looked up, only to find that he had looked away. She returned to the roast,

18

sensing that there was something happening that was beyond her understanding.

"Will you do that?" said Heer.

"It is my job," Cira answered indifferently, stacking slices of meat.

"Sure it is," he said. Then, "What's your name?"

"Mex," said Cira curtly.

Her knife swept through the stacked slices of meat, halving them neatly. Heer's lips thinned in spite of his careful control. Then his professional manner slipped back into place.

"Please don't forget the sandwiches."

Cira was too busy spreading cold beef on a platter to answer him. Heer watched until she was finished and had no further excuse to ignore him.

"I won't forget," she said, refusing to meet his eyes.

"Thank you." Heer gave her the same half-nod, half-bow that he used on Kaiser. "Señorita."

Heer smiled as he lifted the pails off the counter. Later, Cira would remember that his eyes had never smiled, but at the moment, she was too upset by her unrewarding day to be attentive to her instincts.

She picked up the knife and began cutting bread. As the thick white slices fell away from the loaf, Heer left the anteroom. Cira glanced up after the doors stopped swinging, assuring herself that he really had gone. Then she assembled sandwiches with the ease of long practice. Her father, Terrence McCartney, had had a huge appetite for sandwiches made of white bread and beef. It had taken him five years to teach his wife to make white flour bread as well as she made cornmeal tortillas, but he had persevered, for he was a man dedicated to his pleasures. His only other pleasures were the sea and whiskey. After he jumped ship in San Diego harbor with the proceeds of a loaded dice game, he had concentrated on whiskey with awesome singlemindedness.

During the last few years, McCartney had taken most of his meals out of a whiskey bottle, but Cira could remember a time when he would drink and then eat thick sandwiches made of beef and white bread. She had come to associate gringo bread with drunken, unpredictable men, a fact that did little to make her feel at ease as she hesitated before the door to Kaiser's suite.

She balanced the heavy sandwich tray, freeing one hand to knock on the door. But before her knuckles met wood, her interest was caught by a name. The people inside the room were similarly caught, for no one had heard her approach.

"Buckles will agree, because he has no other choice," said Kaiser. "Roger, get the parchment."

Heer went into the bedroom and returned with a beautifully tooled Moroccan leather box. It was the type of box used to hold jewels or gold or other precious objects. Heer opened it and pulled out a roll of dark parchment.

Kaiser held out his hand without looking away from his audience. Heer laid the roll across Kaiser's palm with the precision of a surgical nurse.

"This," said Kaiser, holding up the roll, "is a fully authenticated Spanish Land Grant of 200,000 hectares to one Don Fernando Cardoza. It is signed by the King of Spain and is dated 1795."

Kaiser looked around, his shrewd brown eyes waiting to see which man would understand first.

"The king," continued Kaiser, "was rather forgetful. Some of the hectares included in this grant were also given away in another, later royal document dated 1797." He paused, smiling at each one of them. "Would any of you care to venture a guess as to which document this one conflicts with?"

Moore began to chuckle. "Is the ink dry?"

"Very dry." Kaiser smiled slightly. "This grant—which was recently discovered by my agents in Madrid—covers the Buckles Ranch like a blanket."

Harkness leaned forward, plainly wanting to check the genuineness of the document himself.

"But is it real?"

"Real?" said Kaiser, looking at Harkness. "Of course it's real. You can see it, can't you? That's more than

20

enough reality to cloud Buckles's title, particularly if the matter is submitted to a certain judge." Kaiser tapped the document slowly against the square diamond ring that covered much of his index finger. "And let me assure you, gentlemen, that the conflicting grants will be submitted to Judge Hilms unless Buckles agrees to let my section crews begin laying rails across his land."

The five men stared at Franklin Kaiser with a mixture of admiration and uneasiness, as each man weighed outright fraud against the exigencies of empire and conscience. A slow murmur of approval rose as they settled back into overstuffed chairs and accepted another drink from Heer's deft hands.

Cira's knock seemed unnaturally loud. She grasped the tray tightly and waited for the door to open. When Heer saw who it was, he smiled and ushered her into the room as though she were guest of honor rather than kitchen wench.

"Thank you señorita. The tray goes on the table next to Mr. Kaiser."

Cira looked beyond Heer, avoiding the sudden interest that showed in the men's eyes. Heer's gesture indicated a red leather chair where a white-haired man with curling muttonchop whiskers sat. His large-knuckled hands held a parchment; the hands were still ridged with muscle, in spite of the dark spots that betrayed age. Cira stared at the parchment and the hands, guessing that the man must be Mr. Kaiser.

"Roger," said Kaiser in his husky voice, "help the child. Can't you see the tray is heavy?"

"Sorry," said Heer, taking the tray and in the same motion pinning Cira between himself and Kaiser's chair. "Thoughtless of me not to notice."

Kaiser's brown eyes appraised the young buttocks pressed against the arm of his chair. His nostrils flared slightly as he breathed the mixed scents of soap and fresh bread and youth. Heer moved even closer as he lowered the tray to the table. Cira made a small sound of pain.

21

"Do back up, Roger," said Kaiser. "You're standing on the poor child's foot. Are you all right, my dear?"

Flustered by Kaiser's fatherly tones and Heer's crowding, Cira nodded and tried unsuccessfully to squeeze past Heer.

"You're limping," said Kaiser reprovingly.

His hand moved and her floor-length skirt lifted. There was a brief view of bare, slender legs before Kaiser let the skirt fall back as far as her ankles. On her right foot, between the straps of her leather sandals, was the outline of the tip of a man's shoe.

"Such a tiny foot," Kaiser said huskily. "He must have hurt you."

Kaiser's finger slid between the sandal and her skin, rubbing slowly until the dust mark was gone. Cira was shocked motionless by the strange touch. Just as she would have jerked away, Kaiser lifted his hand and let her skirt hem drop to the floor.

"There," he said. "Better?"

Without waiting for her answer, Kaiser turned his attention back to the men, like a father who had dutifully soothed a child's hurt and now was free to pursue adult matters. The townsmen wondered whether Kaiser had noticed that Cira was not really a child at all.

Heer had no doubt; he had seen Kaiser's fractional nod as Cira walked hastily out of the room.

Kaiser listened to the men as they resumed their talk of crops and inventories, expansion and profit. The thick sandwiches melted away as surely as the ice in the tin pails, but the townsmen did not become bored with their own conversation. Occasionally they even forgot that they were waiting for the man who owned the land their dreams were built on. But each time the chest-high clock chimed another hour, silence fell and the men looked toward Kaiser for their cue. Each time, Kaiser smiled graciously and said a few phrases that rekindled their dreams.

When the clock's brass chimes burned in the slanting afternoon light, Kaiser became impatient with his game.

He had assumed hours ago that Buckles probably would not show up, but had waited because even long shots occasionally win. Now the odds were vanishingly small, even smaller than the slender foot that had been so warm beneath his finger.

Kaiser caught Heer's eye and signaled unobtrusively.

"Gentlemen," said Heer, standing up. "You have been very patient, but there's really no point in asking you to wait any longer."

Slowly, the men stood, taking a last swallow of their drinks while they groped for their ties. Heer helped men into their jackets, distributed their hats and canes, and ushered them out of the room with an efficiency that bordered on rudeness. When the last man had left, Heer looked over his shoulder at Kaiser. Kaiser nodded.

Heer strode down the hallway and stairs to the kitchen. Cira was there, working just out of reach of a fat man who was stuffing pork chops with surprising dexterity.

"Señorita," said Heer.

Harry looked up. Cira, recognizing the voice, did not.

"What is it? said Harry, looking at the greasy clock. whose hands had crept too close to dinnertime.

"There is a room that needs to be straightened before dinner."

"Call the maid," said Harry, losing interest.

"I did. No one came." Heer waited, then said clearly, "Mr. Kaiser dislikes messy rooms."

"Franklin Kaiser?" asked Harry, putting down a chop. "Yes."

Harry took a quick step and pinched Cira very low on her buttocks. "You heard him, Mex. Jump!"

With trembling hands, Cira yanked off her apron and followed Heer. She was as angry as she had ever been in her life. She was tired of scut work and prying eyes and Harry's rude fingers. And she was a bit afraid of Heer.

As though he sensed her fear, he opened the door to the suite and walked in without looking back.

"The room will be empty for about an hour," Heer said, lifting an overcoat off the tall mirrored rack that

23

stood along one wall. He glanced at her when she stopped on the far side of the threshold. "Relax, señorita," he said shrugging into the coat. "I'm going out on the boardwalk."

Cira entered the room, careful to stay well out of his reach. She looked disdainfully at the debris of a futile afternoon. Empty and half-empty crystal glasses, smudged decanters and overflowing ashtrays, crusts and greasy scraps strewn on chairs and tables. And even the bracing sunset wind could not dispel the stink of chewed cigar butts.

"Start in the bedroom," Heer said as he buttoned up his coat and pulled on dark kid gloves. "That way, if Mr. Kaiser wants to dress early, he won't have to wait for you."

Cira nodded, relieved to have an excuse to leave his presence. Heer watched as she shut the bedroom door behind her back. Immediately, he closed and bolted the door to the hall.

Cira looked around the bedroom, seeing nothing out of place, nothing for her to clean up. Then she realized that Kaiser was sitting on the bed, nearly concealed in the heavy blue folds of the damask bed curtains.

"Oh!" Cira backed up. "I'm sorry. Your man said the room was empty."

"Perfectly all right. I don't mind the interruption."

Kaiser swung his legs over the side of the bed and watched Cira try to flatten herself against the door. He sighed.

"You certainly aren't one of Cartier's sluts." He watched her intently. "In fact, I'm rather afraid you're a virgin."

Cira's blush was all the answer Kaiser needed.

"Pity," he said, his eyes more intimate than Harry's rough fingers. "Such exquisite feet. Well, we'll just have to make the best of it, won't we?"

He smiled and slowly stood. "Is everyone gone, Roger?"

"Yes, sir."

Cira started at the voice so close to her back. She half

turned, but the doorknob did not move. When she faced around again, Kaiser was so close to her that she could not take a deep breath without touching him. She was suddenly very frightened. She bolted to her right, but got no more than a step before his fingers wrapped around her upper arms, nails digging into her flesh with a force that made her feel faint.

"Struggles bore me," Kaiser said, his brown eyes holding her as surely as his hands. "Listen to me carefully, because I'll only explain what I want once. If you please me at all, you will be very well paid. First, I am going to take off your clothes and—be still!"

The force of Cira's head hitting the door made an audible crack.

"Everything all right, Mr. Kaiser?"

"Just fine, Roger."

"Are you sure?"

Kaiser laughed and whispered to Cira. "Hear that? He knows that if a woman gives me trouble, I give the woman to him for a time. I would hate to see your perfect body marked up by Roger. Do you understand me?"

Cira understood little at that moment. The pain of her head slamming against the door had dazed her. She looked up at him through lashes as dark as night, too confused to realize what was happening. "No," she whispered. "Please."

He bent down until she was overwhelmed by the smell of whiskey and cigars and sweet lilac water. Sickened, she stood passively while the weight of his flesh pressed against her. When his hand slid up beneath her skirt, she shuddered convulsively, but made no other move.

"Good," muttered Kaiser. Then, loudly. "Take a few turns around the boardwalk, Roger. I won't need you this time."

"Yes, Mr. Kaiser." There was a second of silence, then a laugh. "She says her name is Mex."

As though at a great distance, Cira heard the hallway door shut and wondered if the cold-eyed Heer had really gone. She glanced wildly around her, but was too stunned to do more than whisper pleas that only served to excite Kaiser more. He leaned into her, forcing her against the door until she could not breathe. The room darkened and seemed to retreat, then his groping hand shocked her out of her daze. She tried to twist away from his hand, pull free from the fingers clamped around both of her wrists, but all her twisting did was move her hips under his and wedge his hand more firmly between her thighs.

"So you like that," said Kaiser, misunderstanding. "Maybe you aren't a virgin after all."

His arm went around her buttocks, lifting her, holding her while he forced his body against hers. She had learned enough from Yolanda's giggling confidences to know the meaning of Kaiser's movements. She struggled as he held her, feet off the floor, but she found that struggling was worse than futile for it moved her legs apart.

Kaiser groaned and fumbled at his buttons, but could not undo them while holding her up. With a hoarse curse he stepped back and let her slide down until her feet touched the floor. Though he still held her wrists clamped in one hand, he no longer pinned her against the door with his weight.

Sensing an opening, Cira lunged sideways. Her driving legs brought her knee against his crotch. Though the blow was no more than glancing, Kaiser was acutely vulnerable. He recoiled, dropping her wrists to cover himself with both hands. Cira did not know why her accidental blow had caused him so much difficulty; she only knew that it had won her partial freedom. She lashed out at him again, this time with purpose. The result was as sudden as it was shocking. Kaiser staggered backwards and sank to the floor, his face pale and sweaty and his breath coming in gasps. She looked down at him appalled, then realized that he no longer was a threat to her.

She began trembling in every part of her body as fury replaced fear. Suddenly she wanted to kick him so savagely that he would never get up again, but her body was shaking too hard. All she could do was lean against the door and fumble with the knob.

It took Cira so long to open the door that she began to fear Kaiser would recover. She glanced hurriedly at him, but he had done no more than draw his knees up and groan. With a strength she did not know she had, Cira forced her legs to carry her through the bedroom doorway and into the sitting room. There she leaned against a table until her legs stopped shaking.

As she pushed away from the table, she noticed for the first time the roll of parchment flattened beneath her right hand. She remembered the triumph in Kaiser's voice as he described the downfall of Lee Buckles, a downfall that hung on this crushed document. Her fingers curled around the parchment until they made a tight fist. She laughed, a single high note that was a breath away from hysterics. She had not been strong enough to exact full revenge on Kaiser, but she knew of a man who was. The thought calmed her enough that she was able to walk out of the room and down the hall stairs with no outward sign of what had happened to her.

Cira went through the lobby of the Blue Lagoon Hotel openly carrying the forged Spanish document that she had stolen from Franklin Kaiser's room. No one noticed the parchment in her fist as she let herself out of the front door, but two men on the porch did notice her lovely smile as she thought about Lee Buckles's vengeance.

At that moment, it would have taken very little to move Lee to revenge. It had been a bad day, beginning before dawn when he discovered that three hundred sheep had wandered off from the bluff pasture. He had checked Baja Creek first, and had found nothing except the ugly tent squatting in the sands of Blue Lagoon.

But when he returned to the valley beneath the bluffs, he had found a trail left by panicked sheep, a wide churned swath through valley grass and hillside brush. Along the trail, tufts of gray dotted bushes where wool had snagged and been ripped from fleeing sheep. Far worse, he had found several sheep standing three-legged, eyes dull with pain. He had shot them with a cool efficiency that was belied by his bitter curses as he reloaded his gun.

Then the ragged trail had begun to show sheep lying motionless on their sides, protruding tongues too thick for their mouths. Lee had fallen into a grim silence as the count of dead sheep rose. The lines on either side of his mouth deepened until he looked older than his twenty-three years. The two shepherds who had accompanied him exchanged looks, but were too wise to say anything.

Finally the trail ended in a blind draw at the base of the San Moreno foothills. At the head of the draw, two hundred and fifty sheep were jammed together, bleating their thirst, too stupid to turn around and walk out of the dead end they had fled into.

By the time Lee and the shepherds chased them out of the draw and drove them to the closest water, it was noon. Then began the messy, grueling work of skinning the dead animals. He could have left it for his men, but that was not his way. Nor would he simply leave the skins to rot. He might be Lee Buckles, largest single landowner in California, but he could not afford to ignore the value of sheepskin. If nothing else, the hides would cover the dirt walls of his centry-old adobe ranchhouse.

The clear light of September was mellowing toward late afternoon before Lee had wrapped the last hide into a tight roll and tied it behind his saddle. His big chestnut did no more than roll his eyes at the bloody hide; Lee and the horse had fought over the first three sheepskins and then the chestnut had given up.

Thoroughly sick of his own smell and that of the reeking hides, Lee had slipped off to scrub himself in a sun-warmed slough. The bath made him feel better, but not good enough to take the raw edge off of his temper.

As the sun's color changed from yellow to incandescent orange, Lee had ridden into the yard of the adobe house. To one side, shading the western wall of the house, was a huge jacaranda tree. Its dark, lacy leaves were ragged from the dry wind, yet the tree's elegance was almost startling in the dry land. A lark, disturbed by Lee's horse, flew up into the jacaranda's fan-shaped crown. As it flew, the bird called liquid warning into the dying light.

Normally the lark's superb song would have been appreciated by Lee, but this time he had ignored it while he took care of his horse and then went inside the dark adobe. When he came out again, the sun was more red than orange, its great fires banked for a long night.

Lee did not spare a glance for the flooding reddish-orange light. He leaned against the center post of his porch, sharpening his skinning knife with quick, angry strokes. From time to time he would glance over where piled raw sheepskins made a blot of gray in the dense sunset shadow of the canted barn. Each time he saw the pile he swore quietly, disgusted with an animal so stupid that it would run itself to death long after the initial danger was gone. No other animal on earth was that stupid, not even a chicken.

Lee tested the edge of the knife with his thumb and shook his head. While he rubbed blade over whetstone, he wondered whether a coyote or one of Kaiser's section hands had panicked the sheep. He would have bet the ranch that Kaiser was at fault, but could not prove it. Even if he could, it would not make those thirty-one sheep get up and walk again.

Lee stroked the blade until sparks jumped from the whetstone, asking himself which was more stupid—sheep or the men who tried to make a living off of them. Even when the knife was very sharp, gleaming beneath the dying sun, he had not answered his own question. But he had not expected to. It was a question he had been asking himself at least once a day since he had turned twenty-one and wrested control of his father's estate from rapacious trustees. The banks, emporiums, mines and stock that had made the senior Buckles immensely wealthy had vanished into the trustee's accounts.

Lee's father had mortgaged everything he owned to buy the last tract of undivided land in California, the huge Pico Land Grant. The purchase was made with an eye toward the future, when his children and grandchildren would live in California where good land had become scarce, hence very valuable. In the meantime, Lee's father made plans to transform the land; fenced and divided, planted and husbanded, the land would be made to produce wealth in the form of crops and wool and meat.

Lee's father had planned well and shrewdly, but no man knows the time of his own death. The heart attack that seized the elder Buckles was as unexpected as it was lethal. Half of the mortgages came due at the moment of death. Because the Buckles Ranch had been purchased less than a year before Buckles's death, his plans for the ranch had barely begun to be implemented. The ranch was several years from showing a profit.

Because the conditions of the will forbade selling the ranch for a decade, the trustees of the Buckles estate had two choices. They could sell or juggle assets until the various mortgages were paid off; or they could default on the loans and thereby forfeit everything that Buckles had put up as collateral.

The trustees were the same men who had loaned Buckles the money to buy the Pico land. They knew that the ranch at that moment was worth less than the assets that secured the various loans. They could reduce their personal risks and realize a substantial personal profit by allowing the estate to default on the loans. It was all quite legal, and quite devastating to the worth of the Buckles estate.

By the time Lee was twenty-one, there was nothing left of his legacy but a continental education and 200,000 acres that the conditions of the trust had forbidden the trustees to sell. Along with the unworked land had come hundreds of scrawny, near-wild Merino sheep. Lee still was not sure whether the sheep were a blessing or a woolly curse. If world markets and natural disasters did not intervene, he would make a good profit from the fall shearing.

But he still believed that sheep were the most rancid creatures ever devised by a surly God.

So he leaned against his creaking porch, sharpening his

worn knife and swearing to himself: Leander Champion Buckles III, the last of the great California landowners, his boots stinking of sheep and his back aching from bending over woolly carcasses.

"I was not born to raise sheep," Lee announced to the first star showing in the teal blue sky.

His only answer was the sigh of dry wind through jacaranda leaves and the sound of crickets warming up in the fields around the house. The crickets reminded Lee of the days when he had come to the Buckles Ranch fresh from the satin and champagne world of Paris. The rasping, monotonous crickets had symbolized to him the wild land that was his legacy. In those days, everything about the ranch had disgusted him, from the fact that it was more than a day's ride from the dubious amenities of Los Angeles to the realization that adobe was just another name for dried mud.

But isolation and dirt were all that he had.

For weeks he had ridden over his legacy on a borrowed horse, roaming the unkempt land, half-wild with rage at a God who would play such cheap tricks on the son of San Francisco aristocracy. He cursed the chaparral-covered hills and the wide plain crackling with sun-cured grass. He dreamed of gambling the ranch away, one tax parcel at a time, a long windfall for the seamy bordellos of Colonia Juarez. But somewhere in his roaming, his oaths had given way to calculation and his rage had become a driving will to make the ranch pay. He had ridden his horse up the shoulder of the highest mountain and looked down at the land rolling golden to the distant sea . . . and he realized that it was Buckles land, all of it. His land.

On the way down the mountain, Lee began rounding up sheep. He had never stopped.

With a sigh, Lee pocketed the whetstone and sheathed the lethally sharp knife. His eyes searched the dense blue twilight for the shape of a man on horseback. Gilberto Zavala was supposed to come by this evening to share beans and tortillas and a cribbage board with his boss. Lee had hired Gil nearly two years ago to ride herd on the sheep and on the other men. It was a decision Lee had never regretted; Gil's clowning, easygoing manner and skill with sheep had shortened many a day for both of them; and his guileless brown face and deadpan jokes concealed a mind as subtle as any Lee had known.

The sound of a cantering horse brought Lee off the porch and over to the pole corral that was surrounded by tall jacaranda trees. A few pale stars were showing, but there was more than enough light left for Lee to see that something about the approaching horse and rider was wrong. Gil's tall, straight-backed outline was too thick, his horse's gait too choppy. Lee watched narrowly while a flock of sheep parted before Gil's gray horse like a querulous sea.

Gil saw Lee and swept his wide-brimmed sombrero off, waving it in an arc over his head as he called out. Even though the men were too far apart to discern words, Lee relaxed, knowing by Gil's call that nothing bad had happened.

Nonetheless, Lee watched with unusual attention as Gil's gray gelding cantered closer. He could see by the horse's gait that it was traveling under protest. Every few steps it would try to buck, only to be hauled up short by the heavy, Spanish-spade bit. Then Gil's spurs would dig into the gelding's stubborn hide, sending the gray forward until it tried to buck again and was hauled up short again.

Ordinarily, such a bad-tempered performance would have earned the horse a vivid cussing out, but not so much as a *Dios!* passed Gil's lips. That, as much as a sudden flap of cloth, told Lee that there must be a woman up behind Gil. That would also explain the gray's conduct; few except specially broken horses could abide the restless folds of a woman's skirt.

Lee waited, his face showing none of his curiosity. The gray plunged to a halt in front of him, revealing little more of the woman than a flare of rose-colored skirt and a small face whose tight jaw told of fear and a determination not to show it. Gil held the restive gray in front of Lee without saying a word; he just sat, smiling and waiting for Lee's questions. Lee tipped his hat back on his

32

forehead, crossed his arms over his chest and decided to give Gil a hard time.

"Saw a coyote den in the rocks above the bluff meadow," drawled Lee, carefully not noticing the skirt that floated up on the evening wind and wrapped over Gil's thigh like a hand. "Next time you ride that northeast line, take some poison bait with you."

"*Sí, jefe,*" said Gil, his brown eyes crackling with laughter. "Poison bait and the den of a coyote. Is there anything more?"

A gust of wind caught the skirt, lifting it off Gil's leg. The gray leaped and snorted.

"Yes," said Lee, yanking on the gray's bit to keep from being trampled. "Either teach this sonofa—this nag some manners or use it for the poison bait."

"*Sí, jefe,*" Gil said. "I do not know what is wrong with him. Do you suppose it could be the smell of sheep?"

Lee nearly laughed at the thought of the gray noticing the smell of sheep; the gelding had herded more sheep than either man could count.

"Or," added Gil innocently, as the skirt wrapped around his thigh once more, "perhaps it is the full moon, no?"

"No." Silence, then Lee gave in. "Gilberto, Compadre. Is there something behind your saddle?"

Gil glanced over his shoulder as though he expected to find nothing more than the back of his shirt.

"*Dios!*" said Gil, turning back to Lee with an expression of shock. "There is a girl back there!"

"A girl," Lee repeated tonelessly. He cleared his throat. "Good for you, Gil. You can see the face behind your hand. Now can you also tell me what the devil you're doing with—"

"Oh, *sí,*" interrupted Gil quickly. "*Sí, sí.* I remember now. *Muy claro.* I found this one on the trail out of Baja Canyon, walking hard and mumbling to herself and sure—*muy seguro*—that she has something important to tell you." Gil smiled slyly. "Anything more, *jefe?*"

Lee sighed loudly. "You have failed me again, Gil-

33

berto. I have told you many times that your job is to keep all strangers off my land, and most particularly, to keep off all young girls with long legs and important messages."

Gil's shoulders quivered with silent laughter, but his face was unsmiling as he said over his shoulder, "Chica, this is the man you walked so hard to meet."

Lee stepped closer to the gray and looked up at the girl.

"Are you sure," he asked gravely, before she could speak, "that all this wasn't just an excuse to ride behind the handsome Gilberto?"

The long walk and rugged ride had hardened Cira's emotions, curing them into an unbending determination to make Kaiser regret every second of the attempted rape. She tossed the long hair back from her face and looked down at the man who was laughing at her for the second time that day.

"Are you finished with your little jokes?" she asked in a voice that was older than she looked. "If not, I'll go back to Franklin Kaiser's room."

The name had the effect of an oath. Lee stepped back, looking her over with suddenly narrowed eyes. She seemed too young to be a whore, but he had learned in Paris that one never took a female for granted, no matter how young. And why else would she go to a man's room?

Lee stood so quietly in the gathering night that Cira thought he was going to refuse to talk to her. She leaned forward, ready to blurt out the parchment's importance, but he spoke before she could say a word.

"Gil, help the señorita down," said Lee quietly, all trace of play gone from his voice. "She may indeed have an important message."

Without waiting for a reply, Lee turned on his heel and walked toward the dark house. Gil, as surprised as Lee by the implications of Cira's words, eyed her like a horse at auction.

"Chica, what you have better be worth it. That's a tough man you're playing with."

"Kaiser?" Cira all but spat. "He is nothing!"

"Seguro," agreed Gil, swinging his right leg over the saddlehorn and sliding lightly to the ground. "But I was talking about Lee Buckles."

Gil reached up and plucked her off the gray's back. She stiffened at the hands around her waist, but he let go as soon as she was able to stand. Then he leaped back into the saddle and reined the gray around. After a few steps he looked over his shoulder. She had not moved.

"That is the house," said Gil, gesturing with his arm toward the lightless rectangle that loomed out of the dark evening. "He is waiting."

She did not stir.

"Go," he said impatiently. "You roped the horse, chica. Now it is yours to ride."

"Wait!"

The plea in her clear voice was undeniable. Gil brought the gray around and waited.

"You must stay with me," she said urgently. "I can't go into his house alone."

"Mother of God! First you demand to see him, then you refuse to see him. What is the matter with you?"

"I won't see him alone," said Cira firmly.

"You were alone with me."

"You aren't a damned gringo!"

The venom that streaked her voice surprised Gil. He leaned down, looking at her closely. Even in the vague light, he could see hatred in the flattened line of her lips. Then the line curled into a smile that transformed her.

"Please, señor."

"Mother of God," said Gil in a low voice, but this time there was no anger in his tone. "*Sí,* little one," he said, dismounting. "I will be your dueña." He laughed shortly. "Me, Gilberto Zavela, a dueña. May my father never know."

Cira smiled up at him, trying to express her relief that he was coming with her.

"*Por Dios,* chica!" said Gil, his voice almost harsh. "Don't smile like that!"

Cira pulled away, startled by the change in him.

"I didn't mean—" she began. "I wasn't laughing at you, Señor Gilberto. I was—"

"*Sí*," interrupted Gil softly. "*Sí*, chica. I know. You were just being what God made you." He took off his sombrero and executed a bow that was graceful in spite of its exaggeration. "Forgive me, little dove. I have been alone with my bad-tempered horse so long that I have forgotten how to talk to a beautiful woman. And you are very beautiful, woman. *Muy hermosa*."

Smiling, Gil straightened and offered his arm. As she had been taught to do, Cira put her fingertips on his dusty sleeve. He glanced sideways at her, surprised by the gesture more suited to lace mantillas than to wind-tangled hair.

Cira did not notice his keen interest; she was trying to control her sudden fear as they approached the black house. The closer she came, the higher she held her head and the straighter became her back. By the time she walked beneath the black lace silhouette of the jacaranda tree, she was walking with the haughty grace of a king's daughter.

Gil looked down at her again, sensing her nervousness in the slight quiver of her fingertips.

"Don't be afraid, chica. Lee has a soft heart for girls who need dueñas."

With no outward hesitation, she allowed Gil to lead her into the old adobe house. Light flared from a wooden match as Lee lit a coal oil lamp set in the middle of a heavy plank table. The unstable light made shadows move like black fire across the seamed wooden surface. When Lee straightened behind the table, his thick hair nearly brushed the ceiling beams. The old ranchhouse had been built for a more compact race of men.

Cira slowed when Gil stopped inside the doorway. Then she raised her head even higher and approached the table. Yet the closer she came, the harder it was for her not to turn and beg Gil to stay next to her. Lee Buckles dominated the room and the night as surely as the mountains dominated the plains. It was not just his height or the controlled grace of his movements. It was his eyes, eyes that changed color like the sea. They had been gray in gloomy Baja Canyon, were gold now in the lamplight and too old to belong to a man whose hair shone yellow in the light.

Cira stood motionless, fascinated by his eyes, staring into them longer than she should have, longer than was either comfortable or wise.

Lee adjusted the wick until the light thinned to yellow-white. The new brightness outlined the muscles of his arms below his rolled-up sleeves. Sparks of gold slid across the fine hair covering his arms and his face seemed all angles and darkness except for his eyes, and there was no comfort in them.

Light leaped and swayed in a draft that flattened the lamp's flame. Glass clicked against metal as Lee replaced the lamp's chimney. The tiny sound made Cira jump. She looked away from Lee's sun-browned arms. Only then did she notice the silence and the fact that Lee was watching her.

"I believe there was a message," said Lee, dropping the burnt-out match into a tin can.

Cira moved uneasily, as restless as flame, and her dark eyes clung to him like smoke. Their message was as clear to Lee as it was unknown to her, but he had discovered that what seemed an invitation from a woman often turned into insulted protestations of innocence. That was particularly true of the few Mexicans he had met since he came to the ranch—though none of them had been so lovely as this lithe girl whose hair tumbled to her waist like black water.

Cira turned away from his compelling eyes. She glanced around the room again, as though her message were cut into the thick adobe walls.

"My mother was born in this house," she murmured, more to herself than to him. "Her mother planted the jacaranda trees. She believed they brought prosperity and long life."

Her voice was like an echo of lamplight, warm and soft

and smoky at the edges. Lee felt himself leaning toward her, straining to hear what had not been said.

"What's your name?"

The hard tone of Lee's voice drew a surprised look from Gil. When Cira spoke, her voice was changed, tight.

"Cira Pico McCartney." Her eyes searched all the shadows, measuring the room against her mother's memories. "It's not as grand as she said it was."

Lee followed her eyes to the frayed wood-and-hide furniture, the battered table and the moth-chewed blankets that replaced doors whose leather hinges had long since rotted off.

"It would look better if I replaced a few things," said Lee, both rankled and amused. "But I wasn't expecting the daughter of a Spanish grandee."

His eyes moved slowly over Cira, making her aware of her smudged white blouse and cheap cotton skirt. She flushed and lowered her head. Then she startled both of them by lifting her chin and fighting back.

"I may not be rich, gringo, but I have come a long way to do you a favor."

"Have you?" said Lee. He put his palms flat on the rough table and leaned toward her. "You owe me nothing, Miss Cira Pico McCartney, so I'll bet that your favor will also benefit you."

The truth of his words angered her even more than his blunt appraisal a moment before. She snatched the stolen document out of her waistband and held the parchment practically under his nose. The pressure of her fingers made the parchment crackle as though it were burning.

"Do you want it, gringo man? Do you?"

"I might—if I knew what the hell it was."

As Lee glanced for the first time at the crushed parchment, he felt the hair on his neck stir. He had felt the reality of his land rolling to the sea. Like all men of potential greatness, he had an intuitive grasp of the importance of single events. The primal stirring warned him that he was balanced on a knife edge; what he did or did not do in the next moment would shape all the remaining moments of his life.

Slowly, Lee Buckles reached for the stolen parchment.

The document crackled in Lee's long fingers. He carefully unrolled the parchment, but its arcane Spanish and stilted calligraphy defeated his attempts at translation.

"Here," he said, handing it to Gil.

Gil read the document through twice and then began it yet again, tilting the parchment toward the lamp to catch every bit of light. But no matter how he turned the document, it still said the same thing. Lee lifted his eyebrow in silent question.

"This is an old land grant," said Gil slowly, bringing the paper so close to the lamp's chimney that the deed was in danger of burning.

Lee waited wordlessly. Gil released the bottom of the parchment, allowing it to roll up with a loud snap.

"It says your ranch belongs to somebody else."

Lee's only answer was the silent leap of lamplight reflected in his eyes. Then, "That cunning old bastard."

"It's not real," said Cira hurriedly.

"Of course it isn't!" He looked toward her and saw something close to fear tightening her lovely lips. "Of course it isn't," he said less harshly. "But that won't matter."

"That's what he said. Kaiser." The flecks of gold in her eyes shifted as she leaned over the table and touched his bare arm. "You will punish him, no?" she whispered, sliding into Spanish with the urgency of her question.

Without thinking, Lee lifted his hand and traced the lines of former tears on her face.

"What did he do to you?" he asked, low-voiced in the suddenly silent room.

Cira closed her eyes, but said nothing.

"Did he think you were one of the Frenchman's . . . women?"

He felt the heat of her blush beneath his hand even before he saw her cheeks darken. Her eyelashes made long, ragged shadows across her face when she bowed her head.

"He must be blind," Lee said, suddenly certain that she was an innocent as she was alluring. "You're too beautiful to be one of them."

Abruptly, Lee dropped his hand and turned away from the table, and from Cira who was too young and too beautiful.

"I'll get the horses," he said to Gil. "We have to see that she gets back safely."

Lee strode out of the room, not trusting himself to say more, or to look again at the gold deep within her eyes.

"But," said Cira to his retreating back, "what about Kaiser?"

She was asking the question of an empty doorway. Lee was gone.

"Chica," said Gil, "you've done enough for one night."

He crossed the room and blew out the lamp. The rising moon tinged the night with silver, making it easier for Cira to follow Gil through the dark house to the porch.

"Señor," began Cira, then stopped as she looked up at his face. When Gil was not smiling, his moonlit profile looked as closed and hard as Lee's had. After a long silence, she gave voice to her confusion. "I didn't mean to make you angry. Or him."

"No one is angry with you, chica."

"Then why—"

The sound of two horses approaching cut off Cira's half-formed question. Without a word, Lee rode into the moonlight at the edge of the jacaranda's dense shadow, leading Gil's gray. When Gil moved as though to put Cira up behind Lee, he reined his chestnut back.

"No!" Then, hearing the harshness of his own voice, he said, "Your gray should be used to her by now."

Gil looked up at his boss for a moment, not knowing whether to laugh or swear. In the end he did neither. He mounted and pulled Cira up. Cira's long, three-tiered skirt lifted as she settled behind the saddle. The gray snorted and side-stepped suddenly. Cira's arms went around Gil's waist with surprising strength. He could feel the warmth of her body pressing innocently against the length of his spine.

Gil swore, but very quietly. Much to his relief, the gray stopped prancing almost immediately and Cira's hold loosened.

The wind off of the ocean had died at moonrise, so that Cira's skirt did not lift nearly as freely or as often. But after one sight of her foot and bare calf pale in the moonlight, Lee kicked his horse into the lead. In spite of his restlessness, he kept the pace at a walk for Cira's comfort.

They rode without talking through tall grass silvered by moonlight, dry grass that writhed and whispered as it slid beneath their horses' bellies.

Cira rode gracefully, her dark eyes searching moonlight and shadows, looking everywhere but toward the man who rode slightly ahead, his lean body swaying to the chestnut's long walk. Once she thought she saw a flash of light, his eyes watching her as Kaiser had, but somehow different, for Kaiser had disgusted her and Lee had not. For an instant she wished it was Lee's back so warm against her breasts. Then she pushed away from Gil, suddenly feeling hot in spite of the cool darkness. The gray shied, forcing her to grab onto Gil again.

"Easy, chica," murmured Gil and laughter slid just beneath his words.

Cira blushed as though Gil had read her mind, not realizing that the electric quality of Lee's silence and her own told Gil all he needed to know about their private thoughts. But Lee and Cira were too much aware of each other to be aware of Gil, a fact he accepted with wry humor.

In time, the scattered lights of Colonia Juarez glittered out of the empty land ahead. A mile beyond Juarez, the concentrated lights of San Ignacio bloomed. Night was kind to the colonia, hiding the drab adobe houses. A hungry dog yapped sharply, and was answered by more dogs barking. A shout from one of the adobe houses silenced the dogs and peace reclaimed the darkness.

Off to one edge of the quarter-mile square that was the

colonia, newer homes were set beneath the few tall trees in the area. Two of those houses were constructed of sawed lumber; several others were adobe that had been plastered over and whitewashed. The new homes were separated from the lights of San Ignacio by a mile of flat, sandy plain, and by an ever-widening cultural gap.

In the beginning, Colonia Juarez and the town of San Ignacio had been equals, but as California became more and more a gringo land, the colonia sank into sand and indifference. Once a center of culture and color and wealth, Colonia Juarez was now shabby and poor and aspired to no higher entertainment than weekly Mass and nightly cockfights. The town of San Ignacio, however, had progressed from a collection of shacks and hopes to a sizable sprawl of homes and stores and boardwalks that bustled by day and glittered by night. Most of the two-story buildings along Main Street were false fronts, but here and there a light gleamed through the windows of a genuine second story, unmistakable sign of prosperity.

Even in the darkness, it was clear that the town of San Ignacio was thriving and Colonia Juarez was not. The new, gringo-style lumber homes of the colonia were mute tribute to the town's success. Boards and shingles were singularly ill-suited to the hot, arid coastal plains, but San Ignacio had succeeded with just such buildings; if the colonia imitated the town, perhaps wealth and growth and life would come again to Juarez.

The horses crossed over to a narrow wagon road that ran like a pale ribbon toward the colonia. The dust of the roadway muffled the sound of hooves and the random clumps of brush served to blur the outlines of the riders. As the two horses walked quietly toward the colonia, the closest house shone in the moonlight, ghostlike and serene. But the appearance was deceptive; by daylight, the white board house was wind-scoured and forlorn, offering scant comfort or peace to its inhabitants. Only the nearby jacaranda tree remained unchanged, as beautiful beneath sunlight as it was beneath the moon.

42

"Your mother's house stands out even at night," Gil said, finally breaking the unnatural silence.

Cira said nothing for a moment. Then, "My mother would be pleased to hear that."

"Why?"

Gil turned slightly in the saddle when he asked his question, but the girl looked past him at the house her father had built before whiskey consumed him and her mother.

"She doesn't want to be part of anything Mexican," Cira said expressionlessly. "She's the daughter of Spanish aristocrats."

"She's not the only one," said Gil, laughing. "If you believe the people of the colonia, not one of their ancestors was Indio. White as oysters, every one."

Cira laughed shortly, a sound too brittle for her years. "*Sí!* But my mother truly belongs in neither the colonia nor the town. She belongs in another world where people are not real."

"And you, Cira," said Lee softly, "where do you belong?"

She turned toward his voice and was surprised to find him close to her, close enough to touch. "I am the daughter of a drunken Irish seaman and a woman descended from Spanish kings. I don't know what I am, but I know what I'm not. I'm not what my mother wants me to be."

"What is that?"

"Her dream," said Cira bitterly. "La Princesa. But I'm not a princess and she is not a queen." Cira's impatience with her mother's obsession showed in narrowed eyes that reflected the hard light of the risen moon. "And keeping me on my knees in my room won't make me as white as her dream!"

"You're neither too dark nor too light," Lee said, his voice as warm as his hand sliding down her hair. She shivered slightly and her eyes searched his face for something she could not name. "You're cold," he said. "You should be inside."

She stared for a moment longer, then said quickly,

43

"Not my mother's house. Tía Inez, my aunt. Do you know my mother's sister, Señor Gil?"

"It would be best," agreed Gil. "Your mother wouldn't like seeing her daughter ride into the front yard behind a man who is as dark as me." He turned toward Lee, half-smiling. "Perhaps we should put Cira behind you," he teased. "Underneath that tan, you're as white as a Spanish king."

"My mother doesn't want me riding behind any man," said Cira curtly.

"What about your aunt?" asked Lee.

Cira shrugged, thinking of her cousin Yolanda. "My aunt has seven daughters and all of them go where they please with their *novios*."

"And others," said Gil under his breath, smiling. "Pretty girls, your cousins."

Lee looked at Gil sideways, but said only, "Lead the way, compadre."

Gil turned the gray away from the colonia, making a wide circle beyond the lights until scattered brush gave way to a dry stream bed. After several minutes, Gil spurred his horse up the bank, across a flat open space and into the shelter of an ancient jacaranda tree whose feathery leaves seemed to touch the gleaming stars.

When the two horses stopped, Cira suddenly realized that she was within one hundred feet of her aunt's house and no one in the colonia could possibly have heard or seen her arrival.

"You certainly know the secret ways," she whispered to Gil.

Gil smiled broadly, his teeth white in the moonlight. "Your cousins are very pretty, chica. Almost as pretty as you."

Without dismounting, Gil offered his arm to help her off the gray. But Lee was already off his horse, standing close to Cira, his arms reaching up for her. She leaned toward him without a word and her hands went to his shoulders. Without conscious thought, her fingers sought the warmth of his skin above his open collar. The shock

44

of feeling muscle sliding beneath her hand made both of them freeze. Then, very slowly, Lee lifted her off of the gray. The horse shied away from the flutter of her skirt, but neither Lee nor Cira noticed. She was staring at him, lips parted with an invitation she neither knew nor understood.

He bent over her until she could see nothing but him, feel nothing but the shocking warmth of his mouth moving over hers. For an instant she was his, fitting perfectly into his arms, then she twisted like a flame and his arms were empty.

"Cira—"

But she had vanished into the darkness, leaving him only memory and the fragrance of jacaranda.

Gil waited a long moment, waited and watched the spot where she had disappeared into the night. Finally he whistled softly.

Lee remounted and sat motionless on his horse until a faint square of light appeared in the house. Cira's figure stood outlined against the light as she looked back toward the jacaranda tree and the man she could still taste on her lips. Then both light and Cira disappeared.

Lee reined his horse gently, turning back toward the dry wash. After a moment, Gil brought his gray alongside, disturbed by Lee's silence.

"Well, *jefe*," said Gil lightly, "what now?"

"Will she be all right?"

"*Sí.*" Gil smiled. "Inez will be a little angry, but she understands what it is to be young."

"What about Cira's mother?"

Gil shrugged and his voice turned sour. "That old crow." Gil lifted his hands, palms up. "Señora McCartney goes from pious saint to drunken queen and back again. *Loca.* Crazy."

"Is Cira safe with her?"

"She knows when to go to Inez. And Inez is a good woman." Gil smiled and amended. "Well, she is a kind woman. *Muy simpática.*"

They rode in silence until Gil realized that they were angling away from the ranch trail.

"*Jefe—*"

Lee glanced over as though startled to find out that he was not alone.

"This isn't the way home," said Gil patiently.

"No, it isn't," agreed Lee. He lifted his hat and his fair hair burned nearly white in the moonlight before he yanked the hat back into place. "Thought you might like a drink."

"*Seguro*. But this isn't the way to San Ignacio, either."

"The Frenchman has a bar of sorts."

Gil laughed softly. "He has more than that, compadre. He has a redhead who will make you forget a certain dark-eyed—"

Lee's chestnut went from a walk to a lope in a single muscular bound, cutting off Gil's words.

"You're losing your sense of humor," called Gil, kicking his gray into a gallop that quickly brought the two horses even again.

"You have enough for both of us," said Lee.

But he pulled his horse into a trot more suited to the uncertain light. Gil looked over at Lee's unsmiling face and sighed dramatically.

"For months," said Gil, pulling his face into tragic lines, "for months I have spoken to you of the redhead and always you say, Mañana, compadre, mañana. And now you say—"

"Mañana," laughed Lee.

Gil smiled widely.

"But," added Lee, "you don't have to stay and drink with me tonight. I'm old enough to drink alone."

"You're a funny man, *jefe*. Maybe this Kaiser will kill himself laughing at your jokes."

"He's very old," said Lee dryly. "Maybe your redhead will kill him before we get there."

Gil laughed and thumped Lee's shoulder. "Compadre, I would not have missed this night for a new pair of leather pantaloons."

46

With that, Gil began singing a courting song of old Mexico, a song of passion and jealousy and a wounded bird calling its death to the moon. Gil's voice was sure and supple, the voice of a balladeer, and Lee was haunted by memories of dark eyes flecked with sudden gold. He wanted to tell Gil to stop, but found himself singing instead, his deep voice blending with the foreman's tenor.

When the last mournful note dissolved into silence, Gil smiled slyly and launched into a song describing the charms of a famous border whore. Because her attributes were as numerous as they were incredible, the song barely left them enough breath to climb up the balcony outside of Franklin Kaiser's suite. Fortunately, whatever sounds they might have made were amply muffled by the rhythmic surge of waves sweeping up the crescent beach just beyond the hotel.

Kaiser heard the waves without really being aware of them, or of the damp salt air that was sending pain lancing up from his arthritic knee. He was propped up on the bed, resplendent in a brocade smoking jacket that was the color of fine French burgundy. His hands, stiffer now than in the afternoon warmth, held a crystal tumbler of whiskey. He stared into the amber liquid as though he could find his youth reflected on the whiskey's flat surface. But his hand trembled, transforming his reflection into meaningless streaks of color.

Kaiser set the tumbler sharply on a polished rosewood bedside table and reached to summon a maid. The lavishly brocaded bell pull was stiff and slippery; it slid out of his grasp, but his fingers caught in the long silk tassle knotted at the end of the pull. He yanked down, freeing his fingers and summoning the maid in the same motion.

The sudden movement caught Roger Heer's attention; though he was studying several proposals for the most profitable development of Buckles Ranch, Heer's attention was never far from Kaiser's needs.

"May I get you something, sir?" said Heer through the open door to the bedroom.

"I want the window closed, but the maid can do it," Kaiser snapped. "Go on with your work."

Heer returned to his papers, deftly turning his face so that Kaiser could not see his slight, disdainful smile. This was the third time Kaiser had rung for the maid. Each time she came he was visibly disappointed. Heer assumed that Kaiser was waiting for the one he called Mex, but when Heer had offered to go out and find her, Kaiser had refused with an anger that Heer had rarely seen. He wondered what the little Mex had done to get Kaiser in such a heat. She was pretty enough—beautiful, in fact—but Kaiser had had a lot of beautiful women without any fuss at all.

Heer looked at Kaiser's set, flushed face and decided that Mex must have taught the jaded old dog a few new tricks. Heer's speculation as to what those tricks could have been was interrupted by a knock on the hallway door.

"Enter," said Heer crisply, curious in spite of himself as to which maid it would be.

The door opened slowly and a girl came in. Heer glanced at the ragged hem of her long skirt and the faded red of her peasant blouse and knew without looking further that she was the same dark Indio girl who had been there twice before. He waved her toward the bedroom where Kaiser sat staring into his whiskey glass as though reluctant to look up and be disappointed yet again.

She hesitated just beyond the doorway, seeing a man who was physically imposing in spite of his age and the near-empty whiskey decanter on the table. Each time she had come, less whiskey remained.

"Señor?" she said, asking Kaiser's attention.

Her voice was young and she had black hair and she was a female shape haloed by the flaring gas lights on either side of the door; for an instant Kaiser thought she was the girl with gold in the center of her eyes.

When she saw his expression change, the maid came toward him with an exaggerated roll of hips, but when she moved, the illusion vanished and Kaiser's heart beat normally again.

"Your wish, señor?" she asked, but there was no question in her voice nor in her thigh moving slowly against his arm.

Kaiser withdrew his arm with insulting haste and gestured toward the window at the end of the room.

"Close it."

With a pout that blurred her strong Indio face, the maid went toward the balcony doors.

"No," said Kaiser curtly, in spite of a slight slurring of his voice. "The other one."

"Is close already," she said; her accent was a parody of Cira's delicately flavored English.

"Open it."

The girl looked over her shoulder and saw Kaiser take a drink, watching her over the rim of the glass with unnerving intensity, especially when she stood between him and the hissing gas lights. She knew that the strong light outlined every inch of her body, naked beneath the thin cotton of her blouse and skirt. With a smile she stretched as she slowly opened the window.

"Is good, no?" she asked, turning slowly toward him.

"Close it."

The girl closed it with a vigor that betrayed impatience. She faced him again, hands on her hips.

"Señor?" she asked in a voice that tried and failed to be seductive.

"What's your name?"

"Maria," she said, and they both knew it was a lie.

"Your name is whore," he said coldly, taking another swallow of whiskey. Then he snapped his fingers with an impatience that would have warned her if she had not assumed he was drunk. "Come here, whore."

She moved toward him with the exaggerated walk that would have made him laugh had he not been so angry. He raised the crystal tumbler to his lips and drained the whiskey before he could see his age reflected in its unwinking amber eye. She was close to him now, too close.

49

Even the yellow light of the lamps could not soften the graceless lines of her clothes or the coarseness of her skin. Kaiser studied her with an expression that said he could smell her in the room and he did not like what he smelled. Then his hand moved beneath her clothes without heed for her pride or her pleasure.

"You're not even a whore," said Kaiser, twisting her flesh. "You're a common slut."

She rubbed against his hand as though his insults and his cruel fingers pleased her; and perhaps they did, or perhaps it was simply that he was rich and she was not.

"Lift up your skirt, slut," said Kaiser hoarsely, sitting upright, beyond the soft reach of the pillows.

She smiled and raised her long skirt, revealing sturdy feet wedged into stained satin slippers. Her feet were broad, blunt, calloused, the feet of someone who had spent most of her life carrying heavy loads barefoot over rough trails.

With a sound of disgust, Kaiser snapped her skirt down.

"What is wrong?" she said, surprised.

"Where is the other maid?" he said pouring himself another drink.

"Is no other," she protested.

"The one who brought the sandwiches earlier?"

"Oh." Maria dismissed the idea with a gesture. "She not one of us. She—" Maria paused, stumbling over her limited English. Then she shrugged contemptuously. "She is nothing, señor. *Nada*. Una virgin." She bent over, letting the peasant blouse fall away from her full breasts. "She know nothing about men."

"Yes," said Kaiser, looking coolly inside her blouse, "but she didn't have feet like a cow."

"Feet?" Maria straightened and her lips flattened when she understood what he said. And then she laughed. "A man does not fuck a woman's feet!"

"Not yours, certainly," agreed Kaiser with a cold smile, but she was too astonished at being rejected to measure

50

the barely restrained rage in his response. "What is the virgin's name?" he demanded.

Maria's answer was laughter that made her breasts shake. "Feet!" Then, "Mañana I ask—for a price," she said, snickering. "Is only fair you be good for something, no?"

She laughed at her joke until Kaiser's hand moved beneath her skirt and she went to her knees with a gasp of agony. Too late she realized that Kaiser was neither as drunk nor as stupid as she had believed.

"No," she said. "I no mean—"

"Shut up."

The suite became very quiet, so quiet that Heer was afraid to lay aside the paper he had finished and thereby risk attracting Kaiser's wrath.

"You will find out who she is," said Kaiser softly, clearly. "But not tomorrow and not for a price. For free and right now. Savvy, slut?"

She looked into his eyes and felt nausea rise in her throat.

"*Sí,*" she said, backing away from him on her hands and knees. "*Sí!*"

Then she was beyond his reach, on her feet and running into the hallway as though she feared pursuit. But all that followed her was the sound of laughter.

Very carefully, Heer put down one sheet of paper and picked up another; he was no more eager to face Kaiser in this mood than the maid had been. The click of decanter meeting glass was loud in the silence. By the extended gurgle of liquid, Heer judged that Kaiser had poured himself a good four fingers of whiskey. The bed creaked, the bedroom lights went out, then the bed creaked again as Kaiser lay down, staring toward the well-lit sitting room as though it were a stage.

When a gentle tap came on the hall door, Heer got up hastily to answer it, grateful for any excuse that would take him beyond the range of Kaiser's cold eyes.

Heer opened the hall door, expecting to find a cowed Indio maid. But all he saw was empty hallway. Puzzled, he stepped forward to look around. He caught a glimpse of a strong brown arm as it shot out from behind the potted palm beside the door. A leather-clad hand clapped itself over his mouth before he could voice surprise or alarm.

Though Heer was not a weak man, he was totally unprepared for Gilberto Zavala's whipcord strength. Before Heer could set himself for a fight, Gil yanked him out of the doorway and into the deep shadow between hallway lights.

"Señor," whispered Gil, "that is a castrating knife you feel on your backbone. One word, one sound, and I will cut you like a calf."

Heer's right hand made a reflexive twitch toward his waist, then he was utterly still. But Lee had seen the movement. He searched until he found a gambler's gun hidden behind Heer's hand-sized silver belt buckle. Lee hefted the tiny gun, barely larger than his palm. He broke open the gun and removed two tiny bullets.

"You better be careful," said Lee very softly, tapping the gun with his fingernail. "You shoot a man with this and he'll be mad enough to kill you." The gun and bullets clinked slightly as they landed in the damp earth of the potted plant. Lee glanced at Gil. "Inside. Keep him quiet."

"*Seguro,*" said Gil, grinning and leaning lightly on the knife.

Heer twisted suddenly, but only succeeded in getting a mouthful of foul leather glove. Guessing at the glove's past uses, he fought an impulse to gag. Then he stared with narrow-eyed intensity at the tall, soft-voiced man who had taken his gun and who moved so silently, so easily. Heer had seen only one other man move like that, the man who had picked him up and thrown him into a rented buggy.

When Lee moved into the light of the sitting room, Heer needed only the glint of Lee's fair hair beneath the battered hat to be certain of his identity. With a final flexing of muscles, Heer tested the alertness and strength of his captor. Then Heer relaxed, accepting the fact that he was not going anywhere until the Mexican let go of him.

Lee went rapidly, silently, across the sitting room's thick carpet. Heer's reading lamp threw long shadows, pools of blackness alternating with heavy yellow light from an ill-trimmed wick. Lee stared into the bedroom just long enough to see Kaiser slumped in shadows beneath the bed's canopy. His massive torso was propped up by pillows and his thick-knuckled hands were pale against his smoking jacket.

Lee scooped up the reading lamp and cat-footed into the bedroom. The faceted crystal decanter blazed, transforming light into shards of primary colors. Lee glanced at the crystal, and at the muted gleam of gilt lettering on a large book lying near the decanter. Holding the lamp at eye level, he looked more closely at the book. It was an Italian edition of Dante's *Divine Comedy*. Lee ran his fingertips over leather binding that was smoothed by much use, as though Kaiser read the *Comedy* as religiously as Lee's Scots mother had read her New Testament.

With sure fingers, Lee opened the book. The Italian style of print was ornate, nearly impenetrable, but the graphic drawings of tortured souls needed no elaboration. Frowning, Lee closed the book.

"Wake up, Kaiser," he said softly. "Wake up, you drunken son of a bitch."

Kaiser's eyelids flickered. He squinted against the glare without moving to turn aside from it. "Get that damned thing out of my face, Heer."

The precision of Kaiser's speech warned Lee that Kaiser was not nearly so drunk as he appeared. Lee moved the lamp until the light fell less harshly across Kaiser's face. Other than the sudden narrowing of Kaiser's eyes, he made no sign that he was surprised to find a stranger by his bed. Kaiser's black glance swept from Lee's stained hat to his dirty boots, then settled on the pale eyes that seemed yellow in the lamplight.

"Do I know you?" said Kaiser, his voice more amused than curious.

"You've been trying to break me for a year."

Kaiser smiled faintly and pulled a cigar out of his smoking jacket. "That's hardly a distinction, son. I broke a lot of men last year."

"You didn't break me."

"Oh?" A match flared and hissed. "Then you must be Mr. Leander Buckles."

Lee bowed with a grace that belied his rough clothes. "I apologize for calling you a drunken son of a bitch," said Lee smoothly. "Obviously you aren't drunk."

"But I'm still a son of a bitch?"

Lee smiled with neither warmth nor humor.

"I assume," said Kaiser, breathing out a fragrant plume of smoke, "that if I called Mr. Heer, he would not answer."

Lee's smile widened.

"Did you damage him?" asked Kaiser dryly.

"No."

"Pity. Roger is getting above himself." Kaiser waved a hand toward the decanter. "Drink?"

"No."

Kaiser waited, but Lee said nothing more, merely stood and stared down at him with eyes that were as yellow as a cat's. For the first time, Kaiser felt a vague stirring of fear. Lee Buckles was not at all what he had expected. But fear only sharpened Kaiser's appreciation of the situation; he had learned long ago to make fear a servant rather than a master.

"Sit down. Unless standing over me helps you to feel superior."

Lee neither moved nor spoke. Kaiser nodded minutely, approving of Lee's style while regretting the difficulties it caused.

"I like you, young man."

"Then God help the people you love."

The hand that held Kaiser's cigar trembled slightly, a current of anger that quickly passed. He sighed softly.

"You're young, Lee. You haven't learned that it's unnecessary and sometimes dangerous to insult a man whose neck is under your boot." Kaiser's cigar glowed and dimmed in a rhythm that echoed the ebbing of the tide. "That's something that I'm afraid Roger will never learn."

Lee's shoulders moved in a gesture that betrayed his tightly leashed impatience, but still he said nothing.

"As you obviously don't care for my conversation, my chairs, my whiskey or me," said Kaiser sardonically, "why did you come here?"

"To return this," said Lee, holding the rolled parchment in his left hand, just within the circle of bright light.

Kaiser immediately recognized the rolled document. He looked at Lee with renewed speculation. "So she's a friend of yours. Perhaps I underestimated both of you."

"No, Kaiser. I didn't send her. You drove her to me."

Kaiser's smile became a grimace that distorted his aged, handsome features. He rubbed his fingers through his thick silver hair. When he dropped his hand, he was no longer smiling. "What do you want?"

"Nothing." Lee set the lamp down on the table, just out of Kaiser's reach. "I thought you'd want to watch this."

Lee held the dry parchment across the top of the lamp's chimney. Both men watched while the paper darkened, then flared into flame. When the parchment was all but consumed, Lee released it. The glowing remnants were ash by the time they touched the polished rosewood table.

"Rather like fireworks," said Kaiser. "Pretty, but pointless. I can always have another grant made up. Paper is quite cheap and judges to enforce the paper, while more expensive, are nonetheless well within my means."

"You really must need my land."

"Need?" Kaiser shrugged. "I won't deny that your land lies exactly in the path of commercial progress, in the form of a rail connection between Los Angeles and Mission San Diego." He smoothed the burgundy brocade of the jacket across his flat stomach. "But I'm not the one who needs your land. It's your neighbors who do. They taxed themselves to raise enough money to make it worth my time to build a railroad here." He smiled to himself and added softly, "Your neighbors are generous people; they agreed to pay your part of the levy."

"Your railroad and my ranch can't exist on the same land," said Lee bluntly. "You know it and I know it. In five years, maybe. But not now, not while I make my living from the sheep that would be killed by your crews, your locomotives and the squatters who follow both."

"I appreciate your problem," said Kaiser, examining the ash on the end of his cigar. "But it is just that . . . your problem. You were born too late, Lee Buckles. The days of vast ranchos are finished. You can preside over the cutting up of your ranch for a modest return or you can keep your ranch in one piece and go bankrupt. Your choice."

Lee nodded slowly. Kaiser was only saying what Lee himself had often thought. But there was a third alternative. There had to be.

"I'll hold onto my ranch because I have no real choice," said Lee. "The land is all I have to work with."

Kaiser's cigar glowed vividly. "Have you considered that a railroad will make you more money than your sheep?"

"No thanks. Your railroad will make you ten times—a hundred times—the profit that it will make me." Lee smiled thinly. "That's the nature of monopoly."

"And you believe you can win against it."

Lee did not say anything. The fact of his presence was all the answer either man needed.

Kaiser shook his head. "You have much to learn, Mr. Leander Champion Buckles the Third. You should have figured out by now that your fine neighbors aren't going to let you hold onto that ranch. With or without my help, they will cut your land into pieces and then they will cut those pieces into smaller pieces and still smaller until finally your ranch is no larger than their dreams." He turned suddenly and fixed Lee with dark eyes that compelled attention. "You see, they don't really like you.

They don't like either one of us, but they need me and my railroad. You they neither like nor need."

The black eyes looked away, focused on a place only Franklin Kaiser ever saw. "Those fine people don't understand what it is to be where we are. All they see is us at what they think is the top of the world . . . you with your ranch and me with my Goddamned steel road."

He looked again at Lee until Lee stirred uneasily beneath the knowing black eyes.

"Have you guessed how much they hate you?" asked Kaiser softly, smiling. "No, I can see that you haven't. Too bad, Lee Buckles. We have more in common that you can admit, but my railroad is more important to me than your ranch.

"You lose, Mr. Buckles."

Lee's face tightened until shadows made dark slashes beneath the planes of his cheekbones. Kaiser watched, waiting for Lee to lose his temper. But Lee did not.

"You're older than I thought," murmured Kaiser. "Perhaps you're even old enough to understand that there is nothing personal in either your loss or my victory. A simple exercise of power."

The shadow lines on Lee's face did not soften.

Kaiser sighed and turned his hands palms up in an elegant gesture of resignation and regret. "Then, young man, you will learn the hard way not to stand between the dragon and his wrath."

"First," said Lee coolly, "we'll have to find out who is the dragon."

The lamp swung, making shadows dance. When the shadows were still once more, Lee was gone.

Gil was waiting in the sitting room, out of sight of the open bedroom door. He leaned against the wall, apparently relaxed, but he reminded Lee of a hunting cat. Perhaps it was the feral alertness in Gil's eyes as they measured Heer.

"Finished?" said Gil without looking up.

"Almost."

Gil remained as he was, arms crossed on his chest, his

57

hat pushed back on his thick black hair, his lined brown face impassive. Lee nodded to the man on the loveseat.

"Mr. Heer, isn't it? Sorry for the inconvenience."

Heer studied Lee through eyes that were like bits of blue china, weighing Lee's tall, lean build against his own shorter, bulkier body. Whatever Heer's conclusions were, he kept them to himself.

"Let's go, Gil."

Heer waited until he could no longer sense the silver chiming of Gil's Mexican spurs. Then he went to the bedroom door. Though he could barely see into the darkened room, he knew that Kaiser was waiting.

"Should I go after Buckles?"

"No," said Kaiser absently. "You might be unfortunate enough to catch him." He rapped the tabletop with his knuckles. "Send for the special crew tomorrow. We've waited long enough. Too long."

A match flared as Kaiser lit the bedside lamp. When it burned brightly, he lifted the heavy book onto his lap and turned the thick, stiff pages until he found the depictions of the inmost circle of Hell.

Heer hesitated, then spoke softly. "Anything else, sir?"

Kaiser, engrossed by the writhing bodies of the damned, did not answer.

Cira awoke as she had the day before, with a restlessness that was born of half-remembered dreams. A look at the light pouring through the window told her that she had slept late again. That meant that her mother had also slept late or had gotten up early enough to drink herself into a different kind of unconsciousness.

With a frown she was not aware of, Cira blotted out the picture of her mother, slack-jawed and snoring, lying fully dressed in a tangle of bed sheets and alcohol. Cira turned on her side and looked out the window, east, toward blue-black mountains jagged above the golden heat of the plains. Her eyes followed the hard rise of ridges with inarticulate longing. All of her life she had wanted to lie on the top of the highest peak and feel the land roll away while the hot sky turned overhead. But she was on the plains, now and always, where it was flat and the sky never turned.

Cira lifted off the clinging sheet and flapped it soundlessly, wishing that she were in her aunt's house where the thick adobe walls kept rooms cool on even the hottest days. She stretched, turning her body to take advantage of the desultory breeze from the open window. Then she let go of the thin cotton sheet, shivering as it drifted down, stroking her skin. She smiled with the sheer pleasure of being alive, in spite of the fact that her mother would be furious if she found out that Cira had slept naked again.

With a defiant gesture, Cira swept off the sheet and lay on her back, but the restlessness which had haunted her dreams was only increased by the tantalizing play of breeze over her skin. She became aware of a pleasant, powerful feeling spreading through her, an inner tension that made her acutely aware of her own supple body. She rolled slowly onto her stomach, stretching, and her breasts tightened with a feeling like that when Lee's lips had moved over hers.

The feeling increased, a wire of sensation tightening and vibrating through her, and with each vibration the wire grew tighter and more potent until the feeling was no longer pleasant but an intolerable restlessness born of a need she neither recognized nor understood. What little she had learned of men and women had been whispered to her by giggling cousins beneath the covers at night or under the cool jacaranda tree during summer days when all but children's primal speculations were hammered flat by the sun.

A tall shape moved against the mountains. Cira strained forward, seeing a powerful man on a half-wild horse, a man whose mouth tasted like her own. Then she realized that there was nothing beyond the window but heat twisting light into the shape of her dreams. She shivered and withdrew from the window, but the room was suddenly a cage closing around her and tightening.

With hands that shook she pulled a black dress over

her head. The cloth covered her neck and wrists and feet in dull folds. The dress was meant to be worn with a corset and layers of petticoats, but Cira had no intention of subjecting herself to that torture on such a hot day. She would have preferred to wear her cousin Yolanda's skirt and blouse again, but her mother had found Cira in peasant dress and had destroyed the clothes in a drunken rage.

Cira hesitated at the doorway, listening for sounds of her mother. She heard only the wind ruffling the jacaranda tree, a sound as familiar as her own breathing.

With a sudden movement, Cira pulled the door open and slipped through the house, making no noise with her sandals. No voice called out to her, demanding what she was doing out of her room when she should be on her knees praying for her tainted soul. Cira eased the front door shut and ran toward her aunt's house.

As soon as she had put a screen of brush between her and her mother, Cira slowed to a walk. But instead of being relieved to have escaped her mother, Cira found that her inner tension had only increased. She grew even more irritated at the thought of listening to Yolanda's breathless descriptions of the moon, the night and the hard body of her *novio*.

Cira made a small sound of impatience; her own reactions baffled her, for if she did not go to her cousin's house she had nowhere to go but home, and she would not go there until driven by darkness. She refused to spend another afternoon kneeling in her bedroom, pretending to pray. She glanced around almost frantically until she saw the mountains. So many times she had stared at them, fascinated by their mystery and promise. Now she could not look away from their sinuous ridges and peaks thrusting into the soft blue sky.

Without conscious decision, Cira began walking toward the twin peaks that had brooded over so many of her awakenings. She moved quickly, impatiently, as though all the years of her childhood were inside of her demanding to be free. The light became brighter, harder, hotter, the white noon of an arid land, but she walked on, obsessed by the mountain growing closer with every step until the land humped up beneath her feet, ridges and ravines and rocks broken by more time than she could imagine. But time did not matter, whether it was the mountain's time or her own. All that mattered was the peak so close that it had become a trail beneath her feet, a trail twisting higher, always higher as though it knew her need.

Cira stumbled and realized that she was thirsty and her legs ached with the speed of her ascent. She sank down into the shade of a huge boulder. For the first time she looked behind her; Colonia Juarez was little more than a roughness on the surface of the plains. Her house was merely a pale blur and her mother less than that, invisible.

Cira leaned against the cool granite and unbuttoned the front of her dress until the breeze could slide between her half-bare breasts. For a moment she was almost dizzy with a feeling she could not describe, then the moment passed, leaving a strange weakness in her. She closed her eyes, letting sun and shade and wind caress her while she slept.

Far below and miles away, Lee Buckles rode alone on a tall horse that was the same dry, dusty tan as his leather vest and chaps. He wore the brush-scarred leather with as little thought as he wore his battered hat—both were necessary equipment for anyone whose job was chasing stupid animals through canyons thick with chaparral. Which was exactly what he had been doing when Gil brought word that B. Eliot Fulton wanted to see Lee at his earliest possible convenience.

The late autumn sun still had the power to make heat waves dance off of land and animal alike. Where Lee's shirt clung to him, sweat made the faded blue cloth almost bright again. Lee lifted his hat and wiped his forehead. The way he yanked his hat into place said more about his mood than his impassive, tanned face. Whatever Fulton had to say, Lee suspected he did not want to hear.

The wagon road Lee was following was dusty, rutted

and had only its lack of brush to recommend it. The dust-colored horse had a walk that was both easy to ride and very fast; somewhere in the animal's bloodlines was a Tennessee Walker. It was equally important to Lee that the horse was calm to the point of unconsciousness. No amount of wagons, buggies, shouts of general chaos disturbed the tall animal.

A covey of quail burst out of the brush alongside the road with a whirr of wings and flecks of gold light flashing off their feathers. The mixture of brown and gold, flight and grace reminded Lee of Cira. The memory sent desire twisting through him. He spent the remainder of the ride to San Ignacio trying to forget that instant when she had fitted perfectly into his arms. Trying, but not succeeding. Only the chaos of San Ignacio's streets finally diverted his unruly mind.

Noise, dirt, flies and people shared the streets of the town in nearly equal parts. The last time Lee had been on Main Street, there was one vacant lot for every three buildings. Now there were few lots that did not bristle with the wooden skeletons of tomorrow's stores or shops or restaurants. The smells of fresh lumber and boiled coffee vied with those of outhouses and horse manure.

A young black dog rushed out from under the new boardwalk and barked ferociously at Lee's horse.

"Easy, Walker," said Lee.

The horse twitched an ear at his rider and totally ignored the dog. Chagrinned, the dog slunk back under the boardwalk, not to reappear until three half-wild chickens started scratching through a pile of garbage.

Lee tied Walker to a cast-iron hitching rail near a water trough. Walker sank his muzzle into the tepid water, sucked loudly, and slobbered on Lee's sleeve. Lee pushed the horse away and studied his reflection in the disturbed water. As the water calmed, he saw that shaving this morning had only made the rest of him look more shaggy. He considered the promise of a brightly striped barber pole half a block up past the bank, then shrugged;

a haircut would not change the due date of the Buckles Ranch mortgage.

Lee's boots and spurs rang on the boardwalk as he walked up to the only two-story building with plate-glass windows in San Ignacio. Straight gold letters marched across the glass, spelling out "San Ignacio Bank and Trust." Beneath the proclamation, in letters that were smaller but no less bright, was "B. Eliot Fulton, President."

Lee swept off his hat and used it to beat trail dust out of his pants before he stepped through the bank's impressive door. Like the raised boardwalk, the polished mahogany door was new since Lee's last visit. As San Ignacio prospered, so did B. Eliot Fulton's bank.

The interior of the bank had also changed. It was more quiet, cool. The tellers' cages were of brass and beveled glass that made the wooden floor look even more scuffed than it had before. Lee did not recognize either teller; both men ignored him after one glance at his clothes. With a shrug, Lee pushed aside the waist-high swinging gate that separated patrons from bank personnel.

"Just a minute, cowboy," said one clerk.

Lee kept on going. Fulton was nowhere in sight, but Lee guessed that the corner of the bank that had been partitioned off would be a good place to look for the bank president. Lee rapped once on the new door, opened it and walked in. The scandalized teller was only a step behind.

"Sorry, Mr. Fulton," said the teller hurriedly. "He just—"

Fulton jerked his head in an unmistakable gesture of dismissal. The teller left, closing the door behind him. Lee said nothing, just stood there looking unreasonably big and fair in the windowless office, radiating the smells of dust and leather and sun.

"Sit down, Mr. Buckles."

Though Fulton was perhaps eight years older than Lee, the banker was already going bald. His body showed plainly that he was unaccustomed to any activity more rigorous than pulling open the vault door five mornings a week.

"Since when am I Mr. Buckles to you, Eliot?"

Fulton flushed at the soft question. His fingers nervously sought a sterling silver letter opener.

"Sorry," said Fulton. "Lee."

Lee sat in a chair that was too small for him. He crossed his arms against his chest, waiting. In the gloom of the office, the sun-gold hair on Lee's forearms gleamed as though it were alive. Fulton cleared his throat and threw Lee a look that was half defiance, half appeal and wholly uncomfortable. The silver opener slipped out of his fingers and cracked against the solid oak desk.

"It's about your mortgage."

Lee waited, unmoving.

"It's due in twelve days."

Silence.

Fulton flushed again and Lee almost took pity on him. Then Lee decided that if Fulton was going to be a predator, the banker would have to learn that prey were rarely grateful.

"But," muttered Fulton, "I suppose you know that."

Fulton waited. Lee sat and watched him out of eyes that were never the same color twice.

"Dammit, Lee—"

"Eliot," interrupted Lee gently. "Tell me something I don't know."

"There won't be an extension," said Fulton in a rush.

"I know."

"Now I know that we—what?" said Fulton, realizing that Lee had spoken.

"Go on, finish your speech," said Lee, suddenly tired of the town, the bank and the man who had wrestled with his conscience. And lost.

"I know that we had discussed the possibility of an extension," said Eliot hesitantly, not liking the look on Lee's face, an older, harder face than Fulton remembered. "You've made your interest payments on time and to the

64

penny and naturally expect an extension. But there won't be—can't be—an extension."

"Why?"

The letter opener flashed when Eliot picked it up and then set it aside almost immediately.

"It would be a bad investment, Lee," said Fulton finally. "Working land on the scale of your ranch just isn't economically feasible any longer. And you refuse to divide the ranch into acceptable parcels."

"Acceptable to whom?" said Lee softly.

Eliot sighed. "Lee, you can't stand in the way of progress."

"Progress—or Franklin J. Kaiser's Great Western Railroad?"

Fulton looked levelly at Lee. "The two are the same. We need that railroad. Without it, San Ignacio will die."

"The town looked healthy enough this morning."

"Only because of the promise of a railroad going through."

Fulton smoothed his thinning hair, choosing his words carefully, for it was very important to make Lee understand that the banker was acting for the greatest good to the greatest number of people.

"I've been empowered to make a final offer to you from Great Western. The railroad will settle for every third alternating section along the right-of-way, and the right-of-way itself, naturally. In addition, you'll sign an open note for the capital costs of the track. This bank will hold the note, and I've demanded that it not come due for five years. That will give you more than ample time to sell the sections you retain, pay off the note and give you an excellent profit in the bargain." Fulton again looked directly at Lee. "Frankly, that's the most generous offer anyone has gotten out of Great Western. Ever. As your banker, I'd advise you to take it."

"It's better than a patch of burned grass," drawled Lee. "Or didn't Kaiser mention that offer to you? I thought not. My foreman found a quarter-ace burn in the center of the plains. A warning."

"I doubt that, Lee. Probably just a squatter's campfire that got out of hand."

"It burned the neatest square you ever saw."

"Oh," faintly. Then, "It still could have been a squatter."

"And pigs could fly. Tell Kaiser to shove it."

"Think it over more carefully, Lee," cautioned Fulton. "It's a very generous offer."

Lee swore with a softness that was more shocking than a shout. When he leaned forward, his eyes were gray-black in the gloom, and his voice was uninflected. "Eliot. Have you ever seen my ranch."

"Ah . . . some of it."

"The wagon road."

"Yes."

"Let me tell you what you haven't seen, the parts of my ranch that chew hell out of leather clothes, the ocean cliffs and the canyons and the mountains and the brush, always the Goddamned brush. Even sheep have a tough time scraping a meal off of most of my land. The only part of the ranch that's really worth a damn is the land lying between the ocean and the mountains. The flat, fertile plains that are the guts of my ranch.

"The plains that Kaiser wants me to give him for the honor of having Great Western cut my ranch into two worthless halves." Lee's voice rose and fell like a whip in the stuffy room. "But we all have to make these little sacrifices to the Great God Progress, right, Eliot? My ranch and your word. I wonder what else that steel road will cost before it's done."

Fulton's narrow hands closed around the letter opener. "I understand your disappointment," he said in a tight voice, "but there was no written agreement on an extension."

"How much did Kaiser pay you?"

"Kaiser?" said Fulton, obviously surprised. "Nothing."

"At least the price was right."

"Now look here, Lee! I made the only possible decision, given the circumstances."

Lee sat forward suddenly. "Did you? You think the railroad is good for San Ignacio and your pocketbook, and my ranch is good for neither. You're scrambling for Kaiser's pennies while silver dollars bounce out of your pockets. Kaiser will take a hell of a lot more out of this land than he ever puts back!"

"At first, yes," conceded Eliot. "But we have to be far-sighted. Think of it as an investment in the future." Fulton leaned forward, his narrow face drawn with his desire to make Lee understand. "I don't really care for Kaiser, Lee, but there's no way I can stand against him. Nor do I want to. San Ignacio must have a railroad."

Lee stood with a savage grace that made Fulton sit back.

"Write out a receipt for this."

Lee tossed a packet of bills onto Fulton's desk. Fulton reached out and riffled the corner of the stack.

"The mortgage payment?" asked Fulton, more than half unbelieving.

"Every bit of it. I was going to use the money for wells and check dams and reservoirs," said Lee, his voice bitter for the first time. "I believe you call it capital investment in the future."

"Yes," said the banker faintly.

"Now I'm back where I started—praying for water in a dry land."

"Lee—"

"Good-bye, Mr. Fulton."

When Lee reached the boardwalk, his angry footsteps were drowned out by the clatter of a freight wagon piled high with fresh-cut lumber. It was past lunch time, but the thought of stale bread and mutton sandwiches flattened by hot saddlebags was enough to drive Lee away from the dust-colored horse standing asleep while children and chickens ran beneath its belly.

Lee passed up his usual town favorite, a café owned by the French chef who had tired of cooking for whores and their drunken customers. He went instead to one of the three beer halls that had been opened by German immigrants. The place he chose was of the sort frequented by working men and drifters.

With his rough clothes and work-hardened body, Lee appeared the same as the other patrons. No one even looked up, much less recognized him, when he sat down at a half-empty trestle table with a mug of beer and a thick sandwich that did not smell of sheep. While he ate, he listened and watched, for there was an undercurrent of tension in the room that he sensed but did not understand.

Then he saw the men who had claimed the center table that was tacitly reserved for regular patrons. One look at the men told Lee that they were not from San Ignacio. He had seen their hard-shouldered counterparts in every port in Europe and America, men whose fists and iron-toed boots were their pride and pleasure and passport to jobs wherever force was preferred over finesse.

Lee watched and knew that Kaiser was calling in all bets. He must have guessed or known or perhaps not even cared that Lee had money to repay Fulton. Or like the burned square, the mortgage might have been nothing more than a way of showing how many ways Kaiser had Lee beaten.

Without appearing to, Lee listened to the rough-voiced men. He found out that they had just come in from Long Beach, that their leader was a brawler called One-Ear Mike and that they expected to start laying Great Western track within a few days, as soon as the rest of the men and equipment were gathered.

Lee sipped beer and admired Kaiser's pragmatism, if not his ethics. Kaiser would gather the crew on the spur track that ended just at Buckles's land, the spur that had been built a year ago and seemingly abandoned. Then, with a large crew, work locomotive and flatcars of equipment, the track layers would simply strike out across country, driving their great steel nails into Buckles's land, laying track and defying anything short of God Himself to stop them.

It would be a classic exercise in might making right-of-way. Kaiser had done it before up and down the state, whenever landowners disputed Great Western's chosen routes. The courts Kaiser owned or influenced would dally over the ensuing suits until the contested route was finished. Whether it was in the control of the land, the courts or the freight rates, Great Western played a bare-knuckle game that did not bow to politics, commerce or society.

Great Western's steel road would come to the Buckles Ranch as surely as winter rains.

Lee let the last of the beer slide down his tight throat. He set the heavy mug on the table with deceptive gentleness and left the beer hall as anonymously as he had come. He mounted the dust-colored horse and rode through a town teeming with railroad dreams, money dreams; and the death of his own dreams shouted from every half-built structure redolent of pitch and sunshine.

Once before Lee had felt this way, the day he had learned the true position his father's executors had left him in. Once before he had turned his horse toward the low granite peaks that marked the eastern boundary of his land. Once before he had been driven by despair and rage to ride up nameless canyons, higher, always higher as though a solution would come to him if only he climbed high enough.

Far up on the shoulder of the mountain, on a ridge where the first pines grew, Lee saw fresh tracks made by small feet. At the same moment, the horse's head turned and its ears pointed toward a large boulder just off the game trail Lee had been following.

Cira lay asleep in the shadow of the granite, until the horse's steel-shod hoof struck stone. Then she woke up all at once, like a cat, and looked up to see a man sitting on a dust-colored horse, sitting and watching her with eyes that made her forget her quest for a mountaintop.

Lee did not ask any questions or seek any answer or say anything at all. He simply reached out to her. She accepted his silence as she had accepted his presence, with a wordless sense of completion. She took his hands, felt his strength when he lifted her up in front of him. The horse snorted at the swirl of black cloth, but made no further protest.

As the horse started up the trail, the movement and the swell of the saddle made Cira slide back against Lee. She felt the heat of his body through her dress, felt his thighs against hers and his arms holding her when the trail was steep. The tension that had driven her away from the familiar plains was stronger now, a bittersweet pressure inside her when he touched her or when she watched his sun-browned fingers tighten on the reins, guiding the tall horse.

"I wanted to be on a mountaintop with only sky around me," she murmured, as much to herself as to him.

"Yes," he said, bending over her, lips touching her neck. "I'll take you there."

Cira trembled as she had two nights ago, but this time she had no desire to flee. She wanted only to be closer to him, to feel his lips and the power of his arms holding her. With half-closed eyes she relaxed against him, letting go of all sensations except those caused by his presence.

The trail wound up a narrow canyon and over a steep, rocky ridge. Sunlight was like pale-yellow fire consuming the mountain, driving out moisture until the brittle chaparral almost smoked with intense heat. In a few weeks rain would transform the land, bringing out more shades of green than anyone could count or name; but until then the land would remain golden brown, the color of toast or ripe wheat, the color of Cira's breasts half-bare against the black cloth of her dress.

The trail went deeper into the throat of the canyon, rising toward a huge outcrop of granite that was like a heavy brow over the eye of the mountain. Beyond, the mountain rose further, rock and no trees, but the outcrop itself was the watershed between east and west, desert and ocean.

The trail widened as it climbed and was joined by other smaller trails, dusty tributaries to the sand river they followed. Random sycamore and oak appeared, suggesting water not far beneath the rock and sand skin of the canyon bottom. The trees became larger and more lush the closer they grew to the rocky outcrop. Then the trail turned around an ancient landslide. A flash of pure green drew Lee's eye, and he turned to see ferns the color of jacaranda leaves growing in cracks between boulders.

He looked down at Cira, so close, yet he was able to see only thick black lashes against cheeks flushed by more than the sun. Her breasts rose and fell with each slow breath and glistened with a heat that made his body ache. He spread his fingers across her flat stomach, pulling her closer, and felt the soft weight of her breasts against his hand. She tilted her head back, looking up at him with eyes that condensed sunlight into flecks of gold. And she smiled.

Brush gave way to grass imperceptibly, mellowing the quality of the light. Squat, twisted toyons and thick-trunked sycamores were replaced by graceful, tall trees whose leaves made a thick canopy rarely pierced by the hot sun. Beneath the leaves was a glade radiant with golden-green light.

"Where are we?" asked Cira in a voice hushed by the beauty of unexpected green.

"I don't know."

Then Lee realized with a stirring across the back of his neck that his words were almost a lie. It was as though he had ridden under the hot sun to find her and to bring her to an oasis he had never before seen. Never seen, but somehow he had known it was here, waiting, green, and his awe was not that such a place existed but that he recognized it in the first instant he saw it.

The trail ended in a rock wall that was like a garden turned on end. Moss and ferns and grasses spilled in vivid profusion out of crevices and hollows. A stream of crystal water no wider than his hand tumbled down the black rock wall into a small pool whose overflow gave life to the glade.

For a moment Cira and Lee were utterly still, absorbed by the simple miracle of water in a dry land. Then the horse stepped out through knee-deep grass to the edge of the pool. Lee let the horse drink from shaded water while leaves drifted down like great butterflies. One leaf came close enough for Lee to pluck it out of the air, smiling as he recognized something he had not seen since he was a child. A maple leaf touched by frost.

He let the leaf sail away from his palm, wondering how maples came to grow in Southern California's harsh mountains. He glanced around, seeing more trees than he could count. Maples dominated the closed end of the small canyon, their existence owed to a whim of nature or to an anonymous wanderer who had longed for the bright leaves of his childhood.

Lee picketed his horse well back from the water. Together, he and Cira slowly walked back to the tiny, tumbling stream and silent pool. The surface of the water was as motionless as a mirror, reflecting in perfect detail the myriad leaves and the splinters of golden light that reminded Lee of Cira's eyes.

They knelt together and drank water that was sweet and cool and clear, sliding silver between their fingers, over his neck and her breasts, exhilarating. Lee drank again, then stood and unbuttoned his shirt. When he pulled off the faded cloth and rinsed it in the water, Cira turned to him, her fingers and eyes tracing patterns of muscle down his back and ribs and stomach. His breath caught and he captured the slim fingers that burned more deeply than any flame.

"Cira," he said raggedly, "you don't know—"

"Then teach me."

He looked at her eyes and saw a woman awakening behind a child's innocence, saw the fear and anticipation and above all the hunger that were driving her unknowing out of childhood.

"Yes," he said, and his lips on hers were as gentle as a falling leaf.

He drew her to her feet, holding her lightly, letting her make and remake her choice with each breath, each kiss, until her tongue moved over his and then he held her as though she were water sliding between his fingers.

His hands moved over her body, slow caresses that made her arch against him, inviting and then demanding more, to be closer, to feel his touch unhindered by black cloth. He opened her dress to her waist, fingers stroking her and his eyes burning with a knowledge that made her writhe slowly beneath his hands.

Her dress drifted to the ground and the laces of her chemise melted away at his touch, his clothes gone and her own until she felt his lips slide like wind over her bare breasts. Then his tongue teased her slowly and she clung to him, her body moving with a hunger that would have shocked her if she had known what it was.

But he knew. His arms tightened around her until they should have hurt, yet did not, for the woman inside her was fully awake and powerful and glorying in the knowledge of a man's passion. Even when she was lying naked, open to his eyes and hands, even then she was not afraid. She arched against his hand in a blind seeking that snapped his control.

Lee moved suddenly and her eyes opened with the shock of feeling him slide into her. He thrust once, hard, but whatever virgin's pain she might have known was overwhelmed by the intense pleasure of his body moving inside her. She arched again, trying to match his motion with an eagerness that made him laugh deep in his throat. He slid his arm beneath her hips, lifting her to him at the same moment that he went deep into her. He held her, closer than his own breath, and watched her face transformed by passion with each sure movement of his body. She moaned and closed around him convulsively, demanding, and he answered until they both cried out, discovering ecstasy in their joined bodies.

He held her while their breathing slowed. With a gentleness that made Cira feel weak again, he kissed her, whispering her name and her beauty and searching her face for reassurance that her cries had been born of pleasure rather than pain. He saw gold turning deep within her eyes, lips full and soft, smiling. Her head moved toward him, black hair tumbled over his arm in silky caress and her fingers stroked the muscles of his chest with a sensual delight that made breath thicken in his throat.

"Cira—"

She moved in his arms, turning her body until she fit perfectly along his hard length.

"Yes?" she murmured.

Her hands slid down his body with a devastating mixture of curiosity and resurgent passion. He groaned when she touched him.

"I'm sorry," she said, retreating. "I didn't mean to hurt you."

"You didn't," he said thickly, pulling her hands back down his body, teaching. "Yes, like that. Ahhh, you're a witch, Cira, gold in your eyes and fire in your hands."

"Fire?" she said, laughter in her voice. "I thought this was called—"

But his hand moved between her thighs, driving away her teasing words as sudden hunger shook her, frightening her with its violence.

"Lee—!"

"Hush," he said, entering her with a need as great as her own. "This is what you wanted to learn."

His mouth closed over hers and he moved silently, fiercely, and her flesh answered his until both of them were spent and they slept in each other's arms.

Walker's long snort woke Lee. He propped himself up on his elbow to look down at Cira, almost afraid to touch her, wake her, because the grass and the water and her beauty seemed impossible in a dry land. Then she murmured his name and molded herself more firmly against his length. He buried his lips in her fragrant hair, beginning to believe that he was not dreaming.

Smiling, he lifted his head and looked over her shoulder where brilliant shards of sunlight touched the still face

74

of the pool. She moved, following his glance, then she turned back and he felt her breath against his neck.

"What are you thinking?" she asked almost shyly.

"I'm wondering if I have enough strength to stand up."

Cira laughed against his skin and touched him with a woman's pride. "You are strong enough for anything."

He kissed her before he stood up, pulling her with him.

"I promised you a mountaintop," he said, putting on his pants. He shook out her dress, then tossed it aside in favor of his half-dry shirt. "Here," he said. "A dress would trip you."

Cira wriggled into his shirt, flapping the too-long sleeves and giggling.

"I'm a scarecrow."

She turned in a full circle, inviting Lee to laugh with her, but the damp cloth clung to her breasts and hips in a way that made Lee's mouth too dry for laughter. When she bent to strap on her sandals, he had to look away or he would have pulled her down into the silky grass again.

Quickly, Lee stamped into his boots and set off around the small pool. His continuing response to Cira surprised him. He had felt nothing like it before, though he had taken many women, some of them very beautiful and all of them experienced. But not one of them had aroused him like Cira.

She caught up with him at the face of the black rock wall where the tumbling white song of the stream was enveloped by the pool's green silence. Lee climbed up the brow of rumpled rock with clean, sure motions, pausing only long enough to be sure that no rattlesnakes sunned on the warm rocks. Cira watched his easy progress, then rolled up her sleeves and followed with the lithe grace that was as much a part of her as the gold within her eyes.

Lee gained the flattop of the rock promontory and leaned down, taking Cira's wrists in a grip that lifted her over the last rock. Then he stood between her and the world falling away at her feet.

"Close your eyes," he said, his voice low and as warm

75

as his hands. He moved behind her, supporting her. "Now," he whispered against her neck. "Look."

Her eyes opened an she saw their tiny green canyon open onto a mountainside that was harsh with chaparral and rocks baking beneath the flat yellow eye of the sun, a land the color of dust and heat, a land turned in upon itself, waiting for rain.

Beyond the brown foothills was the tawny plain, radiant with sun and curing grass, a great spreading fan of fertile land, the heart of Buckles Ranch. At the western edge of the plain was the gentle swell of coastal hills. The slanting light gave the hills depth and beauty, the textures of warmth without dryness. And beyond the hills was the sea, shimmering with sun and distance.

Lee stood with his hands on her shoulders, telling her of his ranch and his dreams, of the land he loved more than any man should. With his words came a vision of groves and fields green against the sere hills, wells and reservoirs and water, always water bringing life to a vast land that was tamed but not broken, its staggering fertility intact, unlocked by his hands.

The wind rose, dry and hot and heavy with dust. His words faded, replaced by the reality that had driven him out of San Ignacio. Because the thought of Kaiser breaking the land was like acid, Lee tried not to tell her, tried not to destroy the beauty of the moment. But she was so close that she sensed the change in him, life draining out of him like water into sand.

"Tell me," she said, drawing his arms around her with newly found wisdom.

At first she was afraid that he would say nothing, then he spoke slowly, voice devoid of emotion.

"Without the plains, my ranch is worthless. Kaiser will take the flat land as the price of his railroad."

In the same, emotionless voice, Lee explained just how Kaiser would take the plains, nailing his way across the body of Lee's dream.

"But it's your land!" said Cira, eyes black with indignation. "Can't you stop him?"

"I could kill him," said Lee indifferently, "but that wouldn't stop Great Western for long. You see," he said, fingers digging into her without realizing their strength, "nothing can stop the coming of the steel road."

"Then build one of your own," said Cira simply.

Lee started to laugh, then was silent for a long time while he stared east, beyond the brown shoulder of the mountain. The land he saw was like his own, largely untouched. From the mountaintop he could not even see the small herds of sheep and cattle he knew were scattered across hundreds of thousands of acres of dry, unfenced land.

And off to the northeast in back of him, just beyond the limits of his sight, was a town growing tight against the base of another, higher range of mountains. Like San Ignacio, the town of Sierra Leon was just beginning to thrive, thanks to the magic of steel rails. Although the railroad was not the Great Western, Sierra Leon was as much captive to its rail line as was San Ignacio; both towns were growing only because of the promise of wealth roaring down to them on a steel road.

Almost two decades ago, Great Western and Pacific Coast railroads had divided California between them. The piece that was the Buckles Ranch, as well as vast sections of raw desert that bordered it, had been all but ignored. The assumption was that the area was not worth the trouble of specifically including it in the negotiations. If the time came that the land was worth something, the stronger railroad would simply take it.

In the years that followed, Kaiser's shrewd choices became more and more evident. Great Western's land and service area prospered and grew each day, while PacCo was stalled in Sierra Leon, seventy miles from the ocean that gave the railroad its name. The line had done so badly, in fact, that it had succeeded in doing the impossible: Pacific Coast Railroad had lost enough money that its control had been transferred to new owners by the courts.

Lee looked inland and wondered what the new owner

of PacCo would give to have the right-of-way across the Buckles Ranch. Or more importantly, what the railroad would not take from him. He smiled thinly, thinking of Kaiser's various offers.

Cira turned in Lee's arms, watching his eyes, so pale, almost like ice. She shivered, hoping that he would never look like that at her. Then his eyes turned to her face and his expression changed, hard lines melting into a smile that made her breath catch.

"Not only are you beautiful," he said, bending over her, "you're damn smart."

He kissed her long and gently, trying to tell her what it was to have a broken dream return more whole and vivid than at the moment of its loss. Somehow, she understood. When he lifted his mouth he saw tears on her cheeks. He cupped her face between his hands until his lips were wet with her tears and he knew that he could no more let go of her than he could let go of the land.

Lee led her back down the wall to the still pool. There they bathed each other while gold moved in the water and her eyes. Then he carried her to the grass and loved her with a controlled languor that consumed both of them.

By the time Lee and Cira started down the mountain, the sunlight was the color of honey. The chaparral slowly came alive with the rustlings of creatures released from the sun's blinding cage of light. Cira rode silently, relaxed against his chest, eyes nearly closed. She yawned once with the delicacy of a cat; and like a cat, her teeth were small and white and sharp. With a sleepy smile, she turned and rubbed her cheek against his shirt. Neither he nor she spoke, for neither wanted to say the words that would end the day.

But steep hills gave way to long alluvial fans spreading over the plains, and Colonia Juarez condensed out of the sunset in front of them. With gentle fingers Lee lifted her hair and kissed the smooth gold skin of her neck.

"Promise me you'll be careful."

She moved languidly, increasing the pressure of his lips. "Why?"

"Kaiser doesn't like to lose."

"No one does."

Lee sighed and gathered her more closely against him. He had wanted to wait until the future of his ranch was settled before talking to Cira's parents, but if she was too young to understand the potential danger from Kaiser, her parents would not be.

"I'll speak to your father," he said, and even as he spoke he wondered why Gil had not mentioned Cira's father at all.

"My father is dead. And my mother is . . . sick . . . most of the time."

"Even so, I must talk with her."

"No. Please," said Cira, twisting around to face him. "She wouldn't understand."

"Then you must. *Claro?*"

Cira smiled at the Spanish word. "*Sí.* But I'd rather you kissed me and—"

Lee kissed her with a force that left her breathless. He looked at her flushed cheeks and smiled. "Now will you listen?"

Cira put her lips on his chest where a shirt button had come undone.

"Cira—"

"I'm listening." She looked up and her eyes were not laughing. "Truly. I'm listening, though you don't like what you will say. I can tell by the tightness of your body."

Lee's eyes examined her face slowly, surprised by her combination of childlike earnestness and adult perceptions.

"You're right," he said softly. "I don't like what I have to say." He frowned as he remembered Kaiser and the maid and the somber book enclosing Hell. He tightened his hold on her. "Kaiser warned me not to stand between the dragon and its wrath. Can you understand that?"

"Yes," she said slowly.

"If you were in the wrong place at the wrong time with me . . . he's a cruel man, Cira. I don't want you to be caught between me and Kaiser." He tilted her chin up until she met his eyes. "No more rides for a little while. And don't walk out alone. If you need me, send one of your cousins to Gil. They do know Gil, don't they?"

Cira's sly smile answered more questions than he had asked.

"So that's where he's been spending his nights," laughed Lee. "Which one does he like?"

"Juana, the prettiest."

"Seguro," said Lee in dry imitation of Gil. "Of course."

In front of them, Cira's house rose out of the land with its jacaranda tree like a torch held against the coming night. They rode slowly until they were beneath the tree. There, Lee slid off the dust-colored horse and lifted Cira down to stand beside him.

"I'll come to you as soon as I can," said Lee.

He kissed her as though for the first time, or the last, and she fit perfectly into his arms. Then she turned and went toward the house while he stood tasting her on his lips and hearing jacaranda leaves combed by a dry wind.

The next morning Gilberto Zavala rode quickly through the dry dawn. His gray horse was already streaked with sweat and trail dust. San Ignacio and Colonia Juarez receded behind Gil as the horse loped toward the ranch boundary. When the gray would have slowed, Gil's spurs drove him back into a ground-eating lope.

With a steady light pressure, Gil put the gray in a wide arc past the Great Western spur line. When he saw that the track was still empty, he reined the horse back onto the shortest possible route to the old adobe house.

But long before he reached the house, a shout brought him up short; with a profound sense of relief, Gil pulled the gray to a stop, waiting for the dust-colored horse and its rider to break out of the brush by the wagon road. Soon Lee appeared riding a tall horse and leading a chestnut carrying bedroll, grain and extra water.

"Ola, jefe," called Gil, casually rolling a cigarette while Lee's horse came to a dust-raising stop.

Lee's eyes did not miss Gil's horse sweating into the

hot dawn, nor the hard lines of his foreman's normally smiling face.

"All right, Gil. Let's have it."

"I had breakfast in Frederico's boarding house." Gil blew out a plume of smoke as he shifted in the worn saddle. His face was closed and his voice was flat, remembering the drunken men he had overheard between mouthsful of frijoles and eggs. "Great Western starts laying track in two days. Three at most." Gil spat out a piece of tobacco, then glanced at Lee's face. "You aren't surprised."

"I ate lunch at Helm's beer hall."

Gil's cigarette glowed raggedly.

"I had hoped," said Lee in a carefully uninflected voice, "for at least a week."

"To do what?" said Gil bluntly.

Lee smiled. "To build my own railroad."

Gil squinted against the smoke curling off his cigarette. *"Seguro,"* he grunted. "I'll shout and you'll swear and the little sheep will shit railroad tracks."

"I think Pacific Coast Rail Lines would do it better," said Lee mildly.

Gil's nearly black eyes probed the other man, then Gil laughed bitterly. "You mean it. You really mean it." Gil broke off, removed the almost consumed cigarette and watched its glowing tip. When the glow died he crumbled the cigarette between his fingers and let the cold ashes sift to the ground. "Compadre," he asked softly, "does it make that much difference which railroad rapes you?"

"Think of it as a shotgun marriage," said Lee. "Not ideal, but better than rape and no marriage at all." Lee's saddle creaked as he crooked his right leg around the saddle horn, settling in to explain to his proud foreman. "I'm going to have a railroad shoved down my throat," he said bluntly. "Kaiser's or some other. Now, it's not the tracks I mind—it's giving away the center of my ranch. PacCo might be hungry enough to drive steel and leave my ranch to me. I'm going to Sierra Leon to find out."

Gil rubbed his hands along his thighs, removing the last of the pungent ash. "And if that doesn't work?"

"I fight."

"No," said Gil, anger replaced by a grin. "We fight."

"Gil—" Lee sighed and began again. "Compadre, there's no pleasure in a fight like that."

Gil laughed. Lee shook his head silently; his foreman's zest for guns and knives was something that Lee did not share. Lee would fight if he had to, even kill if he must, but he did not enjoy it. And because of that, he was a deadly fighter.

"Tell the men to start carrying arms," said Lee abruptly.

"*Sí, jefe*," said Gil, teeth shining.

"And remember that the track layers will have guns too."

"*Seguro*." Gil shrugged. "That is what makes it interesting, no?"

"Gil, have you ever killed a man?" asked Lee quietly, watching the dawn.

Something in Lee's voice made the foreman look at Lee closely. "No."

Lee looked directly at him. "I hope you'll never have to."

Gil waited, but Lee said nothing more, for he was remembering Paris and a hotel room where dawn had come for only one of three men. Gil saw death reflected in Lee's eyes and looked away. He did not look back until Lee spoke again.

"The plains are impossible to defend with the men we have. There's no natural funnel, no canyon or river course that the track will have to follow." Lee's eyes raked the surrounding brush as though angry at the land for not protecting itself better. "So if we fight, it will be as bandits—guerrillas—not as blazing heroes. *Sabe?*"

"*Sí.*"

"No one will shoot unless in self-defense or under my direct orders."

"*Sí.*"

"We can't win, Gil."

"*Seguro*. But we are men. We can't lose without a fight."

The two men sat silently, watching early morning light flood through brush while quail called from a thousand long shadows. The soft, throaty cries brought memories to Lee; for a moment he lived again in a world of water and Cira moving in his arms. He shut his eyes and thought of something else, anything else, for he could not go to her today, nor tomorrow, and the hours were like summer days, hot and long with no hope of rain.

"Gil—"

"*Sí?*"

"I told Cira to stay out of sight until this is settled. I don't want to remind Kaiser how I found out about his plans. If Cira needs anything, she'll send one of her cousins to you." Lee smiled briefly. "Probably Juana."

Gil smiled. "I look forward to it. And *jefe*—"

The laughter in Gil's voice made Lee glance up. "Yes?"

"Next time you bring Cira home, don't go by the home of Lupe Verdugo. The whole colonia knows that Cira was riding with a man."

"Was I recognized?" demanded Lee with an intensity that killed Gil's laughter.

"No." The foreman's eyes narrowed. "But is it such a bad thing for a gringo to be seen with a—"

"Shut up, Gil."

Gil traded a long look with Lee, then the foreman smiled again. "I'll watch over her like a brother, compadre. And I'll leave a man in the brush to watch the spur line."

"Gilberto," Lee said, "what would I do without you?" He straightened and reined the dust-colored horse aside, tugging on the chestnut's lead rope at the same time. "I'll be back tomorrow night."

"To Sierra Leon and back in that time?" said Gil incredulously. "*Hijo!* I don't envy you."

"Neither do I."

Lee touched spurs to his horse. The chestnut fought the lead rope for an instant, then gave in and cantered alongside the fast-walking horse.

Lee alternated gaits and horses throughout the hot morning, resting each animal from the burden of a rider. But there was no rest for him. He skirted the foot of the mountains until he came to a wide, dry riverbed that cut the low mountains in half. There he turned inland while the day and the sand grew so hot that sweat burned on his skin and grit coated his throat, and to move at any pace faster than a crawl would kill the horses.

In the distance he saw what seemed to be two men walking. As he came closer, he saw that the heat waves had disguised the outline of a man and an animal. Closer still, and Lee recognized the one-armed man and his mouse-colored burro. Lee pulled the horses off to one side of the trail and waited.

"Morning, Luther."

The old man looked up at Lee out of a face that was as worn and seamed as the mountains. Normally Luther had only curses for his fellow man, but he spoke civilly to Lee because Lee was one of the few people who did not call him Crip.

"Morning." Luther spat a red-brown stream of tobacco juice at a distant rock. "Kinda far from your sheep, ain't you?"

"So are you. Last time I saw you was in one of the canyons halfway up my mountains."

Luther chewed reflectively, making his stained beard jerk like a goat's. "Yeah. 'Bout three weeks ago. Pretty place. Know there's silver there, just waiting." He peered up at Lee and added half-defiantly, "I'm headed there now."

Lee looked levelly at the old man. "So long as you don't bother my sheep and keep your campfires under control, you're welcome to prospect on my land."

The old man grunted. "Townfolk told me you'd been leaning on tres-pass-ers," he said, contempt riding each syllable of the last word.

"That's right. But," said Lee, half-smiling at the old man, "I doubt if you're planning on running my sheep into the ground or settling in that canyon and raising a litter of kids on my land."

Luther laughed soundlessly, thumping the stump of his arm against his chest at the thought of a man his age having either the desire or the ability to conceive children. Then the old man leaned forward confidentially and his sharp eyes pinned Lee with surprising force; whatever Luther was now, he once had been a man of considerable presence.

"You be careful. This here country's filling with riffraff." He nodded once, sharply, agreeing with himself. "Passed a fellow yesterday. He was smack in the middle of the trail, big as you please, squattin' and gruntin'. I told him that other people used the trail and he oughta use the bushes. He just laughed and said he didn't care, he wasn't going this way but once." Luther shook his head in disgust. "It didn't used to be like that. No one has any respect, nowadays. No respect at all."

The old man moved down the riverbed muttering to himself, followed by a fat burro with one bent ear.

"Thanks for the warning."

There was no answer, nor did Lee expect one. He took a small swallow of water from his canteen, then urged the horses into the searing riverbed.

By the time Lee came to the huge dry bowl that held Sierra Leon, the moon was rising and the immense heat of the day had vanished into the always surprising chill of desert night. In the distance was the pale gleam of weathered wood buildings and the brighter shine of whitewash. Farther on, against the base of the foothills, light streaks of mine tailings gleamed against the dark bulk of the land. But the mines were nearly spent, their highgrade silver ore just a memory. If it had not been for the railroad, Sierra Leon would have been nothing more than a few abandoned buildings hunched against the withering desert wind.

Lee turned off the road. Rather than search a strange

town for lodging in the middle of the night, he found a stock tank, watered the horses and wrapped up in his bedroll. The rising sun woke him after too few hours of sleep on ground that was too hard. He washed in the trough, ate mutton jerky and a can of peaches and headed for Sierra Leon.

The September sun sucked every bit of the cool night out of the ground. The wagons and men who were dispersing freight from the railhead at Sierra Leon spun clouds of dust that Lee could see miles away. The PacCo freight yard was on the western edge of town, where the flatlands began their slow, inexorable rise to the twisting slot called Highpass. The long, nearly flat valley that paralleled the foothills was the railroad's last chance to gather steam for the rigorous pass. Even with many miles of running start, it took at least four engines and a skilled engineer to bring a single train through Highpass.

By the time Lee arrived at the freight yard, he was coated with sweat and dust and sand grated between his teeth. With his clothes, his tired horses, his battered hat and worn boots, Leander Buckles looked every inch a saddle tramp.

Lee left his horses in a cool stable and set off on foot for the freight yard. The closer he came, the more obvious it was that David Arthur Carrington, PacCo's new owner, had put a lot of money into his acquisition. New track, new roadbeds, new culverts and cars and engines converged on the freight yard. Carrington's investment seemed to be succeeding; the southern route across the desert was siphoning off an appreciable part of Kaiser's Great Western business. But that alone would not ensure PacCo's success. Carrington had gambled that Southern California, Nevada, New Mexico and the Oklahoma Territory would grow as their northern counterparts had. And as they grew, they would make Carrington as rich as Franklin J. Kaiser.

All Carrington had to do was to survive the slow strangulation of lean times.

PacCo had offices in a building that was half weathered

and half under construction. In spite of the exterior bustle, Carrington's section of the building was clean, cool and surprisingly quiet. Lee jerked his hat more firmly in place, hooked his thumbs in his jeans and in his best continental voice spoke to the secretary who guarded the entrance to Carrington's office.

"Would you be so good as to tell Mr. Carrington that there is a man here to see him."

Lee's cultured accent and his trail-stained appearance were so at odds that the secretary was momentarily immobilized. Then he recovered with an alacrity that suggested he had learned that in the West, men were not always what they appeared to be.

"Who shall I say is here?" asked the secretary with careful civility.

Lee smiled and said nothing. The secretary moved uncomfortably, liking neither the smiling lips nor the unsmiling gray-green eyes.

"See here," said the secretary sharply. "Mr. Carrington is a—"

"—very busy man," finished Lee with a cool arrogance he had rarely used since France. "So am I. Take my message to him."

The secretary wanted to be snide, but something in Lee's look made that seem unwise. Without a word the secretary turned and stalked through a door at the back.

Outside, from not too far away, came the sharp, rhythmic sounds of a steam engine making headway against the first gentle rise leading to Highpass. Lee crossed to the front door and watched while four coal-black locomotives pulled wooden boxcars along the rigid steel road. Black smoke boiled out of straight-sided smokestacks and white steam shot from traveling cylinders. The train passed in a gathering fury of force and noise.

Lee watched the train until its passage no longer shook the ground, until the train was a thin, dark line drawn precisely over gleaming silver tracks. When Lee turned back to the room he saw that he was being studied by a man who was perhaps ten years older, smaller and every bit as uncompromising as Lee. The quietly elegant clothes and confident posture told Lee who the man was.

"David Arthur Carrington," said Lee softly.

"You have me at a disadvantage."

Carrington's glance took in Lee's clothes, the way he stood, moved, spoke, smiled or did not smile, the many subtle signals that Carrington had learned to read unconsciously. There was a long silence while the two men appraised each other. Lee looked from Carrington to the secretary who was plainly fascinated by the confrontation. Carrington followed Lee's glance, then reacted with the swiftness and accuracy that was responsible for much of his financial success.

"Thank you, Joseph. That will be all," said Carrington.

The secretary looked startled, flushed slightly and returned to his desk across the room. At Carrington's gesture, Lee followed him into an inner office that was cool, spacious and appointed with an understated elegance that was lean rather than lush—and more intimidating than velvet and gilt. Everywhere in the room was the unobtrusive presence of rare wood, fine leather, and superbly made furniture. Carrington was wholly a part of the room, at ease in his three-piece, lightweight suit and cream silk shirt. On the smallest finger of his right hand an emerald glowed. He gestured Lee into an informal grouping of chairs.

"Your name," said Carrington mildly, but there was nothing mild about the hazel eyes that watched the cool, rough-looking stranger.

"Leander Champion Buckles."

Carrington's eyes flickered over to the door; it was safely closed. He nodded briefly, then looked back at the tall cowboy who was so much more than he seemed.

"You've had a long ride," Carrington said. "May I get you anything?"

"Coffee, if you have it," said Lee, having spotted the large silver samovar set discreetly back from the chairs.

Carrington drew a mug of coffee for Lee with the practiced motions of a bachelor used to entertaining. The fragrance of the Turkish blend filled the room invisibly.

"Sugar? Cream?"

"Neither, thank you."

Carrington gave the mug to Lee, lifted the top off of a silver bun warmer and extended it to Lee. Inside, crescent-shaped rolls nestled against each other invitingly. Lee looked up at Carrington with a light of real appreciation in his eyes.

"I haven't seen croissants since Paris," said Lee, taking one. "Thank you."

Carrington smiled at the younger man's pleasure.

"You are more than welcome, Mr. Buckles. I was beginning to think I was the only man west of the Mississippi who knew a croissant from a corn tortilla."

Carrington got himself a mug of coffee, sat in a chair next to Lee and sipped at the brew as though it were common for a railroad tycoon to serve breakfast to every stranger who wandered in looking hungry. But he watched Lee unobtrusively, noting that nothing escaped Lee's restless eyes, not even a glass case of silver ore along the far wall.

Lee finished eating, wiped his fingers neatly on a napkin and silently toasted Carrington, the room and the freight yard with an upraised mug of Turkish coffee.

"You have a fine railroad, Mr. Carrington."

"Thank you," said Carrington dryly. "I rather thought that you disliked railroads."

Lee looked at the older man's unlined, tanned face and the body that spoke of health and hard work as clearly as the finely made gold watch-chain and emerald ring spoke of wealth and taste. Like the room, the man was an unusual combination of efficiency and elegance.

"I only dislike railroads that are being rammed down my throat."

Lee watched the minute changes that occurred in Carrington's face as he examined the ramifications of Lee's ostensibly casual remark. Few men would have seen the moving shadow that was not quite a smile on Carrington's full lips. But Lee saw it and began to relax for the first time since Gilberto Zavala had read the forged deed aloud in a room swirling with shadows.

"I was told," said Carrington, more to himself than to Lee, "that you were too young, too raw and too stupid to recognize a railroad's inevitability."

"I'm all of those things from time to time," drawled Lee, taking off his hat and hanging it on his knee. "But I do try to be careful about the times."

Carrington's smile flickered. "Anybody who believes your cowboy . . . act . . . will be badly fooled."

"As will anybody who believes you are a drawing-room dandy," said Lee equitably.

Carrington laughed softly, making the watch-chain turn and shimmer in the light.

"But appearances shouldn't be disregarded," added Lee. "The façade is, after all, attached to the building."

Carrington set down the mug and held out his right hand.

"Leander, I believe it's going to be a rare pleasure."

Lee took the hand in a firm grip that was equaled by the other man. Then Carrington settled back, selected a croissant and waited for Lee to tell him precisely what Lee hoped to gain from his long ride to Sierra Leon.

"I assume," said Lee, "that you know about Kaiser's attempts to back me into a corner."

"The last year has been very instructive," said Carrington with a smile that was gone almost the instant it touched his lips.

"That's one way of putting it," said Lee. "I'm like a man who has to cross a river, but I can't swim and the ferryman wants two arms and a leg to take me across. The choice between drowning and dismemberment is not an attractive one."

"But if it's the only choice you have. . . ?" murmured Carrington when it appeared that Lee was not going to continue.

"Not quite." Lee sipped his coffee while steam rose and vanished before it reached his sun-colored hair. "I could always kill the ferryman, but that still wouldn't get me across."

Carrington's hazel eyes probed Lee for long moments before the older man nodded once. Lee, his eyes on his coffee, did not notice.

"So," continued Lee softly, "I decided to find someone who could build me another ferry."

Carrington's lips curved into an easy smile of appreciation. "Most people would have been frozen between the first alternatives like the proverbial ass between two haystacks."

"That's why most people spend their lives carrying other men's burdens." Lee looked up; in the muted light of the office, his eyes were almost as colorless as the steam curling off of his coffee. "Can you build a line through my ranch and make a profit?"

Carrington steepled his hands, displaying fingers as long and supple as a concert pianist's. He stared over his hands as though he could see through the room to Buckles Ranch.

"I would come in through the southern canyons, cross your land on the plains and then push through to Los Angeles, or branch off to Sierra Leon. Or both, if business warranted. Profitable? Not immediately. But the railroad would bring Mission San Diego into the nineteenth century and then the line would earn back its costs."

"I thought so," said Lee softly, setting his empty mug aside. "Kaiser is not a fool." He looked at Carrington. "I'll give you the right-of-way and a note against my ranch for half the capital costs of constructing the line. In return, you'll put the line where I want it and guarantee equitable freight fees."

Carrington frowned. "The fees are no problem. The line, however, would be too expensive unless it crossed the flatlands. And that would cut your ranch in half, an act that I believe you objected to in rather blunt terms."

Lee smiled sardonically. "If you build at the coastal edge of the plains, I can live with it. I'll have to."

Carrington was silent for a long time, weighing possibilities. "You realize," he said finally, "that it is customary for the railroad to get land in addition to the right-of-way? Selling land to settlers who will in turn depend on the railroad is the source of much of our profit. And of the ranchers' profits as well. Land becomes more valuable because of the presence of a railroad. Settlers come and build towns, creating markets for ranch and railroad alike."

Lee said nothing. Nor did he need to.

Carrington's fingertips pressed together lightly, then relaxed. "I know what you would get out of this partnership you're proposing. But what of me?"

"You'd get the same thing I would. Survival." He gestured to the glass-front case that held samples of the very rich silver ore that had been mined out of the nearby foothills. "The good mining is about gone. You have to get into the mainstream of California growth or you're finished. Or do you think you can make a profit hauling Kaiser's leavings across deserts no one gives a damn about?" Lee paused, giving Carrington a hard, almost amused look. "Frankly, I'm surprised you didn't come to *me*."

Carrington returned the look in kind, not the least insulted by Lee's blunt appraisal of PacCo's probable future in relation to Great Western.

"Would you have listened if I'd come to you?"

Lee smiled ruefully. "I doubt it."

"What changed your mind?"

"Great Western will begin laying track tomorrow."

Carrington's face became as expressionless as polished wood. "Then you've had a long ride for nothing. I can't get the agreement of my backers in less than a week."

"But Kaiser will be halfway across my ranch by then!"

"I know." Carrington shrugged expressively and spoke with real regret. "I'm sorry. For both of us."

Lee was on his feet with a cat's speed. He ranged around the elegant room like a newly caged animal, restless, seeking, radiating a savage energy that was one instant away from violence. Then he stopped in front of the case holding the silver ore, staring at the muted gray rocks as though he had never seen their like before. Carrington let out his breath slowly, only then realizing the tension that had built since Lee had surged out of his chair.

"If I guarantee you a week," said Lee in a deceptively calm voice, "can you guarantee the rest?"

"Yes." Carrington eyed Lee with renewed speculation, remembering the past moments when violence had seethed in the young man's eyes. "I can get you an injunction against Great Western."

"How soon?"

"Before you leave."

Lee smiled coldly. "It's the best legal system that money can buy."

"That's preferable to violence, isn't it?" asked Carrington blandly.

"So long as you have money." Lee turned back to the ore samples. "I need these."

Carrington started, then stared, but did not ask why Lee required the ore. Without a word he stood, walked over to the case and unlocked it. Then the realization hit him and his full laughter rang in the room. Lee glanced up, smiled and then began laughing in spite of himself.

"You're sure that there's no silver on your land?" asked Carrington, still chuckling.

"Only this—and what the fools will carry up in their pockets."

Carrington laughed and shook his head in admiration. "I was right, Leander. It has been a rare pleasure."

It was dark before Lee rode up to the corral beneath one of the old adobe's five jacaranda trees. The trip to Sierra Leon and back, plus a day spent combing Moreno canyon for Luther and his lop-eared burro, had worn out both Lee and the spirited chestnut.

"Find him?" asked Gil from the darkness.

"Yeah. Way up. Damn near over the mountains."

Gil took the reins and gently shoved Lee toward the

adobe where yellow lamplight glowed invitingly on the porch.

"Coffee's hot. I'll take care of your horse."

"Thanks."

"De nada."

Lee left the lamp on the porch, preferring to find his way around by the light of a candle. He sank wearily into a kitchen chair and gulped coffee out of a cracked earthenware mug. Then he wrapped a cold tortilla around colder beans and ate, staring with unfocused eyes at the pure yellow flame.

A handful of moths circled, drawn to the light. They danced and darted, daring the flame until finally one came too close and was devoured with a tiny hiss of sound. The other moths danced on, oblivious, until another and yet another spiraled into the flame.

The sound of a running horse brought Lee to his feet. He stuffed the last of the tortilla into his mouth and ran to the porch, waiting for the rider who was pushing his horse too hard over a dark road. Silently, Gil materialized out of the night and stood next to Lee. Lee noticed for the first time that his foreman was wearing a handgun and carrying a rifle.

A horse burst out of the shadows beneath a jacaranda tree. With a fine disregard for safety, the young Mexican rider yanked his horse into a rearing halt. There was a burst of Spanish so rapid that Lee caught only the word for train. Lee was back in the house, reaching for his rifle, before Gil could translate.

"They've started. Pulled out the bumper stop on the spur and they're laying track."

"How many?" asked Lee, checking and loading the rifle with sure motions.

"My cousin stopped when he ran out of fingers and toes."

Lee reached for a shotgun, broke it open and shoved a fat shell into each barrel. The shotgun made a sharp metallic sound when Lee closed it.

"What about our men?"

"Miguelito will tell them to meet us on the hill."

The sound of a distant whoop came to Lee and in his mind he saw a small Mexican spurring a wildly running horse.

"If he doesn't break his neck first," muttered Lee.

He grabbed rifle, shotgun and a box of shells and began running toward the corral. Within minutes, he and Gil were galloping toward San Ignacio and an illegal railroad line.

The light from the huge, coal-oil lamp on the work train could be seen for more than a mile across the plains. The train was already several hundred yards onto Buckles's land, a tribute to the organized frenzy of a crew that numbered more than sixty. In front of the engine, twelve mule teams worked by torchlight, pulling wide blades over the dry ground, smoothing it enough to accept a burden of ties and rails.

The construction crew had dispensed with the time-consuming process of laying down a roadbed of crushed rock. Instead, they were putting wooden ties directly on the earth and then nailing the rails into the ties with long spikes. The land was flat enough to support such an arrangement, so long as the engine speed was kept to the pace of a walking man. Obviously, Kaiser had decided to lay as much steel as he could and then worry about replacing it later, after the courts reinforced his claim to the right-of-way that he was ramming across Buckles's land.

Lee watched Great Western's progress with a cold calculation. Included in his calm equations was the impact of bullets fired from darkness at men who were as tied to light as moths to candle flame.

Out of the night around Lee, his ranch hands began to gather, watching the mile-distant crew with a silence that matched Lee's. There was a fascination about the track-laying process: the mule teams and their single-blade earth scrapers sliced down through pale grass to dark soil, tearing a wound that was stitched closed with ties and rails almost as quickly as it was made.

The progress of the work train was inexorable, more like a natural force than a creation of man. The steel road grew while they watched, measured by black ties and silver rails and the engine muttering to itself while it inched forward, pushing a flatcar from which the working men snatched wood and steel. From Lee's vantage point, the men flitting in and out of the cone of light looked no larger than moths.

But even distance could not conceal the progress of the train over land that moments before had never supported anything heavier than a good horse. Lee watched and knew that his intuition was correct; the railroad and the impulse it represented was stronger than any one man's ability to withstand. Now it remained to see if his intuition had come in time.

"Follow me in a few minutes. And remember—no shooting unless I give a direct order."

Without waiting for an answer, Lee kicked his horse into a lope and rode down the small hill with a double-barreled shotgun across his lap.

Fifty yards beyond the leading edge of the work crew were two outriders; the engine light silhouetted them and the rifles they carried at the ready. Other armed riders were fanned out behind on either side of the advancing locomotive. The effectiveness of the guards was limited by the glaring light, which ruined night vision, and by the piercing clang of steel sledges meeting steel spikes, a noise which effectively masked the sounds made by Lee's horse.

The point man finally heard the galloping horse. As he had been told to do, he fired a warning shot into the sky.

"Go back!" he shouted, firing again.

The shout and the flat reports sent most workers racing for the safe darkness behind the engine. The men who remained were One-Ear's crew. They continued to drive steel, but they no longer shouted and they watched the darkness very carefully. The point man and the guard who rode up beside him also watched the darkness, though they were confident that the shots had stopped the rider.

Instead, Lee put spurs into his tall horse. The animal flattened out into a gallop. It was the last response the guards had expected. They had been told to fire shots to scare away anyone who came near the work crew, but they had also been told to make damn sure their shots were high. They had not been told what to do with a man who kept on coming.

By the time the ex-cavalrymen realized that they were in a situation not covered by their orders, Lee's horse was plunging to a stop in front of them and the shotgun across Lee's lap was pointed exactly between them, where a single shot would take both men out of their saddles.

"Just so we don't misunderstand each other," said Lee, "you're on private property and this shotgun is loaded for bear."

The guards sat very quietly on their horses, their rifles still pointed at the sky.

"You've gotta be Buckles," said one outrider finally.

Lee's sardonic smile made the man shift uncomfortably. His horse took a step and suddenly the ex-cavalryman was looking down both barrels of the shotgun. The guard began to sweat.

"Look here, Mr. Buckles," said the other man. "This ain't private land no longer. We got a court order that says so and we're coming through. Everything's nice and legal."

"Then why did you wait until dark?"

In the silence, the rhythmic ring of steel on steel was painfully loud. The second man stirred and spat a pungent arc of tobacco juice. "Mr. Buckles, you can't stop this many men by yourself."

Lee smiled and moved the shotgun so that its barrel once again pointed between the two guards. "All I have to stop is you."

The two men were very still, watching each other and waiting for something to break the silence that had become dangerous. The sound of a horse trotting from the darkness behind the train came as a relief to the guards.

The horse stopped between them; even in the difficult light, Lee saw that the third man was Roger Heer.

"Get out of the way, Buckles," Heer said, ignoring Lee's shotgun.

"Glad to." Lee smiled. "Just as soon as you back that Goddamned engine off my land."

"I have a court order from Judge Hilms," said Heer, and Lee did not misunderstand the amusement in Heer's voice.

"Heard about that," drawled Lee, pushing his hat back with his left hand. "What does it say?"

Lee's slow speech and his easy seat on the tall horse did not mislead Heer; he had seen that Lee's pale eyes missed no movement, however small, made by the three men in front of him. For the first time, Heer believed that Buckles might kill for his land. But not yet. Certainly not tonight.

"The order says that Great Western is going to lay track across your land whether you like it or not. The order was signed three hours ago. Satisfied?"

"No," said Lee, smiling in a way that angered Heer. "I've got one of those court orders too. Mine was signed yesterday afternoon. Want to know what it says?"

"Yes," snapped Heer.

"It says that Great Western is not going to build one damn thing on my land." Lee laughed softly and reached up with his left hand to pull his hat back into place again. "Guess we'll have to start bidding on a third judge to break the tie."

Heer's horse started forward, but the sound of both hammers going back on the shotgun stopped Heer as effectively as a wall.

"All right, Buckles," said Heer. "You've had your little party. Now get the hell out of my way."

While Heer spoke, railroad riders closed in behind their boss, adding twelve new silhouettes between Lee and the light of the train. Behind them, One-Ear's men continued driving steel, but at a much reduced pace. The locomotive moved up another length of rail, coming so close that its light seemed hard and almost white.

The steam hissing from the engine's traveling piston and the clang of steel spikes being driven into ties muffled the sounds made by Gil and his half-dozen riders. They stopped just behind Lee.

The sudden appearance of more men did not surprise Heer; he had guessed that Lee was not foolish enough to come alone. But when Heer recognized Gil as the Mexican who had humiliated him in the Blue Lagoon Hotel, Heer's diffuse anger at being under Lee's shotgun focused into rage. His blue eyes raked over Gil with unmistakable intent.

"Well, well," said Heer slowly, "if it isn't Buckles's faithful greaser." He raised his voice so that it carried over the sound of track being laid. "Know how greasers got those dark skins?" he asked. "They eat so much gringo shit that they're brown from the inside out!"

Lee spoke in hard, rapid Spanish to Gil. Slowly, Gil's hand moved away from the butt of his pistol. Heer's disappointment was almost painful; he knew that at least one of his men had a rifle trained on the big Mexican.

"What did you say?" asked Heer sarcastically. "I don't speak greaser like you."

"I told him there was no point in killing a man he had already castrated."

Before Heer's rage could be translated into action, Lee spurred his horse until it crowded up against Heer's horse and the shotgun was a cold fist in Heer's stomach.

"Any man who whores for Kaiser," said Lee softly, "can't afford to have a thin skin."

Lee waited, leaning on the shotgun until Heer's face became that of a rational man. The work train moved closer, so close that its light bleached the men's skin and made even the thinnest shadow indelibly black. The smell of oil and dirt and railroad ties coiled through the tight silence. Steel no longer met steel, for the crew would not go further until the horses moved aside. One-Ear had silently signaled for his men to get out of the light.

"I'm going to enjoy watching you lose your land," said Heer distinctly, his voice resonant with barely controlled rage. "Your land and everything else you care about. I'm going to enjoy that very much."

"Don't count on it." Lee spoke to the men behind him without looking away from Heer's eyes. *"La casa! Pronto!"*

"But—" began Gil, then he saw the white flash of Lee's glance and decided to leave without comment. He spoke in rapid Spanish to the men behind him, half of them shepherds on rawboned horses and half of them vaqueros on horses as fine as any Lee rode. Slowly, the men put away weapons that ranged from percussion revolvers to .50 caliber buffalo guns. Compared to Heer's fourteen ex-cavalry guards, Lee's men were a ragtag force.

Lee waited until he could no longer hear the sound of horses going away. He increased the pressure slightly on the shotgun while he eased his horse around until only Heer was between him and the white flood of light from the train.

"Men like you should work in the dark."

As Lee spoke, he moved the shotgun slightly and fired both barrels. Pea-sized shot slammed through the thick glass lens of the train's headlamp and shattered the mirrored reflector behind the flame. Before Heer could recover from the sudden noise and recoil that had bruised his ribs, Lee spurred his horse and vanished into the night. A few of the guards got off shots, but they were wide and too high. Gil's answering shot whined off of the locomotive, scattering workers.

"Hold your fire," Heer shouted angrily to his guards, realizing he was at a tactical disadvantage.

In the sudden silence, Heer heard two horses galloping away. He swore in disgust.

"Should we go after them?" called one of his guards.

"And leave the track unprotected? Don't be more stupid than God made you," said Heer coldly.

As soon as Lee and Gil were beyond rifle range, they

stopped to listen for sounds of pursuit. They heard nothing but wind blowing over dry grass.

"Damn!" said Lee. "I was hoping to lead them up the mountain and over on the dry side while you tore out track."

Lee turned his horse, listened with fierce concentration, but still heard nothing.

"What now?" asked Gil, sliding his rifle back into its scabbard.

With the need for action past, Lee felt suddenly tired. "Sleep. And pray."

"What?"

Lee yawned. "Pray that Luther puts on a convincing show."

"But if he doesn't?"

Lee turned his horse toward home. "Then we stop wasting bullets on locomotives."

The following morning, Cira woke to the sound of people moving past her open window. She stirred slowly, then sat upright when she realized that someone was tapping at the glass. For an instant she thought it was Lee and a ripple of excitement went through her. Then she saw the round face of her cousin Yolanda. Irritated, Cira snapped the sheet off and stalked to the window in her heavy nightgown.

"What is it?" she whispered.

Yolanda smiled and her black eyes shone with excitement. "There was a big fight last night!"

"There is one nearly every night," snapped Cira. "Knives and tequila and those stupid fighting cocks. Is that any reason to—"

"Not in the colonia," interrupted Yolanda. "At el rancho grande. With guns!"

"What?" Cira said, her fingernails digging into the window frame. "Tell me!"

Yolanda smiled slyly. "But maybe you're right. What is so interesting about a fight? Go back to sleep, cousin, I'll—"

Cira's hand shot out and her fingers twisted through her cousin's coarse black hair. Yolanda's surprised yelp did not drown out Cira's hissed words.

"If your mother heard you say such things, she—ow!" Yolanda's head jerked and she said placatingly, *"Basta,* cousin. I was only teasing."

Cira let go with a mumbled apology.

"The railroad," said Yolanda hastily. "They started building it across el rancho last night. Señor Buckles and his men fought with guns. Many people were shot."

Cira leaned forward. "Was Lee—Señor Buckles—hurt?"

"Some say yes, some no." Yolanda shrugged. *"Quién sabe?"*

Cira let go of the frame and leaned against the side of the window, feeling almost dizzy.

"Where is Juana?"

The quality of Cira's voice made Yolanda forget her cousin's hot anger and her own desire to tease. "Are you all right, Cira?"

Cira laughed, a half-wild, half-frightened sound. "I am fine, cousin. *Muy bien, gracias.* Now tell me where your sister Juana is."

"When she heard last night, she left to find Gilberto."

"Did she find him?"

"She must have," snickered Yolanda. "She did not come back."

Cira said another word that shocked her cousin.

"I'm going to where they are building the track," said Yolanda. "Do you want to come? Your mother is still drunk. Asleep," amended Yolanda quickly. "She won't wake up for hours."

Cira thought of Lee's warning to stay out of sight, then she thought of spending hours wondering if Lee was hurt.

"I'm coming."

"Señor Gomez just went by. I'll ask him to wait. Hurry!"

While Yolanda ran after the Gomez wagon, Cira jerked off her nightgown and pulled a dress over her head. The

102

cloth was so dark that it was almost black, but in sunlight it had a blush of blue across its surface that made Cira's skin glow. With a series of yanks that made her wince, Cira combed her hair and twisted its length into a large knot at the nape of her neck. She jammed in two elegant tortoiseshell combs just above the knot, strapped sandals on her feet and was turning toward the window when she realized that her mother was standing in the doorway.

"Where are you going in such a rush?"

Señora McCartney's voice was harsh, clouded by whiskey, but her dark eyes were penetrating. Cira blushed and unconsciously retreated. Her mother closed in, standing so near that the smell of stale alcohol made Cira turn her face aside. Señora McCartney swayed slightly, leaning toward the daughter who shrank away.

"Have you so little shame that you are meeting your lover in daylight?" demanded the señora. "Look at me, *puta!*" she said, slapping Cira's face. "Look at the mother you have shamed!"

Cira backed up a step, only to find retreat blocked by the bed. Before she could move, Señora McCartney's hand descended on Cira's other cheek.

"No," said Cira, shielding her face with her arms.

The señora's hands closed over Cira's shoulders, shaking her.

"You say no to me? To your mother? But to men you say *sí. Es verdad, puta. Madre de Dios!* I should have given you to the nuns while I could. I told you what men are, but do you listen to me? No. You lift your skirt to every man who asks!"

"Let me go," said Cira suddenly, wrenching away from her mother's foul breath and accusations. "It's not what you believe. You're wrong."

Señora McCartney staggered when Cira freed herself. The older woman would have fallen if she had not caught herself on the bed.

"*Niña,*" whispered the señora hoarsely.

She reached out for Cira with hands that shook, but Cira was three steps away, sliding out of the window.

"Don't trust them," called the señora after her. "They take your honor and leave you nothing, nothing. I know, *niña*. Please believe me, I know. I have been left . . ."

Señora McCartney's voice died into a harsh whisper as she realized that she was alone. She walked slowly to the window and through an alcohol haze saw Cira running toward a wagon. Not once did Cira look back.

By the time Gomez and his wagon arrived at the edge of the ranch land, both the wagon and the area around the track were filled with people. Word of last night's fight had swept through San Ignacio's gossips; as in the colonia, the bloodiness of the fight had grown with each retelling. An hour after sunrise, men in business suits, workers in rough clothes, women in long skirts that caught on the tall, dry grass, and shrieking children had gathered around the mule teams and work crews.

Great Western men watched the gathering people with a total lack of enthusiasm. The crews had begun laying track before the sun had cleared the northeastern mountains. Heer had held his crews on the plains all night, patrolling the track and sleeping in shifts. He watched the laborers very carefully, knowing that they were uneasy at the thought of working under guns.

Except for the ex-cavalrymen and One-Ear's crew, the workers had been recruited from the ranks of the unemployed immigrants who crowded the streets of Los Angeles, lured West by railroad fares as low as one dollar and by railroad lies about easy living west of the Mississippi. The immigrants quickly learned that life was no easier in California than in Boston or Kansas City, but the dollar fares only went one way. So the desperate men worked for whatever pay was offered, at whatever job they could find, but they were ill-trained, ill-disciplined and loyal only to their stomachs. Heer knew that, and wanted the track laid as quickly as possible.

Cira had not been along the track for two minutes before she spotted Heer. He had detached half of his outriders to ride herd on the crowds of people, trying to keep them out of the way of the crews. But even rough words from the guards could not discourage boys from playing tag among the big metal scrapers, scaring mules, muleteers and themselves in the process. The big blades slowed to a crawl until the children became too bored or too tired to continue their dangerous game.

Cira watched the direction Heer was taking, then slipped into the crowd without saying a word to Yolanda. But Heer was not easy to avoid. He was everywhere, his presence a constant goad to his men to work as fast as possible. Breakfast had been brought out to the crews by wagon. They ate in small shifts, quickly, hardly daring to take a second cup of coffee under Heer's cold eyes. Heer had not relented until midmorning, when the last crew had finished eating. Then, with brisk movements that showed no fatigue after a sleepless night, Heer paced the length of the chuck wagon, sipping coffee and eating doughnuts.

After Heer dismounted, Cira slipped from her inconspicuous spot at the side of the crowd and pushed through, trying to get to the front where townspeople and work crew were talking about last night's fight. But the men said nothing she had not already heard from Yolanda on the ride over. Discouraged, she wove in and out of the crowd, hoping to see Gil, or at least Juana.

As she looked around, Cira sensed someone staring at her. She turned to her left and saw Heer facing in her direction. Instantly, she faded back into the loose crowd, no longer looking for anything except a means of staying away from the man whose dead blue eyes frightened her. Without seeming to, she watched Heer while he set down his cup and started through the knots of watchers.

Cira edged diagonally through the people until she was at the head of the track. From the corner of her eye she caught a flash of sunlight on fair hair. For a moment Cira froze, then realized that the man was too short and too clumsy to be Lee. But her pulse was still racing when she looked away from the stranger. Heer was no longer in sight. She glanced around quickly until she spotted him halfway through the crowd, coming her way.

With growing unease, Cira looked for people she knew or even a group of strangers to put between herself and Heer, but it was too late. The crowd had moved with the advancing engine and Cira was nearly alone, with no place to run but the empty dry plains. She glanced around once more, then straightened and walked quickly toward the front of the track where people crowded thickly. Heer cut her off within six steps.

"Good morning, Mex," he said in a low voice.

Cira looked with more than a little fear and anger at the man who was blocking her way. She turned to step aside, but he moved with a speed that surprised her.

"What's your hurry, Mex?"

Heer smiled, a gesture that made Cira step back involuntarily. He noticed her reaction and his smile became even wider. He moved, and again his speed caught her off guard. She spun away, frightened, but his hand was around her wrist in a grip that paralyzed her. She gasped, but no one heard or noticed; everyone was riveted by the sight of men hammering a steel road into the plains.

Still holding Cira in a ruthless grip, Heer's hand moved until her wrist was hidden in the folds of her skirt. He stood so close that she could smell the coffee he had just drunk on his breath. With a small sound, she tried to wrench away.

"Mr. Kaiser wasn't pleased when you stole that deed," said Heer, squeezing her wrist until she was forced to lean toward him.

Cira wanted to scream or cry or do anything except stand almost touching a man who made her sick with fear. But she sensed that to show any emotion would be to encourage Heer's abuse. She raised her head and stared over his shoulder as though he did not exist.

"Uppity, aren't you? I'm going to enjoy beating that out of you, bitch. You won't be half so pretty when I'm done with you."

Heer's attention was so consumed by Cira's beautiful, expressionless face that he was not aware of the tall man who walked up softly behind him. Heer saw Lee only as a

106

reflection of relief in her eyes, and he heard only a cold, low voice.

"I should have killed you last night."

Heer let go of Cira's wrist but kept on watching her. He had seen that look on a woman's face before, but never for him. Slowly, he turned to face a man he had come to fear.

Lee's eyes were nearly white with suppressed rage. "Touch her again and you're a dead man."

Heer's lips twisted into a smile that was as ugly as Lee's voice. "Leander Champion Buckles the Third," said Heer, dragging out each syllable sarcastically and unobtrusively bringing his hand up to his belt buckle. "Are you offering to kill a man over a piece of Mexican ass? What will the good people of San Ignacio say when they find out you have a taste for dark meat?"

Cira had watched Heer's hand move to his buckle and remembered that her gambler father had often worn a concealed gun. Before Heer was finished speaking, Cira leaped between the two men.

"No!" she cried to Lee. "He has a gun!"

With one hand Lee spun Cira away. His other hand closed around Heer's fingers with crushing force. The silver-plated gun never got out of its hidden clip.

"Some day that toy is going to get you killed."

Lee released Heer's hand. So great was Heer's fury that he almost went for the gun again.

"Go ahead," said Lee. "Today might be your lucky day."

Heer's hand stopped as he read Lee's willingness to kill in the flat lines of his face. "You'll get yours, Buckles," snarled Heer.

"Maybe, but you won't be the one to give it to me."

Heer's lips tightened until they all but disappeared. He turned away and walked back to the chuck wagon. Even after he mounted his horse, he did not look in Lee's direction. Nonetheless, Lee watched until Heer was lost on the far side of the train.

Lee's gray-green eyes swept the people nearby, but no

one seemed to have noticed anything unusual. He looked down at Cira, curled within his arm, looking up at him with gold in her eyes. He wanted to pull her against him, bury himself in her special warmth and fragrance, but there were too many people. Cira saw desire move in his eyes and she trembled in response.

"Did he hurt you?" asked Lee, misunderstanding.

She shook her head without looking away from his eyes, then she smiled slowly, feeling joy turn inside her because she was young and alive and touching him.

"My God, you're beautiful," said Lee hoarsely. Nearby voices reminded Lee where he was; there was no way of knowing who might be watching. Gently, reluctantly, he released her. "You shouldn't be here."

"I heard you were hurt," she said simply. "I had to come."

"Are you alone?" Lee asked, looking around swiftly, but Heer was still out of sight, apparently no longer interested in either of them.

"Yolanda, my cousin, came with me. And if Gil is here, Juana won't be far away." Cira smiled wistfully. "She did not spend the night alone."

Lee reached out and slowly brushed her lips with his fingers. "I'll come to you tonight, *querida*. If you want me . . . ?"

"Yes," she whispered against his fingers. "Yes. Beneath the jacaranda tree."

Lee moved as though to hold her, but shouts from the crowd made both of them turn toward the town. At first, all they could see was dust curling up from the wagon road that paralleled the Great Western spur line. Beneath the dust were several buggies and wagons pulled by running teams. Alongside were mounted men whose yells were quickly distracting attention from the scrapers and track layers.

"Quickly," said Lee, turning Cira toward the closest knot of people. "Go and wait over there until this is over."

"But—"

He squeezed her shoulders gently. "Go, *querida*."

With a puzzled look, Cira walked away and stood inconspicuously at the fringe of the townspeople. Lee waited until she had blended in with the watchers, then he strode away and stood alone, just beyond the edge of the trampled work area.

The buggies, wagons and mounted men were close enough that shouted words could just barely be understood. The crowd of watchers began to stir as though moved by invisible currents.

"—old Crip."

"Saddle bags full of—"

"Gold!"

The crowd gathered and flowed to the wagon road, engulfing the dusty strip in a colorful tide while the wagons clattered to a halt. Driving the first buggy, looking proud and slightly drunk, was Luther Horton. The townspeople who did not know Luther on sight were informed by neighbors and strangers who vied to have a moment of importance in the midst of excitement.

By the time Luther opened his mouth to deny the rumors of gold, everyone in the crowd knew that he had come West in 1849, he had made and lost at least three gold fortunes, he had discovered the San Gabriel Creek Glory Hole north of Los Angeles only to lose the claim to a crooked surveyor, he had been prospecting the Moreno mountains on the Buckles Ranch and he had just made the strike of the century.

"C'mon, Crip, tell us where it is!"

Luther looked in the general direction of the voice, spat an impressive stream of tobacco juice and rubbed beneath his canvas miner's shirt as though the weight of the saddlebags over his shoulder was painful.

"Ain't got nothing to tell." Luther shifted his chaw to his left cheek and searched the crowd. "Where's the damned land clerk? Supposed to be in his goddamn hardware store at nine and ain't even a damn dog there to greet a man."

People in the crowd yelled for Luther to tell about his

109

strike, but he sat up on the buggy seat with the stubbornness of the granite he had spent so much of his life prospecting. Then, believing they would not have their curiosity satisfied until the land clerk was found, the crowd seethed and mumbled and finally pushed out Jackson Moore, part-time land clerk and full-time owner of San Ignacio's biggest hardware store. Moore had been out at the track since dawn, watching Kaiser implement Moore's dreams of a bigger, wealthier town.

"Okay, Crip," said Moore with open skepticism. "Where's the big gold strike?"

"Ain't no gold," said Luther, spitting emphatically, "and ain't none a your damn business nohow."

"Listen here, old man," began Moore coldly, only to be distracted by a late arrival riding a tired, heavily sweating gray horse.

Gil pulled up, sending dirt flying, and gave Luther a disgusted glare before spurring the gray over to where Lee Buckles stood. To the townspeople, it looked as though the two men were exchanging bad news. When Lee and Gill were recognized, a buzz of speculation arose, but no one was close enough to eavesdrop.

"Everything on schedule?" said Lee softly, his face grave and his eyes alight with suppressed enjoyment.

Gil hid a smile beneath a ferocious scowl. "That old bastard is having the time of his life."

"I noticed," said Lee dryly. "Is he going to stay sober enough to remember his lines?"

"He better," snapped Gil, frowning in earnest and staring at the old miner before turning back to Lee. "Think it's time?"

Without appearing to, Lee measured the mood of the people pressed around the borrowed buggy.

"Yes, Gilberto, it's time. But slowly, compadre. Your horse's legs are longer than mine."

People stepped aside as Lee preceded Gil's horse to the buggy. Lee walked down a gauntlet of staring eyes and whispered speculations that grew more excited with every moment. He stopped at the side of the buggy, put his foot on the step and pushed his hat back as though there was nothing more urgent on his mind than exchanging a few pleasantries.

"Morning, Luther."

Luther started to spit, then glared at the people crowding in on all sides. The closest men stepped back hastily, giving Luther room to rid himself of the tobacco juice. In the spreading silence, the liquid sound was audible to people who were standing ten feet away.

"Morning, Leander. Kinda far from your sheep, ain't ya."

Lee smothered a smile, realizing that Luther was a good deal less drunk than he seemed. After a sidelong glance at Moore, Lee spoke softly, with just enough emotion in his voice to insure Moore's complete attention.

"I'm surprised that you didn't come to me, Luther. You know I've always treated you fairly."

Moore laughed. "Gold doesn't know fair from fart, Buckles. That'll teach you to let a crazy old cripple run around your mountains."

"It ain't gold," snapped Luther.

"But it's in his mountains, isn't it," Moore said smoothly, more statement than question.

Luther's beard twitched. He did not answer, but his half-ashamed, half-triumphant glance at Lee said more than words. Moore grinned as Lee yanked his hat back down, obviously disgusted by Luther's treachery. Moore pushed past Lee, stepped into the buggy and sat beside Luther. Before the miner could protest, Moore took the reins into his own hands.

"All right," shouted Moore. "Clear the road. We've got business back in town. Out of the way." He looked down at Lee. "And that most surely includes you, Mr. Godalmighty Buckles!"

"Wait a damn minute," bellowed a voice from the rear of the crowd. One-Ear himself shoved forward with a grand disregard for the feet and feelings of the people around him. "You ain't going nowhere until I know what that old buzzard found and where he found it."

One-Ear's men shouted their approval and pushed after their leader. Moore looked at One-Ear's huge, scarred hands wrapped around the reins and at the six other tough men backing him. One-Ear grinned, showing the ill-fitting store teeth that were as much the legacy of his brawls as the chewed stump of ear that had given him his name.

"Let's see the gold."

"It ain't gold!" yelled Luther, at the end of his patience. He bent over and let loose a stream that splashed near One-Ear's foot.

"Then what is it?" yelled several people from the crowd.

One-Ear ducked around the horse and scooped the saddlebags off of Luther's shoulder, ignoring the old man's outraged screech and flailing stump. With a yank, One-Ear opened the flap, dug into the bag and came up with a jagged chunk of ore bigger than his fist. He held the rock up to the sun, turning his hand and peering at all sides of the ore with the intensity of disappointed avarice. The rock moved and shimmered with the hard brilliance of quartz and the softer gleam of nearly pure silver.

"It ain't gold," One-Ear said in a disgusted voice.

"That's what I been saying, you stupid mick," said Luther, snatching the sample out of One-Ear's hand. "Give me the bags back."

One-Ear smiled and dropped the saddlebags on the ground. "Get them yourself, Crip."

One-Ear started to turn away, then realized that Moore was staring at the rock in Luther's fist. Moore's hand shot out, taking the ore before Luther could protest. Moore's admiring whistle rose above the disappointed buzz of the crowd.

"What are you so damn happy about?" One-Ear asked sourly. "It ain't gold."

Moore smiled and cradled the sample in his hands, turning the ore so that sunlight ran down it in silver streams.

"No," agreed Moore, "it sure as hell isn't gold. But my

daddy was a hard rock miner and I can tell you this is better than a few lousy placer nuggets."

Moore's voice and excitement rose while silver light ran down into his cupped hands. He looked beyond the ore, searching the upturned faces for understanding.

"You fools," he said softly. "This is the richest silver ore I've ever seen, richer than the Sierra Leon, richer even than Virginia City!" Moore jerked on the reins, startling the horse. "Out of my way. Mr. Horton has business in town."

"Not so fast," said One-Ear, grabbing the horse's head. "Where's this strike?"

"None a yer damn—" began Luther belligerently, but he was cut off by Moore.

"Only one place silver like this could be," said Moore, looking down at Lee with pure dislike and pointing to the twin peaks rising in the northeast. "There, in those granite mountains, is God's own silver mine!" Moore smiled down at Lee while the crowd broke apart, torn between the mountains and the town where the claim would be filed. "I hope it isn't on your land, Buckles," said Moore. "But either way, you're going to have a lot of trouble raising sheep while you're chasing squatters."

Moore yanked on the driving reins, pulling the horse in a tight circle that threatened to overturn the buggy. Then he snapped the whip along the horse's spine, sending the animal into a plunging run while people scattered.

Within minutes, the work area was almost deserted. The immigrant workers were streaming toward the mountains along with many of the townspeople. Heer shouted and threatened until he realized that short of shooting, there was no way to keep his men working on the track. One-Ear's crew was gone and the ex-cavalrymen were leading the charge across the plains to the mountains. Heer swore and put spurs to his horse.

Lee watched the lone figure racing toward the west while everyone else ran east toward the mountains or north toward the town. Gil, still mounted on the gray, followed Lee's amused glance.

"Kaiser will be unhappy," murmured Lee, keeping a frown on his face for the benefit of the few people milling about.

"Seguro."

Gil hid his laughter by bending over and lifting up the forgotten saddlebags of ore. Lee watched the smooth retrieval, remembering the time he had seen Gil do the same thing from a running horse. Then Lee's attention shifted back to the ragged wave of people heading for the mountains.

"Sure hope we found all the sheep," said Lee.

"The men are holding them in the beach canyons as you ordered." Gil tied the bags in place behind his saddle. "If some of the sheep were too shy or too stupid to follow their compadres, then they deserve to be eaten," Gil muttered, yanking the rawhide ties that secured the saddlebags behind the saddle.

Lee glanced around again. Almost the only people who had not left were two girls. Cira caught Lee's eye, cocked her head questioningly, but did not call out to him. Standing next to her was Juana, a pretty girl with chestnut hair that was like a fire beneath the autumn sun.

"I hope your gray is too tired to fret over flapping skirts," said Lee. "We have two girls to escort back to the colonia." Lee watched Gil look around. When he spotted Juana, there was a perceptible softening of the foreman's expression. "Juana is very pretty," said Lee. "I don't blame you for spending your nights away from the ranch."

Before Gil could answer, Lee strode out beyond the trampled area where a dust-colored horse waited patiently out on the plains. They took the girls home, riding slowly. Later, in total darkness, Lee returned alone.

The moon was whole, a flawless silver circle that teased shadows out of the jacaranda's feathery foliage. The wind that had blown hot by day had subsided at sunset to a restless murmur of warmth permeated by the scent of chaparral and grass and dust from a far desert.

114

Lee tied the chestnut in a clump of brush where it was almost impossible to see the horse, even with the aid of the brilliant moonlight. There were open spaces between brush and jacaranda; Lee knew that he could be seen crossing them, but there was no other way to approach the house at the edge of the colonia. With the animal grace that characterized all his movements, Lee moved through moonlight and shadow until he stood beneath the whisper of jacaranda leaves stirring in a restless breeze.

Though it was late, Cira was not there. Even as disappointment washed through Lee, he heard a faint sound from the house. Moonlight shifted over Cira's bedroom window while the glass slid upward. Soon she was out of the room and running across the bright open space between the jacaranda and the house. Lee shrugged the bedroll off his shoulder and quickly spread the blankets over the sandy soil at the base of the tree. When he stood up, Cira ran into his arms and clung to him with a strength that surprised him.

"It's so late," she whispered while her lips moved over his face almost frantically. "I was afraid you weren't coming and I wanted to scream but I couldn't and the room kept getting smaller and—"

Lee caught her face, silencing her with a kiss that left her trembling. His hands went from her shoulders to her hips before he realized the harshness of her nightgown scratching his palms.

"What is this?" he said. "A hair shirt?"

He held a heavy fold up to a patch of moonlight, but still could not guess what made the material so harsh.

"My mother makes me wear it."

Lee thought of the rough cloth abrading Cira's softness and was suddenly angry enough to tear the nightgown into shreds.

"Does she wear one like this?"

"No," said Cira, surprised. "She isn't beautiful," added Cira, as though that explained everything.

"Hold still."

The anger in Lee's voice froze Cira. She watched fearfully, then with growing wonder while he slowly undid the many square buttons and eased the stiff cloth off of her shoulders. His mouth touched everywhere that the harsh material had chafed her skin. As the nightgown and his caressing tongue moved down her body, Cira's fingers worked through his thick, fair hair, holding him even closer.

The nightgown and his mouth slid down and she moaned with shock and a passion that was nearly pain. He held her immobile until she knew nothing, felt nothing but him and then he pulled her down and silenced her cries with the driving power of his body.

They lay together while jacaranda leaves floated on silent streams of moonlight. Lee's eyes searched her still face and he cursed himself for making love to her as though she were an experienced woman, when, in fact, she was only a few days removed from virginity. He wanted to apologize, but did not know how to without driving her further away. With a cold feeling of loss, he rolled over on his back, closing his eyes against the memory of her face utterly still in the silver light.

After a few moments Cira stirred, stretching with a slow appreciation of the night and the man who lay so close to her. She rolled onto her side and looked without embarrassment at her lover naked in the pouring light and sliding shadows beneath the jacaranda tree. Soon her hand was following the patterns of light over his body.

At her first touch, Lee's eyes opened and he saw her kneeling over him, wholly absorbed in the feel of him beneath her hands. Her face was unbelievably beautiful, silver and shadow and a dreamy sensuality. He lay unmoving, not daring to disturb the perfection of her smile. Her hands moved slowly, surely, and he knew the acute pleasure of being touched by a woman who was discovering the beauty of a man's body.

Cira murmured wordlessly and he felt the coolness of her hair sweeping across his skin. Her lips touched his shoulders, but when he would have lifted her mouth to his, she slid like water between his palms. Her lips parted and he shivered at the touch of her tongue savoring his skin. He called her name, reaching for her again, but she evaded him, laughing. Then her head bent and the world shrank to the soft heat of her mouth moving over him.

The moon had set and the stars were almost transparent before Lee could force himself to look beyond Cira. He wanted nothing more than to spend his life in her arms, talking to her about his dreams and hers until their bodies once more sang with passion. It was the same on the second night and the third and all the others until the tenth when he told her he had to go to Sierra Leon the following night.

"Then hold me once more," she whispered.

Lee pulled her over his body as though she were a blanket. She shaped herself bonelessly to him, then her tongue was between his lips, demanding. His hands kneaded down her body until she arched against his fingers with slow, sinuous movements that made him forget the pre-dawn light tinting the sky. Even after their passion was wholly spent, he held her with aching force, suddenly afraid to leave her. As though she shared his fear, Cira held him with all the strength of her young body.

"You'll be here when I get back," he said against the curve of her neck, and his words were more demand than question.

"Yes," she whispered fiercely, "yes! Come back to me soon, my love. A day is so long . . ."

She brushed her lips over his, then was on her feet, running for the open window with the hated nightgown flying from her hand like a black banner.

Slowly, Lee dressed. He rolled up the blankets, scuffing over the signs of two people beneath the jacaranda tree. With a last, long look at the silent house, he turned and slipped through the dawn.

Lee mounted his horse and eased through the dry, brown brush until he was far enough away from the colonia that no early riser could hear the sound of a running horse. He kicked the chestnut into a long lope, heading for the Great Western spur line as he had every morning.

When he approached the little hill from which he had first watched the track layers, Lee saw that another rider had passed ahead of him. A single line of bent grass went to the top of the hill where an almost transparent ribbon of smoke climbed into the rosy light of early morning.

When Lee breasted the small rise he saw Gil bent over a fire no larger than his hand; the rich smell of coffee rose upward, tantalizing. Without looking away from the fire, Gil held out a steaming clay cup. Lee dismounted, took the cup and sipped the strong coffee.

"Compadre," said Lee gratefully, "I think you just saved my life."

Gil's grin flashed while he handed Lee a tortilla rolled around hot, spicy beans. *"De nada.* A man who spends the nights as you do needs—" At Lee's startled look Gil's grin widened. "Oh, *sí,* compadre. I know. But I'm the only one. You would have made a good Apache." Gil laughed softly and wrapped Lee's fingers around the tortilla. "Eat. The only reason I know is that I leave Juana at the first hint of light. Once I thought I saw someone, but he lost me in the brush."

Lee smiled slightly, remembering that night. If he had known it was Gil behind him, the ride home would have been a lot shorter.

"If I lost you, how did you know it was me?"

"I went back the next day."

"And?"

"The chestnut's left rear shoe has a notch in one side. If the moon had still been up, I would have known it was you by the tracks."

Lee shook his head and chewed the spicy beans. "Gilberto, I wish I could afford to pay you what you're worth."

Gil made an exaggerated expression of surprise. "What? A wealthy landowner like you? Aiee! I even heard that a crazy old man discovered silver on your land."

"A vile rumor," said Lee, taking a huge bite out of the tortilla. "No truth at all."

118

"You only say that to keep poor but honest men from crossing your precious land to stake out claims. Or to keep the silver for yourself."

Lee looked toward San Ignacio, ghostly pale in the early light.

"Do they really believe that?" Lee asked softly.

"That's what Moore was saying, until his hardware store was sold out down to the dust in the corners. Then he changed his song."

Gil separated the few coals carefully, letting the fire die. "You should have seen it. Men threw away their jobs and bargained for pickaxes and shovels and pry bars—even pans as though they expected to wash silver out of streams like gold nuggets." Gil poured more coffee into Lee's cup. "They even begged me to lead them up the canyon they've named Silverado. *Por Dios,* they are such sheep."

The two men squatted on their heels, sipping coffee and watching the nearly deserted camp below. Seven men came out of a tent that was big enough to hold thirty. They were carrying sledgehammers and steel bars, but it became apparent that they had no intention of laying track. Heer, who had been sleeping fully clothed in a smaller tent, heard the men and came out in a rush. Though Lee and Gil could not hear the distant conversation, it became obvious from Heer's flailing arms that whatever he said was having no effect.

More men came out of the tent. They hesitated, then joined the first men who were flowing around Heer like a stream around a rock.

". . . nine, ten . . . twelve . . . fifteen, sixteen . . . twenty . . ." Gil laughed triumphantly "Twenty-two! I heard that Kaiser could only find thirty in the whole of Los Angeles and those were right off the train. All the rest of the poor dumb sheep went looking for silver." Gil saw Lee's skeptical glance out of the corner of his eye. *"Es verdad, jefe.* Over on the dry side are hundreds of men, trampling the cactus and each other. I'll bet that only one or two of them would know silver ore if it were crammed down their throats."

"What about the townspeople?"

Gil stretched and yawned. *"El viejo* registered his claim like you told him to. The markers are on the far side of the mountains, at least a mile from the watershed. Clearly not on Buckles's land. *Por Dios!* Have you ever been up the canyon and over the top?"

"Once, a long time ago. It's a rugged piece of land."

Gil snorted. *"Seguro.* The townspeople are having a very hard time. They are soft from weighing words and flour. I think that they will be back soon. It's very difficult to dig holes in a stone mountain."

"Some have already come back," said Lee. "I'm glad Carrington will start driving steel tomorrow. The silver fever has about run its course."

Below the hill, Heer stood watching while the last of his men headed for the purple line of mountains. He turned and looked up at the small rise; although it was too far away to be certain, he sensed that the two watching men were Lee Buckles and his tough Mexican foreman.

Heer stared long and hard at the two men. Then, with an obscene gesture, he mounted his horse and rode west. Both Lee and Gil watched until Heer's black clothes and bay horse blended inextricably with the autumn colors of the land.

"He's a snake," Lee said, sending the dregs of his coffee into the tiny fire with a snap of his wrist. "Kaiser and Heer should leave as soon as PacCo starts laying track. But until then, compadre, watch your back."

"Seguro." Gil poured the dregs of his coffee over the cooling ashes, then said quietly, "Your back is broader than mine, Lee."

"I'll be out of reach."

But in spite of his words, Lee was uneasy as he watched the spot where Heer had vanished. Even after Lee mounted and rode toward Sierra Leon, there was a coldness on his spine when he thought of Heer.

Lee's malaise was nothing compared to Heer's. Heer knew that Kaiser's fury was growing with each day, each defection to the lure of silver. And now this last crew had not driven even one spike before heading toward the twin peaks.

Heer knocked twice softly, then waited outside the hotel room that Kaiser had turned into the temporary headquarters of his railroad empire. He expected to live and work in the hotel for the months that would be required to ensure the success of his latest acquisition.

"Enter."

Kaiser's office was a study in scale and subdued tones of rose, cream and wine. The desk, the chairs, the drapes and even the vases of fresh flowers were individually selected to accommodate and enhance Kaiser's physical stature. The result was that men of normal height and bulk felt subtly dwarfed as their eyes were irresistibly drawn to the man who loomed behind the long desk, his thick silver hair and dark brocade jacket the only highly contrasting colors in the muted room.

Heer had never been able to decide if vanity or pragmatism had decreed the office décor, and whether the effect was merely clever or completely brilliant. But he had no doubt that the effect worked. From behind the desk, Kaiser dominated the room like a richly robed cardinal dominated a roomful of acolytes; he was force and power and even his closest associates rarely were allowed to forget it.

Kaiser's dark eyes flicked over Heer, noting the small signs of anger and unease in the way Heer stood as though the heavy carpet were a fragile skin of ice stretched over a black lake. Normally Heer was familiar to a fault, accustomed to controlling men and situations by knowing intimately the weaknesses of both. Kaiser understood and used this, even though Heer's perceptivity was a double-edged sword.

"When you approach so deferentially, my dear Roger, you must have bad news."

Kaiser's insight did nothing to set Heer at ease; Heer

liked to believe that Kaiser never knew when his assistant was manipulating him. For the thousandth time, Heer regretted that Kaiser was not a stupid man.

"The new crew . . ." said Heer, his voice almost tentative in the oppressive silence.

Kaiser knew what Heer was trying to say, but offered no encouragement.

"The new crew," repeated Heer, both uneasy at and angered by Kaiser's treatment of him, "it, uh, left."

"Left?"

"Yes."

"Do explain what you mean, Roger."

Kaiser leaned back in his chair while Heer stood uncomfortably, dwarfed by the desk and the room and the man whose brown eyes never softened.

"They went off to look for silver," said Heer tightly, his voice less subdued. "But they'll be back quick enough. No one except the old man has found anything but grief. I'll have those shiftless bastards laying track within three days. And they'll work—how they'll work! I'll see to it, sir."

"It doesn't matter," Kaiser said quietly.

"I'll see that they lay track faster than—what?" asked Heer, belatedly realizing that Kaiser had spoken.

"It doesn't matter."

"But—"

"It doesn't matter," said Kaiser for the third time, "because I had a visit from Sheriff Bensen just a few minutes before you arrived."

Heer's face became totally expressionless as he measured Kaiser's fury in the very softness of the voice and the almost imperceptible trembling of his hands.

"Sheriff Bensen," continued Kaiser's dry voice, "left these." His long index finger flicked against two sheets of stiff paper, separating them with a sound like a snake sliding over sand. "This one is from Judge Hilms. He no longer believes that the interests of justice would be served by condemning a strip of Buckles Ranch for Great Western's railroad. The original order is henceforth null and void."

Heer watched Kaiser's finger send the first sheet sailing off of the desk.

"The second one," said Kaiser, his voice thick with the effort of controlling himself, "is a copy of an 'agreement to agree' signed by Buckles and Carrington. It gives PacCo a right-of-way across Buckles Ranch. The copy was sent by Buckles's judge to my judge. Purely for the sake of information, of course; it had nothing to do with Judge Hilms's reversal of his own previous order, as the good sheriff very carefully explained to me."

Heer stood with increasing discomfort. He would have preferred that the older man swear or yell or do something other than talk in that dry, soft voice. Then Heer decided that he would rather listen to Kaiser's voice than to the absolute silence that followed the second paper's descent to the wine-colored carpet.

"Won't the townspeople—" began Heer, but Kaiser interrupted with that same chilling softness.

"The townspeople will get their steel road. They don't give a cold turd who builds it."

"Then there's nothing we can do?"

Kaiser smiled. "Not quite, Roger. I will pack up my office and return to San Francisco to oversee the continued growth and prosperity of Great Western."

"You mean you're going to let Buckles get away with it?"

"What would you do, Roger?"

"I'd make that son of a bitch regret the day he was born!"

"Just how would that profit Great Western?" At Heer's look of confusion, Kaiser added dryly, "Profit, my dearest Roger, is all that separates Great Western from the general herd. If I could deposit Lee Buckles's misery in a bank, it would give me great pleasure to 'make the son of a bitch regret the day he was born.' But misery is not negotiable and I always keep pleasure separate from business." Kaiser paused, then smiled very slightly. "Well, almost always. I must confess to some small pleasure in firing you.

"Close the door on your way out, Roger. The sea wind is rather brisk today."

Heer close the door softly.

Two hours later, Heer was in a beer hall, sitting alone at a long table and drinking beer in amounts that were astonishing for a man his size. The only other customers were a few townspeople and drifters. From their appearance, most of them had just come down off the mountain.

Heer ignored everyone. His self-absorption was like a wall separating him from the others in the room. His thoughts were focused on Lee Buckles and the many ways a man could be brought to his knees. But none of the ways were without substantial risk, and Heer had learned to be cautious with Leander Buckles.

Three of One-Ear's men came into the hall. The grinding canyon called Silverado had taken all of the bluster out of them, leaving only a bitter frustration. Not only was their lust for wealth unconsummated, but they were exhausted, half-starved and the butt of jokes told by townspeople who had stayed home. Twice the three had jumped bystanders who had made sarcastic comments about gullible idiots who went looking for God's own silver mine. Twice the three men had been beaten by townspeople.

Heer immediately recognized the men's frustration, humiliation and inchoate drive for revenge. All were emotions he was accustomed to focusing and then manipulating in others. All were emotions he now felt himself.

He looked at the three beaten men and saw the possibility of revenge on Lee Buckles.

Smiling, Heer signaled for the men to join him. Slowly, reluctantly, they sat down across from the man whose last words to them had been epithets and threats. Heer waited until the sullen men had eaten and drunk deeply before he began talking to them in the low-voiced, confident tones of a man among men.

"No hard feelings about what I said, men. Buckles made fools of us all that day."

124

"What do you mean?" snapped Red, whose name came from his bald head which seemed to sunburn right through his hat.

"You mean nobody told you?" Heer asked, taking a swallow of beer. "Guess the dumb city boys haven't figured it out yet."

"Figured what?"

"Yeah," said the smallest of the three. "What the hell are you yammering about?"

Heer put his mug down with just enough force to remind them who was boss. He did not know whether what he would say was true; he suspected it was, but did not care. True or false, he hoped it would focus the men's bitterness.

"Did anyone but that old fart find silver?" asked Heer.

"Hell, no," said Red, his voice rising.

Heer leaned forward and lowered his own voice, forcing the others to move closer in order to hear.

"No point in letting the townspeople in on it, is there?" His cold eyes pinned each man for a moment; when he spoke again, each man was listening. "No one is going to find silver because there is no silver to find."

"But I saw that ore—!" Red choked off his anger at a look from Heer.

"Any horse's ass can buy a bag of silver ore," said Heer. "Do you see Buckles or any of his men going up that canyon? Hell, no. And you won't, because he and those greasers of his are laughing themselves sick watching all the suckers scrambling after a silver mine that isn't there, never was there and never will be there!"

The three men shifted and made inarticulate, angry noises.

"Yes," Heer said, "Buckles made fools of us all that day. He's still making fools of us. We don't even have a railroad to build anymore—he went and gave the land to PacCo."

Heer smiled thinly, reading the seething emotions on the three men's faces. Now they felt foolish, childish, impotent. Now they were ready.

"I'll beat the shit out of him," snarled Red.

"First you'll have to catch him alone and unarmed," murmured Heer, turning his mug in circles on the table. "That will be difficult."

"You got a better idea?" challenged Red, his voice hard because he and everyone else suspected that Buckles could hammer all three of them into the ground.

"Maybe. Buckles has this Mexican whore he's real touchy about."

"So what?" said Red. "I don't care if—ohhh."

Heer nodded minutely as he measured the change in Red's expression.

"Thinks a lot of her, does he?" said Red slowly.

"Yes."

"Jealous?"

"Yes."

"Where is she?" said Red.

"In a whitewashed frame house on the eastern edge of the colonia. Of course, she might not be willing . . ."

Red shrugged and stood up. "That's her problem."

"Yes, I suppose it is."

Heer watched the three men walk to the door. When they opened it, the honey light of evening glowed; semidarkness returned when the door swung shut. Silently, Heer toasted the three men. His only regret was that he would not be the one to make Cira bleed and beg. But Buckles had said he would kill Heer if he touched Cira again, and Heer believed that Buckles was a man of his word.

The three men walked quickly toward the colonia, but even so, by the time they had skirted the scattered adobe buildings, it was dusk. They hesitated, then spotted the pale frame house set off from the rest of the colonia. Just as they started for the house, they saw Cira coming from her aunt's adobe. As one they waited, making sure that Cira was alone. Then Red walked out of the brush and stood between Cira and the house.

Cira was so surprised to see Red that she did not notice the two men sneaking up behind her. She spun around to leap away from Red, only to run into his friends. Before she could scream, Red's hard hand was over her mouth and nose, suffocating her.

"Into the brush," grunted Red, struggling to hold Cira. "Way back where nobody can hear." He jerked his head to the side, swearing when her fingernails scored across his cheek. "Grab her hands!"

Before they could subdue her, Cira marked Red again and again, breaking her nails off at the quick and clawing Red until blood ran down his cheeks onto the collar of his stained shirt.

They dragged Cira through the brittle brush and into the dry wash. There they pulled her down in the sand and swarmed over her while she screamed until her voice broke and then she fought with silent ferocity against the horror of men forcing their hatred into her again and again, fouling her in a grotesque travesty of the act of love until at last she lay unmoving, staring at a star-swept sky with bruised, uncaring eyes. Her indifference infuriated Red. He began tearing at her flesh with teeth and fists and boots, shouting incoherently. The other two men pulled him away, fearful that his raving could be heard far beyond the dry ravine.

Long after the men had gone, Cira slowly returned to partial consciousness. Her eyes were so caked with blood that only one could open, and then only as a slit. In the distance she heard an animal whimpering and she would have wept for its pain but the men had left her nothing, not even tears. She rolled over and pulled herself along the sand, trying to find the source of the cries.

Gil heard the same cries as he rode to meet Juana. Even when he saw someone face down in the sand he did not want to believe that the sounds he heard came from a human throat. He dismounted and gently lifted Cira up, not recognizing her, for there was nothing of grace or beauty or youth left in her beaten body.

Cira felt a man's hands, a man's cruel strength and she tried to scream, heard herself screaming in her mind. But only a hoarse moan came from her raw lips. With an im-

127

mense effort she twisted. Bloody hair fell away from her cheek and lay in sticky strands across Gil's arm.

"Easy, chica," Gil said in rapid, soft Spanish. "I won't hurt you."

Then Gil recognized her sandal and tiny foot and remembered a beautiful girl whose skirt had made his gray horse shy.

"Mother of God," Gil said hoarsely.

Not believing, not wanting to believe, he turned so that moonlight lay across Cira's battered face. The sound he made was indistinguishable from her earlier cries.

Gil lifted her onto the gray and mounted behind her. The horse made no objection this time, for this time there was no flapping skirt, only the smell of blood and the gray had smelled blood many times before. Gil held Cira with all the gentleness he had, but still she moaned and shrank away, not recognizing anything but the male strength she now feared.

"Cira," he said in soft, urgent Spanish, "it is Gilberto. I will not hurt you, Cira. You are safe."

He repeated the words again and again during the ride to her house. He carried her inside, still murmuring reassurances. The first open room that he saw was hers. He laid her on the bed and lit the oil lamp that was on her dresser. He made no sound when he saw her in the pitiless yellow light.

There was a pitcher of wash water, a basin and a rag on the table. He bathed Cira with great gentleness in spite of the rage and sickness that made his hands shake. While he soaked away clots of blood and sand and semen he thought of the small, slightly curved knife he wore and the many ways he could punish a man.

"What are you doing to my daughter!"

Gil glanced up, saw that Cira's mother was in one of her sober periods and curtly explained.

"Cira has been raped and beaten."

"I told her! I told her! Why did God curse me with a slut? Why did—"

"Shut up!"

The sheer rage in Gil's voice silenced Señora McCartney for the moment. Cira's throat worked and her swollen face turned toward her mother, but no words came. Gil poured a glass of water from a small, stone pitcher. Gently he propped Cira up, helping her to drink. He could tell by the tightness of her body that the mere act of swallowing was agony, but she drank anyway, tiny sips and drops.

"Cira," said Gil softly, "do you know who I am?"

Her head moved in what could have been a nod.

"You're safe now, Cira," he said, smoothing her matted hair away from her face. "Everything is all right."

Señora McCartney laughed. "All right? All right? What man will have her now? What man will take another man's garbage? What man would even bother to piss on—"

Gil's slap silenced the señora's hysteria, but Cira had already heard. Full consciousness had come with the water she drank, and with consciousness came memories that sickened her. She vomited wrackingly, helplessly. It was Gil who held her and washed her again. It was Gil who was relieved that she did not vomit blood. It was Gil who bandaged her tenderly when she tried to scream at the mention of a doctor to examine her.

When the last bandage was in place, Gil covered Cira and turned to reason with her mother, but Señora McCartney was gone. He sat next to Cira then, holding her hand gently, trying to ignore the blood oozing beneath her torn fingernails and her bruised eyes staring at the ceiling.

"In a few days, a week, you will be healed," he said quietly, stroking the back of her hand with gentle fingers. "You are lucky he didn't cripple you, Cira. You will recover."

Cira turned her head slowly and looked at Gil. Her eyes were no longer shut by dried blood; though they were swollen half-closed, he could see the gold flecks that made her eyes unique. She said a word that he could not understand.

"What, little one? What is it?" he asked, bending over her.

". . . three."

"Do you mean there were three men?"

". . . *sí.*"

Gil took several slow breaths before he trusted himself to speak. His voice was calm, almost soothing, asking her about the men he intended to kill.

"Did you know them?"

Her head moved to the side slowly, and he understood that she did not know the men. His disappointment was so consuming that it took a moment for him to realize that she was trying to get herself another drink. He filled the glass with water and held her upright until the glass was empty again. This time she did not throw up.

"Were they Mexican?" he asked, setting the empty glass aside.

"No."

Her voice was raw, but oddly clear.

"Are you sure you never saw them before?" Gil said, remembering Heer's threats and Kaiser's cruelty to the Indio maid.

"*Sí.* One was—"

Cira's eyes closed. She wanted to forget, yet knew that she would remember until she died. She wished for death with all the intensity she had once reserved for life, but her heart kept on beating in answer to its own animal imperatives. Then she knew the worst of the night; she knew she would live, and living, remember.

"One man was bald," she said tonelessly. "His hat came off and his skin stretched over his skull and it was shiny under the moon, sweaty shiny and jerking up and down, up and down while blood and spit dripped up and down and up and—"

At first Gil thought she was crying. When he realized that she was laughing he tasted bile in his mouth and had to fight to control himself. The pain of laughing cured Cira's hysteria. She drew a ragged breath and stared at Gil with eyes that were too sane and too old.

"He will have blood on his face," she said hoarsely, holding up her torn fingers.

"What about the other two?"

"Only him, shiny, up and down and—" She shuddered. "Only him."

"Did you hear any names?"

"No."

He sat silently, stroking her hand, wanting to mention Lee but afraid to disturb the terrible sanity in her eyes. The sound of a buggy sliding to a stop in front of the house made Cira try to get up.

"No! No doctors! No more men pulling at my legs!"

Gil tried to hold her on the bed until he realized that being restrained by a man was sending her into a frenzy. He let go and stood well away from her. Cira got almost to the door before she collapsed. Gil waited for a moment, then knelt beside her.

"Little one, will you let me help you?"

She looked at him, sane again, and made no protest when he lifted her onto the bed. But both felt her involuntary shrinking away from his hands.

"I'm sorry," said Gil miserably. "I don't want to hurt you."

"You didn't. I just don't want to be touched."

Señora McCartney burst into the room just as Gil pulled the sheet up over Cira's bruised body. Her mother yanked open the wooden wardrobe and began stuffing Cira's clothes into a carpetbag. She threw a dress and underclothes across the bed.

"Get dressed," she said curtly.

"She can't."

"Then you dress her, hombre. It certainly won't be the first time you've touched her. Slut."

Señora—" began Gil threateningly.

She looked disdainfully past him to her daughter. "Were you a virgin before tonight?" she demanded.

Cira closed her eyes and whispered, "No."

"Es verdad," hissed her mother. "I know. I saw your

131

tall lover. Well, my daughter, what do you think of your fine man now?"

"You stupid cow!" Gil yanked the sheet off of Cira. "Look! Look at her! Is this the work of a lover? *Por Dios*, woman! Have some pity on the girl!"

Cira's mother looked away. "I do. I'm taking her to Mexico, to the cousin of my father's cousin if the old woman is still alive. Then no one will know my shame."

Gil could not believe what he was hearing. He watched Señora McCartney empty drawers into the bulging bag.

"You are *loca!* Cira is hurt. She can't take such a long trip."

Cira pulled herself into a sitting position and began fumbling with the dark dress her mother had thrown across the bed.

"Cira, you can't," said Gil. "What about L—"

"Don't!" she said, her raw voice almost a shout. "Don't say his name."

"But—"

Señora McCartney brushed Gil and his protestations aside.

"My daughter is a slut," she said harshly, "but she isn't stupid. She has learned what men really are. After tonight, this lover of hers wouldn't use her to carry slops."

"That's not true," said Gil, turning to Cira almost despairingly.

Señora McCartney laughed, a sound as raw as Cira's voice. "Tell him, daughter," she urged, her eyes black and shrewd and filled with pain. "Tell him that your lover plans to marry you. Tell Señor Gil the date of your marriage."

Cira turned her face away from both of them.

"*Sí,*" said the old woman. "It is as I thought. Did he even say that he loved you, my foolish daughter? Did he promise you the love of angels while he pulled you down into mortal sin?"

Señora McCartney saw the truth on her daughter's

swollen face. When the old woman turned back to packing, her eyes were wet.

"Poor little one," she whispered. "I tried to save you, but you were too beautiful, too much like I once was. Too much passion. Too little prayer. God punished me for my sins. Now he punishes you. But the men who soiled us . . . who punishes them?"

There was no answer to her question, nor did she expect one.

Gil turned back to Cira, who was trying to button her dress with fingers that were slippery with blood.

"Cira," said Gil, bending over to help her with the buttons. "Is this what you want?"

Cira did not answer, merely sat while he buttoned the long dress around her. But she watched him with eyes that he could only meet for an instant before he had to look away.

"At least let me talk tó him," said Gil so softly that her mother could not hear.

"Look at me, Gilberto," said Cira.

Her voice was hoarse, yet each word was as distinct as the bruises on her face. Gil looked at her.

"If he finds out, I will kill myself."

"Chica, you can't mean . . ."

But his words faded because she did mean it. There was no mistaking the truth in her half-closed eyes.

Gil finished dressing her without argument, carried her to the buggy beneath the jacaranda tree and set her gently within.

He tied his gray behind the buggy and drove the two women across the Buckles Ranch, around farms and towns to the Mexican border. Then he gave the reins to Cira's mother, mounted his gray and spurred it north, racing to find a bald man before the scratches healed on his face.

1897

Marjorie Todhunter Buckles disliked dirt and mud and
vast stretches of land unadorned by cities. The winter of
1897 had intensified her dislike into a feeling that was as
close to passion as her nature permitted. Each morning
she had looked out of her house, hoping, but each morning the rains had slanted down, transforming dry, ugly
land into wet, ugly land, a sea of mud and knee-high citrus trees lapping around the elegant house that had been
her father's wedding gift to the daughter he called Joy.

With restrained impatience, Joy lowered the lace win-
dowshade, softening the outline of gray rain and brown
mud, if not the knowledge that she was marooned in a
sloppy wasteland far from the exhilarating society of her
San Francisco home. Almost as depressing was the
knowledge that a five-mile swath of mud lay between her
and the town of San Ignacio. Although the town was dis-
tressingly rural, it was a decided improvement over the
ugly land that drained away all of her husband's time and
energy.

Frowning, Joy looked through the lace. Try as she
might, she could not reconcile the handsome, continental
gentleman she had married in San Francisco with the

rough, hard man she had lived with for nearly five years. Surely no gentleman would attempt the liberties that he had with her person. No true gentleman would even know of such unspeakable practices.

She closed her eyes and her translucent skin flushed with the agony of shame that came whenever she remembered their first weeks of marriage. Only after an excruciatingly embarrassing talk with her mother had Joy realized that what she abhorred was necessary in order to conceive children; it was also the duty of a wife in the eyes of God. Following her mother's pained hints—and armed with a vial pressed into her hand at parting—Joy went back to the bridal suite, opened the vial of oil and dutifully presented herself to Leander. The oil, at least, made the humiliating ordeal less painful, as did her insistence that nothing occur that was not absolutely required for conception.

Unfortunately, she had not yet conceived, and thus was faced with the monthly recurrence of her duty. For in spite of her innate fastidiousness, she was determined to be the most complete wife a man could have, just as she had been the most complete belle of several San Francisco social seasons.

Joy turned away from the window and the thoughts called by rain and mud. She leaned over a sterling silver matchbox shaped like a surprised dragon, struck a match and lit one of the room's many lamps. As she replaced the yellow silk lampshade, a warm light permeated the room, a color not unlike that of the absent sun. The light created a subdued rush of color in the parlor. Settees and divans covered with embroidered silk shone richly, their jeweled colors repeated in the Persian carpet and brocade drapes. A closely patterned wallpaper graced the upper half of the walls; the lower part was of curved, hand-rubbed cherry panels. The subtle glow of polished wood was repeated in the clawed feet of the furniture, in the glass-windowed curio cabinets, in the ceiling beams and in the few inches of floor not covered by carpet and throw rugs.

Little of the wall panels or the carpet was visible. As well as settees and divans, there were wicker and over-stuffed chairs, ottomans, ornate tables of all sizes, lamps and clocks, a superb piano, framed photographs, oils done by her school friends and continental artists, and knick-knacks from her continental tours. All of the furniture was draped with tatted lace in shades of white and oyster and cream. On top of the piano and tables and in what-ever floor space not taken by furniture, plants flourished. Amid their greenery, elegant china dogs sat, perpetually alert.

Smiling, Joy touched the narrow head of one of the three china whippets. The nearly waist-high sculpture was the pièce de résistance of her recent trip to San Francisco. The graceful white china dog was a perfect accom-paniment to the teal-blue brocade armchair and the arched fronds of a large fern. The glistening white of the dog seemed to unify all the disparate elements of white in the room's décor into one harmonious whole that bound together the cascade of shapes and patterns and colors.

The rest of the three-story house was furnished with the lavish abundance of the parlor, except for the west wing, Lee's office suite on the second floor of the house. Once she had tried to soften the suite's sterility by adding just a few things—trailing plants in wicker baskets, lamps with stained glass or silk shades, lace throws to soften the outlines of plain furniture. The next morning, everything except one lamp was neatly stacked in the hallway.

Joy had been on the point of protesting, when she remembered what she called the Jacaranda Argument. Lee had all but ignored the myriad details and intensive planning that went into furnishing a proper house. Nor was his lack of interest distressing to her; she had been schooled to create and manage a fashionable, wealthy household and she knew she was very good at it. Lee himself acknowledged her skills. So she was shocked when Lee flatly rejected her plans for an elegant, informal garden built around a jacaranda tree. When she pressed for a reason, he had looked at her out of a stranger's eyes, pale and remote, and she had never forgotten what he had said.

"Your father gave you this house, Marjorie, and the money to furnish it according to your own taste. But the land is mine, and will be furnished to suit my taste.

"There will be no jacaranda trees within sight of this house."

Joy frowned when she remembered his cold voice, but her frown quickly faded. She was too busy for unhappy thoughts. It was a new week and much needed to be done. The downstairs china needed washing, the plants required dusting and watering, the parlor rug needed beating and it was time to plan the weekly menu, as well as to begin deciding on a spring wardrobe for herself and Leander. Not that he cared; he rarely wore anything fashionable. But it was a wife's duty to see that her husband at least wore clothes that were decently made . . . and he could look so handsome when he took the trouble.

Without realizing it, Joy again slipped back into the dazzling weeks of her San Francisco courtship. Leander had been so utterly proper, yet such a dashing beau that all her friends had been drawn with envy. But now her friends were presiding over society in San Francisco, New York, London and Paris, and it was she who was envious.

Briskly, Joy started for the kitchen and her weekly wrangle with Elena, the young Mexican cook. The cook Joy had brought from San Francisco had stayed less than a month before declaring life to be impossible beyond San Francisco's city limits. After several disastrous attempts to turn Irish or English or French immigrants into cooks, Joy accepted Elena as a temporary measure until a more cosmopolitan cook could be found. That was four years ago, and Gil's cousin Elena was still cooking. Arguments over continental versus Mexican cuisine had become an institution in the Buckles household. Though neither Joy nor Elena would ever admit it, they both looked forward to their weekly wrangles with the enthusiasm of a bullfighter waiting for the corrida to begin.

Before Joy was out of the parlor, she heard the sound

137

of someone coming up the muddy stretch of unplanted land that she had not yet managed to turn into a proper driveway. Joy turned back, lifting the long silk skirts of her house dress and reaching the window with more speed than dignity. She saw an ebony, high-wheeled buggy drawn by a matched pair of black trotters. With a sound of delight she rang for the maid, gave a string of rapid, precise orders and opened the front door just as a middle-aged man of medium height and great elegance stepped onto the broad front porch.

"David!" Joy said, smiling with a pleasure that pinked her cheeks. "What a wonderful surprise!"

Carrington took her outstretched hands in his own, bowed over them, then hugged Joy with the familiarity reserved for childhood friends of the family. He held her at arm's length, noted the incipient lines of unhappiness tightening her lovely, pale face and silently cursed the cruel law that insisted that children grow up. Yet, he had to admit that the lines enhanced her ethereal, ash-blond beauty.

"You are more ravishing each time I see you," said Carrington, tucking her arm into his and leading her back into the warmth of her house. Then, over his shoulder, he called to the stable-boy, "Just hold them there for a moment, Felipe. We'll be going out soon."

"I have no intention," she said, giving him a sidelong look from her pale violet eyes, "of going out in this ghastly weather. Nor do I intend to let one of my favorite people catch his death of cold out there."

She turned and surprised Carrington by giving him a delighted kiss on his cheek, just above his seal-smooth beard. She smiled at him like a child who has just received an unexpected present.

"Oh, David, it is so good to see a civilized man!" Then, realizing that her words could be taken as criticism of her husband, Joy blushed. "Not that Leander isn't civilized. It's just that he's so busy he never has time to talk and he's always covered with dirt. Of course, I know he has to

138

oversee the hired men and no one can stay clean in this miserable—"

Carrington's indulgent laughter did not anger Joy as her husband's laughter did. She faced Carrington confidently, knowing that he would never find serious fault in her.

"Well," she said with spirit, "that collection of rags and sticks he so proudly calls an orange grove is disgusting. We could have had acres and acres and acres of gardens, but he ruined it by turning it into something so—so—" She hesitated, trying to find a word that would be forceful without being unrefined.

"Useful?" offered Carrington, a teasing smile in his eyes.

"Mundane," said Joy finally. "And ugly. Yes, ugly! It looks like the rag man emptied his bags all around the house."

Carrington laughed, enjoying the indignation that made rosy highlights beneath her flawless skin.

"I hope you didn't say that to Lee," chuckled Carrington, looking back over his shoulder at the drenched ranks of knee-high saplings that were tied to supporting stakes with rags.

"I most certainly did," said Joy, forcing a smile, determined not to let yesterday's argument spoil today's visit. "He was rather abrupt about it," she continued lightly. "I'm afraid he's losing his sense of humor on the subject of oranges and rags."

Carrington did not doubt it. Lee had extended himself to the hilt in a huge gamble on citrus. But money was never a topic of conversation between a gentleman and a lady, so Carrington shrugged gracefully and allowed himself to be ushered through the house to the parlor.

"What an elegant piece," said Carrington, immediately noticing the china whippet that seemed to hum with civilized vitality.

"Isn't he marvelous?" said Joy, delighted that Carrington had immediately noticed what she had had to point out to her husband.

"Perfect," murmured Carrington, looking around the room. Although the décor was not in keeping with his own preferences, Carrington nonetheless appreciated the room for what it was, the essence of the era's artistic expression. "You're a marvel, Joy. Nowhere have I seen a better melding of fashion and taste. How do you manage to do it out here, by yourself . . . ?"

"Leander advises me," she said, lying easily because it was a social lie, a polite fiction that her husband cared about or even particularly noticed the interior of his house.

Carrington smiled, but did not disagree; he understood the necessity of social fictions too well to disturb them without compelling reason. After a final appreciative look around the parlor, he said, "Get your wrap, child. I've come to take you on a ride."

Joy tapped Carrington's cheek and delivered a devastating look through lowered eyelashes. Both the touch and the look were gestures that came easily to her; she had been trained to be a coquette as thoroughly as she had been trained in other required social graces.

"Dearest David," she murmured, looking up at him with wide, violet eyes. "You notice a trifling china dog and ignore the fact that the child who used to beg you for sweets has become a woman."

"How very rude of me," said Carrington, bowing to conceal the sudden sadness that had pulled his smile apart. When he straightened again, his smile was correct to the last fraction. "I must blame the lack on an old man's eyesight."

"Nonsense!" said Joy almost fiercely. "You are not the least bit old!"

Carrington's hand touched Joy's fine, fair hair in a gesture that recalled the first time he had seen Byrd Todhunter's silver-haired child and had instantly been entranced by her.

"You're a beautiful woman, Joy. More than any one man deserves." He smiled. "I'm going to have to rap your
140

husband's knuckles for not bringing you to San Francisco more often."

"Do that," responded Joy with more fervor than was strictly polite.

No longer smiling, Carrington rang for the maid and requested Joy's wrap. She pouted, then gave in gracefully.

"All right, Mr. David Arthur Carrington. I will go out into that horrible rain. But only for a dear friend, and only if that dear friend promises to visit me more often."

Carrington smiled, pleased that Joy liked his visits as much as he did. But, though he would never have admitted it to Joy, this time he had come to the ranch for more than the pleasure of her beauty and conversation.

"I'll do my best," he said, bowing slightly. "But promise not to be too angry with me if I have to leave soon."

Joy's delicate hands tightened inside the dark fur muff that matched the wide band of fur trimming her long coat. As she looked back at him quickly, her eyes sparked like amethysts against the dark sweep of her hat.

"Oh, David, you're teasing me, aren't you? You'll at least stay the week?" At the regret she saw on his face, she said quickly, "Then just a few days. Three? Two? David, please don't tease me like this. You don't know how lon—how much I enjoy your visits."

"I'm sorry."

Carrington saw the pleading in her lovely eyes, the flush of her translucent cheeks and her lips as delicately curved and pink as a shell.

"How could any man resist such beauty?"

"Then you'll stay?"

"I'll think about it," he temporized.

Joy's smile changed her expression from desolation to delight. She kissed his cheek and snuggled against his arm as she had ever since she could remember.

"What is that marvelous scent you're wearing? I must buy some for Leander." Her nose wrinkled delicately. "I'm afraid my husband often smells of sheep."

Carrington laughed as he opened the front door for

her. "That's why he insisted that I take you for a ride in the rain."

"Whatever do you mean, David?" she asked, accepting his help in entering the high buggy.

"Lee wanted you to witness a bit of Buckles history."

"I've witnessed quite enough of that, thank you," she said glancing around from her vantage point in the nearly enclosed buggy.

Carrington climbed up beside her, followed her glance, and became lost in the view. Behind the buggy, the three-story Victorian house bristled with architectural incongruities, an exuberant pastiche of cultures crouched on a long swell of land. Around, on all sides, knee-high rows of orange trees stuck out of raw, muddy furrows. Beyond them the plains fanned out, almost transparently green with the first tint of new growth. The eastern mountains were all but obscured by filmy clouds and to the west the coastal hills were concealed behind distant, twisting curtains of rain.

"Lee certainly chose the site carefully," remarked Carrington as he gathered the reins. "Even in this weather he can see half of his ranch from the parlor window."

Joy, busy arranging her rustling skirt, said nothing.

"The plains are beautiful," continued Carrington. "Have you ever seen a color to equal that green? Eden must have looked like that on the seventh day."

"I rather think that Eden had less mud," muttered Joy. She looked out, but her eyes rose no further than the raw groves. "Rags and rain. Rain and rags."

Carrington's smile faded. He looked at the fragile woman beside him with real concern.

"Joy, do you want me to ask Lee if you can return to San Francisco with me? Your parents would be delighted."

For an instant Joy's cheeks leaped with color, then the instant was gone and her voice was as pale as her skin.

"I tried to persuade Leander to stay over after our Christmas visit, but he said that there was too much to do here."

Without realizing it, she sighed and sadness shadowed her eyes. The effect was more devastating than any careful coquetry. Carrington picked up the reins, but did not let the horses move faster than a walk.

"Does Lee know how lonely you are?" he asked gently.

Joy seemed on the verge of protesting, but did not. She had been laying small hurts and large problems in Carrington's capable hands for twenty-one of her twenty-three years. She saw no reason to stop now.

"Yes. He suggested that I stay in San Francisco at least through the February rains."

Carrington relaxed subtly, relieved that he would not have to intervene in order to make Lee realize Joy's needs. Such an act would have been distasteful in the extreme to Carrington, but he would have done it for Joy without hesitation.

"Why didn't you stay?"

"A wife's duty is to her husband."

There was nothing he could say to that statement. He flicked the reins and spoke sharply to the horses. Mud began to snap off of the high, black wheels. The rain thinned to a sporadic drizzle as the buggy turned onto the San Ignacio Wagon Road. In spite of its impressive name, the road was still little more than muddy ruts studded with fist-sized rocks.

"Where are we going?"

Carrington turned to Joy and smiled in a way that made him look years younger.

"That, my lovely child, is for Uncle David to know and you to find out."

Joy giggled into her soft muff, then began trying to tease the truth out of him. It was an old game between them, quick questions and quick answers that never lied and rarely told enough truth to be useful. Even when the horses turned off the wagon road and onto a narrower strip of dirt, she still had not guessed where they were going, much less which piece of Buckles history she was required to view.

The narrower road paralleled PacCo's tracks, though

any sign of the railroad was minimized behind a ten-foot-high line of young eucalyptus trees. The graceful, slim-trunked trees glistened with colors of cream and green and beige and the air was pungent with the trees' exotic scent. But even eucalyptus oil could not disguise the odor curling off of a road that had been churned by hundreds of small, pointed hooves.

"Ugh!" Joy shuddered and held a cologne-drenched handkerchief to her nose, attempting to shut out the wet, oily, overwhelmingly organic smell, a smell so overpowering that she could not even identify it, only try to escape its effect.

"What is that?" she asked, choking slightly.

"That?" Carrington said in obvious surprise. "That's the source of your husband's wealth. Sheep."

Joy shook her head until the black feathers on her hat danced. "I've smelled sheep before and it was not like this!"

"Was it raining before?"

When the buggy turned and went between the trees, Joy saw what the eucalyptus had concealed; a railroad siding with several boxcars, loading pens, men—and sheep.

"Sheep!" She turned on Carrington like a cat. She was offended by the rain and the mud and the bleating and most of all by the unbelievably rank smell of wet sheep. "You brought me out of my house for this? I've seen sheep before, David. Too many of them, even if they are—as you so indelicately stated—the source of Leander's wealth. I loathe sheep!"

Carrington refrained from smiling while he gestured toward the siding. "That must be why Lee wanted you here. These are the last sheep you'll ever have to smell." Carrington's smooth, handsome face settled into thoughtful lines as he added softly, "Take a good look, Joy. It's the end of an era. Lee wanted to share it with you."

"My husband," said Joy tightly, her voice muffled by the lace handkerchief pressed to her nostrils, "doesn't yet believe that I have no interest whatsoever in anything to

144

do with his sheep, his oranges or his miserable ugly ranch."

In silence they watched Lee, a dozen men and several swift, silent dogs maneuver the water-logged sheep into the last stock car. Lee, riding a horse whose chest and flanks were coated with the same mud that speckled its rider, caught a glimpse of the buggy out of the corner of his eye. He waved a greeting and signaled to Gil to take over supervision of the loading. Gil, his face wrinkled in unconscious comment on the smell that hung in the air, spurred forward when Lee turned his muddy horse toward the elegant black buggy.

Before Lee had a chance to say anything, Joy leaned toward him, her cheeks red with cold and anger, her handkerchief pressed against her nose.

"Did you actually force David to drive me out here just to watch you chase sheep into a railroad car?"

Lee's lips tightened, but the pleasure of ridding himself of sheep overrode the displeasure in his wife's voice. "Precisely, Marjorie. But these aren't just any sheep. These are the last sheep that will ever crop Buckles grass or get pneumonia in Buckles pastures. When the boxcar closes, I'll be a gentleman rancher. Cattle, oranges and barley. Knowing how much you despise sheep, I thought you'd enjoy watching them go."

He looked at her and he smiled in a way that reminded her of the man she had met in San Francisco, the compelling stranger she had determined to marry. And had.

"Well, I suppose it will be worth something to be done with sheep," Joy said finally. "But it was most uncivilized of you to make me come all the way out here. I know you seem to relish discomfort, but not everyone is so . . . earthy."

Lee raised a sun-whitened eyebrow and looked meaningfully at Carrington's elegant buggy.

"I had no idea it would be such an imposition, my dear," said Lee. "I guess that's why ranch wives need to be hearty stock."

"Really, Leander! You insult me, implying that I have

145

anything in common with those—those brood sows who—" Then, realizing the content of her indelicate allusion, Joy blushed and said in a strained voice, "May I go home now?"

Lee sat in the saddle for a moment while the smile on his face thinned to nothing and was replaced by a look that more nearly matched hers. Except that Lee's dominant expression was distance rather than anger. He tipped his hat and bowed with an elegance that matched anything she had ever seen in Europe.

"Of course you may go, Mrs. Buckles. I am terribly sorry to have imposed on you." Lee looked at Carrington, who was plainly unhappy with the crosscurrents afflicting two people he loved. "I'll see you back at the house, David. We need to talk."

Lee's heels dug into his horse. The animal spun, dancing, unable to run because of the iron grip Lee had on the reins. Caught between Lee's heels and hands, the horse sidestepped back to the boxcars.

Joy rode silently until they were beyond the reach of the odor of sheep. She sniffed the air tentatively before putting away the filmy handkerchief. The damp air had made her hair nearly transparent as it curled closely around her temples. She fluffed her hair absently, anger and frustration etching small lines around her mouth.

"Sometimes men amaze me," she finally said, turning toward him and consciously smoothing her face until only an echo of irritation remained in the tightness of her mouth. "Leander is eight years older than I am, but sometimes I think he is twice the child I ever was."

Carrington studied her face and saw that the beguiling little girl who had been so sure of herself and the world had become a beguiling woman who had retained all the black-and-white verities of childhood.

"Joy," said Carrington slowly, trying to make her understand the enduring truths about the vices of man's virtues and the virtues of man's vices. "A great part of Lee's success—and he has had great success—is due to his willingness to treat serious matters with a certain

146

lightness. He knows their full weight, but if he let himself feel that weight fully, he would sink like too many other men.

"And you, my very dear Joy, with your infallible taste for lovely things, had better hope that Lee maintains his attitude, because it is all that stands between you and poverty."

"Don't be dreary," she snapped, then said contritely, "Oh, David, do forgive me. But if Leander needs money he simply can sell off some land like everybody else does. And if that isn't enough, there's always my money, or even father's." She frowned suddenly, as though she still smelled sheep. "The whole subject of money is terribly distasteful, David. I insist we speak of more pleasant things."

Carrington was stunned by her dismissal of Lee's land as just another form of money. He realized then that she was very young in some ways. Willfully young. He thought of telling her about Lee's obsession with the land and the consequent dangers of her treating the land so lightly, but a glance at her perfect, tight-lipped profile convinced him that it was the wrong moment.

"Joy, you have a great deal to learn about your husband," murmured Carrington.

"Perhaps. Or perhaps he has a great deal to learn about me."

Carrington flicked the reins. The black horses trotted swiftly through the mud and the increasing rain. When Carrington spoke again, it was about mutual friends in San Francisco. He was an excellent raconteur; his wry intelligence wove incidents into a cloak of amusement which Joy folded eagerly around herself, shutting out the gray day and the raw land and the husband who thought so little of her that he demanded she come out in the rain to be nauseated by the smell of sheep.

Before she was out of sight of the siding, Joy was laughing helplessly at Carrington's wit. The clear music of her laughter floated up from the buggy, delighting the shepherd who heard it.

But Lee was too far away, and too angry to be charmed even if he had been able to hear her laughter. He did not know which irritated him more—Marjorie's hauteur or his own stupidity in expecting anything better. During the first year of marriage, he had been very sensitive to her whims and pleasures; he had believed that if only he courted her carefully, thoroughly, she would no longer be rigid every time his hands strayed below her waist.

At some point during the years of their marriage, Lee had begun to realize that from the trivial to the essential, Marjorie's pleasures and displeasures rarely coincided with his. Rarely did her mind or her oiled, dutiful body edge further than the threshold of response, and then only when wine rather than desire flushed her cheeks.

Though she could not bring herself to speak of it, her every gesture told Lee that she had never forgiven him for the first weeks when he had tried to arouse her to the sensual possibilities of the marriage bed. He had finally accepted her near-total lack of responsiveness, though he still hoped that someday, somehow he would find a way to unlock a passion just half as great as her beauty.

But in the gray clarity of the rain he knew that he would not, that such a woman comes only once to a man and he had had that passion, held that ecstasy and then lost her for a reason he had never been able to discover.

Lee dismounted swiftly near the chute that led into the last boxcar. With a muddy, dung-crusted boot he jammed the last stinking woolly into the wooden car. Leaning against the sheep, he reached over, slid the door closed and snapped the latching bolt into place just as Gil rode up to help.

"Vaya con Dios," said Lee softly, his smile reflecting nearly a decade of animosity.

Gil saw the smile. He pulled his horse up near Lee and began rolling a cigarette.

"You know, compadre," said Gil, licking the thin paper, "I hate sheep with a hatred that is as great as the one

I reserve for the fish oil my sainted mother forced down me when I was a boy." Gil struck the match with his thumbnail, inhaled and grinned at Lee. "I think you do not care for sheep either, *es verdad?*"

Lee crossed his arms and leaned against the chute. "Compadre, I hope mutton is the main course in Hell."

"No, no," said Gil hastily. "Then we will surely spend eternity eating sheep!"

"Beats raising them in heaven," drawled Lee. Then he added, "Don't tell my Basques, but the only time I ever felt sorry for those damned animals was when Kaiser's yahoos ran them to death."

For an instant Lee saw behind his eyes not only Kaiser's abortive railroad coup, but a slender girl whose memory was like a knife twisting.

Gil saw Lee's eyes change and answered before the question could be asked. "No, I've heard nothing about her."

The lie came easily; he must have told it a thousand times by now. But in spite of its age the lie still hurt, like the stump of an amputation in cold weather.

Lee nodded almost curtly. Cira's memory was as much a part of him as his eyes or hands, but he had worked very hard not to think of her too often, for the comparison between past memories and present loneliness had once nearly destroyed him. After Cira had disappeared, he had searched for her with a singlemindedness that had surprised and finally appalled Gil. Then both men had searched for her until they were as finely drawn as wire, searched until one day Lee came back from Mexico and saw the edges of his land overrun by squatters and the corpses of sheep.

The sight had shocked him into paying attention to his ranch again. By the time the last of the squatters had been thrown off, Cira had been gone for more than a year.

Lee never gave up hope of finding her, never stopped seeing her in the golden light that danced over secret springs, never stopped feeling her in his arms when he heard a jacaranda tree combed by restless winds. When the pressure of need and memories became too great, Lee would saddle his dust-colored horse and roam his ranch from beach to mountaintop until Gil found him. Then they would drink mescal until there was neither past nor future, only a present seething with bar brawls and seamy bordellos on both sides of the border.

Gradually, so deftly that Lee realized it only in retrospect, Gil deflected Lee from the black explosions that could have destroyed first the ranch, then Lee himself. Lee rarely drank himself blind anymore; nor did he fight with the savagery that had shocked even the toughest border bars.

"That's about it," said Lee, turning back to Gil. "You can tell the men to—damn! I almost forgot." Lee slogged over to his horse, pulled a carefully wrapped bundle out and held it up to Gil. "For Raul. Wish him a happy birthday."

Shaking his head, Gil took the package. "Compadre, you are a miracle. There are days when I forget the names of my six children, but you—you never forget a birthday or a christening. I thank you in behalf of my oldest son."

"*De nada,*" said Lee smiling and thinking of the ten-year-old boy whose black eyes, shy smile and quick hands seemed to combine the best of Gil and Juana. "It's my pleasure to watch him grow. How's Juanita? I heard she was running a fever."

"*Sí,*" said Gil, a flash of worry darkening his face; he had already lost one of his children to sickness. "Juana says it will turn into chicken pox soon, because Yolanda's youngest girl had it two weeks ago." Gil shrugged glumly. "Then there will be Hell to pay. All of them sick and Juana pregnant again."

"Gilberto, I think you'd better get some more of your cousins up from Mexico to help Juana." He gave Gil a sideways look out of eyes that sparkled with silent laughter. "That is, unless you've run out of cousins at last."

"I'll run out of cousins when Mexico runs out of Mexicans," said Gil dryly. "But you're right. I'll send for one of Manual's older girls. They've been begging to come to Los Estados Unidos, where the streets are paved with gold."

"Looks more like sheep shit from here," observed Lee. "Smells like it too. She's going to be disappointed."

"She'll get over it. My cousin Felipe has a boy who is strong, handsome and wants a wife from Old Mexico."

A yell brought both men's attention to the head of the train. The railroad worker waved and shouted again.

"Ready to move out, Mr. Buckles!"

Lee acknowledged with a wave and listened while the glistening black engine worked up a head of steam.

"There it goes, Gilberto. Ten years. I couldn't have done it without you. Hell, without you, I'd be dead in a bar someplace."

"Not you, Lee. Twenty other men, maybe, but not you." Gil smiled, but his tone was far from laughter. "Don't ever get mad at me, compadre. Juana is too young to be a widow."

Lee snorted, remembering the times Gil's quick strength had made the difference. "Flattery won't get you more than a ten percent raise. Come on. I've got to pay off the shepherds who want to leave."

"Only the Basques left, and you paid them yesterday."

"What about Frederico? And Pedro. Your cousins loved those damn sheep as much as any Basque."

Gil shrugged. "They love their life here more than a few smelly sheep. Between your funny red-and-white cattle and your skinny little orange trees, the men figure you'll need all the help you can get."

Lee chuckled, then noticed that several of the shepherds had gathered along the loading chute while he and Gil talked.

"Frederico," called Lee, "is it true that you want to trade sheep for orange trees?"

A nearly toothless, wiry man looked up from his friends. His face was burned almost black by fifty years of sun and his beard was the color of clean lamb's wool. He smiled and gestured hugely.

"*Es verdad,* Señor Buckles. I am too old to chase the sheep anymore, but your little orange trees—aiee—they are not going anywhere, no? *Pobrecitos.*"

The shepherds all laughed at the expense of Lee's ragged citrus groves, but Lee did not get angry. He felt that these men had earned the right to laugh or curse or cry over his land.

"And you Alfredo? Pedro?" asked Lee.

The two brothers looked up and smiled gravely. As always, it was Pedro who spoke.

"We were born here before the Bear Flag was raised. We will die here. Our loyalty is to the land." Pedro paused, then added slowly, as though examining a familiar truth in a new light. "And you are a good man to work for, señor. *Muy fuerte.*"

"*Gracias,* Pedro," said Lee. He walked over toward the small group of men, removing his leather gloves. First he stood in front of Pedro, then all the rest of the men, offering his hand. "I'm only as good as the men who help me."

Behind the men, the train hissed gouts of steam into the cool air and slowly moved off of the siding and onto the main track, towing a segment of Buckles history down the shining steel road.

Lee waited until the train had disappeared into the mist before he mounted and rode toward what he called the "grove house," in spite of Marjorie's dismay at the name. He had tried to explain that he only used the name to distinguish the mansion from the "other house," the small, thick-walled adobe that had sheltered him for much of his life on the ranch. But Marjorie refused to see the distinction; she believed that "grove house" was a deliberate denigration of the structure that was her pride and pleasure.

As he rode, Lee searched the landscape with eyes the color of rain, looking for the sheep that were no longer there. When he realized what he was doing, he smiled wryly. He could have shipped the last sheep out weeks before, but he had waited until today, the anniversary of the day he had first come to the ragged sprawl of land called Buckles Ranch. Once, a few days after he had met Marjorie, he had tried to tell her about his dreams and his work and most of all his land, the crackling brush and hot winds, the smell of surf and grass cured by the sun, and always the dark mountains arched against the sky.

She had listened with a total concentration that he had mistaken for interest. Later he realized that her alert gaze was as much a part of her training as the slow smile that seemed to promise so much. Both the flattering intensity of her eyes and her sensual smile were like gloves—articles to be worn or doffed as the occasion required.

With an effort, Lee tried to pin his wandering thoughts in a present where things could be accomplished, rather than in a past haunted by futility, misunderstandings and regret. But the past called to him as surely as the fading whistle of the engine pulling boxcars of Buckles sheep through the rain. The distant keening made him think of his first meeting with Carrington, when four engines had screamed against the long grade of Highpass. He had gone back to Sierra Leon a second time, signed papers a second time and returned to the ranch with golden earrings in his pocket. . . .

His mind refused to live again the hours when he found that Cira was gone; memory leaped five years, to the day when he finally agreed to go to San Francisco. Carrington had been delighted. He had wanted Lee to meet more of San Francisco's important financiers. Lee had already met one of the most powerful, Byrd Todhunter, one of the three men Carrington had turned to for capital to construct his railroad north from San Diego and across the Buckles Ranch to Los Angeles.

Lee had found Todhunter to be a shrewd, quick-minded man, but not particularly a companionable one. Todhunter was too fond of ostentation for Lee's comfort. But the two men got along in spite of their differences. During those early years, when Byrd had visited the ranch from time to time, checking on his investment, Byrd had spoken with a father's pride of his daughter, Joy. Though barely seventeen, Joy was already one of the brightest gems in San Francisco's social diadem. Between Carrington, who was enormously fond of Joy, and proud Papa Todhunter, Lee was thoroughly lobbied in behalf of Marjorie Todhunter long before he arrived in San Francisco.

Apparently, both Todhunter and Carrington had not been hesitant in pointing out Lee's attributes to Marjorie. He came from an excellent family; though he lacked liquid assets, his potential wealth and power were as great as the ranch he owned; and until he realized his potential, there would always be her father's extremely generous allowance to amuse her.

From the moment of Lee's introduction to Marjorie, her violet eyes had not strayed from him. She had permitted him to pursue her while she pursued him with a skilled subtlety far beyond her years. For his part, Lee was hardly unwilling. He had spent too many nights alone and he had held too many of Gil's laughing children not to want a wife and children of his own. He had looked at Marjorie's inviting curves, her translucent skin and her lips which seemed to approve of him without reservation. She was an exceptional child of wealth whose natural gift for social interplay had been as carefully and beautifully polished as the amethyst necklace that sparkled against her neck. Most important of all to Lee, nothing about her fragile coloring, her impeccably fashionable dress and conversation, her cool reserve with suitors, or her wealth reminded him of Cira.

Only later, too late, did Lee realize how well he had chosen Cira's opposite.

Marjorie was as unresponsive as a polished china doll. And as friable. Lee was faced with the choice of shattering her or living essentially by her rules. The result was a luxurious house set in the middle of raw land, three to four months of every year wasted in San Francisco or Europe, a separate bedroom whose sanctity was breached

154

only by invitation, and Lee's growing despair of ever having children.

In addition, Lee had a powerful father-in-law, a socially impeccable wife and a dowry that in his more cynical moments he compared to Marjorie's ubiquitous vial of oil; both lubricated painful and humiliating adjustments.

Lee's horse snorted and shied when a covey of quail exploded out of a low clump of brush. The number of quail had increased in the last few years, as had all animal life on his ranch. Marjorie's dowry had allowed Lee to begin implementing his ambitious plans for bringing water to a thirsty land, plans that had been stymied first by a banker's refusal to extend the mortgage and then by the new mortgage required to underwrite the cost of building the PacCo line.

But today, stock tanks and check-dams and reservoirs dotted the hills, holding back the winter rains, storing them until summer when water was the difference between life and death for the four thousand small orange trees he had planted three months ago. Not very many dams, and the reservoirs were too small and too few, but their sum would be the difference between bankruptcy and wealth for Lee Buckles.

Unlike Marjorie, Lee did not resent the rains that came over the land like a great, sweeping blanket. He welcomed the water with upturned face, thinking of all the countless drops sinking into the land, his land, water that was as good as wealth and far more necessary to life.

He opened his mouth to the cool mist. It was the first time he had tasted rain since his childhood. Rolling the drops on his tongue like a connoisseur, he decided that at least rain had not changed; it still tasted pure and almost sweet. Grinning at his own foolishness, Lee adjusted his hat and turned onto the swath of unrelieved mud that was the driveway to the grove house. Deep marks from Carrington's buggy were still pressed into the stiffer stretches of mud.

The house looked both eerie and inviting in the mid-afternoon gloom. The ghostly aspect of the house came from its odd, white-painted curves and angles glowing against shadows that ran out of every depression like black liquid. Yet light poured invitingly out of windows where lamps were lit, light as warm as a summer evening. Lee pulled his horse to a stop for a moment, watching the house change as rain brought darkness. A new light glowed suddenly, transforming a black rectangle with light. Then another light glowed, and another, and more as lamps were lit against the premature fall of evening. The interior of the grove house became a many-centered pool of honey light.

Lee urged his horse down the driveway to the stables at the rear of the house. There he turned the animal over to one of Gil's omnipresent cousins and ran through the increasing rain to the back porch. When he gained the shelter of the tiny entrance off the kitchen, Joy's voice came to him above the sudden beat of rain.

"Oh, Leander, those awful boots!" She pulled her scented handkerchief out of the long sleeve of her magenta afternoon dress. With a pained expression, she pressed the small, silk square to her flaring nostrils. "Go back outside and remove them."

"It's raining," he said shortly, suddenly realizing that he was chilled beneath his sheepskin jacket.

"Your boots are offensive, Leander."

Lee's eyes swept the entry way. Muddy boots from Carrington, the servants and his wife were stacked in neat rows, waiting for the houseboy to scrape them clean.

"I trust you didn't make David go out and take off his boots in the rain?"

Joy stiffened as she measured her husband's voice, finding anger and something less defined, more disturbing.

"David is our guest," she said quietly, then added with a vague irritation of her own, "Besides, the—"

"—shit on his boots doesn't smell," finished Lee.

Joy's pale skin became even more white. "David and I will be in the parlor. When you have removed your filthy clothes, bathed and dressed in a civilized manner, we would appreciate your presence."

156

Joy turned, gliding away in a rustle of magenta silk. The scent of violets stayed with Lee, as did the shimmer of her hair. For a vivid instant her flawless beauty was framed in scent and light, then she was gone.

Lee pulled off his boots and hurled them out into the rain.

An hour later, bathed and dressed in a fine, three-piece black cashmere suit, supple black leather boots, white silk shirt and a cravat held in place by a magnificent ruby, Lee entered the parlor. Joy looked up as he crossed to the divan where she and David were talking quietly. She could not help but look; Lee's lithe walk and fine clothes were everything that she had wanted in a man. Though his grace was due to an unfashionably strong body, she nonetheless admired it. That same whipcord strength assured that his clothes hung perfectly, a fact that made him a favorite with her tailor. Above all, her husband had an indefinable aura that automatically made his presence the focal point of any room.

Joy smiled and held out her delicate hands. "Leander, I hardly recognize you."

Lee bowed over her fingers. "You look beautiful, Marjorie. Your dress is a darker echo of your eyes."

Startled by the well-turned compliment, Joy really looked at her husband's face. His eyes were almost yellow in the hissing gaslight, yellow and narrow and unreadable. His eyes had always been opaque to her, and the cabochon ruby in his cravat was the color of fresh blood. In its unwinking redness she vaguely sensed a resonance of his anger. But she ignored her insight; he had bowed over her hands, complimented her dress and left his coarse language in the entry way with his disgusting boots. She smiled slowly, her lips approving, promising.

"Thank you, Leander."

Lee bowed again slightly and turned toward Carrington. "David, what—"

"Leander," said Joy coaxingly, resting her fingers on the back of his hand. "Dear, please don't talk about

157

business just yet. I've had so little time with David and there is so much to tell him about our trip back home."

"Home?" said Lee. "Isn't this your home?"

Joy laughed breathlessly. "Of course it is. David knows what I mean."

Lee cocked his eyebrow. "I'm sure he does. I'm equally sure that David did not drive all the way from Los Angeles merely to talk about parties and fashions and the Queen of Cities."

"But I did," said Carrington quickly, smiling at Joy. "Your wife is without doubt my favorite social butterfly. I missed so many of the best events this Christmas, and she relates their essence so charmingly that it's better than being there. There's nothing that would please me more than an evening of Joy's conversation." Carrington sighed and frowned. "But there are a few small business matters . . ."

The pause floated in the air while they listened to the crackle of black oak logs burning in the fireplace and rain blowing against the thin windows. Finally Joy surrendered to Carrington.

"But first there will be business to attend to," she said lightly, smiling as she stood in a rustle of silk. "I understand, David."

"You needn't leave," said Lee, taking her hand. "My business is—should be—yours. It affects both of us."

Joy looked up at him, wide-eyed. "You can't be serious, Leander. Isn't it enough that I give up David, my sole distraction in this dreary country? Do I have to listen to men's talk as well? I wouldn't understand a word and would be horribly bored." At the objection she saw forming in his lips, she added firmly, "No, Leander. It would be most unseemly." She gave Carrington a slow smile. "Please reconsider staying the night, David. I'm starved for human talk."

"I wasn't aware that I spoke Chimpanzee," Lee said softly.

Joy turned to him with a baffled expression. "That was unnecessary, Leander. David knows what I mean."

158

"And I don't?" Lee let go of her hand. "Send the maid to my wing, please. I can't think in this clutter."

Without waiting for an answer, Lee turned and led Carrington to the west wing, the part of the house where Joy rarely ventured and never stayed for long. The wing had a washroom and a huge, high-ceilinged room with French doors opening onto a balcony. Part of the roof was given over to long skylights slanting back to the smaller third story. Watery gray light filled the room. Lee lit lamps until their gentle hiss blended with the rain and the room was bright. A hearty fire, and wine brought by the maid, routed the clammy afternoon chill. Lee settled into one of the low-backed chairs that was covered with tanned sheepskins, remnants of the day Kaiser men had run Buckles's sheep to death.

There were several pieces of furniture from the old adobe, including a large desk of solid oak planks that had been hand-rubbed on one side and left rough-textured on the other. At one corner of the desk sat a large oil lamp with a shade composed of hundrds of pieces of colored glass. When Lee lit the lamp, the shade shimmered and sparkled as though it were alive.

"Cigar?" said Lee, indicating a polished ebony box with sterling hinges and clasp.

"Beautiful," murmured Carrington, stroking the flawless grain.

"Joy found it in London, I believe."

Lee watched Carrington prepare his cigar with a small, curved knife and clippers made of solid gold, except for the sharp blades. The elegant tool was a gift from Joy on Carrington's forty-first birthday. He selected a match from a plain silver box. The sound of the match scratching into flame was very loud in the room. Slowly, with due respect for the fine leaf, Carrington breathed the cigar to life. When it burned to his satisfaction, he walked behind the desk and stood by the French doors, staring out into the slate-gray evening.

"Let's have it, David. You didn't take a long drive in the mud just to witness the passing of an era on the

159

Buckles Ranch, particularly when you've been trying to get me to sell off those merinos for the last five years."

Carrington's smile was reflected in the window. "That was mainly for Joy's sake. The sheep were profitable enough, on the whole." Then his smile gave way to concern. "Roger Heer is back again."

Lee looked at Carrington's reflection and shrugged. Carrington frowned.

"Don't dismiss him so lightly. Since Kaiser's death, Heer has amassed a formidable fortune, as well as some uncomfortably strong allies." Carrington turned away from the rain. He paused, then probed Lee's face with shrewd brown eyes. "What did Heer do to you, and you to him?"

"We passed a few insults over a shotgun barrel."

Carrington laughed softly. As he lifted his cigar to his lips, his emerald ring winked. "Was that before or after PacCo won the right-of-way across your ranch?"

"During."

Carrington blew a perfect smoke ring. "You were holding the shotgun?"

Lee's lips turned in a half-smile. "That's right, David. I was holding the shotgun."

"Lee," murmured Carrington, trying to sound disapproving but betrayed by the smile that struggled at the corners of his full mouth. "Ah, damn it, Lee—I wish I could have seen that!"

"It wasn't much. And it was ten years ago. Nobody cares what happened that far back."

But as he spoke, Lee looked away from Carrington, not able to face those knowing hazel eyes with an outright lie on his lips.

"You care," said the older man softly. "You must. You've never told anyone about some of those years—not your wife, not your business partner and friend, no one. Except, perhaps, your remarkable foreman?"

Lee's eyes focused on a horizon shrouded by time, seeing a past where he had held Cira, felt her lips and laughter and warmth, then had been left with an emp-

160

tiness that even mescal and rage could not fill. Carrington saw echoes of ecstasy and grief and fury flicker over Lee's hard face like colored shadows thrown by the lamp.

"What happened, Lee?" said Carrington persuasively. "What did you lose and how was Heer involved?"

When Lee looked up, Carrington almost retreated out of sheer reflex.

"Lee," Carrington said urgently, "I'm not asking out of vain curiosity."

Slowly the fury drained out of Lee's pale eyes, but his voice was clipped, harsh.

"What I lost matters only to me. If I had been certain that Heer was involved, I would have killed him." Lee ashed his cigar with quick, precise motions. "Does that answer your question?"

"Hardly. But it will have to do, won't it."

"Exactly, David. It will have to do. Although, if it comforts you, I probably wouldn't kill Heer today. There are other ways to destroy a man."

Carrington met the white appraisal in Lee's eyes without flinching.

"It does comfort me, for it appears that the good Mr. Heer is out to poison your wells, so to speak. He's seen to it that you don't have many friends in Los Angeles."

Lee watched blue-gray cigar smoke rising and waited. "I'm not in business to raise friends," he said curtly. "Just cattle, barley and oranges."

"And money?"

"Of course."

"If your taxes were increased, if special levies were passed for massive road and coastal improvements, could you make a profit?"

Lee stood with the almost violent grace that Carrington had first seen in Sierra Leon and never forgotten.

"Go on," Lee demanded.

"Heer learned a great deal before Kaiser fired him. I'll bet that the old genius is laughing in Hell right now, laughing and watching his former protégé at work." Carrington ashed his cigar. "Heer has a grand idea, Lee, fully mature and ready to bear fruit. He's going to use it to destroy you. Only you know why."

"But I don't know how."

"He bought out the county courthouse—judges, county supervisors, road commissioners and anyone else who has the power to condemn property for the public good and to raise money by taxation for that same public good."

Lee smiled. "I wonder if that son of a bitch got a special rate, buying by the dozen."

"Probably. But they're staying bought."

"You've already tried?"

"It was my failure that brought me here."

"Hell's fire!" Lee stalked around the office, thinking rapidly. "The taxes. When and how much."

"A hundredfold by next year."

"What? They can't get away with—" Lee bit off his own words, knowing that they could and would get away with that. And worse. "The roads. Where and how many?"

"Six. They'll divide your land into sixteen very unequal segments, suitable only for being subdivided into many small parcels and sold."

Lee swore with a ferocity that would have appalled Carrington, had he not said precisely the same things to his horses all the way from Los Angeles. At last Lee was silent except for the whisper of his leather soles across the thick, charcoal rug.

"How did this get so far?" mused Lee to himself. Then, realizing that Carrington had heard, Lee turned quickly. "I'm not blaming you, David. Christ knows that—"

"I should have kept a closer watch on Los Angeles politics," he said bitterly. "But like my provincial peers, I believed that if it didn't happen in San Francisco, or New York, it didn't happen at all." Carrington rubbed the tight muscles of his neck. "All I can say in my own defense is that a local power broker died a few months ago. Apparently, Heer and his money moved into the vacuum. The result was a new county board that plans to tax you into oblivion."

"What about you?"

Carrington grimaced. "I can escape the same fate if I raise your freight rates ten times over." He looked at the rain patterns on the skylights. "I can give the money back to you under the table, of course, but that doesn't answer the main difficulty."

"No, it doesn't." Lee picked up his cigar and stood next to Carrington, staring up at an evening that was all but drowned by sweet-tasting rain. "How in bloody blue blazes did Heer get so much money?"

Carrington frowned. "I'm not sure, but there were some rather sordid whispers. Gambling, prostitution, blackmail."

Lee's eyes narrowed. "Find out, David. Get proof. Do you have anyone who can get next to the new supervisors?"

"My last . . . ally . . . died in a fall from the balcony of Los Angeles's leading whorehouse two weeks before the election," said Carrington, watching one of his smoke rings expand and flatten against the skylight. "He won the election anyway, but Heer's men took the majority of the seats. They lobbied the governor into appointing an antirailroad advocate of property tax. This man, John Marcus, is a paid reformer. Fifty dollars a week, to be precise." He looked at the end of his cigar. "Kaiser and Leland Stanford may be dead, but their methods linger on."

Lee's eyebrow lifted and his lips curled slightly.

"Yes," nodded Carrington in response to Lee's unspoken question. "Marcus is another of Great Western's false prophets. Down with railroads and big landholdings. Up with the little man."

"A pot of gold for every rainbow and a rainbow for every man who follows me. Sweet God," muttered Lee. "How many times will the voters fall for the same old crap?"

Carrington laughed sardonically. "My grandfather got rich selling snake oil. My father got poor drawing to inside straights. People will believe whatever comforts them."

"And never notice that for all the shouting, Great Western gets the gold and the little man gets the pot." Lee made a sound of disgust. "I presume that this champion of the underdog will be named chairman of the county board, and as such will blaze new trails for public policy to follow."

With precise steps, Carrington moved away from the window and sat in one of the comfortable sheepskin chairs.

"I do believe," murmured Carrington, settling back, "that you're wasted as a rancher. You should have been a politician. Not only are you properly cynical, you also have a highly developed jugular instinct." He laughed dryly. "Rainbows and pots, indeed."

"I learned from two masters." Lee's eyes narrowed as he remembered an old man's dry voice telling of hatred in a room lulled by the sound of surf. "One of them was you."

Carrington touched his forehead. "I'm honored."

"As one son of a bitch to another, I doubt it."

Carrington's laughter was surprisingly deep for a man of his stature. He held a beautifully manicured hand out to Lee, who shook it with a mixture of affection and respect and the ambivalence people reserve for those who have taught them something necessary that it would have been more pleasant not to know. Carrington smiled; the quality of his smile told Lee that the learning had been mutual.

"What do you suggest we do?" asked Lee, refilling Carrington's wineglass.

Carrington's face changed and it was as though he had never smiled.

"I don't know. Heer's combination of fear and favor is potent. By all the unwritten rules of power politics, he's won." Carrington's hard, shrewd eyes looked at Lee. "But ten years ago Kaiser had beaten you too. Your instinct for breaking the rules saved you then, and me as well."

164

"I didn't break any rules," said Lee softly. "I just enlarged the game."

Carrington's eyes narrowed. He nodded in appreciation of Lee's acumen.

"I'll remember that," said Carrington slowly. "What does your instinct say now?"

"Think. Long, hard and without flinching."

"Not too long," cautioned Carrington. "Once entrenched, taxes are harder to extirpate than lice."

Lee lifted his glass of wine in agreement. Through the silence came the soft, impatient sound of Joy's footsteps in the hallway.

"My most immediate problem," said Lee very quietly, "is Marjorie, hovering like a moth around a lamp, seeking your light."

"Or your flame," suggested Carrington with a smile.

"No, not mine. She prefers a polished glass shield between her and the possibility of flame." Lee set his wine on the desk abruptly. "I'll need time, David. Stay at least the night?"

"As long as you require," said Carrington simply. "It's my pleasure to be here."

"Good. Entertain Marjorie tonight so she won't be insulted if I don't."

"Now that, my dear partner, is the best idea you've had."

Carrington stood with an alacrity that made Lee chuckle. Smiling, he followed Carrington to the door. Before either man reached it, there was a discreet knock.

"Leander?" called Joy softly through the door. "I'm sorry to interrupt—"

Lee's smile widened at the transparent lie.

"—but Elena should know how long she must hold dinner."

"Very considerate of you," said Lee dryly, opening the door, "to worry about Elena's convenience."

Joy flushed and looked down like a guilty child. Lee put his finger under her chin, tilted her head and kissed

165

her on the tip of her nose in silent apology for teasing her.

"We were just on our way down," Lee said. "You may tell Elena that we will have a guest for at least one more day."

"Oh, thank you, Leander!" Joy threw her arms around him in a quick hug. "I knew you could talk David into staying if you only would try."

Lee returned her impulsive hug with the beginning of fervor. Joy stiffened, and instantly Lee dropped his arms.

"I need to wash before dinner," he said. "Would you escort Marjorie to the table?"

"A pleasure," said Carrington, holding out his arm. "Your dress, madame, would be the envy of Paris."

Joy curtsied gracefully. Only then did Lee notice that she was wearing a new dress of dark lilac velvet trimmed with lace that was the precise shade of her hair. The dress accentuated her fragile waist and full breasts swelling against the low, soft neckline. Abruptly, Lee felt angry that anything so alluring could be so unresponsive. But as quickly as it occurred, the anger passed. If the embryonic plan he was carrying came to full term, he would need every bit of Marjorie's skill as an actress.

Eyes narrowed, Lee watched his wife glide down the hallway, her very feminine curves framed in light. When he turned toward his bedroom, the lovely sound of her laughter followed.

By the time Lee sat at the table, Carrington and Joy were deep in conversation concerning balls, ballets and the hilarious social gaffes of one of Joy's childhood enemies. Relieved of the necessity to partake in a conversation that bored him, Lee spent the dinner and the ensuing hours examining his plan for flaws. Finally, his thoughts fell into a futile circling; he could go no further until he knew whether Marjorie would help or hinder his plan.

At an appropriate pause in the conversation, Lee suggested that Carrington might be tired after his long drive. Joy looked at the clock and gasped.

"Dearest David, whatever was I thinking of? You must be exhausted." She stood in a graceful flow of lilac velvet. "I'll show you to your room."

"Nonsense, child. You're as tired as I am." Carrington stifled a yawn. "I know the way by now." A yawn slipped past his guard. "Apologies," he said, standing and stretching as much as good manners would allow. "I'll see you at breakfast, Lee?" he said, looking at his host with eyes that were anything but tired.

"Unless those damn skinny groves wash out to sea."

Carrington grimaced at the thought and at the sound of rain bouncing off of the French windows. He bowed to Joy and disappeared with the noiseless walk that always reminded Lee that Carrington was no ballroom dandy. With a graceful bow, Lee offered his arm to Marjorie and escorted her to the door of her room. There, he paused.

"May I?" he asked, gesturing with a tilt of his head toward her room. "Or would you prefer to talk in mine?"

Joy heard his slight emphasis on the word talk. She searched his face closely, but found none of the signals of desire that she had come to dread. Relieved, and more than a little curious, she treated him to one of her slow smiles.

"Of course, Leander. We can talk while I prepare for bed."

He opened the door and followed her into the rose-and-cream bedroom that was dominated by a satin canopy arching over a large, tall bed. Plants and lace trailed everywhere and the essence of crushed lilacs permeated the room. Lamps with rose-colored shades cast pools of pink light. There was no chair large enough to accommodate Lee comfortably. He pulled the coy bed curtains aside and sat on the high bed. The softness of the mattress and satin coverlets was like a lullaby. He nearly groaned aloud as his tiredness caught up with him.

"Do you mind?" he said, pulling off his boots, loosening his collar and propping himself up on several large, silk-embroidered pillows.

In spite of her unease, Joy smiled at the picture of her

167

husband's lean masculinity, surrounded as it was by satin hearts and lace and plump cupids peeking out of the folded bed curtains.

"Not at all, Leander. You look so tired."

He watched through half-closed eyes while Joy unfastened multitudes of buttons with deft fingers, but the few inches between her shoulder blades defeated her. She bit her lips in irritation. Usually one of the maids helped her undress, but it was far too late an hour to ask for help.

"Why are dresses made so that a woman can't undress herself?" said Joy in exasperation.

Lee held out his hand and motioned her over. She came slowly, until she was sure that consideration rather than lust prompted him.

"Men designed women's dresses," said Lee, unbuttoning the tiny buttons slowly, "so that women need men to help them undress. There," he said yawning. "What about the corset? Although I'll never know why you punish your lovely body with all that whalebone."

Joy flushed, both pleased by the compliment and flustered by the intimacy of the subject. "I only wear what any decent woman does," she said faintly, ducking behind a rice-paper screen and emerging in a pale-rose dressing gown from China.

The very slight slurring of Joy's words, and the color that remained in her cheeks after the blush passed told Lee that his wife had had more wine than usual. Without seeming to, he watched her closely while she took down her carefully coiffed hair until it made a shining, almost silver curtain over her shoulders. She began brushing her hair, counting each stroke; it was another chore that the maid usually did. Before she was beyond sixty, Lee saw that her arm was tired from holding the big gilded brush. But he waited, hoping she would ask.

"Leander?"

"Yes, Marjorie?"

"If it wouldn't be too much trouble, would you . . . ?"

She held the brush out to him hesitantly.

"Of course."

Lee sat up on the edge of the bed, took the brush and turned her so that she was between his legs, with her back to him. He brushed her hair with a sensuous appreciation that Joy shared. It was almost the only intimacy that he and Joy agreed on.

"You are a lovely thing," he murmured, pulling her closer. But he felt the sudden tension in her body and continued brushing without missing a count. "Very lovely. Easily the most beautiful woman in two hundred miles, and perhaps the most beautiful woman in the state."

She looked over her shoulder, lips pursed and a frown wrinkling her delicate forehead.

"Have you been drinking whiskey?" she asked, puzzled and pleased in equal measures.

"Not drinking. Thinking."

Lee smiled, but his eyes held her.

"About what?" she asked softly, unable to look away.

"You."

Lee put the brush aside. She would have moved away then, but the truth in his gray-green eyes held her as surely as his hands on her shoulders.

"Don't run away, Marjorie. I just want to talk with you." His eyes searched hers for response as he repeated slowly, "Just talk."

Slowly, she turned to face him completely. She thought she had seen all of his moods, known all there was to know about the paradox that was her courtier-barbarian husband. But this controlled, searching glance, as though she were newly discovered and of great importance, this was a new aspect of Lee. She rather liked being the sole focus of those handsome eyes.

"Thank you," he said, reading acquiescence in the subtle shift of her posture. "I won't bore you with explanations. I'll just say that what I ask is necessary to the continued prosperity of the ranch."

He hesitated and she nodded encouragingly, missing his flicker of disappointment that she still did not care about the exigencies of business that made up so much of his life.

169

"If you're willing," he continued, "I would like you to become the center of social life. Just this area, to begin with. That will require teas and dinners and parties, joining or creating clubs, expanding your church and charity work, dances." He stopped, misreading her expression. "I know it's an imposition—"

"Imposition?" she said unbelievingly. "Imposition? Leander, my dear, dense husband, I've been trying to do just those things since I came here. But I stopped after you humiliated me by missing my soirees in order to coddle your sheep."

"That won't happen again," he assured her grimly. "I finally understand the importance of parties."

She laughed and threw her arms around his neck in a quick hug. Then she backed up and looked at him with troubled violet eyes.

"You're not teasing me, are you? I know you felt left out this evening with all the San Francisco talk, but honestly, Leander, I do so love to—"

Lee's indulgent laugh sounded remarkably like Carrington. It surprised her into silence.

"I'm not teasing you," he said reassuringly.

In an attempt to make her believe, Lee absently stroked her arms beneath the Chinese wrapper. His eyes were focused inward, sorting through the best opening moves in the political chess game, where power was king and all else was pawn. Now that Marjorie had agreed to help him, he would have access to a greater range of moves. And pawns.

"You should know at least this much," he said quietly, his gray-green eyes still focused beyond her. "The stakes are higher than just getting return invitations to the right homes."

"What is more important than that, Leander?"

"Power. The power to keep my land intact. You see, they—the political powers in the county—want my land."

"Why in heaven's name would they want hundreds of thousands of acres of dirt?"

"Land is a way of generating money, and money is

170

power," said Lee patiently. "So long as I hold on to the land, it will not generate power for them."

"You make it sound so impersonal . . . a force like rain or electricity."

"It is. A very tough man taught me that there's nothing personal about power. It is the deciding force wielded in a war where the names of the dead are listed in bankruptcy courts and the casualties are bled by usurers. It's not pretty or polite, but now that you're my wife, it's your war too."

"But it can't be," said Joy faintly. "I'm not a man."

Lee saw the shadow of fear pale beneath her skin, heard it trembling in her voice.

"Of course not," he murmured, pulling her onto his lap and rocking her soothingly. "Of course you aren't." His hands stroked her, comforting her as though she were a frightened child. "All of your skirmishing will be done in drawing rooms and over dinners where you're better armed than anyone I've ever known.

"There will be a lot of men coming to see me in the near future. It would be a great help if you would make the men feel welcome. You're a very charming woman, Marjorie. Charm them for me."

"Is that all I have to do?" she said, relief in every syllable.

Lee laughed gently. "That's all. No knives. No guns. No blood. Not even a shout. Just a well-bred woman's lethal charm."

"You're making fun of me," said Joy, but her smile told him that she was basking in his compliments.

She sighed and snuggled against his shoulder, her head full of lists and parties and people and occasions.

"I can do it," she said, hardly realizing that his hands still stroked her, although she no longer needed comforting.

She smiled, knowing that finally her talents were not only going to be used, but appreciated. She would show her barbarian husband how a true lady organized a high social life.

Marjorie never knew quite the moment that Lee's hands slid beneath her wrapper, touching her neck and shoulders and breasts with warm fingers. All she knew was an odd, tingling breathlessness that pulled her out of her social reveries. She trembled then, acutely conscious of her breasts and her nipples as hard as though she had taken a cold bath.

"Leander," she said, cheeks burning. "You promised . . . just talk."

"Then talk to me."

Lee kissed her chastely on the cheek, but his fingers teased her breasts until she felt almost dizzy. Just as she was gathering herself to push away from him, his hand slid up from her breasts. Strong fingers rubbed at the base of her neck, then kneaded her scalp in a way that sent waves of pleasure through her. He felt her relax and smiled. Because her eyes were closed, she did not see the light burning in his.

She sighed deeply. "That feels so good, Leander. All those pins and tight coils scrape and pull so."

"I know." He kissed her again, lightly, on her cheek. "But you do look elegant with your hair piled high."

His fingers worked slowly through her hair until she was fully relaxed. Then his free hand slid beneath the rose China silk to the softer silk of her breast. He caressed her until her breast was full and taut and her nipple was again hard between his fingers. She stirred, pressing against his hand, but the movement was protest rather than invitation. Reluctantly, he lifted his hand. Never before had she let him touch her so freely; he did not want to spoil it so quickly.

"Leander . . ."

Marjorie turned slowly in his arms, facing him instead of reclining across his lap. Her movements opened her wrapper, but she did not notice. In the rose light of the room, her curving flesh gleamed like white jade. Lee closed his eyes for a long moment, brutally recalling all of the times she had refused him.

"Leander, what kind of a party do you want first?"

172

Slowly, Lee opened his eyes. When he looked down, his glance did not go below the small oval face turned up to him. Nor did his hand stray, though her hip rose so temptingly above the pale triangle of hair only half-concealed by the loose wrapper.

"Party?" said Lee. "Oh, a big one," he said gathering his thoughts. "A fiesta."

Joy stiffened. "A Mexican party?"

"No." Remembering her antipathy to all things Mexican, he improvised quickly. "Remember your history books? When the kings had huge feasts and the aristocracy ate in great halls while the commoners ate in the courtyards?"

Joy became completely still. He looked down and saw the intense concentration on her face. Smiling at her absorption, he moved his fingers lightly across her breasts. Almost absently, her hand came up to brush away his, then her fingers stopped in mid-air as she was struck by a thought.

"Should we have costumes?" Then quickly, "No. San Ignacio isn't ready for that yet. Perhaps by next Christmas."

Lee tucked her hand inside his unbuttoned shirt. Her hand slid down his chest until her fingertips rubbed the flat muscles of his stomach idly, as though his skin were a fabric she was considering for a dress.

"It will be wonderful," she whispered, eyes half-closed.

She no longer really noticed the long fingers that moved over her breasts. She arched her back, shifting into a more comfortable position. His lips touched her nipple so briefly she did not know whether she had imagined it. Certainly she had no time to object.

"What will be wonderful?" he asked in a low voice, lips tickling her ear.

"My gala," she sighed. Lost in thought, she arched against his hand again, not knowing why or even caring.

The wine and his hands and the longed-for opportunity to preside over a full social life combined to sidetrack her automatic withdrawal from a man's touch. Lee looked at the beautiful woman lying across his lap and ached to

173

touch her without restraint, to know her body as intimately as his own, as intimately as he had once known another's. His hand slid from her breasts to her tiny waist, her flat stomach and the softness of her inner thighs. For a few moments she lay passively, then she sat up with a little gasp.

"I don't know what—I wasn't thinking—the wine!"

Lee looked at Marjorie's cheeks, bright with shame and wine, but not passion.

"You were just planning your gala," said Lee, voice soft in spite of the frustration gripping him.

"Yes," she sighed, leaning against him again. "What a pity San Ignacio isn't San Francisco!" Her fingers absently traced patterns on his chest. Then she shrugged as elegantly as any Frenchwoman. "It will be wonderful, anyway. I'll give parties that will be the envy of the state." She laughed softly, the laugh of a woman aroused. "Thank you, Leander."

She pulled his head down and kissed him with her lips parted just enough for him to sense the sweetness of her breath. He wished she would yield her mouth to him just once, just for a moment. But he accepted what was offered, just as Joy accepted that San Ignacio was not San Francisco.

"Leander . . ."

The odd hesitancy, almost fear, of her tone pulled him out of his disappointment.

"Yes, Marjorie?" He tilted her chin up. "Is something wrong?"

She looked up at him, then glanced away, blushing scarlet.

"What is it?"

The concern in Lee's voice was obvious; her cooperation was too new, too fragile and too important. Guessing what was embarrassing her, Lee moved his hands back up to her shoulders.

"Is that better, Marjorie?"

His voice was so gentle and somehow weary, that she looked up, surprised.

174

"I thought that you wanted—" Her throat closed in embarrassment and her hand moved from his chest. She squirmed uneasily, opening the wrapper still further. "I thought—" she began again, then sagged in defeat. Her hand slid down until it rested in his lap. She jerked back from the unmistakable hardness she felt beneath her fingers. "Then you do want it?"

This time he did not misunderstand her blush. His gray-green eyes looked at her with veiled intensity. Already her body was less relaxed, more rigid and he knew she was regretting her stumbling words that could have been construed as an invitation.

"Of course."

Joy was too embarrassed to notice that his voice was soft without being gentle. But nonetheless, Lee was careful to choose words that would not offend her.

"I know of no other way to have a son. Do you, Marjorie?"

Silently she shook her head, spilling her pale hair over her breasts. Her lower lip was white where it was caught between her teeth and her hands were curled into futile fists. Lee measured the rejection in her tight body, rejection and fear and humiliation. With a bitterness that went no further than his eyes, he rocked her in his arms.

"It doesn't have to be tonight, Marjorie. It doesn't have to be tomorrow night. It doesn't have to be. Ever."

Joy had expected anger or contempt or any of the harsher emotions he had shown in the past when she refused him. His acceptance made her as dizzy as the wine. She threw her arms around his neck.

"It will be a fine gala," she said intensely. "The finest ever!"

"Of course," he said, rocking her mechanically.

"And—and we will have a son," she said in a rush. "We must. All the best families have them."

Lee did not know whether to laugh or swear, so he sat without moving while she reached resolutely for the perfumed oil she kept in a drawer of the bedside table. He

175

recovered his wits enough to take the vial from her fingers.

"Let me," he said, catching her hand and muffling his smile by kissing her palm. "I know you don't like the feel of oil on your delicate fingers."

"But—"

"But not yet," said Lee, setting the vial aside. As he rubbed her scalp and gave her the undemanding kisses she was able to enjoy, he quickly removed his clothes with one hand and dropped them to the floor. "First, tell me how soon you want to have your gala," he kissed her neck slowly, "and how many will be invited," his lips warmed her ear, then brushed her eyelids, "and how many hearts you'll break before the season is over."

Joy laughed breathlessly, trying to answer his questions all at once, grateful, very grateful to have something to think about besides his alarming nudity and her own. But before she could stiffen against the long caress of his body, he asked more questions, distracting her, until she felt his fingers warm with oil, touching her more intimately than she had believed possible.

"Leander!" she said, reaching down to push his hands away.

"Careful," he said, low-voiced, almost laughing, "you'll get your lovely fingers oily."

But she had already jerked her hands up after inadvertently touching him.

"Put your arms around my neck," suggested Lee, laughing soundlessly. "You won't need to worry about what you touch up there."

When she complied, his fingers resumed their slow savoring of her flesh.

"Leander," said Joy, squirming with embarrassment, "that isn't necessary."

"But it is, my dear Marjorie," he said smoothly. "I know that far too often I hurt you. You are so . . . fastidious . . . that you don't apply the oil properly." He smiled gravely at her while his fingers moved slowly,

176

stroking. "But I don't mind the oil and I very much mind hurting you."

"Surely that is enough!" said Joy firmly, evading his lips.

"Almost."

He poured a few last drops into his palm. The smell of lilacs became almost overwhelming as the oil spread over his heated flesh. To her surprise, he did not hurt her, not even in the last few instants when his need made him forget to be gentle. The fact that she neither gave nor received real pleasure was unimportant. For both of them it was enough that there was no pain.

She fell asleep, relieved that her duty had been accomplished without argument; and she dreamed of a season that never ended. Lee tucked the covers around her, gathered his clothes up and left his wife's bedroom as silently as a shadow. Even while he climbed into his own bed, his mind was polishing the framework of the plan he would share with Carrington over breakfast.

Both men arose early the following morning. By tacit consent, they ate their breakfast quickly and quietly, knowing that if Joy were to waken, business talk would have to be delayed. After the last bit of chorizo and eggs had disappeared, Carrington looked up quizzically. Lee nodded and instructed the maid to bring coffee to his office.

When the office door closed behind the maid, Lee took his coffee over to the French doors and opened them wide. Sunlight flooded the office, picking up blue highlights deep within the charcoal rug.

"Look out there," said Lee quietly, stepping onto the balcony.

Carrington followed him. "It's beautiful," he agreed.

The land was both clean and bright, softened by rain and the slow blush of new grass growing. Even the mountains suggested new green beneath the brown tones of chaparral.

"Beautiful," said Lee blandly, "but too big."

177

Carrington made a surprised sound and turned to stare at Lee.

"Think about it," Lee said, pointing as he spoke. "It's more than a hundred miles from Los Angeles to Mission San Diego. We in the south of the county have to travel too far for the privilege of being robbed by laws and lawmakers who have never seen the land between those two big cities.

"And do those high-living city folk care about us? Hell, no. They only see us as a tame cow to milk whenever the cities are thirsty for cream. The only answer is to make our own county—and milk our own damn cow."

A slow, admiring smile spread across Carrington's lips when he realized what Lee's plan was. He laughed softly, shaking his head. "I'll say it again, Lee. You're wasted as a rancher."

Lee bowed, smiling sardonically, and his eyes were the color of mercury. Then he straightened swiftly. "I don't have the stomach for that kind of manipulation."

"Nobody asked you to like it," observed Carrington.

"It's a damned good thing."

"You're good at it, Lee. Very good."

Lee grimaced. "I'd rather raise sheep."

Carrington ignored Lee's comment. For several minutes he looked out into the clean yellow day, examining Lee's idea from many angles, trying to foresee rewards and difficulties. At last he sighed lightly and his hazel eyes focused on his friend.

"The idea of making our own county is brilliant," said Carrington simply, "but it won't be easy. Heer undoubtedly has some power in the state capital, as well as in Los Angeles. The formation of a new county would require the approval of both the legislature and the governor."

"I can think of ways to enlist the towns on our behalf," countered Lee. "And the other ranchers would be grateful for the chance to get out from under a city-oriented government." Lee paused. "The new county would receive a helluva lot more support than we could hope for if all we tried to do was scotch the idea of taxing Buckles Ranch and PacCo. Face it, David, the idea of taxing the devil out of us has a natural appeal for everybody but you and me."

Carrington smiled but the smile quickly vanished into his beard. He put his palms flat on the damp balcony railing and said hesitantly, "It might be better if I maintained public neutrality in the matter of a new county. If this is supposed to be an upwelling of popular sentiment—a poor man's Manifest Destiny, as it were—I should be well back in the woodwork."

"Amen. And the new county's biggest landowner will be right back in the woodwork with you."

"Then who will lead the charge for a new county?"

"One of San Ignacio's leading opinion-makers. Probably a certain I. Edward Prufrock."

Carrington closed his eyes and smiled, apparently lost in enjoyment of the sun. "And just why would the editor and owner of the San Ignacio *Clarion* be interested in having his own county?"

Lee smiled over at the other man. "Oh, he'll be interested, all right. Just as soon as he realizes that a new county would generate enough captive legal advertising to provide his floundering journal with an instant yearly income." Lee's deep voice suggested depths of irony that were still untapped. "The beauty of this plan is that it allows a great many people to support it for reasons ranging from pride to profit, stupidity to greed. That, after all, is the essence of good political policy, isn't it?"

Carrington studied Lee's handsome face, but saw nothing beyond an impenetrably bland smile. "What a waste," sighed Carrington again.

The blandness vanished; Lee's face was suddenly grim. "Not if I keep my land."

Carrington nodded in silent agreement, stroking his sleek brown beard with sensitive fingertips. "The legislators could probably be made to understand the necessity of a new county. For a price."

"Then it's up to us to find out what price each one attaches to his understanding," said Lee softly, leaning on

179

the balcony with complete disregard for the wet railing. "How long will it take you to draw up a shopping list?"

Carrington pursed his lips. "A week. Buying the items will naturally take a bit longer." His lips twisted in a smile. "Are you very sure that you wouldn't like to be governor?"

"Horseshit." Lee made a sound of complete disgust. "I don't want to be anything that's bought and sold like sheep."

The silence was broken by the susuration of wind blowing up the shallow rise of hill below the house. Carrington listened, sighed and turned back toward the office. As he turned, Lee noticed for the first time that his friend's sideburns were frosted with gray and his clear eyes were rimmed with dark lines of fatigue.

"How long," said Carrington, "will it take you to convince Mr. I. Edward Prufrock of the divine necessity of a new county?"

"One meeting. Maybe two. If he doesn't bite by then, I'll start peddling the idea of being a county seat among the inflexible progressives of the town."

"Your approach to him," mused Carrington. "Landed gentry visits peer in town?"

"Something like that," Lee said uncomfortably, disliking the outright statement of manipulation, but conceding its necessity.

"Then do yourself a favor," Carrington said dryly. "Wear that black suit and take a fancy buggy into town."

"I don't own a fancy buggy," Lee said, remembering that lack was a sore point with Joy.

"You do now."

Lee looked at Carrington.

"You don't think," said Carrington, "that I drove that rig from Los Angeles for the exercise, do you? I have a perfectly fine—not to say sumptuous—private car and an engineer who will take me anywhere there are steel rails.

"And, if you remember, there are steel rails on Buckles land."

Lee laughed softly, shaking his head. "Joy put you up to it, didn't she?"

Carrington shrugged and reached inside his jacket for a cigar. "She's right, Lee. It's time that you stopped looking and acting like a saddle tramp."

"Two days ago I would have told you to eat lunch with the Devil," said Lee, his gray eyes narrow. "But two days ago I didn't know about Heer."

In spite of his soft voice, Lee's mouth was a rebellious line. He muttered a curse, then turned and faced his always elegant, always shrewd partner.

"How much do I owe you for the damn buggy?"

Carrington's hand moved negligently, making his emerald ring flash in the sunlight.

"Call it my gift to you on the occasion of your coming out."

"David—" began Lee, tightly.

But Carrington had left the balcony and was walking quickly across the office.

"I believe I heard Joy calling," said Carrington over his shoulder. "Shall we join your lovely wife for coffee?"

Lee stood very still for a moment, knowing that he had just been manipulated by an expert. And Lee understood the depth of Carrington's finesse, when he realized that Carrington was due thanks for the lesson.

Shaking his head, Lee followed his partner back into the house.

The wide, dusty Main Street of San Ignacio was crowded with delivery wagons, teamsters and shouting children. Dozens of commercial buildings spread out north and west of the railroad depot that had become the hub of commerce. More than one hundred houses were scattered on the narrow streets that branched off of the downtown area; in the last ten years, San Ignacio's population had quadrupled to more than one thousand, and it was still growing. With Citrus City to the northeast, as well as the coastal villages of Santo, Minton and Blue Lagoon, plus various colonias and scattered farms, San Igna-

181

cio serviced a population that was three times as large as the number enclosed within the city's limits.

It seemed to Lee Buckles that every man, child and dog had chosen this sunny morning to walk the streets of San Ignacio. The crowds churned bare dirt into dust that hung in the air, choking man and animal alike. Then the fine dust sifted inexorably down, giving everything a matte finish that was as fine as talcum powder.

Lee found an open spot in front of a feed store that had just been repainted barn red with the obligatory white trim and lettering. He stepped out of the buggy he had owned now for a week, loosened the harness on the blacks and tied them to a hitching post. With short, sharp motions, he brushed the worst of the clinging dust off of his black trousers and tailored coat. Then he snapped his sleeves over his silk cuffs, straightened his new black hat and walked across the street to the offices of the San Ignacio *Clarion*.

The clanking of the small double-sheet press was nearly overwhelming, even after the noise of the street. The office itself had a closed, vaguely offensive smell— ink and raw paper and cheap cigars penned in by windows that were never opened. Lee closed the door quickly. Though he assumed it was impossible to hear the tinkle of the bell fastened to the door frame, the clanking of the press suddenly stopped. A man with thinning gray hair, huge ink-stained hands and a permanent stoop stepped out from behind a tall case of type. He wiped his hands on a ragged piece of already black toweling and fumbled in the pocket of his work apron until he found a battered pair of wire-rim glasses.

"Mr. Prufrock?" said Lee, holding out his hand. "I'm Leander Buckles."

Prufrock peered through the smudged lenses, then wiped his right hand carefully on his apron.

"A pleasure, suh," he said, taking Lee's hand in a calloused grip.

Prufrock's soft Southern voice was almost colorless, a striking contrast to the fiery tones of his editorials and his

182

always opinionated, sometimes ill-informed news stories. But in spite of his biases, or perhaps because of them, Prufrock was one of the few locals who at least attempted to learn what was happening in the world beyond San Ignacio. That in itself made the man interesting to Lee.

"Is this a bad time for you?" asked Lee politely, glancing around at the clutter which suggested deadlines as often missed as made.

Prufrock reset his glasses firmly on his rather large, whiskey-tinged nose. "I'm just printing flyers for the new restaurant. Small job, but it helps to pay the rent. It can wait." He smiled slightly. "The job, not the rent."

Lee chuckled.

Prufrock cocked his head and looked at Lee with old blue eyes that had abandoned both hope and despair. "What can I do for you, Mr. Buckles?"

"A few minutes of your time would be appreciated."

"Of course." He gestured toward two scarred oak chairs and waited until Lee sat before he sat down himself. "I'm sure you're not here to argue with my editorial stand on squatters . . . ?"

Lee smiled appreciatively. Over the years, Prufrock had been more vociferous than the ranchers about the sanctity of property rights.

"Hardly," murmured Lee. "As a matter of fact, I usually find your editorials to be most stimulating. You have a gift, Mr. Prufrock."

"I have bills to pay," said the editor with a tiny smile. "Beyond that necessity, there is no more gift or mystery to my work than to a carpenter driving nails. I have opinions, paper and a printing press. *Voilà!* The San Ignacio *Clarion.*"

Lee looked at the old man sharply; Prufrock was more intelligent than his editorials suggested. "And few illusions?" suggested Lee.

"Pray God, no," Prufrock said softly. "I'm neither young enough nor rich enough to support illusions."

"Then you're a rare man," said Lee. "And a wise one. I very much need a wise man's advice."

Prufrock looked surprised, then subtly gratified. Unconsciously, he nodded, as though Lee had indeed come to the wise man of San Ignacio. Lee measured the editor's response and knew that he had found the key to Prufrock's support; the simple gratification that came from being appreciated.

"San Ignacio has been good to me," said Lee, hesitating as though choosing words, when in fact he knew precisely what he was going to say. "I have prospered reasonably, and I'd like to share that prosperity."

"Reasonably." Prufrock spoke with a touch of asperity that made Lee want to smile.

"Yes."

"There are the usual ways—libraries, scholarships, statues of civic leaders." Prufrock stopped. "Not too appealing to you, Mr. Buckles?" he asked with a smile.

"Would you be offended if I said those suggestions bore me?"

Prufrock's hoarse laugh perfectly matched his low, almost furry voice. "No, Mr. Buckles, I wouldn't be offended. There are more interesting things in life for grown men than ungrateful children and bronze statues dripping with bird shit."

Laughing, Lee took off his hat and settled back for a talk that was going to be both more interesting and more difficult than he had assumed.

"Is it public office you're after?" asked Prufrock, his voice so hoarse that at first Lee did not think he had heard correctly. "No, don't bother to answer," said Prufrock. "The look of surprise and distaste on your face is more honest than any words. If not public office, then what do you want?"

The respect of my neighbors," Lee said with disarming frankness.

"You're respected. But you're not very well liked. Some have even called you unneighborly."

"I know I've not been as quick as I should be to hold out my hand. I can only plead youth and overwhelming work. I'm older now. I realize that my future and San Ignacio's are as completely joined as branches on a tree trunk." Lee smiled slightly. "I'd like that joining to be as pleasant as possible."

Lee shifted his hat to his knee and leaned forward. His eyes were gray, steady, flattering in their intensity. "San Ignacio and the Buckles Ranch have had their differences in the past. But no longer. This is a good city, Mr. Prufrock. It could be a powerful city as well, if it weren't treated like a stepdaughter."

"Cinderella," offered Prufrock, "caught between two ugly older sisters called San Diego and Los Angeles."

"As I said, Mr. Prufrock, you have a gift."

"And bills to pay. Civic pride sells almost as many papers as a double murder."

Lee looked at the editor narrowly, weighing his cynicism. In spite of his hard words, Prufrock's face was thoughtful. Suddenly Lee guessed that Prufrock's rough veneer owed as much to whiskey as to age; the lined, gray-haired, stooped man in front of him was probably no older than David Carrington. Did he, like Carrington, nurture a few frail illusions beneath his cynical façade? And was one of those illusions called Progress and the Betterment of Man?

"I bow to your cynicism," said Lee, "though I'm too young or too foolish to share it."

"You will." Wearily, Prufrock rubbed the bridge of his red nose. "Cynicism—or whiskey—is the inevitable refuge of intelligence."

"Then there's nothing I can do for San Ignacio?"

Prufrock sighed and reached for an inky, age-encrusted black pipe. As he filled its disreputable bowl with black shreds of tobacco, he mused aloud. "I don't know that San Ignacio deserves better than she has." He reached in the desk drawer and rummaged for something to pack the tobacco down. In the end, he settled for an oily lead slug containing a fragment of an old advertisement. "I'm not so sure that Cinderella deserved the Prince, either. Insipid wench, if you believe the story."

Lee laughed in genuine amusement; it was an opinion

of the fairy tale that he had wanted to voice since child-hood and had never dared. Prufrock looked up, grinned like a conspirator and resumed cramming odorous black shreds into the charred bowl. At the appropriate moment, Lee leaned forward, offering a light from the solid gold lighter that Marjorie had given him for Christmas.

"Thank you, Mr. Buckles."

"Lee."

"Then thank you, Lee. The few people who can toler-ate me call me Ward."

Lee nodded, trying not to show his distaste at the rather incredible stench arising from Prufrock's smolder-ing pipe.

"Bad, isn't it?" said Prufrock cheerfully. "But after a day of ink and a night of rye, this is the only thing I can taste."

"Perhaps you should upgrade the quality of your rye."

Prufrock laughed until he began to cough on the acrid smoke. "My wife used to suggest the same thing." A shadow of old sadness crossed his wrinkled face. He shrugged almost irritably. "But that won't help San Ignacio."

"What will?"

"Burn Los Angeles to the ground."

"Too drastic," smiled Lee, "although every time I have to take two days just to transact legal business, I do get a bit angry."

Prufrock nodded. "You're not the only businessman who feels like that. After the weather, the distance to the county seat is the favorite gripe." Prufrock coughed, sending bitter smoke across his desk. "And like the weath-er, nothing can be done about it."

"Weather," observed Lee absently, "is made by God. Counties are made by men."

Prufrock's watery eyes squinted through the smoke, but to all appearances, Lee was merely thinking aloud.

"Out of the mouths of babes," said Prufrock, clearing his throat.

He reached for a chewed pencil and started scribbling

rapidly. Lee watched with apparent indifference, but his gray eyes missed nothing. And revealed nothing. After a time, Prufrock remembered Lee and looked up.

"Sorry. Here you come to ask my advice and instead I steal your idea. Good one too. It will keep this damn dinosaur in hay for a few months at least."

"My idea?"

Prufrock poked at the dead ashes of his pipe. "For a new county."

Lee looked politely puzzled, then allowed himself a small smile.

"With San Ignacio as the new county seat?" suggested Lee.

"Of course. Do you have any idea how much revenue is guaranteed to a county seat?"

"Yes," said Lee dryly. "I've often wondered why it was our fate to go on paying another city's way into the twentieth century." Lee leaned forward again, his eyes clear, intense. "You've had an excellent idea, Mr. Pru—Ward. Much more exciting than a statue. In a few weeks, San Ignacio will be twenty-five years old. What better way to cap a quarter century of progress than by becoming the center of a new county?"

"A quarter-century of—are you sure you're not running for public office?" said Prufrock, smiling and watching Lee with eyes that were more alive than they had been.

"Quite sure." Lee paused, then took a calculated risk. "But if you know of good men who are, I might be persuaded to help."

Slowly, Prufrock sucked on the foul pipe. "I'll think on it, Lee." He chuckled hoarsely. "Life looks to be a bit more interesting around here."

"Life is always interesting," said Lee mildly. "And to do my part in keeping it that way, what would you think of a celebration of San Ignacio's twenty-fifth birthday? Perhaps with a barbeque for several hundred of the town's leading citizens? Just a small way for my wife and myself to thank the community for all that it has done for us."

"And will do?" suggested Prufrock slyly.

"What benefits the trunk, benefits the branch."

"Are you positive you're not running for—"

"You have my word on it," said Lee coolly, fixing the editor with an unwavering gray glance.

"Good enough. Even your worst enemy admits that you're a man of your word."

Lee's blond eyebrow lifted.

"Mr. Roger Heer."

"That was a decade ago," said Lee.

"To the good Mr. Heer, it's as fresh as tomorrow."

Lee said nothing. Prufrock lit his pipe yet again and leaned back, sending a stream of smoke up to the dirty ceiling.

"I would like you to print the invitations for the barbeque," said Lee quietly. "I would also like to put up a modest sum—say, fifty dollars—to be awarded to the person who suggests the best name for the new county. I would take it as a personal favor if the *Clarion* sponsored the contest. Naturally, I'll pay for your time and trouble."

"The contest will pay for itself in increased circulation," said Prufrock, puffing on his pipe thoughtfully. Then he nodded several times. "I like it, Lee. But who will decide the winner? You?"

Lee held his hands up. "Oh, no! You will. Or a committee of citizens. Not me."

Prufrock laughed dryly. "A committee of citizens . . . perhaps the same ones who are having such difficulty raising money to pay for a Founder's Day parade."

Lee repressed a smile. "Would I be permitted the honor of contributing?"

"Permitted?" Prufrock snorted. "They've been drawing straws to see who had to bell your cat."

"And you were chosen?" said Lee, reaching inside his jacket pocket for his wallet.

"No, Eliot Fulton."

Prufrock did not know Lee well enough to realize that

his smile concealed considerable animosity for the banker Fulton. Lee counted out one hundred dollars. The new notes looked very green against Prufrock's cluttered desk.

"And fifty for the contest," added Lee, making a second pile. "Will that help the parade?"

"It will. It will also assure you and your wife of two seats in the judges' section."

"We're honored."

Prufrock grimaced. "Tell me that afterward. Nothing more boring than a small town parade. Ah well, it's all part of Progress."

Lee smiled and rose to his feet.

"I won't take any more of your time, Ward." He held out his hand. "It's been a pleasure. Let me know if there's anything at all I can do to help your battle for a new county."

Smiling widely, Prufrock shook Lee's hand. Then, as Lee opened the door, he turned and looked meaningfully at the pile of money on the editor's desk.

"Someday you must play poker with myself and my partner," said Lee. "Until that day—thanks for the lesson."

The clear metal sound of the door's bell blended oddly with Prufrock's hoarse laughter.

"I look forward to it, Lee," he said as the door shut. Then he added softly, "I'll bet you play a mean hand of poker."

Still smiling, he walked slowly over to the press. With the years-old motion that had stooped his back, he began to work. The rhythmic clanking of the press made the office shudder slightly.

In the ten weeks leading up to Founder's Day, Prufrock wrote a series of editorials that began with paens to the beauty, nobility and moral superiority of the south part of the county over the rest of the world in general and the north county in particular. Lee found the editorials to be almost as insincere as the obituaries that had the deceased being "wafted to heaven on the wings of angels."

Yet, Lee had to admit that Prufrock had accurately calculated the sentiments and sophistication of the majority of his audience; San Ignacio talked about little other than the editorials. By the time Prufrock alluded to the cash benefits of being a county seat, the readers were in such a fervor of indignation that arguments broke out over who had been insulted worst and most often by the greedy county government in distant Los Angeles.

Under Carrington's gentle prompting, Lee spent much of his time in San Ignacio, buying lunches and drinks, listening to merchants, lawyers, bankers and churchmen. Slowly he realized that the men were like himself in that they were feeling their way through life, and at the same time trying to reach beyond themselves and their routines for something more exciting, more demanding and more meaningful than the trivia of daily living.

At the same time, almost all of the men lacked something that Lee found difficult to isolate. He listened and watched and probed while the weeks passed, until he finally decided that the other men's sense of scale was largely different from his own. While he was comfortable thinking in terms of international money, markets, and power plays, most of San Ignacio's leading citizens found it difficult to see beyond either end of their dusty, crowded Main Street. Often, even within these limits, their view of the world around them was clouded, confused and narrow.

Lee suspected that it would be no different if San Ignacio were San Francisco. When he had suggested as much to Joy, she had curtly refused to listen, feeling somehow insulted by his observation.

Although Prufrock's editorials never overtly mentioned the formation of a new county, by the third Saturday in April, San Ignacio was ready to march on Los Angeles and demand equality, or at least a more even distribution of the county dollar. The Founder's Day parade promised to make up in spirit what it lacked in size or polish, as people traded phrases of what had become the new conventional wisdom. But not until the parade was over, and

190

people had come to fill themselves with Buckles's beef and Buckles's beer, would the possibility of petitioning the governor for a new county be officially mentioned in Prufrock's carefully written speech.

Lee looked forward to that speech with a feeling that was compounded equally of anxiety and anticipation. The future of the Buckles Ranch rode on the townspeople's unstinting approval of the idea of a separate county. But in spite of his inner worries, Lee was careful to appear attentive throughout the morning's festivities in San Ignacio. He applauded the Queen of Founder's Day, voted for the San Ignacio Improvement League's float and exchanged careful comments with the citizens who sat near him during the parade.

The socializing that was a burden for Lee was a pleasure for Joy. Dressed in pale lavender silk, hair shining like the spring sun, Joy charmed even the most proper maiden aunts into liking her. The men crowded close for the chance to compliment and talk to her, a fact that the other women did not seem to resent. It was as though they realized at some instinctive level that Joy's beauty was not—and never would be—an invitation for their men to stray beyond the rigid boundaries of social flirtation.

While he drove Joy back to the ranch, Lee spoke rarely, worrying about the coming afternoon. Joy was equally withdrawn, but for different reasons. In her mind, she was making and remaking lists of things that must be done for the success of the barbeque. When the black buggy swept up the driveway behind the high-stepping horses, Joy looked around as though aware of her surroundings for the first time. She smiled and accepted Lee's help in getting out of the buggy. Impulsively, she kissed him on the cheek when he set her on the ground.

"It will be such fun, Leander. And what a perfect day!"

Lee smiled in return, pleased by her unusual show of affection. He put his hands on her shoulders, pulling her closer as he bent over to return her kiss more warmly.

191

She put her lace-gloved hands on his chest, gently but unmistakably pushing him away.

"There are so many things I must do yet," said Joy, slipping out from beneath his hands. "The first guests will probably arrive before I have a chance to change."

Lee turned and stepped back into the buggy to drive it to the stables.

"Leander?"

"Yes?" he said automatically, picking up the reins when the black horses moved restlessly.

"There's something I—" Joy flushed and looked away.

"What is it?" said Lee, consciously making his voice gentle.

"I—that is, we—" She looked up at him quickly, a flash of pale violet, then she glanced down at her lace gloves. "May we talk later, Leander?"

"We can talk now," pointed out Lee reasonably.

"No. Not now," she said, blushing again.

Lee measured her blushes, made a swift mental calculation and decided it must be the time of month that Joy was most likely to conceive. Since he had enlisted her aid in organizing their social life, she had been very conscientious in trying to give him a son. He would have preferred an ounce of pleasure to her pounds of duty, but said nothing, knowing she would not understand. Sensuality was simply foreign to Joy's nature.

"I must change," she said breathlessly, "and then see to the kitchen help. Those Mexicans can be so lazy unless you keep them under your eye all the time."

With a brilliant smile at him, Joy turned and walked quickly up the broad stairs to the front door. But Lee had to admit that she had been right; he barely had enough time to turn the team over to the stableboy before the first buggies and wagons arrived filled with eager guests.

By noon, nearly five hundred people had gathered, most of them in an area to one side of the house where Joy had once suggested planting a jacaranda tree. There, under Gil's supervision, barbecue pits had been dug and kegs of beer and tubs of lemonade and fresh oranges had

192

been set out. Children played tag among their parents, most of whom were tradesmen, carpenters, cowhands and small farmers.

Closer to the house, near the only formal garden to survive the dry winds of summer, Joy had set up striped awnings and tables large enough to seat fifty people. Orange blossoms and ferns graced the long, linen-covered tables. In addition to beer and lemonade, there was punch and a bar overseen by a smiling German bartender from San Ignacio. Standing around the garden, wearing dark suits and bright silk dresses that swept the first blades of a new lawn, were the social, political and religious leaders of the south county area. It was to this group that Joy addressed herself, after a gracious, brief tour of the barbeque pits.

At first, Lee divided himself equally between the awnings and the pits. But when he realized that Joy planned no more than a single foray among the working class, Lee grabbed a mug of beer and concentrated on the crowds who had gathered around the fragrant barbeques. He mingled easily, naturally, stopping to talk with farmers about the weather and with tradesmen about the land boom that was bringing hordes of speculators into Southern California.

Gil and the Buckles ranch hands had been drafted as chefs and beer tappers and bouncers. They had organized an informal, rather rowdy baseball game and a dismounted roping contest. Children and adults were equally entranced by the skill of the vaqueros in making their long rawhide ropes dance and lift. The baseball game drew a large audience that cheered impartially for town and ranch players. Lee stood with a group of his men, beer in one hand and a plate of succulent beef in the other, cheering when one of Gil's cousins fielded a difficult grounder and threw the man out at second base to end the game. As Lee turned to go back toward the awnings for the beginning of the speech, he spotted Gil at the edge of the crowd.

The foreman was resplendent in a black sombrero,

black vest, plum-colored silk shirt embroidered with black silk thread and close-fitting black pants. Lee realized that he had not spoken to Gil other than a few hurried instructions on the way to San Ignacio's parade. When he caught Gil's eye, Lee raised his mug in silent congratulations for Gil's skill in making the barbeque go smoothly. But to Lee's surprise, instead of responding, Gil looked aside instantly, as though to deny that he had seen Lee at all.

When Gil turned away, tugging his hat lower as though to shield his face from Lee's eyes, Lee put down his beer and beef and started walking toward Gil. Intuition and more than a decade of friendship told Lee that Gil's evasion was important. With the patience of a hunter, Lee unobtrusively tracked Gil through the dispersing crowd, past the cooling barbeque pits to the edge of the fledgling citrus groves where several horseshoe games were raising puffs of dust with each throw.

"Gil?"

Gil turned as though surprised to see Lee.

"*Ola*," he said, grinning engagingly, his brown eyes very dark and his face lined with the effort of appearing normal.

Lee looked at Gil with eyes that the spring day made seem almost blue. Gil met his friend's look with a mixture of emotions that he could no longer hide. Lee paused, wondering if he had any right to pry; then the skin of his neck stirred in a warning as old as man. With a small jerk of his head, Lee motioned Gil out of the crowd of players. Gil followed, saying nothing. Lee waited until he was certain that no one would overhear.

"Let's have it," Lee said softly, turning to face Gil.

Gil closed his eyes as though the soft spring sun was suddenly summer-hard and fierce. With a sigh that was nearly a groan, Gil opened his eyes again and looked at the man he was closer to than a brother. But before Gil could speak, both men saw someone walking quickly toward them, a man coming from the direction of the pits, although he was dressed to eat under striped awnings. At the same moment, Lee and Gil recognized him.

"What is that *cabrón* doing here?"

Lee's peremptory gesture silenced Gil.

"Hello, Buckles, It's been a long time."

"Heer," said Lee in a noncommittal voice, greeting and dismissal in a single word.

Roger Heer stopped a few feet away, as though reluctant to get within reach of either man. His brilliant blue eyes flicked over Gil with palpable contempt.

"Your faithful greaser dog isn't so faithful after all," Heer said, rolling the words on his tongue as though they had a unique flavor. "Or has he told you?" Heer's eyes narrowed intently as he looked from one man to the other. "No, I can see that he hasn't."

Lee waited, apparently indifferent, sensing that Gil's silent rage and Heer's oily pleasure were opposite faces of the same coin. Disappointed by Lee's lack of reaction, Heer stepped closer, smiling with a savagery that he usually took care to conceal.

"I'd horsewhip a friend who didn't tell me when a certain woman came back," Heer said in a voice that was so throaty as to be nearly a snarl. "Especially if it was a woman that I was . . . interested in, shall we say?"

Involuntarily, Lee turned toward Gil. The foreman's dark eyes closed in helpless apology and affirmation. Though neither man spoke, Cira's name stretched between them like a wire. Heer saw, and laughed.

"Yes, Buckles. Your little greaser whore is back. She's only going to be here today, Buckles. Just today. She's too ashamed to stay any longer. And you know why, don't you?"

Heer waited expectantly, sure of Lee's rage. But Lee was older than the man who had shoved a shotgun in Heer's stomach. Lee sensed that Heer was taunting him to a purpose; Heer hoped for violence, for a fight that would attract embarrassing attention. Lee gave him nothing, not even a word.

"Or do you know?" snapped Heer, realizing that Lee was not going to fight.

Lee said nothing, did nothing. His every instinct warned him not to be drawn into Heer's game.

"What? No questions?" Heer's voice was suddenly harsh. "Don't you want to know why she left, why you couldn't find her? Or don't you care anymore?" Heer stopped, as if the thought was new and unwelcome. Then he laughed unpleasantly. "It can't be your wife—you're well-known in California's better whorehouses."

Lee's arm moved with the quickness that rage always brought to him. Heer ducked, lips stretched thin in anticipation of an ugly scene, but all Lee did was signal to Frederico. The old man left off poking among the barbecue ashes and walked quickly toward Lee.

"*Sí*, señor?"

"See that this man," said Lee, indicating Heer with a flick of his finger, "finds his way off of Buckles property."

Coolly, Lee turned his back on Heer. Only Gil knew Lee well enough to read the rage that swelled beneath Lee's controlled exterior.

"You can throw me off your goddamned ranch," said Heer loudly, "but what about her? The speeches start soon. If you want your goddamned county, you better be up front, applauding. If you clap hard enough, Buckles, you won't hear the sound of the afternoon train taking your whore back to Mexico."

Though his neck was corded with the effort of not striking out at Heer, Lee stood without moving until he was positive that Frederico had taken Heer out of sight. But even then Lee felt Heer's malevolence as surely as though the man's half-mad eyes were still inches away from his own.

"He's gone," said Gil, turning to face Lee.

Gil stepped back suddenly, the reflexive move of a man trying to evade a blow. But Lee had done nothing more than look at his foreman.

"How much of what that prick said is true?"

"All of it," said Gil very softly.

"Louder!" said Lee harshly. "Christ knows you usually can be heard all the way to the beach!"

196

"All of it," said Gil, accepting Lee's anger, knowing he had earned it and more, more than he hoped Lee would ever discover. But that hope was almost gone now. Soon he would have no half-truths left to hide behind.

"All of it," Gil repeated evenly.

Lee said nothing, merely watched his friend with eyes the color of mercury.

"Juana," Gil said, "Juana told me just an hour ago. Cira's mother has been sick for months. Cira arrived late last night from Ciudad Obregon. Too late. Her mother died last week. The funeral was this morning."

"Go on."

Lee's voice was tight, hard.

"There's nothing to keep her here," said Gil finally, his voice almost hoarse with the effort of hiding the emotions that he sensed tearing at Lee. "She's leaving on the train to Los Angeles this afternoon."

"Nothing to keep her . . ."

Lee looked down, flexing his hands without knowing it, remembering the black lace of jacaranda leaves against a white moon.

"Have you seen her?"

Lee's voice was a whisper, but Gil heard.

"No. No one has but Tia Inez. Not even Juana. Cira refused."

"Why?" said Lee, as much to himself as to his friend whose face reflected the pain that Lee's control refused to reveal. "Why?"

Gil knew the answer, knew it and prayed that he would not have to reveal it and his own part in keeping Cira's secret. Then Lee's eyes swept up, compelling Gil to speak the truth. To Gil's relief, it was not the question he had feared, the one he had promised Cira never to answer.

"Would you have told me before she left?" asked Lee.

Gil held his friend's eyes for a long, long moment.

"It would have been better if I had not told you," Gil said at last, "but I would have. I am weary of secrets." His smile was sad, filled with the pain and uncertainty of a man who had outgrown the black-and-white truths of childhood. There were no easy choices any longer, but choices must nonetheless be made. "What are you going to do, compadre?"

Lee did not answer immediately. His gray eyes moved searchingly among the crowds of people walking toward the platform that had been set up beyond the colorful awnings. Soon he must introduce Prufrock to the crowd, Prufrock who would give a speech that was a watershed in the political life of these people, a watershed that Lee had contrived because he had seen no other means of keeping his land intact.

But behind his eyes he lay again on a mountaintop, listening to the sweet fall of water with a girl who fit perfectly in his arms.

"I'm going to be the fool that Heer expects me to be," Lee said, squeezing Gil's shoulder quickly. "But not nearly the fool I'd be if I didn't go."

Ten minutes later, Gil led one of Lee's horses from the stable and tied the animal with the rest of the guests' horses. Lee, watching from the podium, quickly finished his speech introducing Prufrock. When the editor came to the platform, Lee unobtrusively stepped down, backing into the crowd that pushed forward, letting the crowd divide and reform around him as though he were a boulder in a slow-moving river.

Unnoticed, Lee eased out of the back of the crowd and angled over to the area where his horse was tied. There he swapped Gil's jacket and hat for his own, and mounted swiftly.

"Lee—" said Gil, hand out, holding Lee back. When Lee looked down at him, Gil spoke quickly, as though he did not trust himself to say the necessary words. "She's married."

Lee's horse tossed its head, protesting the harsh hand on the reins. Then Lee's lips closed over unasked questions. He spun the horse toward the wagon road and the scattered houses of Colonia Juarez.

Gil watched until horse and rider were no more than a

dot moving against the newly green plain. With a silent prayer, Gil turned away, holding Lee's hat between lean brown fingers.

While the horse loped across the flatlands, Lee's anger drained into an almost wondering realization of his own foolishness. He was abandoning ten years of work for a girl with gold in her eyes, a girl who had abandoned him without so much as a word, a ten-year-old memory. And he was riding toward her, so sure of the welcome that he had often dreamed of, a welcome that he was in no position to expect or accept, nor she to offer. Yet he could no more turn his horse aside than he could control the urgency that was driving him toward her.

Lee realized then why Heer had acted so recklessly; somewhere in Heer's twisted mind was the full knowledge of what Cira had meant to Lee, a knowledge that had come to Lee too late, after Cira had vanished beyond the reach of the love he had never spoken aloud to her. He did not understand how Heer had known about Cira, but Lee did know that Heer would use Cira against him. He already had. At best, she would distract Lee from what must be done for the county and the ranch; at worst, she would be the means of his destruction. But even knowing that, Lee galloped toward the colonia and the remembered beauty of a jacaranda tree growing near a white frame house.

Inside the house, carefully remembering nothing at all, Cira McCartney de Vasconcellos sat in a straight-backed chair that was draped with dense black crepe. The same crepe covered sawhorses that had supported her mother's coffin. Though Cira held a black silk handkerchief between her fingers, her eyes were dry. She had not cried for her mother, as she had not cried for her recently dead husband. She had not cried at all for ten years.

She sipped slowly from the cup of strong coffee that Tia Inez had brought to her just before Inez left. Inez had noticed Cira's utter calm, a control that Inez had found disconcerting in one so young. Cira had ignored the mixture of concern and curiosity implicit in her aunt's comments. Ignoring emotions, whether her own or another's, was an essential part of the armor Cira had constructed against the world. Emotions once had ruled and nearly destroyed her; it would not happen again.

The cup clicked firmly into its chalk-white saucer. Not so much as a tremor escaped the cool control that had made Cira somewhat of a legend with the men who had courted the beautiful widow of Felipe de Vasconcellos. A few of the men had seen flashes of the warmth that Cira could not wholly suppress, whether it was her fingertips lingering over the softness of a rose or the time she held a ragged child in her arms until the loss of his pet was eased by a storm of tears. The men who had seen her face pressed against the child's dark hair had been baffled by the woman who scorned them, yet cómforted a beggar child as though he were a prince.

Cira's eyes moved slowly over the room, her mother's room, heavy with religious iconography that culminated in a writhing Christ multiply impaled on a cross of gold. The three-foot icon had once given Cira nightmares; now it was merely a symbol of the religion that she had withdrawn from after a priest had decreed harsh penance for the young woman whose wantonness had lured three men into mortal sin.

With a quick movement that made her black mantilla ripple, Cira looked away from the cross that she had come to associate with punishment and humiliation, brutality and hatred. Her eyes finally settled on a blank stretch of wall, soothing in its palid emptiness. Beneath the heavy mourning clothes, Cira flexed muscles that were weary with too much sitting and too little comfort. When word had reached her that her mother was ill, Cira had had no time to hesitate over whether to return; Tia Inez's message had allowed no room for evasion. Cira had left immediately for the United States.

Her mother was dead when Cira arrived. Exhausted by the seven-hundred-mile rail trip from Ciudad Obregon, Cira had absorbed the news of death with apparent indifference. She had made arrangements for burial as soon as was decently possible.

Tia Inez, who had cared for her sister in the last, long weeks of life, prepared the body alone, refusing Cira's help. Left with nothing to do, Cira had gone from room to room in the house where she had been raised. She had let memories and ghosts test the depth of her self-control and had been unmoved. Nothing broke through her reserve, not even the odor of whiskey from a half-empty bottle she found spilled behind the bathtub.

She slept in the bed her father had built for her, but her memories of him were too faded to disturb her dreams. Nothing disturbed her, except for a brief moment between sleeping and waking when she saw the dark blue bulk of the twin peaks beyond her window. For a second she was on the mountaintop with the man she had tried so often to forget. Then she awoke fully, and the mountains became merely one more memory stripped of emotion and meaning.

Cira closed her eyes, shutting out the only type of memory that had the power to hurt her. Even the hideous memories of rape were not that strong, although they lay thick and dark inside the wall of indifference she had so carefully built.

Unconsciously, Cira sighed and shifted her shoulders to ease an invisible weight. She had come North to bury her mother, and childhood griefs as well. Perhaps now she could forgive the woman who had hated instead of comforted her bleeding daughter; the woman who had blamed her daughter for the viciousness of three men; the woman who had sold her daughter to a man four times her age for two bottles of whiskey and a ticket back to Los Angeles.

Cira tried to stem the memories, then decided there would be no better time to purge herself of remnant bitterness. Emotion of any sort had no place in her life. She had learned to emulate the stone—see nothing, do nothing, feel nothing, and survive. Though she knew she could not attain a stone's perfect indifference, she sought it with a persistence that other women of her time and class reserved for the Church.

Religion was another bitter memory, another voice heaping guilt upon her. Even her husband . . . but he had finally accepted her, accepted the fact that her body would not bring forth the male heir he had bought her for. After her miscarriage, she was no more fertile than his first wife had been. He made few demands on Cira beyond her conversation in the evening when the heat of the desert day had passed.

On those nights when he required more than her words, she had learned to accept his body without screaming beneath the burden of memories of three men tearing at her. When her husband was finished, Cira would lie in the darkness, trying to understand a church that praised her husband's unwanted intrusions into her body, censured her for being raped by three strangers and condemned utterly the moments of beauty she had once known in a lover's arms.

In the last few years of her husband's life, he had asked mainly that she not cuckold him with any of the men whose eyes followed his graceful young wife. So great was his gratitude for her chastity, and for the luminous beauty that permitted his aged body to feel young again, that he became very kind to his reluctant wife. Cira eventually accepted the marriage that had been arranged and repeatedly consummated without her consent. In time, she even came to the realization that she had been fortunate; Felipe de Vasconcellos was a man of modest wealth, wit and culture, and a man of gruff gentleness where his child-wife was concerned.

She had tended him meticulously during his final illness; if she could not pretend to love him, neither did she scorn his needs. When he died, she felt neither joy nor grief, merely a mild sadness that equaled the moderate affection she had come to feel for the kind, disappointed old man who happened to be her husband.

Cira's fingers closed around the china cup. The coffee was cold, but she did not notice. She stood up, sipping at

202

the bitter blackness, swallowing without tasting while she walked to the window. The room was still but for the rustling of her long, black silk dress. Beyond the window the jacaranda tree held its blossom-covered branches to the sky as though in mute sacrifice to the sun.

Engulfed by lavender blossoms, a lark sang solemn, joyous notes that pierced Cira's defenses like a needle through silk; the memories she had suppressed for so long rose like a river in flood, threatening to drown her. For a searing instant she remembered Lee, remembered the incredible beauty of his body moving with hers as they shared all the textures of ecstasy. She fought to control the memories, to make them dull, colorless, lifeless, powerless once more as they had been powerless before a lark sang in a jacaranda tree. But the memories were as sweetly relentless as the lark's liquid song.

A distant rider condensed out of her memories, a lean man with hair the color of the sun, a man who rode his horse with an easy grace that made her weak with longing.

With a half-choked cry, Cira turned away from the jacaranda tree. She felt hot and cold and nauseated and her body trembled so that she had to hang onto the coffee cup with both hands. Shocked that feelings she had thought dead were still potent, Cira leaned against the brick fireplace. She concentrated on the bricks, savoring their cool, hard edges, their rough-textured indifference to the vagaries of mere flesh. They knew what she must learn; the past was out of reach, gone, beyond help or hindrance, ecstasy or agony.

Dead.

Gradually, the habit of indifference returned to her. She could listen to the lark without feeling anything more than a vague pleasure at the purity of the bird's song. Then the sound of hoofbeats silenced the lark.

Cira turned slowly back to the window. Her heart leaped once, painfully, when she saw a rider pull his horse to a stop beneath the jacaranda tree. A sudden anger swept through her, a silent visceral rejection of every moment that had brought her to stand here, trembling; he had no right to affect her like this. He had no right to her at all.

As though he sensed her anger, Lee watched the house for a long moment, as quiet as the pale blossoms drifting down. The lark called again, three notes running together like molten gold. As though it were a signal, Lee urged his horse toward the house.

When Lee dismounted, he noticed that the white paint on the porch columns was peeling away in ragged ribbons, revealing the gray-tan of weathered pine beneath. The windows were streaked by rain and dust and indifference, concealing more than they revealed. The yard was no more than weeds, dirt and cracked flagstones leading to the porch.

For an instant Lee was conscious of his silk pants and shirt and the large ruby stickpin that held his tie. The wind blew, tugging Gil's sombrero off Lee's head, making the black hat snap out to the end of its neck cord. Lee smiled, knowing the picture he must make with his combination of continental and Mexican elegance.

When Lee put his foot on the first step, the front door opened quietly. Cira stood there, looking at him with eyes that still had gold in them, gold and something darker, something that had not been there when he had left ten years ago for Sierra Leon. He wanted to leap the steps and hold her, but the darkness in her eyes was a warning. So he merely stood, looking at her with a hunger neither one acknowledged.

"I was sorry to hear of your mother's death," he said finally.

The sound of Lee's voice sent an invisible tremor through Cira, an involuntary response that fed her anger at the cruelty of a God who would confront her with the one person who still had the power to make her feel emotion.

"She was old. She was old and she had not been happy for a long time. A lifetime." Cira's voice was slightly

204

husky, a huskiness that had never wholly faded since the night she had screamed until her voice broke. "Perhaps she is happy now."

"And you," asked Lee softly, "are you happy?"

Lee's light, changing eyes searched her face for the answers to his fears and hopes. He saw her eyes darken and her face become taut with pain. She did not answer. Nor did she need to. She turned her back on him and walked into a house hung with funeral black. Behind her, the door was open, but Lee could not tell whether that was a gesture of invitation or indifference. He hesitated, but was compelled to follow her, closing the door behind him.

Cira went into the parlor where sawhorses supported crepe and a cup of cold coffee sat on the windows. She walked to the opposite side of a square table hung with Irish lace. When she turned toward him, her face was as tranquil as a portrait of the Madonna.

"You are looking very grand," she said, but her eyes were focused beyond the window, where a jacaranda tree lifted flowers toward the sun.

"And you, my Cira, are more beautiful than—"

"No." Her voice was cold, angry. "You should not have come, Mr. Leander Champion Buckles the Third. You are an important man now. *Muy grande*. Go back to your pale wife, señor. Go now."

Lee's eyes narrowed and the planes of his tanned face sharpened until muscles stood out distinctly along his jaw.

"No, señora," he said, emphasizing her married title, "I will not leave. You owe me something."

"I owe you nothing."

"You owe me ten years," he said harshly, "ten years and an agony that still—"

His jaw clenched around feelings he had never admitted to himself, much less spoken aloud.

"I'm sorry," said Cira, an echo of remembered warmth in her voice. "You must do as I have done, accept as I have accepted that the past is beyond our influence. We must care for it no more than it cares for us."

"Why," said Lee tightly, then with real anger, *"Why!"*

She knew he was not questioning her advice, but asking

the only question she could not answer. She could not tell him why she had left ten years ago. She could not tell him and watch his eyes change, watch contempt replace caring as he blamed her for her own rape. She had borne the calumny of her mother and her church and her husband, but she could not bear Lee's; it would break her.

"I should not have come back," whispered Cira.

She spread her fingers over the back of the chair as though to brace herself. Her eyes looked away from the jacaranda tree until they focused on her own hands. Her head tilted forward, shifting her mantilla until tight coils of black hair gleamed beneath the lace.

"But you did," said Lee, his voice angry with the anger of lost years. "And I should have stayed with my wife and my guests."

"But you did not." Cira almost sighed into the painful silence. "We are both fools. There is nothing we can do that will help, much that will hurt. And I," she added in her husky voice, "have been hurt enough."

"And I—" Lee turned to the jacaranda tree and was silent, as though he were counting its countless soft blossoms. "I loved you."

"Don't," she said, her voice torn between anguish and anger. "You don't know . . ."

"Then tell me."

Lee moved toward her with his hands out, invitation and forgiveness and supplication in a single gesture. Her head came up when she straightened, but her eyes were blind to him, looking beyond him to something he could not see, something terrible that wracked her body in long shudders even as she fought to control herself. Slowly, very slowly, control returned.

Lee stood completely still, watching her, transfixed by the exquisite curve of her neck, the clarity of her profile, the proud strength of her face lifted in battle against something he did not know, had never known because she refused to tell him, just as she had refused even to touch his hands.

His hands dropped and he felt anger racing, anger or desire or both, he did not know. And he did not care.

206

"It is past," she said. "Past."

Lee was too angry to hear the subtle plea in her voice.

"Is it?"

He moved with the animal grace she had never forgotten, too fast for her to evade. For an instant she burned within his arms, then she wrenched free with the strength of desperation. She retreated around the straight chair, holding onto its back with a force that made her long fingers white.

"You have no right," she whispered, "no right at all! I'm no trembling child to be seduced by El Patron." She caught her breath and spoke slowly, carefully. "But I don't blame you for all that happened. I don't blame you for the three who——" Her face twisted·when she realized what she had almost revealed. "For the love of God, go. The past is dead. Let me bury it decently!"

"Cira."

Lee reached out to comfort her, but she shrank away with a rejection that was somehow more total, more humiliating than any he had ever suffered from Joy. A white fury gripped him. He spun around, afraid of what he might do if he had to look for one more moment at the beautiful woman he had once loved.

Cira listened to the sound of his boots hard on the sagging porch, followed by the sound of a powerful horse goaded into a full run. She hung onto the chair, swaying and shaking while cold sweat pooled beneath her black dress. For a horrible moment the room spun away, retreating as he had retreated in a drumroll of sound, her blood pounding in her head until she could hear nothing else, feel nothing else, see nothing at all. She sank to her knees, instinctively bending over until her forehead touched the cool wood floor.

By the time Lee reached the boundary of his ranch, his fury had congealed into an indigestible clot of emotions that he did not even try to name or number. When he reached the table, Prufrock was just winding up his speech. Lee turned over his lathered horse to Gil; the foreman glanced once at Lee's cold, set face, then silently traded vests and hats. Not for a guarantee of heaven would Gil have asked a question. He had not seen that expression on Lee's face for many years, but in no way had Gil forgotten it.

Wordlessly, Gil donned his vest and hat and began walking the horse cool while Lee slipped through the crowd to the pink-striped awning where Joy sat, surrounded by south county society.

"Why, Leander," said Joy. Her voice had enough edge to overcome the last of the spirited approval the crowd was giving to Prufrock's speech. "I was beginning to think you had abandoned me."

Lee's anger leaped, but he knew she had not earned it.

"I'm sorry you felt abandoned," he said evenly.

Lee watched the speaker mount the platform.

"Leander," began Joy with asperity, wanting a better explanation of his absence.

The woman who was sitting next to Joy leaned forward. "Now, Mrs. Buckles," she said in a surprisingly deep voice. "You'll have to get used to sharing your husband with others. My husband tells me that Mr. Buckles has begun to take his natural place of leadership at last. I'm sure he has been seeing to important matters. Haven't you, Mr. Buckles?"

Lee's cold gray eyes studied the woman for a moment, but her round face showed only a guileless need to please.

With a slight bow, Lee murmured, "I would never contradict the words of a handsome lady." He turned back toward his wife. "Have I told you how radiant you look, dear?"

Joy blushed, surprising him; usually his compliments drew smiles and bright glances. In the background, the speaker's thin tenor tried and failed to embrace the crowd while he described the county name contest.

"I've heard," Joy said, leaning toward Lee and speaking in a constrained whisper that went no further than his ears, "I've heard that women often look especially well when they're—that is, when they are with child."

Joy looked down, scarlet with embarrassment, twisting

her fingers in her lap. Lee realized that there had been little pleasure in her voice.

"Are you all right? Is this what you wanted to talk to me about?" he asked.

She nodded without looking up.

"Marjorie, aren't you happy?"

"Are you?"

"Of course." He lifted her hands to his lips. "Of course I am."

Joy smiled and glanced brightly around. No one appeared to be looking at them. Her fingers tightened around his with almost painful force.

"I'm frightened," she said, her eyes almost purple with distress. "I'm so frightened."

"Don't be," said Lee soothingly. "You shall have everything you want."

"I want to go home."

The crowd applauded and cheered the speaker's shrewd platitudes. The last line of his speech was a request for signatures on the petition to the governor. In a single, ragged surge, the crowd drained away toward a long table where the Improvement League had petitions and pens at the ready.

"Then you shall," said Lee simply.

He kept both anger and resignation out of his voice. Not by so much as a tightening of his lips did he show his disappointment as he finally accepted that his home was not hers, and never would be.

Automatically, Lee and Joy smiled and traded pleasantries with the people filing past them. When they were alone, Lee helped Joy to her feet.

"It was a wonderful party," said Lee. "I don't know how you managed all the work."

Joy smiled slowly. "It was pleasure, not work. And don't worry, Leander. I won't go home—that is," she corrected herself guiltily, "I won't go back to San Francisco right away. I have so many parties, teas, fashion shows and even a charity ball planned in the next few months. I couldn't abandon them, could I?"

She looked at him like a child eager for praise.

"Are you sure that won't be too much trouble for you?"

"Nonsense." Joy tapped his hand coquettishly. "I told you, it's play, not work."

"Whatever you say, dear," replied Lee, smiling automatically.

Lee looked around at the men lined up eight deep at the petition table, and at the richly dressed women who were waiting for Joy's attention. The barbeque was an unqualified success.

Lee looked out over the land, radiant beneath the pouring spring light, the land that would become the center of a new county. And he looked at his lovely blond wife, invisibly carrying his first child. His land. His county. His wife. His child.

Lee looked and wondered if success always felt so cold.

Gilberto Zavala shifted position wearily, pulling his sheepskin jacket higher on his neck. It was cold, near freezing, in spite of the earlier spring warmth. He had been waiting outside a colonia saloon for more hours than he cared to count. Even the cockfighters had finally given up and gone to bed. With a deep sigh and deeper reluctance, Gil walked to the saloon door.

The Golden Cock was not the sort of place frequented by the leading citizens in the southern half of the county. The interior was little more than a few primitive paintings overlooking a short bar and five tiny tables. The room was small, dank and empty but for a very quiet bartender and a lean, handsome man who was killing a bottle of Scotch whiskey one slow sip at a time.

Gil eased the door shut behind him. Lee did not look up from the double shot glass that he was rolling slowly between his palms. Gil measured the emotions seething beneath his friend's expressionless exterior and sighed again; he would be lucky to get Lee out of that chair without a bloody fight.

"*Ola,* compadre," said Gil quietly, sliding uninvited into the chair opposite Lee.

Lee looked up with eyes the color of ice.

Gil met the look calmly, not showing the adrenaline that went through him, honing his reflexes; Lee was ready, waiting, needing only the excuse. And Gil would probably give it to him. With a silent prayer that Lee was much more drunk than he appeared, Gil reached for the bottle, tilted it and drank. He let the bottle thump lightly back onto the table. Lee reached for it, but Gil's fingers were wrapped around the neck.

"You can't sit here the rest of your days," said Gil reasonably.

"Try me."

Lee's hand snaked out, jerking the bottle from Gil's fingers. Whiskey gurgled and made an amber rainbow as it poured into Lee's glass.

"I dislike mixing in your private business," began Gil.

"Then don't."

"Compadre," Gil said evenly, "we are too old for this. What is time for, if not to learn from past mistakes?"

Lee laughed softly, bitterly. "What is time for? To destroy us."

The empty shot glass banged onto the scarred tabletop.

"Go on," said Lee coldly, pouring himself another drink. "Tell me what a stinking bastard I am to be here in the middle of the night with a pregnant wife at home."

Gil concealed his surprise beneath a shrug. "You say it so well, compadre. Why should I bother?"

Lee stared at Gil for a long moment, but the foreman's face showed no hint of laughter. At last the squeak of cloth against the glass that the bartender was polishing distracted Lee. He picked up his drink.

"Why are you here?" asked Gil, believing he knew the answer but needing to be certain beyond doubt what had driven Lee to a colonia bar.

"Go to hell."

"Cira?" Gil said, more statement than question.

"Don't push me, Gil."

Lee's voice was low and cold, a warning clearer than the words. Suddenly Gil had a flash of memory, of the moment he had stumbled across a bleeding, whimpering girl who had been beaten almost beyond recognition. Anger whipped through Gil, anger and a pain that was ten years old.

"Did she tell you why she left?" said Gil savagely, leaning toward Lee. "Is that why you're sitting here on your ass, wallowing in Scotch and self-pity?"

The unexpectedness of the attack shocked Lee out of his self-absorbtion.

"No."

Then the implication of Gil's first question hit Lee like a blow.

"She told you! She told you but she wouldn't tell me!"

"Holy Mother of God," Gil said, realizing that he had been wrong, that Lee knew no more tonight than he had ten years ago. "She did not tell me," said Gil harshly. "I have always known." He raised his eyes, giving Lee a look of such compassion and pain that Lee was silenced totally. "Ten years ago, even five, I would not have told you. I don't even know if I should tell you now. But I will. I am sick of lies, so I will break my word to her." Gil looked at his hands. "May God forgive me."

Lee waited, feeling the skin stir on his neck. In low tones, without emotion, Gil told what had happened ten years ago. Lee listened, pale and still but for his hands clenching and unclenching around the bottle. He heard Gil tell how he had found Cira crawling in the sand, crying mindlessly, her voice as broken as her spirit. He heard, and then he hurled the bottle across the room to cover the sound being torn out of his throat. Glass and whiskey exploded, echoing the raw pain that 'twisted through Lee.

Gil ignored both the cry and the glass falling. Relentlessly, sparing neither Cira nor his friend nor himself, Gil described Cira's injuries, how he had bathed her torn flesh, stopped the bleeding that he could see and prayed that it was enough, for Cira had become hysterical at the mention of a doctor.

"And then I said your name. She became calm, so calm she frightened me. She made me promise not to tell you. She made me promise, and I did; I promised because I believed her. I believed she would kill herself if you knew."

Lee said nothing because he could not, not yet. There was more. He saw it in Gil's face lined by too many sad secrets held in too long.

"Señora McCartney was nearly sober. Perhaps it would have been better if she weren't." Gil sighed. "It was as God willed. She insisted on taking Cira to Mexico. I drove them to the border."

"The men. Who were they?"

The intensity of Lee's voice was frightening, but Gil met his friend's cold gray eyes without flinching.

"It was ten years ago."

"For you it was. For me it just happened. Who were they?"

Gil could not evade the clipped, deceptively calm voice that had neither intonation nor inflection. He would have to keep talking until there was nothing left unsaid.

"One of them was bald. He was called Red." Gil looked at his hands, at the scars across his knuckles, ragged white lines, legacy of the night he had beaten a man to death. "I killed him."

"Gilberto," said Lee, his voice almost hoarse.

"No." Gil looked up with hard, dark eyes. "No. I did not kill him for you or even for her. I killed him for myself. Because I had promised to watch over her and I had gone to Juana instead."

Lee's hand closed over Gil's.

"I wanted to kill the others, but I didn't know who they were. You see," said Gil calmly, "Red wouldn't answer my questions at first. By the time he wanted to, he could no longer speak.

"So while you searched for Cira, I searched for two men. It was impossible. The silver fever was over and men were pouring out of the mountains. Many men. Strangers.

"But I did learn one thing. Those three animals worked on Kaiser's railroad under Roger Heer. They were Heer's men, really."

"Did he send them after her?"

Lee's voice was cold again, without inflection, as empty of feeling as his eyes.

"I don't know. And it doesn't matter. It is past, Lee. Long past. Over."

But it never would be over and both men knew it. Emotion returned to Lee with a wrench. His mouth twisted, tasting the bitter knowledge that even the fullest revenge could not restore the balance of her life and his; nothing could repair the rent in the fabric of their experience.

"Heer will wish that I had killed him ten years ago," whispered Lee, "before I learned how many ugly ways there are to ruin a man."

Gil let out a ragged breath, relieved to be done with brutal secrets, relieved that the animal rage in Lee's eyes had been replaced by calculating intelligence . . . and a sorrow that made Gil look away.

"I wish," said Lee softly, "I wish that I had known this afternoon, before her train left."

Gil sighed and quietly spoke his last secret. "She is still here."

Lee looked up with sudden hope lighting his eyes. "Are you sure?"

"Yes. But she did not stay for you, my friend. After the train was gone, Inez found Cira curled on the parlor floor, too exhausted to move. Inez tried to take her home, but Cira refused. She demanded to be left alone." Gil sighed tiredly. "What was Inez to do? She finally left Cira alone."

Lee stood up quietly, picked his hat off of a nearby chair and looked down at the dark face of his friend.

"Thank you," Lee said simply.

"You are going to her?"

"Yes."

"Does she want you?"

"No. But I have to tell her . . . something. I have to."

"Wait," said Gil curtly, holding out his arm to bar Lee's way. "Do you blame her for what happened?"

"Blame her . . . Christ, Gil, how could I?"

"Easy. Everyone else did." Gil's mouth thinned into an

ugly smile. He dropped his arm. "Be gentle with her. I have enough on my conscience."

Lee put his hand on Gil's shoulder. "Don't blame yourself, compadre. I don't."

Lightly, quickly, Lee walked out of the saloon. The door shut noiselessly behind him. When the last hoofbeats faded into silence, the bartender brought a fresh bottle over and spoke in rapid Spanish to Gil.

"*Gracias*, Señor Zavala. You are a very brave man. I have heard of the rages of your patron. *Muy malo.*"

Gil shook his head in silent refusal of the man's words, but accepted the bottle. He refilled Lee's glass, drank quickly. Leaning back, he pulled a short, crooked cigar out of his vest pocket. He snapped a match into flame, puffed and exhaled a thin stream of aromatic smoke. With a hand that trembled very slightly, he poured another drink.

"Go with God, my brother," he murmured.

"Señor?" said the bartender, looking up from the row of glasses he was polishing with a smudged rag.

"*Nada,*" sighed Gil.

The bartender picked up another glass and resumed polishing. He recognized the signs of a man settling in for a night of solitary drinking and accepted it without complaint. Silence settled over the room, interrupted only by the occasional squeal of cloth on glass and the sound of two men thinking their own private thoughts.

Outside, the night was cold and motionless, balanced on the edge of frost. Lee's breath condensed in silver plumes beneath a half-moon's brittle light. In spite of his impatience, he kept his horse to a slow canter, giving himself time to think about what he wanted to say to Cira. But he could not think of any words that would salve their anguish or even describe it. He could not think of any words at all, only tumbling memories of a girl who had trusted him and been betrayed.

Lee tied his horse under a ramshackle shelter that had served as a stable when Cira's mother could afford to keep a horse. When he walked quietly up on the porch, he had no more idea of what he wanted to say than he had had in the saloon, but the need to say it was even greater than before. He lifted his hand to knock, then lowered it without making a sound. A dim light glowed somewhere within the house.

"Cira?" he called softly.

There was no answer. Long fingers closed on the doorknob, testing. The door swung soundlessly open. Lee's boots made no noise on the scuffed wooden floor. He moved like a shadow across the room and down the hallway, drawn by the soft glow of light.

In Cira's bedroom a lamp was turned low, its shine as subdued as embers. Deep gold light and midnight shadows swayed in the room when the low flame licked from side to side. Cira had been asleep for several hours, time enough to have begun the dream that was ten years old, the dream that always brought her sweating and trembling into consciousness, the dream that was so vague and yet so terrible that she never slept without light.

Lee stood by her bed, watching her as she slept. This afternoon he had seen only the face of his memories; tonight he saw the face of reality. It was more exquisite than mere memory. Serious, shadowed by pain, the face of a woman rather than a girl.

Cira moved slightly, making gold light and black shadow slide across her lips, outlining her cheekbone and the hand resting on a tumble of hair that was darker than night. Her face changed, drawn by nightmare into the face of fear. She moaned so softly that Lee barely heard, moaned and moved protestingly, as if the dream could be evaded. Her hand jerked down and her lips twisted. He thought he heard her say "no" over and over. He sensed then that she lived and relived her rape in nightmare, trying and failing to exorcise its horror.

Lee ached to comfort her, but was afraid that holding her would reinforce her nightmare. But when she whimpered, he could no longer just stand and watch. He knelt by the bed, whispering her name again and again, daring only to touch the black fall of hair that felt like cool silk beneath his hand.

Cira's whimpered words became louder, less coherent,

as the nightmare progressed inexorably to its conclusion. Cold sweat misted her skin. The raw pain Lee had known while he listened to Gil returned, redoubled, wrenching Lee in an agony of helplessness as he listened to her cries. He called out to her with words of anguish and regret and love that ran together like tears.

Cira lay between nightmare and the sound of his voice. Dazed, she turned her head toward the comforting lamp. She saw his head bent as though in prayer, his hair haloed in light, hair brighter than her memories, and she knew that it was his voice that had called her out of horror. Still half-asleep, her hand reached out to touch his hidden face. Then she understood the meaning of his words and knew that he had found out.

"No," she whispered. "No!"

She retreated as far away from him as the bed would allow, trying to evade reality as she had tried to evade nightmare. She saw him lift his head, saw lamplight run down his cheeks like slow tears, his tears. She stared, unable to believe that Lee wept for her.

"I'm sorry, Cira," he said, his voice low. "I just found out. I don't blame you for hating me. But I had to come anyway. I had to tell you . . ." Lamplight shimmered in her hair falling black to her waist, lamplight in her eyes huge and dark, alive with gold. "I had to tell you that what happened was not your fault." Velvet light and shadows slid over her face like caressing hands. "The men, the three men. They were Heer's. It was revenge. My fault. Not yours." Her beauty tore at him, wounding him as she had once been wounded, but tears rather than blood welled from his pain. "I had to tell you . . . you were right. You owe me nothing. Certainly not forgiveness."

Slowly, Lee stood and turned toward the door.

Still dazed, almost unable to absorb his words, Cira watched his tall form dissolve into the shadows by the door. Then she was across the room in a rush and her arms were tight around his waist. She pressed her face against his back, unable to speak, knowing only that he had cried for her when she could not cry for herself, and forgiven her when she could not forgive herself and had loved her when she could love nothing at all.

Lee stood unmoving, afraid to breathe and find out that this moment was just one more of his futile dreams. But the long sobs wracking her were real, the terrible dry sobs of someone who had forgotten how to cry.

Silently, Lee turned and held Cira's shaking body. When she could no longer stand, he carried her to the bed and lay beside her, holding her. Tears came to her finally, wetting her face and his until dark strands of her hair clung to her cheeks and his lips. Gently he smoothed her hair back from her face, stroking her and murmuring meaningless words that soothed as much as his touch. When at last her tears were spent, he kneaded her scalp and neck and back with strong fingers, untying her knotted muscles until her sobs faded to random tremors that came further and further apart.

With a long, ragged breath, Cira closed her eyes, feeling a pressure slide away, a pressure that had been so much a part of her that she noticed it only as it diminished. She closed her eyes and seemed to fall asleep as he watched.

He looked at her as though memorizing her face, serene, beautiful in spite of the marks of too many tears. A familiar longing twisted through him. Gently, he eased his hands out of her soft hair and moved slowly away, trying not to disturb her.

"Lee . . ."

His name was spoken as softly as a sigh. He did not believe he had heard it until her eyes opened, seeking him.

"Lee?"

"I'm here."

She found his hand and pressed it against her cheek, still hot with recent tears.

"You feel so cool," she murmured, moving her face against his hand. "So good."

Lee's other hand went to her face, stroking her with fingers that had never forgotten. Slowly he bent down until his lips touched her once, lightly.

218

"Lee—"

But he had already felt her withdrawal and he knew the final sadness he had hoped never to know.

"I'm sorry," he said simply. "I have no right."

Cira saw the pain in his eyes and thought his words referred to her marriage.

"My husband is dead."

"I'm sorry," said Lee again, knowing no other words.

"No," she said quietly. "His death was like my mother's. A relief."

"Then why—"

"My mother," said Cira dispassionately. "My mother sold me when she found out I was pregnant. But I was not pregnant for long. He was four times my age and had no sons. It was a bad bargain for him. He had neither pleasure nor sons from my body." She looked at Lee unflinchingly. "I'm not what I was, Lee. I'm not what you want."

"What I want . . . A jacaranda tree. A mountaintop. What do you want, Cira. Do you want these things?"

"I want to be seventeen again," she said faintly. "I want to lie in your arms and not be sick with fear."

"I can't give you back the years," he said, his voice breaking. "My God, how I wish I could."

Cira raised her hands to his face, trying to comfort him as he had comforted her. With soft, tumbling words she shared her memories of him, the memories that had kept her sane, trying to tell him that she did not want him to grieve for what could not be changed. Her lips caught at his, imploring, merging past and present in their warmth.

Lee returned the kiss tenderly, hardly daring to believe when her lips opened, inviting a deeper caress. Slowly he savored the sweetness of her mouth. When she returned the kiss his breath caught and he murmured her name, kissing her deeply, gently.

"Are you afraid now?" he asked against her lips.

She shook her head slowly, moving her lips over his.

"Tell me if I frighten you," he said. "I'll stop. I promise you, Cira. I'll stop."

She looked at his eyes, almost wholly gold, lit by passion and an emotion that was both softer and more enduring.

"Will you tell me?" he asked.

"Yes."

"I love you, Cira," he said, bending down to her again. "I have always loved you."

His arms were as gentle as his lips, holding her as though she were made of moonlight, never giving her reason to feel helpless against his superior strength, always asking where other men had demanded, cherishing where other men had forced, giving where other men had taken.

Gradually, Lee undid her long nightdress, pausing over each button, giving her every opportunity to object. She moved her hands and he stopped, waiting. She kissed his hands with a promise that made him weak. Slowly he pulled her nightdress down over her body, kissing the skin that was more flawless than he had remembered and more beautiful, touching her as he himself longed to be touched, passion and love mingling to bring a pleasure that transcended pain.

He touched her only with his mouth, not holding her for fear that she would be frightened by his hands on her nakedness. So it was his lips and tongue that first touched her remembered softness, caressing her until she moaned and her hands pressed against him as though to push him away. With an effort that left him shaking, Lee forced himself to stop caressing her.

Her hands sought the buttons of his shirt. He realized that she did not want him to stop, she merely wanted to savor his skin as he had savored hers.

Lee took his clothes off with an impatience he had not shown for her nightdress. When he lay beside her again, he was almost afraid to touch her. He wanted her more than he had ever wanted anything in his life; but he loved her even more than he wanted her. He stroked her breasts and waist and hips and finally the incredible softness between her thighs. And then he could not control the need to touch her deeply, repeatedly, in a mute litany of desire.

Cira's hands moved down and again he thought that she was pushing him away until he felt her fingers sliding around him and he groaned with the pleasure only she had ever given him. He moved and suddenly she was beneath him. Even as she stiffened he realized his mistake.

Lee rolled onto his back quickly, releasing Cira in spite of the need for her that was clawing inside him.

"I'm sorry," he whispered.

Cira turned until she lay on her side, resting the full length of her body along his.

"No," she said, pulling his hand down her body in a long caress. "You have done nothing to be sorry for. Does that feel like a frightened woman?"

Lee closed his eyes, shutting out all but the sensation of her body beneath his hand.

"You were frightened a moment ago."

"You're so quick," she whispered, moving slowly against his hand. "I had forgotten how very quick you are."

Her body moved bonelessly against him.

"If you are afraid," Lee said between his teeth, fighting for control, "tell me now. I can stop now if you—ahhh, God."

Lee groaned as her liquid warmth surrounded him. His body moved of its own volition and he knew he could no longer stop. Nor did he have to. The heat of her body burned through him and her words were a fire in his blood.

"Love me, my love," she whispered against his throat. "Love me."

They held each other through all the hours of darkness, living in a world where nothing existed beyond the circle of gold light that protected them. Later, when the lamp's flame faded before the onslaught of dawn, they would talk about time, about their past and their future. But time had stolen so much from them that they did not hesitate to steal back what they could. They started with a single night when each lived only for the other.

1910

A wedge of white-cheeked Canadian geese slipped through the low cloud cover. They set their wings, dropping toward a tidal marsh where pools of water the color of mercury trembled beneath a late fall wind. Lee Buckles stopped his car in the middle of the muddy road and listened to the eerie calls of another species asking and answering unknowable questions. Though he was late, he got out and leaned against his Cadillac touring car to watch the geese. They were remarkable birds, deft and strong, wise and wary and wholly wild.

The wedge formation shattered into individual birds, wings flaring and beating frantically as geese flew in all directions; the formation had flown over one of the blinds at the edge of the brackish marsh. The sound of shotguns rolled across the marsh, thick reports magnified by the damp salt air. With a silent cheer, Lee saw that none of the geese had fallen. Then he smiled, realizing that he was more and more on the side of the geese as he grew older. He had hunted long enough to know that the contest between armed man and feathered goose was uneven—if the man had a modicum of skill.

Lee slid back in behind the wheel of the car. After more than forty years, Lee's movements still echoed the smooth power of the wild geese. His hands brought the balky car to life and kept it out of the worst holes in the rutted, muddy road that hemmed the marsh. While he drove, he saw a lone goose glide down nearby, feet outstretched, wings cocked, neck arched for landing. Though the bird descended gracefully, its indifference to the car told Lee that the goose was either too tired or too young to realize the significance of the noisome metal box that lurched along the edge of the marsh.

Though his shotgun was within easy reach, and the goose was within easy range, Lee continued driving. He was not indifferent to the lure of early mornings crackling with frost and the wild calls of descending geese, and he enjoyed testing his eye and reflexes; but he no longer felt compelled or even pleased to kill more than a goose or two each season, just enough to satisfy his taste for meat that had fattened in remote Canadian bogs.

The stone and wood buildings of the Black's Bay Hunting Club appeared on a low bluff that rose along the northeastern arc of the bay. The club took up more than three thousand acres of Lee's land and, lately, an inordinate amount of his time. Though Lee rarely hunted anymore, he had other uses for his club; while other club members waited in blinds for fowl or sprawled in the spacious lounge with potent drinks in hand, Lee quartered the club's rooms in pursuit of game less innocent and more lucrative than wild birds. Nor was he lacking for quarry. An invitation to shoot at Black's Bay was a trophy sought by those who had political, professional or social aspirations. The fact that Black's Bay had some of the best shooting in the states was an added but not necessary attraction.

Lee was both amused and appalled by the scramble to gain his favor. He knew that he had the reputation of being a powerful and sometimes dangerous man, a reputation that sprang from several incidents that were rumored to have taken place over the years. One incident involved the banker, J. Eliot Fulton, who had wanted to be a state senator. In spite of Fulton's intelligence, ambition and malleability in the hands of power, he never was able to get enough backers to swing an election. It was widely rumored that Fulton's problems began two decades ago, when he attempted to foreclose on a certain young rancher. It was also widely rumored that Fulton kept his position as president of the bank only so long as it pleased Lee Buckles to have him there.

A second incident involved an ambitious young minister who had become enamored of Joy. Lee had watched with real indifference while the intense young man went in quest of Joy's porcelain grail. But Lee's amusement had vanished when the minister began weekly tirades against adulterers and whores. One such tirade had stopped just short of naming Lee and Cira. The next day, it was said that the minister visited Cira and forced his way into her house to harangue her on the subject of fornication. Lee whose contributions to the church were both frequent and generous, made a single phone call. The frustrated minister was promptly posted to succor the religious needs of Nome, Alaska.

The third incident revolved around the formation of Moreno County. Most people assumed that the county grew out of a popular mandate. Some people suspected that vox populi spoke with Lee Buckles's soft accent. A very few people knew that Roger Heer's plan to tax Buckles Ranch into penury had resulted in Lee's campaign for a new county, a county to be controlled by him, and a county where Heer's social, political and business plans would be systematically undercut by the very man Heer had hoped to destroy.

When Heer attempted to ingratiate himself among the powerful men in the new county, stories of Heer's unsavory past became public knowledge until Heer was no longer welcome in the better homes of Moreno County. When Heer tried to gain power through blackmail or bribery, the men he bought were promptly purchased again by Lee. Those men Heer blackmailed were sooner or later exposed by Lee. When Heer tried to gain wealth through land manipulation, Lee used his own wealth to ensure that the few of Heer's plans that might have worked, did not.

As Lee became richer, Heer was diminished until he was a bitter, half-mad gambler living on the thin sufferance of the world he had once sought to control.

There were other incidents, but the three entailing the banker, the minister and the gambler were irrevocably entrenched in the hagiology of California power politics. Few people could prove that any of the three incidents had taken place, but that was immaterial. Lee was the biggest private landowner in California and one of the biggest in the United States. Obviously he must have power, even though it was rarely seen and then only indirectly, at second hand, by inference and rumor.

As years and careful management piled wealth upon the land, Lee no longer had to go out and solicit support among the local power structures. He still contributed modest amounts to political and social campaigns, as well as providing free facilities for political and social barbecues, but he did so more out of habit than need. He did not even have to make his desires known to have them met. The varied public officials who depended on Lee anticipated his business and personal needs more closely and more delicately than Lee thought necessary. The men who were dependent on his goodwill were more protective of his interests than he had ever been; the lesson of the banker, the railroad man and the minister had not been forgotten.

Lee took no particular pride in being known as a hard son of a bitch, but neither did he make an effort to ameliorate the impression. Long ago he had discovered that his reputation for ruthlessness saved time, money and energy at the bargaining table. Although he had withdrawn from the daily exercise of political control, he still wielded decisive power on long-range matters that he perceived as important to himself and to his ranch. It was one of these matters that brought him to the clusters of bluff-top buildings that were Black's Bay Hunting Club.

The Cadillac touring car sloshed through a puddle and came to a stop on a gravel pad to one side of the large stone lodge. As Lee parked the car, he saw that Elton Marshall's two cars were ahead of him, parked at opposite ends of the building. Lee smiled slightly, remembering Marshall's complaint about the imposition and the impossibility of doing as Lee requested.

"Those two men have been enemies for years," Marshall had told Lee urgently. "Sam Moore and Ben Meyerson are like fire and gasoline—you're all right so long as they don't get together."

Lee had laughed and repeated his request that Marshall see that both men were at Black's Bay on the fifteenth. And Marshall had delivered, a fact that Lee would not forget. The young lawyer had been helpful in many other ways. Lee made a mental note to repay Marshall soon. It was not a good practice to become indebted to any one man; repay him now and repay him well was a rule that Lee never broke.

The silence that came when Lee turned off the engine was a relief. Though he appreciated the speed and comfort of an automobile, Lee sometimes longed for the dignified silence of a horse. As Lee climbed out of the car, distant shotguns boomed, heralding a new flight of geese. Lee pulled off the supple shearling coat be used to keep warm instead of closing the car's finicky side curtains. Since he was no longer dependent upon the approval of conventional society, Lee dressed to suit his own tastes and comforts. Beneath the sheepskin coat he wore a fitted, white linen shirt that was open at the throat, and thin, straight-legged pants of soft wool that fell flawlessly over his handmade boots. A sand-colored suede vest and a straight-brimmed Stetson completed his outfit.

With his immaculately tailored blend of western and continental clothing, his lean body and his hair that was just touched by silver, Lee looked like what he was—a man who had enough power and independence to choose which social conventions to obey and which to ignore.

Before Lee could mount the steps to the lodge, the massive wooden door opened and Gil Zavala slipped out onto the porch, closing the door behind him. Gil was thicker through the body than he had been ten years ago, and his black hair was streaked with white, yet the changes had served to make him even more attractive; at forty-five, Gil remained a favorite with women of every age, a fact that he enjoyed as much as they did. But at this moment, his handsome brown face was creased with barely controlled irritation.

"What the hell took you so long? It's nearly noon," said Gil. "You know I'm not cut out to play political pattycake. You should have brought in Carrington to hold their goddamn hands."

Lee clapped Gil's shoulder. "Look at it as another form of human manipulation—like romancing a pretty lady."

Gil snorted. "The women I romance don't specialize in nutcracking."

"That bad?" murmured Lee, reaching for the door.

"Worse. Those two are like—"

"—fire and gasoline," finished Lee dryly. "Did you keep them from exploding?"

"Christ, yes! You made it sound like I could take the next train south if I didn't. So I shoved a newspaper down Meyerson's throat and dragged Moore into the blind by the edge of the slough. And I made damn sure his shotgun had blanks in it."

As Lee laughed, his affection for Gil modified the grim lines that both sorrow and triumph had carved on Lee's face.

"Mil gracias, compadre," said Lee softly. "I'm in your debt again. Did you know you are the only exception to my rule?" Before Gil could ask what Lee was talking about, Lee said, "Why don't you retrieve the doubtless frustrated Mr. Moore while I pull the newspaper out of Meyerson's throat." He shook his head in admiration of Gil's duplicity with the shotgun. "If Sam's daddy knew about those blanks, the Buckles Ranch would never be able to buy another piece of hardware in San Ignacio."

Gil made a graceful, decidedly obscene gesture that indicated how Jackson Moore could dispose of the contents of his three hardware stores. Without a backward look, Gill strode off toward the place where Sam Moore potted at geese and wondered if he were going blind. Lee went around to the back door of the clubhouse. He opened the door noiselessly, walked into a kitchen redolent of spice and peppers, and spoke in fluent Spanish with the cook and her two assistants. When he was assured that brunch was proceeding as scheduled, Lee left as silently as he had come.

Lee found Ben Meyerson in the comfortably appointed lounge where a fireplace radiated the pungent warmth of a mixed oak and cedar fire. Meyerson was reading a newspaper while he toasted his polished boots near the fire. His modish hunting clothes had never seen the inside of a muddy duck blind.

"Mr. Meyerson," said Lee in the soft voice that forced people to lean toward him in order to hear, "I'm very sorry to have been such a poor host. It was good of you to come here on such short notice."

Meyerson was tall and thin and restrained by a mixture of ineptitude and unease. He smiled in a way that revealed how little he appreciated being kept waiting. But he accepted the handshake with an alacrity that revealed how much he enjoyed being invited to one of the world's more exclusive hunting clubs. In spite of Meyerson's reputation for boorishness, it was apparent that he was not above enjoying a social coup.

"No need for apology," said Meyerson in a monotone voice that managed to be as abrasive as it was uninteresting. He slouched over the handshake until he realized that Lee was nearly as tall as himself. "I've heard enough about your little club to be curious."

Lee smiled perfunctorily, taking Meyerson's measure as he took the measure of all men he needed. Lee concluded that the advance reports of Meyerson were largely correct; he was a brilliant, socially gauche engineer. He was much more at ease with blueprints than he was with those who drew or implemented them. He wore his expensive clothes like he wore his height, ungracefully.

"Well," drawled Lee, "we'll have to see that you get in some shooting so that your trip lives up to its advance billing. But first, let's hunt up some coffee."

Meyerson looked around, plainly wondering if anyone else would be joining them, particularly a man called Sam Moore.

"The others will be along in a bit," said Lee, leading the way to the dining room.

The room's huge, plate-glass windows overlooked the green and silver marsh, the mercury sweep of Black's Bay, and the slate-gray expanse of the Pacific Ocean. The men seated themselves in chairs that were wide, upholstered in leather, and made for the comfort of big men. The hand-rubbed plank tables were built on a similar scale. While the cook's assistants moved noiselessly about their task of laying out a large brunch, Lee settled back to learn all he would need to know about the defensive, abrasive human being who was one of the most visionary engineers of the new century.

"Tell me the news from Los Angeles," invited Lee as they were seated. "Down here we often find ourselves removed from the main flow of events."

Meyerson snorted. "The way I hear it, Buckles, you're pretty well informed. Matter of fact, I hear you engineer events the way I engineer dams."

The bald statement seemed to make no impression on Lee. He reached for a large, enameled pot.

"Coffee?" asked Lee politely.

"Yes," said Meyerson, nudging his mug with a thin finger. "I even heard," he continued, "that you started your own county down here so you wouldn't have to pay your share of taxes."

Meyerson laughed explosively, short, loud sounds that were almost barks. Lee examined the engineer with eyes that were nearly white. Meyerson finished laughing and began dumping sugar into his steaming coffee, apparently unconcerned that his words could be construed as an insult. Lee weighed the other man for a few long moments, then decided that Meyerson neither intended nor even understood the insult; in his own, incredibly inept way, Meyerson was merely trying to make conversation.

"Events conspired to make this county," Lee said softly, pouring himself a cup of coffee. "Because I live here, I was naturally a part of those events."

Before Meyerson could reply, the outer door opened and Gil entered, followed by David Carrington and Sam

Moore, a blocky bulldog of a man who had a long, bristling moustache that matched his sandy red hair. Moore's eyes immediately fastened on Meyerson; Moore's face, already flushed with the morning cold and frustration, turned a darker red.

"What's that mother—" began Moore harshly, but Lee was up and speaking before Moore could finish the epithet.

"Hello, Sam, good of you to join us," said Lee, his voice overriding the short man's anger.

Meyerson had stood to face Moore, but Lee was already between them. Lee took Moore's hand in a grip that was hard enough to make the man wince. "I know you must be hungry after a morning of hunting. Any luck? No? Too bad. You'll just have to come back tomorrow. You know Meyerson, don't you? Good. Come sit down across from him."

Never giving either man a chance to open his mouth, Lee firmly ushered Moore to his designated side of the table. Without pausing, Lee continued his amiable monologue.

"Good morning, David. Any luck? Good. That fancy English shotgun must have improved your eye—or did all that silver just blind the geese?" He clapped Carrington on the shoulder and risked a brief look at Carrington's knowing hazel eyes; the railroad man was quietly amused by Lee's machinations. Lee looked away before his own amusement broke into a shared smile. "Gil, drag over two more chairs and let's all sit down to eat."

With the help of thick, tender steaks, fresh eggs, Mexican pastries and white flour tortillas, the next fifteen minutes were dominated by Lee's easy conversation. The excellent food, and the considerable personal charm that Lee could exert when he wished to, reduced the two engineers' mutual glares from murderous to merely irked. Between bites of food, the two men gradually began giving more attention to their host than to one another, for Lee's conversation was calculated to interest them in spite of their antagonism.

"You two gentlemen share a fascinating profession,"

230

Lee said, gradually lowering his voice as he spoke so that both men had to pay close attention to hear him. "Without your work on roads, harbors, dams, sewers, bridges and aqueducts—particularly aqueducts—we would still be savages grubbing for roots and grasshoppers."

Lee paused to chew a bit of tenderloin while both men nodded unconsciously, agreeing that their work was indispensible to civilization. Carrington quietly mopped at the bright yellow egg yolk on his plate with a scrap of tortilla. He sensed that Lee's presentation needed no reinforcement; the two engineers were willing to let themselves be seduced away from enmity by the proximity of power, money and flattery. The sole dissent at the table was registered by Gil, whose posture continued to show his uneasiness at having to be polite to men he would rather ignore.

"In fact," continued Lee, "the two of you are responsible for most of the major construction and public works design in California. Naturally," Lee said, eating a fragment of egg, "there is a certain amount of healthy competition between the two of you."

Carrington coughed into his napkin, but so softly that no one except Lee noticed. Lee smothered a smile in his own napkin and pushed his plate aside; as ordered, the cook had given him little food, allowing him to finish eating ahead of the others without appearing to rush. Now he was able to continue controlling the conversation by the simple expedient of being the only man without food in his mouth.

"But," said Lee clearly, "competition should not preclude cooperation. Even Mr. Meyerson's enemies admit that he has no equal when it comes to hydraulic engineering. And even Mr. Moore's most vocal detractors swear that he has a genius for organizing massive construction projects. Together, you've brought this state and much of the West into the twentieth century."

The two engineers raised their eyes and glared at one another, but neither wanted to interrupt Lee's slow, flattering words.

"Throughout history," said Lee, glancing from one man

to the other as he spoke, compelling their attention, "civilization has depended upon the availability and accessibility of fresh water. Every country from the greatest to the smallest depended on water. Rome was no exception. America is no exception. California is living proof of the necessity of water. This could be the most productive agricultural land in the world, gentlemen, but it is limited by lack of fresh water.

"I've been building reservoirs and check dams and digging new wells for the last twenty years, spending thousands upon thousands of dollars just to water a few thousand trees and cattle. My neighbors have been doing the same, wringing the land and their bank accounts in order to grow oranges and walnuts and lemons, praying for rain so that their cattle and sheep and barley might survive one more season.

"Water is the limiting factor on the usefulness of this land. We're within a generation—probably less—of outstripping the natural water supply. This is, after all, a desert that we have chosen to live in."

"That's what I've been saying for years," said Moore, swallowing a chunk of steak to clear his mouth. "That's why I moved my construction company north. Moreno County just can't handle any more growth, so there wouldn't be enough work here for an engineer. My daddy still doesn't accept that, but it's true just the same."

Lee smiled crookedly; Jackson Moore was Moreno County's most avid and unthinking proponent of progress. Moore saw the smile and misunderstood the thought behind it.

"Look, Mr. Buckles. When you first sank a well, how far down did you have to go?" asked Moore.

"About thirty feet," Lee said.

"Thirty-four," said Gil without looking up from his steak.

"How far do you have to go now?" asked Moore.

Lee waited for Gil.

"Seventy-one feet on the last one, and it was on the flats," said Gil, looking interested in the conversation for the first time.

"We're sucking the land dry," said Moore flatly. "A year of light rain would drop the water table another ten feet, at least."

"Twenty," said Meyerson, his naturally harsh voice made even less pleasant by a mouthful of egg.

"I said 'at least,' " shot back Moore. "But the point is that Moreno County can't afford to keep on growing more crops and towns."

"Perhaps," said Lee neutrally. "Let me tell you about a small experiment Mr. Zavala conducted. It was expensive, but very instructive. He planted five acres of tomatoes down on the flatlands. We dug a new well just for those five acres, and assigned a team of irrigators whose job it was to work those acres full time. With plentiful water and labor, the tomatoes grew like Jack's beanstalk. What did we finally decide the yield was, Gil?"

"Six tons to the acre," said Gil. "And if we hadn't run out of horseshit, I could have gotten it up to seven tons."

"Gil is a great believer in spreading horseshit," Lee said blandly.

"I'm not the only one," muttered Gil, biting into a searingly hot pepper with no outward sign of discomfort.

Lee laughed and took another sip of coffee. "At any rate, there were enough tomatoes for every woman in the county to put up a year's supply and still we plowed under tons. Wasteful, but the point was made: with enough water, this is an incredibly fertile land."

"But there isn't enough water," said Moore flatly.

"Not under our noses," agreed Lee softly. "But sometimes we have to look farther than our own noses."

Lee paused, letting his silence emphasize his message, but Moore was the hard-headed son of a hard-headed Missouri father.

"A man would have to see at least two hundred miles northeast to find that kind of water," said Moore sarcastically.

"Three hundred," Lee said. "The Owens Valley, to be exact. There's water in the mountains between Moreno and Owens, but not enough. No, Mr. Moore," said Lee, cutting off half-formed objections, "I have ridden every

233

watershed in Southern California in the past year. The Colorado River might be a little closer, but the delivery system would be too expensive for us at this time. Owens is the only water source that makes sense.

"I might add that I've had this same discussion with a half-dozen other men around California, and they share my assessment of the situation."

Neither Moore nor Meyerson needed to be told that the men Lee had talked with represented the real power in the state. But Moore still found it difficult to accept the idea of going so far away for water. It just was not done.

"Impossible," said Moore. Then, "No, it would be possible, but I don't think that it's very—"

"Dry up, Moore," said Meyerson. His thin face was lit by inner visions of hydraulic design. "Mr. Buckles, that's a hell of an idea. It would be one of the biggest engineering jobs ever undertaken anywhere in the country."

"One of the biggest public works projects in the history of man," said Lee, smiling and turning his attention back to Moore. "The work would be too much for any single company to undertake. Of course, it would be possible for one company to grow into the job," said Lee, his voice neutral and his eyes hard as he looked at Moore, "but it would be preferable to use two experienced companies."

Lee reached for the coffeepot, poured himself a fresh cup and refilled other cups while he spoke.

"Of course, this whole discussion is purely speculative. The state government is not yet aware of the imperative need for more water, and the cost of such a system would be far more than even the richest private citizen could bear. However," continued Lee blandly, "as the need for water becomes more and more pressing, the government will become desperate for technical advice. Naturally—"

One of the cook's assistants signaled unobtrusively. Gil got up and left the room with so little noise that only Lee noticed the foreman's departure.

"—I want such advice to be immediately available. If you men would be interested in investigating the feasibility of bringing in water from the Owens Valley, I would be willing to pay a reasonable fee for your work."

Gil returned, his face an expressionless mask that was as much a warning to Lee as a shout.

"If you will excuse me for a moment . . . ?" said Lee.

Lee smiled and moved his heavy chair aside with a controlled surge of power that was at odds with his soft voice. Only someone who knew him very well would have guessed the extent of his anger at being interrupted at such a crucial point in his conversation. Carrington knew; without a pause, the railroad man assumed control of the conversation before either engineer could remember that the other was an enemy. Gil also knew Lee; the foreman turned on his heel and led Lee to a private office where a phone was off the hook. Gil grabbed the dumbbell-shaped receiver and muffled it with his palm before he spoke.

"It's Joy. She sounds crazy," said Gil bluntly.

He handed the receiver to Lee. Before Lee could protest, Gil was gone. Lee looked at the receiver with the disfavor he usually reserved for poisonous reptiles. Then his face and his voice flattened to utter neutrality as he leaned against a massive desk and addressed his wife.

"Marjorie," said Lee.

The word was whatever she wanted to make of it—a simple designation, a challenge, an acknowledgment of her presence. Her voice came back to him as though from another country, distorted by static and distance and something more disturbing that Lee could not name.

"Hello my dear husband Leander."

The distance was not sufficient, nor the static loud enough, to disguise the unpleasant, almost eerie quality of her unnaturally high voice.

"Are you all right?" Lee asked shortly.

"I'm better than you'll be in a few minutes," said Joy. Her voice carried a mixture of pleasure and malice that was so familiar to both of them that neither he nor she could remember when it had sounded otherwise. If it ever had. "My father died last night."

Lee said nothing for a moment, weighing the implications of her words and the vicious edge to her voice. What was there in her father's death that gave her such pleasure? She had been very close to Byrd Todhunter.

Yet, his death was neither unanticipated nor unwelcome, least of all to the old man who had been bedridden since a stroke three years ago.

"I know that you'll miss him," said Lee. "I'm sorry."

"Not sorry enough to come home at night, are you?" she snapped.

Lee drew a long breath, wondering at the tension he sensed building in Marjorie. "You made it quite clear that living with me was an impossible burden," said Lee evenly. "I'm only trying to conduct our lives in the least destructive way."

Joy's short, ugly laugh was almost like a burst of static. "The least destructive way," she repeated mockingly. "You should have thought of that ten years ago. Husband."

"Ten years ago you couldn't wait to run out on me for the pleasures of San Francisco." Lee moved impatiently, bored with the turn of the conversation. "Is there anything else that must be discussed right now?"

"Yes, dear husband," she said, drawing out her words until she and the static hissed indistinguishably.

Lee sensed incipient hysteria tightening Joy's voice until it was so high that he could barely understand her. The skin on the back of his neck tightened in primal reflex.

"The telegram says Daddy left everything to me," Joy said, her voice higher with each word. "How do you like that, Leander Buckles? Husband. I own part of your precious land. Now I may not understand all that complicated folderol that you and David shut me out of, but I do understand this. If you want your ranch, you'll have to crawl to—"

"Marjorie." Lee's voice was like a whip. "This is not the time. I'll be at the grove house—at home—as soon as I can. We'll continue this discussion then."

"Yes," she said, laughing wildly. "We certainly will, won't we? Husband."

There was a harsh sound when she jammed the receiver into its hook, then the static-filled silence of an open line. As Lee had guessed, the San Ignacio switchboard operator was on the line. Whether or not she had listened, Lee had no way of knowing. Gently, he replaced the receiver.

Conversation stopped when Lee appeared in the doorway to the dining room.

"Gentlemen, I regret that I won't be able to talk further with you at this moment. Mr. Carrington or Mr. Zavala can answer any of your questions. But now, if you will excuse me, I must leave. My wife's father just passed away and she . . . needs me."

Lee was gone before either of his guests could move.

Carrington did not allow the conversation to falter, despite his own intense curiosity about the rage he saw behind Lee's white eyes in the instant before Lee had turned to leave.

Lee's new Cadillac lurched between puddles and ruts as he forced the car over bad roads, heading back toward San Ignacio and the grove house. While he drove, he thought about Todhunter's death, and he weighed possible threats to the dream that had become his obsession—the Buckles Ranch.

The cloud cover descended in long veils that were too heavy to be mist and too light to be rain. Even Lee's shearing coat could not turn away the clinging gray chill. Moisture beaded on the windscreen, sliding down the glass in ragged lines. Lee was thoroughly cold by the time he turned the car into the long, rock driveway that was flanked by densely green citrus groves.

In spite of the gravel, Lee's boots were muddy by the time he walked from the driveway to the house; he suspected that there was not enough gravel in the entire county to subdue the bottomless clay of the flatlands. Though he was shivering from the cold, he walked around the house to the kitchen entrance, peeling off his driving gloves while he skirted mud holes deeper than his boots were high. Real rain began to fall, drawing circles on the brown surfaces of the puddles.

The instant Lee's foot touched the first step onto the back porch, the kitchen door opened. Wrapped in a black wool shawl, Joy stood in the doorway. Lee stuffed his gloves into his pocket and began unbuttoning his coat as he climbed the steps.

"Don't bother," Joy said, pulling her shawl closer in an attempt to blunt the cutting edges of cold and rain. "You're not going inside. Your boots are filthy."

Something new in Joy's voice made Lee stop and look, really look, at the woman circumstance had made his wife and time had made his enemy. She was still one of the most beautiful women he had ever seen . . . and one of the least attractive. Her hair was the color of champagne, soft coils that glowed in the muted light of the porch, emphasizing her pale amethyst eyes. The curves of her body had retained their promise, a promise he knew was as illusory as her manners were perfect.

Lee shivered and moved toward the warmth pouring out of the kitchen door.

"No," said Joy. "Your boots are dirty."

"Don't be ridiculous."

Lee stepped around his wife and paused in the entry way long enough to pull off his boots and coat. On silent, stockinged feet, he strode toward the small sitting room that Joy customarily used. Before he reached the room, a boy with nearly white hair and faded blue eyes came out of the kitchen, a hand wrapped around a pastry that oozed cream between his fingers. He straightened when he saw Lee.

"Good afternoon, Father."

The boy's voice was low and well-modulated, his manners as wholly correct as his mother's.

"Good afternoon, Champ." Lee looked at his son's round pink cheeks and even rounder body. "Your mother said you were too ill to hunt with me this morning. I'm glad to see that you recovered so quickly."

Champ's cheeks reddened. He stared at the sweet cream mounded between his fingers. "Momma says guns are nasty. And I don't like getting cold."

Champ took a big bite out of a pastry; the cream that stuck to his lips was darker than his skin. Lee sat on his heels, bringing his eyes down to the level of his son's face.

238

With a long, tanned finger, Lee wiped cream off of Champ's lips.

"Would you like to go surf fishing with me as soon as it's sunny?"

Champ's eyes went from Lee to Joy and then back to Lee. Before the boy could answer, Joy moved to stand behind him. Her white fingers rested on Champ's shoulders.

"Champ is too frail for such things," said Joy quickly.

Lee cocked an eyebrow and looked pointedly at the fat, healthy boy who bore his name.

"He looks about as frail as one of Gil's tractors."

"How would you know? You've never sat up all night listening to him struggle for breath. But then, you're never here at night, are you?"

Champ moved uncomfortably beneath Joy's suddenly tight fingers. Lee ignored her, looking only at his son, and smiling.

"Then perhaps we could take a ride together. That's not too strenuous, is it? You're big enough for a horse of your own now."

"Do you mean it?"

Champ smiled and excitement animated his face. Automatically, he looked over his shoulder to make sure that his mother approved. What he saw made his smile vanish.

"You are cruel, Leander," said Joy.

"Cruel? But I meant every word."

"I'm sure you did," she said cuttingly. "Don't you remember the beating Champion got the last time he went riding? He came back bruised and bloody."

"You exaggerate."

Lee's voice was low and cold. Champ shrank back beneath his mother's white fingers.

"Besides," said Joy, her voice unusually high, "my son is allergic to horses."

"Since when?" demanded Lee.

He stood with startling speed and grace, seeming to tower over his wife and son. Champ's breathing thickened to an audible rasp.

"May I be excused, Momma? I feel faint."

"Of course, dear," murmured Joy. She leaned down

and hugged Champ. When she spoke, her breath stirred his very fine, light curls. "You're such a good boy. Momma loves good little boys."

In spite of his labored breathing, Champ held out his hand to Lee. But when Lee moved to hug his son, Champ bowed quickly, turned and walked away.

"You could at least cut his hair," said Lee, too low for Champ to hear.

"He's just a baby." Joy looked at her departing son and smiled. "A baby."

"He's almost ten. He should start growing up. To run this ranch he'll need more than perfect manners." Lee met Joy's glare with the cold determination that she hated. "Champ's been in lace and knickers long enough, Marjorie. At least let him play as a boy."

"An animal, you mean. Champion is a perfect son. He is gentle, loyal and obedient."

Lee grimaced. "So are my hunting dogs."

"You are disgusting," spat Joy. "I loathe you."

"Tell me something I don't know," said Lee icily. "Tell me how a mother could turn her son into a soft puppet who needs her permission to shit!"

Joy gasped and pressed her palms against her forehead. Her shawl slipped unnoticed to the floor. "I feel faint," she whispered, swaying.

Lee swore, knowing he had lost again; Joy's headaches were as convenient as they were vicious. He swept her up in his arms and carried her into the sitting room. The room had been rearranged since he had last been in it; the small table that held Joy's headache powders was no longer by her velvet chair.

"Where's your opium?" he said curtly.

"Ivory box . . ."

Lee's gray eyes raked over the room until he spotted the vague gleam of ivory next to a red velvet couch. He laid Joy on the couch, yanked the top of the box off and grabbed a twist of paper. The carafe that had once held water now held wine; there was more powder in the twist than he remembered. He hesitated, uncertain.

"How much?"

Joy's only response was a moan. He bent over her with the twist of paper held between his fingers.

"How much powder? Half?"

"All," she said faintly.

"In the wine?"

"Yes . . ."

Lee bit back his objections and stirred the powder into the wine. He propped her against his shoulder, holding her until she finished the opium-laced burgundy. Soon, the worst of the pain faded. When her neck muscles were no longer rigid, Lee eased her down onto the couch again. As he stood up, her fingers wrapped around his wrist.

"Wait. I haven't told you."

Her smile was as hard and cold as the amethyst pin at the base of her throat.

"You can tell me when you feel better."

"I feel better just thinking about it."

"It?"

"The ranch. My ranch." She laughed in spite of a residue of pain untouched by drugs. "My. Ranch."

With a mixture of anger and pity, Lee gently removed her hand from his wrist. "The opium is confusing you, Marjorie. It always confuses you. You'll feel better if you sleep."

"No." Her voice, like her smile, was clear and hard. "My daddy owned the mortgage on this ranch. He left it for me to hold for Champion. I own the ranch."

"Not quite, Marjorie. So long as the payments are made on the mortgage, the ranch is mine."

"The mortgage came due on my father's death."

"Within thirty days," corrected Lee. "That's more than enough time to arrange another loan to pay off the money owed to your father. To you."

Joy moved restlessly. "But it's mine and you can't borrow more on the land unless I agree to it, and I won't and David promised not to loan you any money unless I said so."

There was a long silence while Lee absorbed the implications of her nearly incoherent words.

"I see," said Lee finally. "Where does that leave us?"

"You'll have to default. That's the word when you can't pay, isn't it?"

"Yes."

"Yes," echoed Joy. "Yes. And then I'll sell your godforsaken ranch. Husband." She smiled, pale lips thinning over white teeth as she struggled against pain and drugs, trying to sit up and throw her victory in his teeth. Her breath whistled with effort, making her even harder to understand. "I'll sell this—damned land you love—and then you'll know what—it feels like to lose and lose and never—never have what you want—what they promised you would be yours—oh, God, to be happy again!"

Joy laughed though tears ran down her cheeks, laughed even when it brought back the pain, then she called for her father, but no one heard. Lee had already gone upstairs to his office to wait for David Carrington. While Lee waited, he made several calls to San Francisco, speaking with men who knew the contents of Byrd Todhunter's will.

By the time Carrington arrived, Joy's hysteria had faded into random fits of tears, then into restoring sleep. Carrington knocked on the front door in his characteristic manner—two sharp raps. The knock was more a way of announcing himself than a request for permission to enter the Buckles house. In the last ten years, Carrington had become a member of the family in all but name. He let himself into the house and called out softly. No one answered. He called out again and heard a muffled sound that could have been his name.

Without stopping to take off his muddy overshoes, Carrington walked hurriedly toward Joy's sitting room. The door to the room was almost closed; though the afternoon was as gloomy as most evenings, no lamp had been lit.

"Joy," called Carrington softly.

"David . . . ?"

He pushed the door open and saw Joy lying on the couch, her translucent skin streaked by past tears and present grief. When Joy saw him, tears again welled out of her eyes.

"He's dead, David. My daddy is dead."

Tears ran down her cheeks and her slender body trembled with the force of her suppressed sobs. Carrington knelt by the couch and took her pale, cold hands between his, warming her fingers.

"I'm so sorry, Joy. I loved him too."

"It's so lonely," she whispered.

Carrington gathered her against his shoulder with wordless comfort. Joy abandoned herself to tears, knowing that he would understand as he had always understood. For an instant she wondered what life for her would be like without his enduring, gentle strength to depend on. The thought of not having him so frightened her that her fingers closed convulsively on his damp coat.

"Don't die," she said in a raw whisper. "Promise me you won't die!"

"Of course I won't," he said immediately, sensing her need. He smiled gently. "I'll live forever."

Joy nodded once, solemnly, then shuddered and buried her face in his wool overcoat. Carrington held her, rocking slowly, murmuring words that had no meaning beyond the reassurance of hearing his voice.

After a long time, Joy's tears diminished. As though her grief had released her inhibitions, Joy began to talk about her loneliness and disappointments, her fears and her need for money, more money, and then more, enough to blunt the teeth of the carnivore called Life.

Shocked at the depth of her bitterness, Carrington could only listen helplessly while she poured out her hates and plans and beliefs. It was not the first time she had confided in him, but it was the only time she held nothing back. Slowly, with utmost delicacy, Carrington tried to deflate the most irrational of Joy's obsessions. But too much had happened for Joy to be easily swayed, even by the man she had trusted all of her life.

Finally, the onslaught of another agonizing headache forced an end to the conversation. Joy lay back and closed her eyes, looking frail against the vivid red of the couch and the multicolored afghan that was draped over the back cushions. Carrington mixed her a very light potion of opium and wine. She drank with her eyes closed, but when she sensed that he was going to leave, she looked up at him with eyes more beautiful than any jewels she wore. Each time she breathed, wisps of her shining hair stirred with dreamlike slowness.

"What would I do without you, David?"

Carrington smiled. He pulled the colorful afghan off of the back of the couch. With gentle hands, he tucked the blanket around her. Then he bent and kissed her forehead.

"Things will be better now," he said softly. "I promise you."

Carrington straightened and went upstairs to face the man who was Joy's husband, his own partner and most of all his friend. With a feeling close to despair, Carrington realized that Lee probably would feel betrayed by what he had promised to Joy.

No light showed beneath Lee's office door, but Carrington sensed Lee's presence the way deer sensed a hidden mountain lion. Carrington pushed open the door, feeling every minute of his fifty-one years like a weight on his back. Automatically he reached into his pocket for a cigar. In the few moments it took to light the long, thin cigar, he gathered himself for a conversation that he feared might end his friendship with one of the people he loved.

Lee saw little more than a glow and a pale stream of smoke expanding into the chilly hallway, but there was something in Carrington's stance, revealed by the instant of matchlight, that warned Lee. With a feeling of sorrow and bitterness, Lee dragged a match into flame, lighting the desk lamp whose shade made pools of color.

"Hello, David." Lee looked away from the lamp. His voice and face were expressionless, giving no hint of his thoughts. "Where are our engineers?"

"Gil took them into Pizarro," said Carrington, trying and failing to achieve a light tone. "As he put it so delicately, 'If they get laid, maybe they'll be too tired to fight.' "

Lee made a short, humorless sound. "If Moore and

Meyerson want to be big boys and build big things for big money, they'll have to learn what Kaiser taught me years ago: animosity is bad business." Lee looked at Carrington and smiled sardonically. "That's your cue, David."

Carrington waited while his hazel eyes searched Lee for the subtle signals he was accustomed to reading in all men. But Lee was as blank as an adobe wall. Carrington walked into the office slowly, pulling off his hat and coat and gloves.

Carrington sighed. "That was good advice twenty years ago, Lee. It's still good advice. Animosity gets in the way of business."

Carrington closed the door and discarded his coat, gloves and hat on a nearby chair.

Lee studied his partner for a long, silent moment, seeing a man years older than he remembered Carrington being. The gray in his hair had silently engulfed the brown; the lines in the handsome face were too deep to be called merely mature. And there was a despair deep in those hazel eyes that touched Lee as no outward sign of aging could. With a realization that was almost painful, Lee knew that he loved Carrington too well to destroy him, and that fact only made Carrington's betrayal worse.

Carrington saw sorrow move over Lee's face like mist over the face of a mountain, blurring lines of strength and endurance.

"I'm sorry, Lee. I did what I believed best for everyone."

For a moment, Lee could not believe what Carrington had said. How could destroying Lee's dream be good for anyone at all? To control the anger he felt uncoiling deep in his gut, Lee sifted words and more subtle signals, searching for kernels of emotion and motivation and reasons. How had he and Carrington come to this moment? What had he done to make Carrington hate him? What had he done that was commensurate to the punishment of losing his land, his dreams?

Lee closed his eyes, the last instant of weakness he would allow himself in his fight for the land. When his eyes opened, they were the color of autumn rain. His smile was all the more chilling because it was genuine.

"Brilliantly done, David. I've built a few boxes in my time, but I'll never approach the elegance of the one you built for me. There's just one thing," continued Lee coolly. "Why? What do you gain when I lose my land?"

"Lose your land?" Carrington's voice rose in confusion. "What are you talking about?"

Lee controlled an angry retort; it was obvious that Carrington's confusion was genuine. And then Lee understood.

"That cast-iron bitch fooled you too." Lee's laughter was a mixture of savagery and despair, but Carrington still did not understand. "She's got both of us and she's going to squeeze until our balls fall off."

"You're not making sense."

Lee stopped laughing abruptly. "I don't have to, partner. I'm not the bastard who sold out a friend."

There was a long silence that ended with Carrington's sigh.

"I was afraid you would take it like this," he said softly. "But is it really so terrible to have Joy hold title to the land? It's just for a few years, until the mortgage is paid off. That's a small price to pay for her happiness. She has felt so insecure since . . ." Carrington's voice died. He had never mentioned Cira before and had no intention of breaking precedent now. "Joy feels unnecessary, like an outsider, never consulted or even informed about decisions that affect her son's future and her own."

Lee listened quietly, holding anger at bay, probing Carrington's words and phrases for all their levels of meaning, for all the things that Carrington was too well-bred to hint at, much less say aloud. Lee realized that Carrington had not built the box alone; Joy and Lee had helped him at every turn. But Lee kept on listening to his partner's voice, a voice that was soft, hesitant, the voice of a man who was uncomfortable with what he was thinking and saying and doing.

"Joy has no parents now, no one to cherish her, for you and she do not . . ." Carrington closed his eyes, groping for a means of making himself understood without referring to Joy's and Lee's private life, a life that Carrington had despaired of for more than a decade. "I only want Joy's security and happiness, and in the long range, yours also."

"Bullshit."

Lee's voice was soft, neither angry nor accusatory, but Carrington flinched as though he had been struck.

"You love Joy," said Lee flatly. "You've loved her as long as I've known you. No—don't turn away, David. It's got to be said. Now. Tonight. No more elegant evasions. No more polite protestations. No more crap." Lee leaned toward Carrington, smiling savagely. "Pretend it's business, David," he suggested. "Nothing personal. Just business. You want Joy's happiness. I want my land. Let's see if we can't get together."

Slowly, Carrington turned back toward Lee.

"Whatever you and Joy are—or are not—to each other, is totally private," said Carrington in a strained voice. "Believe me, I have no wish to know."

"Oh, I believe you, David."

"Good," said Carrington, relieved. "Then we'll have no more of—"

"I believe you," continued Lee harshly, "and I don't give a damn about what you wish or don't wish to know. Our personal lives stopped being separate from our business lives in the exact instant you helped Marjorie to take away my land."

"God above, Lee! You act as though having to share control of the land with Joy is the same as losing it."

"My devoted wife," said Lee distinctly, "is planning to sell my ranch if I don't pay off the mortgage by the end of the thirty-day grace period."

"What! No, that can't—surely you misunderstood."

Lee knew Carrington, knew that the older man was not lying or even evading; Carrington really did not know what Marjorie was going to do.

"David," sighed Lee, wondering how to make the other man understand. "David, you must believe me. Marjorie is deadly serious."

"Borrow the money."

Lee stared speechlessly at his partner, then laughed in spite of his anger. "As you so cleverly pointed out to that—my wife—the terms of her father's mortgage preclude a second mortgage unless the holder of the first mortgage agrees."

Carrington stood without moving, eyes hooded against the rich smoke curling up from his cigar, remembering how he had explained the contract between Byrd and Lee to an unusually attentive Joy.

"Sweet God," said Carrington finally, trying to reconcile the gentle, witty Joy he knew with the vengeful Marjorie who was Lee's wife. "She is so desperately unhappy."

Carrington's eyes narrowed. He moved with the jerkiness of real anger, his voice colder than Lee had ever heard it.

"It ends here, Lee," said Carrington deliberately. "Joy is your wife. It is your duty to consider her well-being before that of any other person alive. And that most particularly includes your paramour!"

In the silence, both men heard the steadily increasing noise of rain pouring over the wet land. Idly, without showing what such control cost him, Lee lit a small cigar and blew rings toward slate-gray skylights glistening with rain.

"If I weren't married to the woman you love, would you care if I had fifty 'paramours'?" asked Lee, his voice mocking Carrington's cultured accents.

"No."

Lee smiled grimly. "Then you admit that—"

"No," snapped Carrington, coming toward Lee with the precise steps of a stalking wolf, "I won't permit you to act as though my love for Joy excuses your whoring after other women."

"Not whoring," said Lee coldly. "There is just one woman. There has never been another. There never will be."

Carrington closed his eyes and the anger visibly drained out of his body, to be replaced by the sorrow that had helped to age him.

"I know. I know. That's why I've stood by and said nothing, watched Joy's unhappiness. Every year it was

248

worse. She is so fragile, so sad." For the first time in their relationship, Carrington allowed Lee to see his private anguish. "My God, Lee," he whispered. "Did you marry her only for her money?"

Lee could not look at Carrington's open grief. He watched instead the slow dance of flame beneath the multicolored lamp shade, watched and heard the echo of a question he had asked himself so many times he no longer noticed the guilt that came with it. The guilt was simply a part of him now, like eyes and tongue and hands.

"I don't know," said Lee finally. "I hope not." He looked up, his eyes reflecting all the colors of the lamp. "And you, David," he asked gently, "why didn't you marry her?"

"I didn't know," whispered Carrington. "I didn't know that I loved her until it was too late."

Carrington stared through space and time, remembering when he was a very young man fascinated by a girl so tiny she had to be helped into his lap. He had loved the funny, sweet child whose matchless eyes always approved of the friend she called her "almost uncle." She had grown older and so had he; he had loved her as an indulgent older brother. She trusted him, always, and he had never betrayed that trust. And then he had loved her as a man loves a woman, but the change had been so gradual, so inevitable that it could be measured only in retrospect and despair.

"Too late," repeated Carrington softly.

A gust of rain drummed across the skylight. The hard sound recalled Carrington from the past. He shook himself as though the rain had actually touched him.

"But it is done and now must be accepted," said Carrington. "Your double life must end."

"I have only one life."

"Lee, this lie must end!"

"What lie? My marriage to a woman I haven't touched since Champ was conceived? Are you telling me that Joy will agree to a divorce?"

"No! That would destroy her!"

"But you were talking about lies," said Lee implacably.

"What do you call a beautiful woman who is as sexually responsive as a stone?"

"Please."

Carrington looked at Lee with a distress so great it could not be distinguished from pain. For an instant Lee almost relented, but the pressure of all the years and lies was too great.

"No, David. We're going to say it all. Maybe you could live on the kind of cold companionship that's all Marjorie can give—hell, you seem to thrive on it—but I can't."

"Stop it. Please."

The room became silent but for the liquid rush of rain over the skylights. Carrington's glance moved slowly around the room, his eyes haunted; Joy was Lee's wife and divorce was unthinkable. He felt Lee's hands on his shoulders and looked up into gray eyes that were luminous with compassion and regret.

"A very elegant box, worthy of a master," said Lee softly. "I can almost hear God laughing." Lee smiled lopsidedly. "And so I add blasphemy to my list of sins. Or is it heresy?"

Carrington's answering smile was faint, but real. "Lee," he began, then stopped as though afraid to tear the fragile web of affection binding them to each other. Carrington sighed and slowly began to speak of things he had pretended for years did not exist.

"You have two families. You have children by two women. If you were to die now, tonight, how would your estate be divided? How would you balance affection and duty? Or is the decision already made in death as you made it in life? Do Joy and your son get short shrift while your paramour and bastard get rich?"

'You have no right to—"

"Right?" said Carrington incredulously. "Right! Jesus Christ! Listen to the adulterer talk about rights!" Carrington put both of his hands flat on the desk and leaned forward, nearly shouting. "What would happen if you died tonight!"

Lee's eyes were almost transparent beneath narrowed lids, but his voice, unlike Carrington's, was controlled.

"Always the calculator, aren't you, David? Always looking at the future and weighing it, balancing one instant against another."

"Of course. And you do the same."

"In almost everything, yes. But there is a single part of my life that is exempt from calculation. Cira is there and I go to her and that is something beyond measure."

Carrington studied the face of the man he had known so long and so well; he saw nothing that undercut the conviction in Lee's words.

"Yes, I see," said Carrington slowly. "And that makes what I must do all the more imperative . . . a very elegant box indeed."

Carrington waited for Lee to respond, to make it easier for Carrington to act, but Lee had learned long ago that the first man to speak at the bargaining table often found himself at a disadvantage later. So Carrington waited in vain, looking around the room as though searching for something that was not there.

"May I?" said Carrington at last, breaking the long silence and gesturing to the logs that had been laid in the large stone fireplace.

"Of course."

"My old bones need warming," Carrington said with a fleeting smile.

Lee said nothing. A match flared raggedly in the gloom by the hearth. Lee watched Carrington stoop to light the fire with an ease that belied his reference to old bones. The kindling burned, sending tiny orange fire flickering and leaping, reaching for the dry logs. Within moments, the logs were all but hidden in the embrace of flames.

"Such a small thing," mused Carrington, looking at the blackened match between his fingers. "Such large consequences."

Absently, Carrington flicked the spent match into the ravenous flames. Without turning back to face Lee, Carrington spoke softly, yet each word carried clearly to the man who waited across the room.

"I have talked with Joy. She is unhappy, with good reason." He paused, seeking words that were both delicate and penetrating. "She fears abandonment. She fears complete humiliation and financial ruin."

Lee waited, but Carrington had finished for the moment.

"Inasmuch as I have contributed to Marjorie's unhappiness," said Lee slowly, choosing his words as carefully as Carrington had, "I have a duty to protect her from unnecessary hurt. Though our marriage is a lie and a farce, I have promised myself not to subject her to the humiliation of divorce. I owe that much to her. As for my estate"—Lee shrugged—"Byrd left Marjorie more money than even she can spend."

"What about her son?"

"The boy's name is Leander Champion Buckles the Fourth," snapped Lee. "He is my son as well as hers, a fact that she denies in practice if not in words! In spite of that, I will be sure that he is not left without resources. I may be an adulterer, but I'm not a monster."

"I know," said Carrington simply.

He turned away from the leaping flames. With slow steps, he crossed the room to stand with Lee beneath the shining gray skylights.

"I know," repeated Carrington, "but I'm not the holder of the mortgage. Joy is. And she is extremely . . . fragile. More so than I had realized until tonight. I doubt if she would believe mere words. I'm afraid she wants something more tangible."

"Vengeance. My land."

Carrington closed his eyes as though it would make the truth less unpleasant. "I hope she will be satisifed with less." He glanced at Lee with almost tangible compassion. "You see, there isn't enough money in the world to make Joy secure and happy, although she doesn't know that. She is so very . . . fragile. Many things that would seem foolish to other people are very real concerns to her. I have tried to dissuade her from the most irrational of her worries. Sometimes I have succeeded. I believe I could persuade her not to sell the land, if you would agree to certain concessions."

Lee felt the skin tightening on the back of his arms and

neck. He wanted to move suddenly, to lash out at Carrington so that neither man would have to speak; but Lee did not move because he realized that only speech could change the nature of the box.

"What must I do in order to keep my land?"

"You must formally and completely and for all time sever your ties with—"

"No."

"—your paramour and her child."

"Never."

"Then you will lose your ranch."

Carrington looked at Lee and was shocked by the violence behind Lee's white eyes.

"I don't think either one of you realizes the cards I hold," said Lee with a control that was more frightening than his eyes. "I could demand that Marjorie become my wife in fact as well as in name. I could require her loving presence in my bed. Tonight, David. Every night. Whenever the spirit moved me. And if the spirit were slack, I would most thoroughly instruct her in the many ways a woman can excite—"

"Stop it," said Carrington, sweating in spite of the cool room. "She's your wife, not your whore!"

"I have no whore," said Lee coldly. "But I do have a wife. And the law is very accommodating on the subject of wives. Short of murder, Marjorie is mine to use as I please. Do you understand me, David?"

Carrington looked at Lee's white eyes and knew that Lee would destroy Joy if he were pushed too far. Carrington shuddered and looked away.

"So you keep your land and your paramour and give Joy nothing but the promise of abuse," said Carrington in a horrified whisper. "She won't accept that, Lee."

"I know."

"But you will still destroy her for selling your land?"

"Yes. Do you finally understand the dimensions of the box, David?"

The sounds of the crackling fire and the windswept rain could not disguise the silence that thickened until it seemed as tangible as the pulse beating in Lee's throat.

"Twice," said Carrington, then swallowed and began again. "Twice in the past you have gotten out of boxes that I thought had no exit."

Lee heard the plea implicit in Carrington's words, but still said nothing.

"Is there no middle ground?" said Carrington.

"Marjorie could go to San Francisco, if she agreed to let Champ spend half of his time here," offered Lee.

"No." Carrington shook his head tiredly. "I suggested that years ago. She does not think you are a suitable moral influence for Champion."

"Oh?" Lee gave Carrington a sardonic look. "'Let he who is without sin cast the first stone.'"

An angry flush swept over Carrington's handsome face. "Joy's relationship with me is above reproach," said Carrington, biting off each word.

"Pity," shot back Lee. "Her relationship with me is beneath contempt."

"That isn't fair to her," said Carrington evenly.

"Fair?" Lee laughed. "Since when has that been a consideration? You've told me all the ways I've shirked my duty to her, but I have yet to hear a whisper from you about her duty to her husband!"

Carrington dropped his eyes and walked back to the fire. He tossed his cigar into the flames, picked up a cast-iron poker and stirred the fire unnecessarily.

"But you don't want to hear about her duty to her husband," continued Lee scathingly. "That particular omission in our relationship is quite satisfactory to your peculiar sense of what is right."

Lee crossed the room with the swift grace he had not lost to time. He put a hard hand on Carrington's shoulder, spinning him around.

"Look at me, David!"

Carrington looked up, but his eyes were unreadable, shadowed by smooth eyebrows that had been transformed by firelight into spun gold.

"Here's your middle ground," said Lee slowly. "I will agree—in writing, if that pleases her—to demand nothing of Marjorie except that which she would give any other

254

guest in her house. In return, she will sign over that mortgage to me."

Carrington shook his head wearily. "That's not good enough, Lee. It does nothing to ease her fear that your other family will supplant your legal family."

"I will not leave Cira."

"Will you sign a paper swearing that her child is another man's issue?"

"No."

"I thought not." Carrington's eyebrows lifted and a speculative light gleamed in his hazel eyes. "But would you swear not to leave your wealth or your name to her child—or any other child you might have by her? Would you swear never to acknowledge her children as your own, whether it be in casual speech or in formal documents?"

Carrington looked away, waiting for an answer. He studied the fire as though their futures burned within it.

"Are you suggesting that I make paupers out of them?" said Lee softly.

"I'm suggesting that if you were planning to settle any money on your bast—on her child, that you do so immediately and discreetly."

"It was done the day Cira told me she was carrying my child."

"Not your child," corrected Carrington softly. "Hers. Champion is your only child."

Lee's face tightened with pain. He stared into the fire, beginning to understand the constrictions inherent in the new box he and Carrington were so carefully constructing.

"The child's name is Magdalena," said Lee harshly. "She belongs to herself. I wish to Christ I could say as much for Champ."

Suddenly the room was too hot and too small and it reeked of the sachet Joy put in every drawer in the house.

"Does that satisfy you?" demanded Lee, turning on Carrington.

Carrington poked idly at the fire. "My feelings are irrelevant."

"Are they?"

"What I have done, I have done for Joy," said Carrington simply. "She is all I have."

Carrington's loneliness dissolved Lee's anger; he could not hate a man who had so little to live for. Feeling suddenly cold, Lee moved closer to the fire, to Carrington.

"Talk her into it, David," said Lee, his voice ragged.

"I hope I can."

"You must, or I will have to."

Sparks showered as Carrington thrust the iron into the fire. He withdrew the poker and faced Lee. Carrington smiled, but there was no softness in his eyes or voice.

"I can't allow Joy to be hurt anymore," said Carrington, tapping the heavy poker against the hearth; a fine spray of ashes flew off of the hot iron. "Surely you realize that?"

Lee was suddenly very still, a coiled stillness that Gil would have recognized and feared. But Gil was not there and Carrington had lost too much to be afraid. For several moments Lee and Carrington measured each other with deadly intent. Then Carrington propped the poker against the wall and left the room with soundless steps.

Lee stood alone in front of the twisting flames, listening to the fire and the rain and the regrets echoing in the lavender-scented room. He knew that it would be wise to stay in the house tonight, but his need for Cira transcended wisdom. It had always been that way. It always would be.

Quietly, Lee banked the fire and left the room. Downstairs, he put on his coat and boots and gloves. He could hear the rise and fall of voices, their voices, but did not hear separate words. He did not care to. He let himself out into the night. Overhead, a brass-gold sun poured between dark mounds of cloud. Wind stooped and leaped, pummeling the low clouds until the evening was a kaleidoscope of sun and cloud and brilliant rain.

Lee walked through black puddles and mud and gravel with equal indifference. He did not feel the cold water seeping into his boots. He was numb, empty. Mechanically, he started his car and guided it down the slippery driveway. Rain blew in with gusts of wind, but Lee did not notice. By the time he reached the edge of the colonia, it was sunset. He was drenched and shaking with cold. But he did not notice. The wind had finally torn apart the clouds, allowing shards of sun to scatter over the land. Ahead, a white frame house glowed in the sudden brightness, and a jacaranda tree tossed in the wind like black flame.

Even as Lee drove into the converted stable, a nine-year-old girl darted around puddles, running toward the garage. Barely waiting for Lee to get out of the car, the girl threw herself into his arms.

"Hello, Maggie," said Lee. In spite of the thin arms almost choking him, Lee smiled and returned her hug. "Where's your coat?" he asked, noticing that her arms were bare, cool, smelling of rain.

"Wet," she said, her hazel eyes sparkling with satisfaction. "Jaime pushed me into a puddle so I grabbed him and we slippped and got all wet and gooey." She giggled, remembering her cousin's shocked expression when he had landed in the mud. "Juana made him apologize to me," she added smugly.

In spite of his weariness, Lee laughed with his daughter. Jaime, Gil's youngest son, had been Maggie's companion and tormenter since the day she had first crawled up to him and enchanted him with a toothless smile.

"I trust," said Lee, carrying Maggie to the house, "that you also apologized to Jaime."

Maggie grimaced; that part of the incident was not nearly so much fun to remember. She buried her face in the damp collar of his soft coat. Even when they were on the porch beyond the reach of mud and rain, she clung to him with unusual tenacity.

"What's wrong, *niña?*" said Lee gently.

"Jaime."

Lee waited, holding her close, knowing she would retreat into stubborn silence if he pressed her with questions.

"Jaime," said Lee neutrally.

"*Sí.* Before we fell in the mud he told me," Maggie's arms tightened, "he told me the gringa bitch would make you go away and never come back and—"

257

Tears which Maggie scorned to shed squeezed her throat shut. Feeling the tension in her thin body, Lee did not scold her for her language.

"Jaime was wrong," said Lee. "I love you, *niña*."

Maggie's arms tightened even more. Lee returned her hug, then lowered her to the porch. She clung to him for another moment, looking up with a heart-shaped face that sometimes made him afraid; she was so beautiful, she seemed not to be real. Her wide hazel eyes had flecks of gold and green that changed with every light, every mood, a display that was almost hypnotic. The bones of her face were fine without being fragile, giving promise of even greater beauty as a woman than as a child. Her skin was pale gold, and her hair was like a moonless night, black, alive with the distant, secret glint of stars. Beneath her sudden, childish movements was an uncanny grace, Lee's gift to his daughter.

Lee shivered with cold and looked away. Only then did he notice that the front door was open and Cira was there, smiling, though her eyes had shadows turning deep within. He looked at her, realizing once again that the mother was even more lovely than the child.

"Come inside, both of you. It's too cold out here."

"I'm all muddy," said Lee ruefully, as Maggie released him and ran through the open door.

Cira pulled Lee inside, ignoring the smears his boots left on the tile floor of the entry way.

"You're cold," she said, seeing him shiver again. She reached up and unbuttoned his coat. "And you're wet."

"Yes," said Lee, touching the streaks of silver in her black hair with gentle fingers. "I guess it was raining."

Lee opened his coat and pulled Cira against him, at first holding her lightly, then with a power that would have been painful had she not held him with equal need. He knew then that whatever gossip Jaime had overheard had also reached Cira.

"I will never leave you," he said against her cheek.

"But your land," she whispered. "Your land."

"You mean more to me than anything else."

Cira pulled away from Lee. Tears squeezed out of her closed eyes. She shook her head.

"She's won," said Cira tiredly.

Lee's hands caught and held Cira's face.

"No. I won't leave you, Cira. I love you too much to even think of life without you."

Cira turned her face to kiss the palm of his hand. "I know. But loving me has cost you your land. Someday— not now, but someday—you will hate me for making you lose your land. The ranch is too much a part of you, Lee. And so she has won."

Lee gathered Cira close again, holding the woman who still fit perfectly in his arms.

"David is talking to Marjorie now. He'll make her see reason."

"What if he can't?" Cira asked.

Lee said nothing. Nor did Cira repeat the question; a single look at Lee's face had told her. She pulled his head down, kissing him without reservation, telling him things for which there were no words.

But Maggie understood only the unanswered question. From the living-room hearth she watched the two people she loved, sensing the depth of their emotions without understanding them. She ran from the warmth of the fire to the greater warmth of their touch. When they felt the thin strength of Maggie's arms around them, Lee and Cira moved to include Maggie in their tight embrace.

"Lee?" said Maggie, her voice muffled against his ribs. "No matter what Jaime says, I love you best!"

Lee's smile did not reflect his desire to lay hands on the too-wise, too-talkative Jaime.

"Lee?" said Maggie again, her voice no longer muffled.

"Yes, *niña?*" answered Lee, bending to kiss the top of her head.

Maggie smiled demurely. "Is there something in your pocket?"

Lee laughed without making a sound. His voice was grave as he answered her. "Why, I don't know. Maybe you'd better check. It might be something important."

Before Lee had finished speaking, Maggie was rummaging in the deep pockets of his shearling coat. One pocket was empty, but the other held a bulging paper bag. With an excited squeal, Maggie pulled out the bag. After sharing a quick smile with her mother, Maggie handed over the bag to Lee.

"What's that?" said Lee, pretending surprise at the sight of the bag.

"It's yours," Maggie said quickly, eyes lighting as she and Lee played a game that was as old as her memories.

"But I've never seen it before," said Lee, a smile playing around the corners of his mouth.

"It was in your pocket."

"Was it?"

"Sí."

Lee shook his head, perplexed. "Then the Good Fairy must have put it there for you."

That was the cue Maggie had been waiting for. She opened the bag eagerly. Even before she peered inside, a distinctive fragrance enveloped her.

"Chocolate!" breathed Maggie.

"Are you sure, *niña?*" teased Lee.

Maggie dug into the bag and came out with a piece of chocolate the size of her thumb. She held the candy under his nose.

"See? Chocolate."

'You're absolutely certain?" asked Lee gravely. "Perhaps you'd better find your cousins and ask them what they think."

"Do I have to share?"

Cira flicked her finger against the bulging bag. *"Sí,"* said Cira firmly. "There is enough there for all of your cousins."

"All?" wailed Maggie.

"Well," Cira said, hiding a smile. "there is at least enough for tia Juana's children."

Maggie hesitated, then accepted the compromise; aunt Yolanda had even more children than aunt Juana.

"Can I do the dividing?" pressed Maggie.

Lee laughed aloud, approving of Maggie's pragmatism. Maggie flashed him a conspirator's smile.

"Of course," agreed Cira serenely. "You divide—and your cousins choose first."

Maggie looked crestfallen. Lee peered into the open bag and fished around until he came up with what was obviously the biggest chunk of chocolate in the bag.

"Open up, *niña*," he said, smiling. He popped the chocolate into her mouth. "There. That will make the dividing easier, won't it?"

Unable to speak, Maggie nodded so vigorously that her long black braids bounced.

"Now," said Cira, tugging gently at a flying braid, "run over to tia Juana. She has dinner ready for you, and little Yolanda wants you to read stories to her tonight."

"Can I stay all night?" asked Maggie eagerly.

"*Sí, niña,*" said Cira, kissing her daughter's cheek.

Maggie started to run out of the door, then stopped, sensing that as soon as she left, Lee and her mother would talk about important things. In spite of Lee's reassurances, Jaime's words still echoed in Maggie's mind. But the lure of a night in the rowdy give-and-take of the Zavala family was too great to resist.

"Will you be here tomorrow?" Maggie asked Lee with sudden intensity.

"Yes," said Lee, bending down to the girl whose feelings were reflected by changing hazel eyes. "I promise you."

"Thank you," she said, giving him a sticky chocolate kiss.

"You're welcome," said Lee, not knowing whether she had thanked him for the candy or for promising to be there tomorrow.

Maggie ran out the front door, not even pausing to grab the jacket Jaime had loaned to her to wear while her own coat dried out. She ran across the yard with long steps, leaping puddles turned molten orange by the falling sun. Overhead, clouds raced and piled up against the eastern mountains.

"She's a wonderful child," said Lee quietly, drawing Cira close. "Thank you."

Cira pulled his arms even more closely around her and

leaned against him, wondering if this was the moment to tell him.

"She's as much yours as mine," said Cira, smiling. "So thank yourself."

Cira hesitated, but the sudden tension in Lee's body told her that she must wait; now was not the time to tell Lee that she was pregnant. She realized that the hands covering hers were cold and remembered that she had seen Lee shiver.

"Come into the kitchen," she said quickly.

Lee let go of her and bent to struggle with his muddy boots.

"Damn the boots!" she said in sudden exasperation. "Getting you warm is more important than clean floors."

Cira found herself swept off of her feet, her body held high by Lee's strength.

"I love you, Cira Pico McCartney Vasconcellos."

Cira laughed with him and buried her fingers in hair that was still thick and the color of the sun.

"Love me in the kitchen, hombre. It's warmer there."

She saw Lee's eyes change and she laughed with the excitement that was as potent now as it had been the first time Lee had made love to her high on a mountaintop. Lee felt the indefinable melting that brought her body closer to his. He whispered her name and his love for her, held her as though she were warmth slipping through his fingers.

"You're shivering," said Cira, concerned again.

"Haven't you ever heard of a man trembling with desire?"

"Yes," she shot back. "But your body is too cold to be on fire. Come."

Lee put down Cira and followed her into the kitchen. There, a wood stove radiated warmth throughout the big room. On top of the stove, a coffeepot and a large kettle sent fragrant steam into the air. While Lee peeled off his damp coat, Cira found a blanket for him. When she returned to the kitchen, she pulled a chair close to the stove and then poured Lee a mug of hot coffee laced with brandy. With strong fingers, she smoothed away the deep lines of his frown.

"Drink that, my love. There is thick soup and hot bread if you're hungry."

Lee sipped slowly at the coffee, relaxing as the stove's heat and Cira's hands loosened muscles knotted by tension. With an unconscious sigh, he closed his eyes, luxuriating in her tangible concern for his well-being. He brushed his lips across the fingers that were kneading his shoulders and neck. He and Cira had sat together in this kitchen almost daily, discussing the intricacies of his ranch and his plans. Many times her quick intelligence had seen solutions before he had; he often teased her, saying that her Pico blood bound her to the land more closely than he was bound by money and dreams. There was a deep trust between Lee and Cira that was the most essential part of their relationship. As always, Lee marveled that the beautiful woman, who could have had any man, chose to have him. And never complained of the cost.

"I don't deserve you," Lee said quietly.

"I know, but you're stuck with me anyhow," said Cira, deliberately misunderstanding him.

Lee smiled crookedly, but the smile slowly faded. Cira could follow his thoughts by the deepening lines of his frown. After a long time of silence, he set the empty coffee mug aside, opened the blanket and pulled Cira into his lap. When he was finished wrapping up again, the blanket made a loose cocoon around both of them.

"Did Gil call?" said Lee, his eyes seeing beyond the gray twilight enfolding the kitchen in a darkness that was more comforting than light.

"Yes," said Cira, looking up at Lee's profile, thinking that time had reinforced rather than ruined the strong lines of his face. "He called, then Juana called. They told me Marjorie's father had died and that somehow his death gave her control of your ranch. Gil guessed that Marjorie would use that against us, that she would force you to choose between me and the land."

"Gil guessed right," said Lee heavily. His laugh was

263

humorless and short. "Gil was against my marriage to Marjorie. I should have listened to him. God, how I should have listened."

"Lee . . ." Cira's voice thinned and she closed her eyes. "Don't give up your land for me. I'd rather be alone than watch you grow to hate me because you gave up your land for me."

Lee's mouth closed over Cira's in a fierce kiss.

"I'll hear no more of that," he said when he finally lifted his lips. "I lost you once because of the land. I won't lose you again."

Cira's lips were soft against his work-scarred hands. When he felt her separate tears hot on his palms, he kissed her tenderly. Then the words that had been burning his throat came out in a hoarse rush.

"There's a price, Cira. I don't know if it's too high."

He looked at her with transparent eyes that were haunted by the knowledge of choices and consequences.

"Tell me," said Cira.

"I can never give Maggie my name or my land."

"But I never expected you to," said Cira simply. What I have, and what you have given to Maggie, is more than enough for her."

"There's more," said Lee, his voice reflecting his pain. "I can't ever tell anyone I'm Maggie's father. Not even her. My own child. Never."

"Maggie . . . Maggie has never asked about her father. It's as though she knows." Cira frowned, catching her lower lip between her teeth. "Sometimes she knows too much for a child; it's as though she reads my mind, all my sorrows and pleasures. But," said Cira, unconsciously bracing herself, "that isn't important now. What else must you do?"

"Isn't that enough?" said Lee bitterly. "I wanted to give the land to you and Maggie. I had it all planned."

"But your son!" said Cira, shocked.

"My son." The rancor in Lee's voice made Cira flinch. "My son will neither need nor want my land. His grandfather's wealth should finish the job of ruining Champ that his mother has begun so well." Lee made a sound deep in his throat. "I have a son I don't care to acknowledge and a daughter I can't acknowledge. Wouldn't you call that an adequate revenge for Marjorie?"

There was only one answer to the bitterness in Lee's question. Cira kissed him slowly, until a desire as intense as any she had ever known shook her. Suddenly she wanted him—now, here, immediately. She moved her hands beneath the blanket and Lee forgot everything but the warm weight of her in his lap. His hand slid beneath her dress until there was nothing between them but love.

Cira's wordless cries were soft, but they covered the tiny sounds Maggie made while she retreated across the living room, clutching the jacket she had forgotten in one hand and the bag of candy in the other. She had returned for the jacket, and stayed to listen.

Noiselessly, Maggie let herself out into the twilight. Though her teeth were bared with the force of her effort not to cry, two tears slid from beneath her lashes. As long as she could remember, she had told herself that the Pico land, Lee's land, would someday be hers, that she would reign like a queen above the colonia children who hurled epithets at her and her mother. But that dream was gone now, snatched away and given to the soft, pale boy she had never seen and always hated.

Maggie slipped through the twilight, planning ways of getting even, trying not to cry, hating the thick taste of chocolate that threatened to overwhelm her.

1937

Clear water brimmed over the edge of the head-high round concrete standpipe and made a musical descent into dark furrows running between rows of orange trees so green they were almost black. Against the dense foliage, pale orange globes ripened by the hundreds on thousands of trees. The sun had almost completed its work; soon the pickers would begin theirs.

Magdalena McCartney leaned back in the rump-sprung seat of an eight-year-old roadster. She thought about the coming harvest while she let wind from the open window play through her shoulder-length hair. The sultry heat and the silky air were familiar, but the landscape was different, like an echo returning, changed in ways both profound and subtle.

In the nineteen years since she had left San Ignacio, scattered groves had expanded, touched, interlocked until they were a fragrant green carpet flung over a once-wild, once-dry land. There were groves everywhere, irrigated by water from the distant Owens Valley. The trees were taller, stronger, greener than she had remembered. Their scent was almost tangible, an overriding fact like sunlight and heat and dark furrows glinting with water. Yet for all the changes, Maggie recognized the land. She could remember when some of the groves had been planted. She had been here before, long ago, when her mother and Lee Buckles went for Sunday drives and brought her down this road to see trees that were shorter than she was, their skinny trunks wrapped in white butcher paper to protect the delicate grafts.

Valencia grafted onto Mandarin . . . after all these years she remembered that. Watching the groves unfurl on either side of the road, other memories returned to Maggie, sensations that she had thought lost to time. The scent and sound and lacy beauty of jacaranda trees. The dry, hot presence of sand between her toes, the softness of the ground as she ran barefoot along the path from her mother's house to her aunt's, the path she had worn, the path her mother had worn before her, the path Andrew had followed after her, always running as hard as he could, always with that serious look on his face, intent on keeping up with his long-legged sister. Never once had he complained or asked her to wait. He simply pumped and ran and kept so much within himself. Little gray-eyed brother, the only person left for whom Maggie gave a single, solitary damn.

Two mourning doves flashed out of the grove, zigzagging along the pavement, moving their bodies with the abrupt grace that was unique to doves. Their tails flashed white wedges as the birds darted into the roadway ahead of the car, perilously close to the windshield.

"Watch out!" said Maggie.

"What?" The driver's response was slow and confused. "Where?"

"*Las palomas,* the doves," said Maggie, watching the birds gain the safety of another grove. "You almost hit two doves."

The driver frowned. He was an earnest Mexican youth whose slowness was equaled by his strength and surpassed by his devotion to Maggie.

"I am sorry," he said, looking around uncertainly. "I did not see them."

His chagrin was so apparent that Maggie impulsively reached out to touch his shoulder.

"It was nothing, Roberto. The birds just startled me."

Roberto smiled shyly. Although he had been born seventeen years ago in a San Joaquin Valley labor camp, he often seemed more like a boy from the rural interior of Mexico than a native American. But three weeks before, in a melon field near El Centro, he had thrown himself in front of Maggie, taking a blow from a highway patrolman's nightstick that had been meant for her. Roberto bore a livid scar across his forehead, a memento of that experience. He also bore his heart on his sleeve for the beautiful woman who had organized the melon strike.

At one time, Maggie would have been embarrassed or angered by such open devotion, but she had discovered that her beauty was a weapon, if she did not use it, others would. It was a lesson she had learned almost two decades ago, on Paris's Left Bank, when her communist lover had dangled her in front of wealthy ideological dilettantes whom he was incapable of moving with his rhetoric.

In the shattering years between fourteen and twenty, Maggie had come to terms with her effect on men. She often thought to herself that there were four kinds of men: those who were disoriented by her presence; those who were destroyed; those who were haunted; and those who were blind. She had left her communist lover before she categorized him, but she had not left the ideology he had introduced her to. The communist movement answered the outrage that came to her when she thought of one man owning so much land while thousands of men went hungry in a Great Depression brought on by criminal greed.

With a smile that was no less haunting for its cynicism, Maggie listened in her head to the sound of phrases taken from her past speeches. If her beauty had got her into the all-male, high-stakes power game of organizing California agricultural labor, her intelligence had kept her there. She used her beauty without compunction, charming reporters until her picture appeared in newspapers, until she became known as the "Workers' Magdalene," symbol of an entire movement. As a result of her notoriety, she was beginning to receive state-wide recognition from union organizers.

Maggie had learned that symbols were more important than truth. Though the San Ignacio fruit pickers were only a fractional percentage of California's agricultural laborers, growers and union organizers alike had chosen to make San Ignacio a test in the organization of citrus pickers: as San Ignacio went, so went the rest of the state. Like two ancient enemies eager for blood, the fact of the impending battle was more important to both growers and union than was the territory over which they ostensibly fought.

Because of the ramifications of the battle, the organizers had put one of their most compelling symbols at the head of their battle column—the woman they knew only as Magdalena. None of the leaders who had agreed on her presence in San Ignacio knew that she had been born there, that her unacknowledged father was Lee Buckles and that her younger brother was Lee's son in all but name.

None of the organizers knew those things, but Maggie did. As she rode in the old car, she wondered how she could deal with Lee Buckles if she came face to face with him. It had been so long since she had spoken to him, so long since her mother had died . . . too long for anything but bitterness to survive. There were times when she wondered if even that remained, if anything remained of her life but the cloying taste of chocolate.

The car swerved suddenly, making a wide arc around a dove perched on a furrow at least six feet beyond the side of the road. Roberto turned to Maggie with a wide, white smile.

"I missed it."

Maggie bit back a sarcastic comment about the only thing she really wanted him to miss—the car that was coming straight down the road at them. By the time Roberto returned to his proper lane, Maggie realized that the oncoming vehicle was a patrol car.

The swerve had attracted the sheriff's attention. Maggie watched as the patrol car passed slowly. Out of the corner of her eye she saw a face turned to look over the car and its occupants. She knew without turning her head that the sheriff would come after them; they were strange Mexicans in a county where war had been declared between Anglo growers and Mexican pickers.

Roberto glanced in the mirror and realized that the patrol car had turned to overtake him. Fear spread across his blunt features like water spilled across a floor, quickly, leaving behind a damp sheen.

"Roberto," said Maggie gently, reading panic in the grip of his hands on the wheel. "He doesn't know who we are." She heard the sound of a siren, high and urgent, a sound like fear. "Roberto. Listen to me. You must do exactly as he says. Don't give him any excuse to take us to jail. Do you understand, Roberto? We must not go to jail."

Maggie reached over and shook Roberto's arm with a gentleness that spoke well for her self-control. Roberto shuddered and pulled his eyes away from the winking red light in his rearview mirror. He drove the car onto the side of the road and parked on the narrow grass shoulder.

The instant that air no longer poured through the window, heat closed over Roberto and Maggie like a cage. Perspiration gathered on her face and slid down between her breasts, perspiration that came as much from fear as from heat. The single glimpse she had caught of the sheriff had been enough to take her back to her childhood. But she suppressed the fear that clawed inside her; if Roberto sensed how close she was to panic, he would be useless.

"If he asks, tell him I'm your sister," she said to Roberto in a low voice. "We're on our way to San Diego. *Comprende? Su hermana.*"

Roberto hesitated, hands working nervously on the wheel. Then he nodded slowly.

"Sister."

"*Sí.* And whatever you do, don't speak to me. I don't want to look toward you. I don't want him to see my face. If you ignore me, he might."

"*Sí.*"

Maggie waited for the sheriff with outward calm, but with every step the man took, she was more certain that she had identified him correctly. More certain, and more afraid. She was grateful that she had spent most of the summer in the fields, organizing the *braceros,* for California's fierce sun had turned her skin deep brown. So long as she hid her eyes, it would never occur to the sheriff that she was not every bit as Indio as Roberto. She slumped in the seat, rounding her shoulders and letting her tangled hair hide her face.

Sheriff Reginald Heer paused by the side of his car. The flashing red light swept across his eyes, eyes as blue and hard as his father's had been before a lifetime of defeat had faded his father into insignificance. With an automatic motion, the sheriff hitched up his heavy gunbelt and walked through the stifling heat, his right hand resting on the butt of his sidearm. Though he lacked his father's shrewd insight into human weaknesses, Sheriff Heer had had enough experience with violence to sense its presence in the county. Lately, his hand had rarely been far from his gun.

When Sheriff Heer reached the window on the driver's side of the car, he put a foot on the running board, leaned over and thrust forward his heavy, flushed face.

"I don't know where you come from, Mex," said Sheriff Heer, his voice deep and impersonally contemptuous, "but around here, we don't let Mexicans start drinking until it's too dark to pick oranges."

A pulse beat rapidly in Roberto's throat, making blood pound painfully through his scarred forehead. But the scar was invisible; Maggie had tumbled his hair over his face, hiding the recent wound that would have aroused official curiosity.

"Let's see your license," said the sheriff irritably, wishing he were in the patrol car and going fast enough to blunt the claws of heat.

Roberto looked at Sheriff Heer with eyes that showed fear and the beginning of an anger born of helplessness. Slowly, Roberto reached into his hip pocket for a worn leather wallet. He pulled out the wallet and removed a frayed card that certified his ability to drive. Sheriff Heer looked casually at the license, then flipped it into Roberto's lap.

"Okay, Mex. How much did you have to drink?"

"Nada."

"Speak English. I'm no goddam greaser."

"I have not had anything to drink," said Roberto carefully, flattening his accent as much as possible.

"Then why in hell were you weaving all over the road?"

"I wanted to miss the dove."

"A bird. You nearly run me off the road for a fucking bird. Jesus." Sheriff Heer shifted the hot weight of his gunbelt. "Okay, Mex. Now you can tell my why you're in Moreno County when your license says you live north of Bakersfield."

Roberto sank back into his seat. "I'm going to San Diego with my sister," he said, adding a quick "sir," as an afterthought. "My family lives there now."

Sheriff Heer hesitated, then decided to accept the boy's words. Roberto looked too scared and too stupid to be much trouble, even if he were lying.

"Just so you aren't one of those communists," sighed the sheriff.

While Roberto shifted nervously, Sheriff Heer lifted his hat, wiped his forehead, and thought of nursing a cold beer in a cool bar. As he pulled his hat back in place, he looked across Roberto to Maggie. She was sitting quietly, eyes lowered, face slack, doing her best imitation of a shy, submissive Mexican woman. She was silently praying that neither her picture in the papers nor her presence in the car would jog the sheriff's memory.

Sheriff Heer looked at Maggie again, caught by some indefinable sense of her presence, but he was too hot and she was too disheveled for him to connect her with the arrogant beauty of the "Workers' Magdalene" or the nineteen-year-old memory of being humiliated by Lee Buckles's beautiful Mexican bastard.

But even Maggie's stillness and the sheriff's impatience and the relative gloom inside the car could not wholly dis-

272

guise her unique allure. Sheriff Heer leaned in a bit further, smiling with an invitation that was just short of a leer.

"How'd a pretty thing like you get such an ugly brother?"

Maggie ducked her head, praying he would look no closer, silently cursing the beauty that could never be wholly disguised. Seeing that he would get nowhere, Sheriff Heer withdrew his face and his smile.

"Stay there," he snapped, pushing away from the car.

As soon as the sheriff's back was turned, Roberto's hand twitched toward the starter.

"No! Don't be a fool!"

Maggie's hissed command stopped Roberto. The two of them waited, dripping sweat, listening to water rushing down furrows, hearing the equally liquid sound of mourning doves concealed in the citrus on either side of the narrow road. In a few minutes Sheriff Heer returned. He looked into the window again, his head nearly touching Roberto's.

"You're clean," said Sheriff Heer slowly, his eyes probing but still missing the truth of Maggie's identity. "Nobody's stopped you in this county before. This is your free one. Next time you're stopped, we'll just have to assume that you're one of those communists trying to stir up trouble." Sheriff Heer's cold smile narrowed his eyes into splinters of deep blue. "In other words, Mex, if you're passing through, pass through. If you aren't passing through, you're in a world of trouble. Around here, we grind up troublesome greasers and use them to fertilize oranges."

Sheriff Heer straightened abruptly and turned on his heel. His thick-shouldered body slid into the patrol car with surprising ease. In spite of his beer belly, the sheriff retained much of the strength and coordination of the athlete he had once been. The engine of the patrol car raced, the red light switched off, and gravel spun from beneath the wheels.

Maggie watched the patrol car's departure with hard eyes. She had recognized the sheriff, even if he had not recognized her. Nineteen years ago she had humiliated Reggie Heer, publicly and repeatedly, with disastrous results. It had happened at high school, out in the muddy yard where students gathered to gossip and flirt. That day was one she had tried to forget, but had never succeeded.

She had been almost out of control that day, driven by an unfocused fear. Her mother was ill, had been ill all winter, her beauty inhumanly refined by chronic fevers. The last few days had been the worst. Sometimes she seemed not to recognize her children, though she always seemed to know Lee. He came and went without warning, bringing a succession of doctors and medicines that eased but did not cure her.

Even little Andrew had sensed the world changing. He sat near his mother's bed, motionless, saying nothing, watching her as if she would vanish if she were not reflected in the gray eyes of her son. Maggie shared her little brother's irrational fear, but she could not stay that close, could not watch her mother's restless burning, her unrecognizing eyes.

Maggie had fled to school, consumed by a fear she would not name. Even her boyfriend Jaime Zavala could not reach past her fear to comfort her. Reggie Heer, watching as he had for two years, had seen Maggie's new wildness, a brilliant edge to the beauty that reduced him to helpless desire. Reggie approached Maggie as he had done so many times before, standing too close to her, his desire as blunt as his features. Maggie focused her anger on him as though he were responsible for Cira's illness.

In the past Maggie had treated Reggie with casual cruelty, calculating his vulnerability with a sure instinct that was older than her years. But that day she forgot everything except the need to lash out, to hurt someone as she herself was being hurt. She taunted Reggie with her contempt for him, told him without mercy that he was a failure in every way, and most especially he was a failure as a man.

At first Reggie bore the searing phrases in silence, but that did not appease her. She berated him until his famous temper outstripped his control. He grabbed her,

274

bruising her with a strength that had been hardened on the football field. Almost as soon as his hands closed on her, she twisted away with a speed that shocked him, clawing his face until blood welled beneath her fingers. Even her quickness would not have saved her from a beating, though, had not Jaime interceded. Jaime, as slim as Reggie was strong . . . it was Jaime Zavala who took the brunt of Reggie's rage.

What followed was too one-sided to be called a fight. When Reggie was finally dragged off of Jaime, Maggie knelt beside her boyfriend, staring at the caricature that had once been a handsome face. She felt his blood, warm and thick on her hands, mixing with the blood she had drawn from Reggie's face. She called Jaime's name, apologizing, but he was too dazed to hear.

Maggie had run then, afraid of Reggie and of herself, afraid of the beauty that had cost Jaime too much. She ran home, wanting to be comforted by Cira's understanding words. But there was nothing at home, not even recognition. Cira was worse. Her skin was unbelievably hot, her body continually stirring with small, random motions.

No one noticed Maggie; not Andrew, not the nurse, not even Lee when he came in and took the cold cloths from the nurse's hands. Maggie watched while Lee cared for her mother with a gentleness he had never shown to another person. Cira's restless movements gradually stilled and her body relaxed. Though Cira's eyes did not open, Maggie was certain that her mother had sensed Lee's presence. Abruptly, Maggie left the room, resenting bonds that she could not understand and refused to share.

Maggie returned to her mother's room again and again that day. Each time Lee was there, watching Cira with an intensity that frightened Maggie. Gil came to take her and Andrew home, but Maggie could not bear to be in the same house with Jaime. Jaime was wrapped in bandages, his face hidden from all but her memory, a memory as destructive as her beauty, as merciless as the fever that was taking away her mother.

Maggie had stolen back to her own house in the hour

after midnight. She had stood in the doorway to her mother's room and watched with eyes that understood too little, and too much. Cira seemed to be neither asleep nor awake. Her head was turned toward Lee and her breathing was as thick as blood. Gently, Lee gathered Cira in his arms, supporting her so that breathing would be less difficult.

Maggie watched them until she could no longer keep her eyes open. She sank to the floor and slept. When she awoke her heart was hammering and Lee's harsh cry was echoing in her ears. Maggie realized that she could not hear her mother's ragged breathing.

For a moment Maggie thought that her mother was better, then Maggie saw Lee's face and sensed the final stillness of her mother in Lee's arms.

Time had taken neither clarity nor pain from Maggie's memories of that one day when childhood had shattered. She had buried her memories beneath layers of sophistication and experience, like cotton wrapped around broken glass. But never wrapped well enough, for every time she remembered she was cut until she bled.

Maggie pressed the heels of her hands against her forehead as though that would push back the painful memories.

"Are you all right?" asked Roberto anxiously, watching her more closely than he watched the road.

Maggie's head jerked upright, as though she were surprised to find herself in a car with a boy who had no part of her memories.

"*Sí,*" Maggie said. "I'm fine."

"Are you sure?"

"Nothing is wrong," she said tonelessly. "*Absolutamente nada.*"

In worried silence, Roberto drove the car through the stifling heat.

Across the flatlands from the dusty roadster, Andrew McCartney lounged in the shade of latticework construction that created an extensive overhang for the Buckles Depot Store. The air was hot, motionless, but less sultry than in the depths of the irrigated groves. Algerian ivy had overgrown the latticework, lending leafy coolness to the area beneath. Andrew tipped his straight-backed chair onto its rear legs, rocking back and forth with uncanny balance, watching sunlight reflecting off of the water spilling down a standpipe across the road. The clear water tumbled down concrete into an intricate system of furrows that watered forty acres of young tomato plants. The air and the day were so still that Andrew could hear the water mumbling to itself as it hurried along dark furrows.

Water held special meaning for Andrew; through all his twenty-six years, he had been fascinated by water, by its uses and its fluid beauty. The miracle of water in a dry land still fascinated him. He came by that fascination instinctively, but instinct had been nurtured by Lee Buckles, whose quiet musings and pointed questions had both informed and honed Andrew's intelligence.

Andrew grew up with a knowledge of water's importance. He had been born in 1911, the year that the preliminary survey had begun on the bold project to bring water to Southern California. Some of Andrew's earliest memories were of hours spent with Lee, riding the ranch on horseback, and the state in Lee's cars, listening to Lee's soft voice describe the consummation of a dream, watching the slow, incredible growth of reservoirs, aqueducts, underground pipes and broad culverts that had transformed Southern California's landscape and future.

The Buckles Ranch became one of the most fertile and profitable agricultural holdings in a state famed for the wealth and diversity of its crops.

With water had come growth and, inevitably, more and different problems. At this moment, the most intractable problem centered in the citrus groves that looked like distant, dark-green water from Andrew's vantage point beneath a canopy of ivy. He rocked absently, waiting for Lee, waiting and drinking a bottle of beer so cold that it made his teeth ache. He drained the last drop of beer, returned the chair to four legs with a snap, and stretched.

Andrew was tall, though not so tall as his father, and well muscled in the manner of a man who had grown up with hard work. His hair was dark and thick and his eyes, Lee's eyes, burned with a hard, searching intelligence. The nearly black hair and compact body were his legacy from his mother; in most other ways, he was Lee's son. Where Andrew was not tanned by wind and sun, he was as pale as his father. Like Lee, he walked with complete assurance, a feline certainty of where he was in relation to his surroundings.

The resemblance between Lee and Andrew was more profound than the merely physical. They thought alike to the point that their communication often consisted of half sentences and companionable silences.

Andrew's relationship with his father was as untroubled as Maggie's was volatile. When Cira had died of pneumonia in the wet spring of 1919, Maggie had taken death as a personal attack. Her anger, the anger of an abandoned teen-ager too old to cry and not old enough to understand, had increased even after she and Andrew moved in with Gil and his huge, loving family. She would sit alone for hours, leaning against the jacaranda's smooth trunk, watching the house that had been her mother's, returning to Gil's house only when driven by cold or hunger.

Andrew, more bewildered than angered by his mother's death, had been shut out by his adored older sister. He had turned to Lee, and Lee had been there, always, holding the small boy who wept for both of them. As Andrew grew closer to Lee, Maggie's self-made exile closed around her with a seamless bitterness that was impervious to human emotions or human needs.

Maggie had left home after high school, and had returned only a few times since. Her education at the University of California, the Sorbonne and the less formal institution of the Left Bank, had removed her from the unresolved angers of her childhood. Her growing involvement with communism, then with union organizing, then with improving the lives of Mexican field workers, had all served to reinforce her renunciation of her childhood. She lived with slogans and anger, an anger whose source she never admitted to herself, but which inevitably divided her from the father she had once loved and never named.

278

On Maggie's infrequent trips home, it was only Andrew she saw, only Andrew she spoke to, only Andrew she permitted herself to love. Nor did they discuss the man she called "Mr. Buckles." The one time Andrew had tried to find the reason for her estrangement from Lee, Maggie had exploded in a bitter torrent of words, blaming Lee for everything, including her mother's death.

Andrew walked the length of the shaded overhang, thinking of his angry, beautiful, foolish older sister; thinking of her was better than thinking of how he would tell Lee the bad news that was spreading across the ranch faster than irrigation water. Just once, Andrew would have liked to tell Lee something good about Maggie.

Even worse, whenever Andrew thought of Maggie today, his instincts stirred with a warning as clear, as primal as the lifting of hairs on the back of his neck. Yet for all its force, the warning was enigmatic, offering no course of action other than an uneasy waiting.

Andrew returned to the chair and to watching water tumble from standpipe to furrows, a scene framed by his muddy boots propped up on a crate of oranges. He had spent the morning out on the ranch, walking the rows and talking to the men, speaking easily in English or Spanish, talking of crops and work and weather. The subject of the strike came up only tangentially, for both Lee and Andrew were well liked and respected by most of the men.

In spite of that, Andrew had come out of the fields and groves with the certainty that the Buckles crews would follow the lead of other pickers and field hands; they would strike. The Buckles workers would not strike from any particular animus for their employer, but from their visceral belief that the strike would be more successful than any of the previous ones had been. Workers who did not go out would face reprisals from their friends, reprisals even more serious than whatever might come from their employer.

With a hollow thump, Andrew brought his feet together, knocking crusts of mud off of his boots. He knew Lee would not be surprised by the workers' decision to strike. Of all the growers, Lee was most able to grasp the international, national, local and purely personal pressures his workers were subject to. Lee would understand, but he would hardly be pleased.

Sighing, Andrew stood again, picked up his empty beer bottle and walked inside. He returned the long-necked bottle to the clerk who waited behind the counter with the sour patience of a barrelful of pickles. Before Andrew had time to buy another beer, he saw a flash of color out of the corner of his eye.

A bright yellow convertible came to a dust-raising stop in front of the store. Though the car was one he had never before seen, Andrew immediately recognized the erect figure of Lee Buckles sitting on th passenger side of the car. Lee's vaguely ill at ease, obviously patient expression was the result of his dislike of being in a car driven by anyone other than Andrew or himself. Nearly last on his list of preferred drivers was his only grandchild, Christina Babcock Buckles.

Smiling, Andrew pulled on a battered straw hat and waited outside where sunlight poured into an unseasonably hot afternoon. The smile on Andrew's face was similar to the one he had worn sixteen years ago when Lee had presented his charming, toothless granddaughter to his charming bastard son. She had grabbed Andrew's finger in her tiny fist, crowed happily, and looked at him with extraordinary purple eyes.

Like another very young man more than a half-century ago, Andrew had been entranced by an amethyst gaze. Carrington could have warned Andrew of the dangers of childhood attachments, but Carrington was dead; and had he been alive, he would never have spoken to Andrew on any subject at all.

In spite of Joy's militant hatred of Andrew—or perhaps because of it—Christina spent the first seven years of her life following Andrew around at every opportunity. Lee, Andrew and Christina became a common sight on the ranch; Lee astride one of the tall Tennessee Walkers he still loved to ride, and Andrew, with Christina in front of him, riding one of the agile quarter-horses he handled

280

so skillfully. During the rainy season, the three often would ride together in one of Lee's cars. Lee drove, pointing out everything from circling eagles to the level of water in a check dam. Beside him, Andrew would sit quietly, listening, resting his chin on Christina's fair head as she sat on his lap in preference to the superior comfort of the car seat.

Eventually, three became two. Andrew went away to school, earning degrees in both business and agriculture. His studies were followed by a twenty-month tour of Europe. The tour was required by Lee, who wanted Andrew to avoid the parochialism that often seemed endemic to America. Time and distance had accomplished what Joy's ultimatums had not: when Andrew finally returned home to stay, the fourteen-year-old Christina seemed to have forgotten her childhood idol.

Christina and Andrew rarely saw each other now. When they did, both seemed unsure how to treat the other. It was as though their past attachment was a river flowing blindly into the present, a river alive with currents that Christina was too naïve to see and that Andrew chose not to acknowledge, much less explore.

Despite this, Andrew was smiling as he approached the car; his affection for Christina was as much a part of him as his memories.

"Good afternoon, Lee. Hi, Sunshine," he said to Christina, smiling widely and using a nickname that he had not used in years.

"Hi," said Christina softly, in a voice that was a feminine version of Lee's. She was startled by Andrew's smile; he was so different when he smiled, so intense. Like lightning. She realized that she was staring at him and blushed. "Do you like my new car?" she said quickly. "Daddy just bought it for me."

Andrew's smoke-gray eyes flicked over the flashy car. It was just the kind of toy that Champ would give to his already spoiled daughter.

"Bright, isn't it," said Andrew in a noncommittal tone. Christina pouted, forgetting that of all the people she knew, both Andrew and her grandfather were immune to that particular weapon.

"Grandfather doesn't really approve," she said, turning toward Lee. "Grandfather is the only one who doesn't approve of everything I do."

"Oh?" said Lee, cocking an eyebrow in Andrew's direction.

"I meant family," said Christina in exasperation.

Lee pulled off his hat, a tan Stetson that was his summer trademark. He fixed Christina with a look that time had not softened. "I've said nothing against your mode of transportation. That's a matter between your father and his rather elastic conscience. But thank you for bringing me here. I know it was out of your way."

Christina's face lost most of the petulance that had blurred its clean lines. For a moment, she looked younger than her years, more vulnerable than any sixteen-year-old should be.

"You don't have to say anything against the car, Grandfather. I can tell. Does it matter that I didn't even ask for this? Daddy just gave it to me."

What Christina did not add was that the gift was an apology from Champ for being too drunk to attend his daughter's sixteenth birthday party.

"I know, child," said Lee softly. He smiled as she bridled at being called a child. "And I also know that you can drive better than the sample you just gave me." He squeezed her hand. "I want you to outlive me, Christina."

Christina returned the squeeze, her eyes sparkling with emotion; he was the only member of her family who touched her. "I'll be more careful, Grandfather Lee."

Andrew watched and realized that Lee's approval was the one thing in the world that mattered to Christina. Everything else came to her without effort, and often without even desire.

"Thank you," murmured Lee. He lifted his hand and stroked her hair, hair that stirred in the wind like pale flames. She was a stunning amalgam of Joy and Lee and Champ, owing little to the mother she rarely saw. Lee smiled again, approving of Christina's vivid young beauty. "Take care of yourself, Sunshine."

Christina felt sudden tears burn behind her eyes. She leaned over and hugged the man she loved more than her father.

"You take care of yourself too," she said almost fiercely. When she released Lee she turned on Andrew. "Does he have to go with you? It's too hot to be working. Remember what happened two summers ago when . . ."

Christina's voice faded. She did not want to remember two summers ago when Lee had been so ill.

"The Growers' League is having a meeting this afternoon," said Andrew, knowing what Christina was thinking about and not liking the memory any better than she did. "Everyone with any pull in the county will be there, discussing how best to turn the tide of Red Communism."

Andrew did not bother to hide the contempt in his voice.

"You don't sound impressed," said Christina accusingly, remembering her father's lectures on the evils of communism.

"Unions aren't the end of the world."

"Daddy says they are. He says we ought to treat union organizers and communists like we used to treat Mex horse thieves—string them up. He says this is the only part of the country where we have greasy brown Reds. He says—"

"Your father," interrupted Lee dryly, "has more opinions of less value than a political rally."

Lee opened the door of the convertible. With a speed and grace that proclaimed Andrew's relation to Lee more clearly than any birth certificate, Andrew moved around the car to hold the door open for Lee. Lee climbed out with apparent ease, moving very well for a man who would be seventy-four in December. But Andrew noted the subtle hesitation and less subtle stiffness that had come to Lee in the last few years. With a mixture of sorrow and helpless anger, Andrew realized that Lee was succumbing to the depredations of time.

The anger came from helplessness, the sadness from

283

having to watch Lee die by fractions, a bit each month, each week, each day, until Lee would be gone and Andrew would be alone in a world where he had no one and nothing except the land—the land that would belong to Lee's other son.

As though he sensed Andrew's thoughts, Lee's gray eyes met and held those of his son. Lee smiled slowly, sadly, sharing the helplessness.

"Are you going to the meeting dressed like that?" said Christina into the silence that seemed to exclude her. Her eyes traveled over Andrew's blue work shirt, the jeans that stretched over his muscular legs and his mud-encrusted boots. "The growers are likely to take you for a Mexican spy, what with your dark hair and muddy boots and tan."

Andrew shot Christina a quick look, but saw only the innocence of a child-woman who knew no more about Andrew's parents than she did about the engine that drove her shiny new toy.

"When I went to the most important business appointment of my life," said Lee mildly, "I was dressed a good deal more roughly than that. David Carrington saw past the clothes."

"I was just kidding," Christina objected. "Nobody would mistake Andrew for a Red. He's much too handsome," she added, looking at Andrew with a frank appreciation that surprised both men. For an instant her eyes were knowing rather than innocent. Then she flushed and said defensively to Lee, "Well, he is! Except for the flecks of gold, his eyes are just like yours, beautiful, and"—Christina's voice faded as she looked between the two men—"and he's just handsome. Is that such an awful thing for me to say?"

"Just don't say it to anyone else," said Lee dryly, imagining Joy's reaction if she heard.

"Oh," said Christina, obviously remembering her grandmother. "I won't. But I don't understand why Grandmama Joy is so mean about Andrew. What did he ever do to her?"

284

Without waiting for an answer—or even expecting one—Christina put the car into reverse, backed up, shifted into low and accelerated down the road without so much as a backward look.

"She's a good child," mused Lee aloud. "But she's on the edge of a very complicated world."

Andrew smiled ironically while he lifted his hat and ran his hand over his hair. "She's not the only one. The world just got a little more complicated for all of us. I finally found out who's going to lead the workers out of the fields."

Slowly, Lee turned and faced Andrew. In the years since Cira's death, Lee's face had thinned and tightened until his weathered skin stretched over the uncompromising bones of his face. Like an aging hawk, Lee's power was in his eyes, and in reflexes that had not yet lost the habit of strength.

"Maggie?" asked Lee softly, fear and regret moving in his transparent eyes.

Andrew nodded.

"Ye gods and little fishes," said Lee irreverently, whistling through his teeth while his quick mind examined causes and consequences. "That is one hell of a complication. Is she here yet?"

Andrew shrugged. "Nobody would say. But the march is tomorrow night. If I know Maggie, she'll be at the head of it, daring mere mortals to throw stones at her."

Lee's lips moved in a smile that came and went as quickly as a thought. He lifted the Stetson from his head and ran his hand through hair that was wholly white. The gesture was a duplicate of Andrew's a moment earlier, right down to which fingertips held the rim of the hat.

"I wonder if she's grown up enough to understand how dangerous life can be," Lee said as though thinking aloud.

Abruptly, Lee turned and walked over to Andrew's muddy sedan parked beneath a pepper tree just beyond the store. He rode silently beside Andrew into San Ignacio. Neither man felt a need to talk, for both knew that

Maggie's arrival was equivalent to striking a match in a world full of gunpowder.

⌇

The conference room of the Growers' League building was crowded with men, heat and speeches. Lee's arrival caused a stir, though he did no more than nod to a few of the men. He sat down unhurriedly, beneath one of a pair of four-blade fans that hung from the ceiling. Though the blades were a blur of speed, the fans were almost useless against the humidity and the relentless heat. Windows and doors had been thrown open, but there was no wind. The sycamore leaves outside the open windows were hanging straight down, motionless. Inside, men had stripped to shirt sheeves, discarded their ties and opened their neck buttons. But there was no escape from the clinging heat.

Sheriff Heer shifted his thick shoulders and selected another section of wall to lean against. He was no cooler in the new position. His khaki uniform showed arcs and streaks dark with sweat. He watched the faces around the long conference table, faces that he had known all of his life, faces flushed by heat and anger and fear. They were talking now, words as hot and empty as the afternoon; come sundown, words would give way to action, growers confronting strikers. Then Sheriff Heer would earn the miserable salary paid to him as he tried to restrain old friends from acts they would regret in the cool days of rain. He knew too well what unbridled rage could do to a man's life.

On the other hand, he despised communists and Mexicans.

"Now, we've all seen what these bastards did in the San Joaquin Valley," shouted Tom Moore, continuing the speech that Lee had inadvertently interrupted. "Hell's fire, they damn near ruined the whole melon harvest in El Centro, even with the Highway Patrol trying to keep order."

Tom Moore, grandson of Jackson Moore, looked around the room. He was a heavyset, normally slow-moving man with a voice that could bend steel. He was president of the League, an office he held by virtue of his voice and of the groves his father had bought with his grandfather's hardware fortune. Tom turned suddenly, singling out Sheriff Heer.

"But we don't need the Highway Patrol in Moreno County, do we? We'll kick ass with our own cops. Right?"

Sheriff Heer smiled wryly, knowing and not resenting the political necessities of what was, after all, an elective office.

"I'll see to it that nothing foolish happens, Tom."

Tom Moore reached out and thumped the sheriff's shoulder, the kind of rough encouragement or approval that would have been at home in any locker room.

"You bet, Reggie," he said. "We'll kick ass just like we used to in school!"

None of Andrew's contempt showed on his face. He stood behind Lee, who sat at the long conference table by virtue of his position as a member of the League's board of directors. It was the only public office Lee had ever held, one which he had chosen for its insignificance. But the League was no longer a social club and its meetings were no longer meaningless. Today Lee sat attentively, his face expressionless while he listened to the discussions with a grim distaste that only Andrew sensed.

"The board of supervisors, the sheriff, the city mayors, all the important people in the county are behind us and against unions," continued Tom Moore. "We're united against foreign agitators. We're going to show them that we won't be told how to run our own business on our own land. Hell, even the folks down at Frenchman's Cove are behind us, and they don't have any oranges to lose. What's your brother offering on our winning this fight, Reggie?"

The men smiled. At one time or another, most of them had gambled in the Blue Turtle, also known as "Heer's Hell."

"Well," said Sheriff Heer, smiling, "you all know that gambling isn't legal in Frenchman's Cove or anywhere else in the county, but if it were, I'm sure my brother would lay you six to five that the strikers won't stay out a week."

"There you have it," laughed Tom, his voice easily overriding the combined laughter of thirty men. "That's the official line. No more than a week and the Mexicans will be back picking. And," he added, his voice suddenly harsh, "any greaser that gets in our way will regret it. We're going to teach them and the rest of the state and the whole goddamned country that we're not taking any shit from any communists, whether they come from Russia or from our own back yard!"

Many of the men clapped or cheered, then subsided into a self-conscious silence that served to underline Lee's quiet voice.

"I am pleased to have the benefit of Tom's wisdom," said Lee. "I, too, would like to see the picking begin on schedule. And I, too, would like to impress the nation with the quality of our politics. As growers, our politics—and our interests—sometimes differ from those of our workers."

Lee's voice was soft, unaccented, oddly compelling. His eyes met and held those of every man in turn. Andrew, watching quietly, sensed Lee's impact without realizing that he had inherited his father's ability to command and hold the attention of men. Fascinated, Andrew was motionless but for his eyes, eyes that were rarely the same color twice.

"So far," continued Lee, "I haven't heard what our workers want. I don't know what the fight is about, and already I find myself in the middle of it."

There was an irony inherent in Lee's words that no man could ignore, for none of the men knew what their workers wanted. Even Tom Moore found himself nodding in unconscious agreement.

"We can hardly expect our workers to be immune to the ideas and emotions that are sweeping the country and the world," Lee said softly. "Unions are the laborers' answer to the Great Depression. Whether we like unions or despise them, we can't dismiss them with rhetoric. We must have information. To get that, we must talk with our workers, rather than fight with them."

Only after Lee stopped speaking did Andrew realize how deftly Lee had defused the situation. Men sat quietly, thoughtfully. The whirring of the fans seemed unnaturally loud. Finally, Sheriff Heer spoke. His voice had an unpleasant edge; speaking to or about Lee Buckles had always had that effect on members of the Heer family.

"Just a minute," said Sheriff Heer. "Are you telling these men to roll over for a bunch of communist greasers?"

Lee gave the sheriff a smile that was somehow more insulting than an upraised middle finger.

"I know these men better than that," said Lee. He chuckled slightly. "Hell, they won't even roll over for their mistresses." Lee waited for the appreciative laughter to die down. "Yes," said Lee again, "I know these men—and they know me."

The implication that Sheriff Heer knew neither the men nor Lee was not lost on the sheriff. His big hands bunched into fists.

"You know the greasers best of all," said the sheriff flatly. "You spend more time with them than you do with us." Sheriff Heer's vivid blue eyes swept over the men. "Remember who his friends are before you sidle up and eat sugar out of his greasy hands."

Lee smiled again, though his eyes were white. "I have many friends in this room, Reggie," said Lee, stripping the other man of rank and stature. "They are men of substance, men who are shrewd enough to see as many cards as possible before they show their own hands."

Hearing the murmur of agreement going around the table, Sheriff Heer knew that Lee had won, knew without having to look around the room. "Someday you'll lose, Buckles. I hope I'm there to see it."

Lee looked steadily into the sheriff's china blue eyes. For a moment Lee lived in the past, heard Roger Heer's hatred echoing, heard Gil's words of rape and retribution, knelt by Cira's bed and felt again the grief that had been surpassed only when she died in his arms.

"I've lost more than you have the wit to understand." Lee stood slowly. "But, does that satisfy you? No. Nothing satisfies you, Reggie. You're like your father in that."

Lee's white glance went around the table. "Thank you for listening to an old man. You will, as always, do whatever you believe right. And some day, when you are as old as I, you will wonder how you could have been so wrong."

In utter silence, Lee walked out of the meeting. Andrew caught up with him at the front door of the League Building. Together, Lee and Andrew walked into the searing afternoon sun. The cruel light revealed every line of Lee's face, accentuated the paleness around his eyes and lips, as though his blood no longer flowed freely. His hands were shaking with anger.

"That son of a bitch is more dangerous than his father ever thought of being," said Lee through his teeth. "Reggie's only solution to a problem is to beat it to death. Christ, how I regret not killing his father when I had him doubled over my shotgun!"

Andrew was shocked by the violent hatred that Lee no longer bothered to disguise. Lee glanced at Andrew and smiled strangely.

"You didn't know about the shotgun, did you? There are many things you don't know about the past. Maybe life will be kind and you'll never have to know."

Lee's smile was subtly transformed by a grief greater than his hatred. Blindly, Andrew reached out to touch his father, but he was no longer there. He had turned away, walking alone to the car, seeing only the past where a jacaranda tree was combed by a restless wind.

A score of *campesinos* were gathered beneath a dusty sycamore at the northern edge of Colonia Juarez, waiting for the results of the Farm Workers' League meeting that was being held in the whitewashed adobe building across from St. Basil's Church. The loud, often disorderly meeting had been going on since late afternoon.

One of the *campesinos* roused himself, went to the screened window of the meeting house and stood, listening. After a few moments, the man returned to his friends and shrugged expressively, telling them without words that nothing had changed. Then he sat again beneath the tree, though the setting sun removed the necessity for shade.

Inside the adobe building, the air was cool. A single lamp had been lit against the gathering gloom. Already, moths circled the lamp's glass chimney, spiraling closer to death with each moment. Maggie McCartney sat next to the lamp, giving the moths more attention than she gave to the deadlocked discussion. Faustiano Barbona and Jorge Valverde, both long-time local union leaders, were going at one another like fighting cocks over who would precede whom in the march through the citrus groves to the San Ignacio Growers League Building.

Eddie Gold, a student from UCLA, was attempting to mediate by pointing out to both men that comrades in the war against the suppression of the masses did not compete for position. When Eddie finally made himself understood through Maggie's bored translation, both labor leaders spared Eddie a single look of contempt before resuming their argument.

Other members of the organizing committee—including three men who were veterans of the San Joaquin cotton riots of 1935 and one man who had been blooded in a vineyard outside of Delano in 1933—were shrewd enough to let Faustiano and Jorge fight without interruption. Both labor leaders were proud and powerful enough to break the twelve-hour-old strike by ordering their followers back into the groves. And that would be the end of months of hard work and years of hopes which had culminated in the San Ignacio pickers refusing to accept the standard penny-a-box increase. Unless the two men agreed, the strike would melt away as had all the other strikes in the past.

In spite of what was at stake, Maggie was bored by the interminable wrangling. She felt as though she had spent her life listening to men argue abstruse points of pride and precedence while human need cried out unnoticed. She bent closer to the lamp, so close that her hair was in danger of burning. She concentrated on the relentless flutter of moths, as though by living only in the present instant she could ignore the past that had threatened to overwhelm her since she had seen Reggie Heer.

With a work-hardened fingertip, Maggie touched the glass chimney. It was hot enough to burn her, yet still the moths beat softly against the invisible barrier separating them from death. She watched without moving until she realized that with each wingbeat, the moths were slowly cooking themselves against the glass while a brilliant, swift death danced just beyond their reach.

The sound of glass shattering cut across the futile argument. Men looked toward Maggie, but did not know her well enough to see the wildness behind her eyes. As though awakening from a dream, Maggie looked around a room lit only by a single naked flame. The many faces she saw were divided by darkness, halved by flame and strangeness, faces out of hell.

With an inner shudder, Maggie forced herself to concentrate only on a single moment. This moment.

"I'm sorry," she said, looking beyond all of them to something she alone could see.

"Quite all right," said Lewis Shreiber quickly. He was an assistant professor of philosophy from Berkeley, accustomed to speaking to a captive audience. "We really should get on to the larger matters of designating proctors and drawing up a list of demands. This bickering over order of march is fruitless—like the growers."

Shreiber smiled, inviting others to join in his appreciation of his own joke. No one smiled.

"The men at the head of the procession," said Maggie, casually stirring hot shards of glass with her fingertip, "will take the brunt of the nightsticks. That's the honor Faustiano and Jorge are arguing over—maybe you would like to take it?"

A dark flush crept above the line of Shreiber's beard. He was one of those men who was disoriented by Maggie's mere presence, much less by her sharp tongue. Maggie looked away from him, staring into the flame where moths no longer danced. Her mouth curved in a smile of unbelievable beauty. In that moment no man could deny her. And she knew it.

"I will lead the march," she said in a voice as soft as flame. "And beside me will march the comrades who have done so much for their men—Jorge and Faustiano."

As Maggie spoke the names, she smiled at each man, seeming to see only him of all the men in the room. Both men nodded, agreeing with her, because to disagree at that moment was as unthinkable as blaspheming in the presence of a saint.

"Well, that takes care of it," said Shreiber briskly, before either man could change his mind. "Let's move on to the matter of drafting a list of strike demands. First, of course, is the growers' ridiculous offer of a penny-per-box raise."

Maggie sat back and stared down at the flame reflected in countless shards of glass. She did not notice the *campesino* who approached her tentatively. When she finally became aware of him, he held out a small envelope.

"For you, señorita," he said, too quietly for anyone but her to hear.

"Gracias."

Maggie took the envelope, turning it over in her hands, but there was no writing on either side. She opened the envelope quickly. The sheet of paper inside was as blank as the envelope. When she unfolded the paper, a single, fresh sprig of jacaranda slipped through her fingers and landed in the broken glass.

Maggie's breath caught in her throat. The feathery green leaves were so much a part of her, a part that she had so long denied. For an instant it seemed that the years that separated her from the jacaranda tree were years without solace or hope; the peace and cool shelter of the tree overwhelmed her. Her eyes closed and her head bent forward, sending her hair toward the flame. Gently, fearfully, the *campesino* swept her hair aside before it could burn.

"Gracias," whispered Maggie again. She gathered herself and gave the messenger a smile he would remember when he had forgotten the names of his children. She retrieved the sprig of green and wrapped it carefully within the paper. "Is anyone waiting for an answer?"

The man shook his head without taking his eyes off of Maggie.

"No," murmured Maggie, tucking the jacaranda fragment into the envelope with gentle fingers, "he wouldn't need to wait for an answer, would he? He knows I'll come."

Maggie smiled, a rare smile, one for herself alone. Unnoticed, the *campesino* retreated beyond the reach of her beauty. Maggie moved slowly through the room, out into the cool night, walking quickly through the colonia toward the house where a jacaranda stood like a torch held against the fall of night.

Andrew waited alone on the porch of the house at the edge of the colonia, waited and savored a small, silky, night wind. Little had changed in the house since his mother had died; though no one lived here, Lee had seen that the house was as beautifully kept as when Cira was alive. Out beyond what had once been the Wagon Road, more houses had been built and more trees had been planted. But neither the new houses nor the new trees could rival the jacaranda spreading above the home where Cira had lived.

With eyes that were almost silver, Andrew watched the dreamlike dance of wind and jacaranda and moonlight. The tree had stretched over his life, as it had his mother's and his sister's. And even Lee's, though Andrew did not understand how or why. But he did know that Maggie would not be able to refuse the message implicit in the soft green of jacaranda leaves.

Maggie arrived so quietly that she seemed to condense out of the night. She paused just beyond the yard, just beyond the reach of jacaranda leaves. Even after he sensed Maggie's presence, Andrew continued to sit quietly, invisibly, in the dense moon shadows of the porch. He watched her stand and look at the house glowing in the pale moonlight, knowing she would not see him. Nor would she see a car, for he had walked, as she had.

Neither of them saw Lee's car, parked in the converted stable.

"I suppose my little brother thinks he's clever," announced Maggie to the tree, "sending me a piece of my childhood wrapped in white paper."

Andrew laughed softly and leaned into the moonlight. "It worked, didn't it?"

Maggie turned toward the porch so swiftly that her hair fanned out behind her. "Hello, little brother," she said, but she did not come any closer.

There was affection in Maggie's voice, and tension, a tension he shared. They had parted in anger seven years ago. Despite the subtle bonds between them, they both were more comfortable talking across the kind of distance that required them to raise their voices to be heard.

Maggie turned away from Andrew, giving her attention to the billowing shadow of the tree. The night was replete with smells and textures that pulled her into the past; and nothing pulled more strongly than the jacaranda tree.

Andrew walked to the edge of the porch and leaned against a white wooden column. He pulled a cigarette and match from his pocket.

"I suppose an olive branch would have been more appropriate," Andrew said, bending over the flaring match.

Maggie looked at the face lit by flame and saw a hard purpose that made her feel suddenly helpless. He looked like Lee, like the past that never receded but somehow slid forward until it came at her out of the future like a train hurtling out of the night.

When the match went out, Maggie walked up to the porch slowly, as though pulled against her will.

"Do you live here?" Maggie asked, mounting the front steps.

"No."

Andrew did not mention that Lee sometimes came here, always alone, never taking away anything but memories.

Maggie glanced around, her face unreadable in the wan light.

"A house that never fit where it was," she murmured, "and us—two kids who never fit either. That's all she ever had."

"She had Lee."

Maggie looked up in the darkness, studying Andrew's face as though it were a list of enigmatic demands.

"You really believe that, don't you?" she said finally, her voice cold and distant. "I suppose you and he are still close?"

"Is there something wrong with that?"

Maggie shrugged irritably, then reached out and touched Andrew's arm so lightly that he could have imagined it.

"There's nothing wrong," she said quickly. "I'm sorry. I'm not trying to pick a fight with you."

"What about Lee?" asked Andrew softly. "Are you trying to pick a fight with him?"

"I don't know," she said slowly. "I hope not. I gave that up a long time ago. After the anger drove me to do things that almost destroyed me . . . and Jaime. So I had to stop being angry with Lee, or wanting him to be angry, or wanting anything from him at all."

Maggie closed her eyes suddenly, her face bleak in the half light and shadow. "Let's talk about something else. How are the growers going to respond to the strike?"

"There was a run on pick handles," said Andrew, blowing a stream of smoke at the moon. "Then the county supervisors authorized Sheriff Heer to purchase everything from spring-loaded saps to machine guns."

"Do they really believe the workers will be scared off by purchase orders?" said Maggie contemptuously.

"Scared off?" Andrew's voice was cutting. "The growers would rather kill strikers than scare them."

Maggie shook her head slowly. "Quit trying to scare me. I don't believe you."

"Grow up, pretty sister," said Andrew, angrily flipping his cigarette butt onto the stone walkway. "This isn't Paris. The growers aren't going to stand around and mark time while you and your loyal *campesinos* sing the Internationale."

"I was in El Centro. A kid got his head broken protecting me. I know all about it, little brother."

"Shit," said Andrew, disgusted.

"Where does the Buckles Ranch stand in this?" asked Maggie when the silence became unbearable.

"We're right in the middle." Andrew smacked his hands together. "Right in the goddamn middle."

"We?" asked Maggie softly. She studied her brother's face. It showed the kind of involvement with the land she had seen once on another man's face, a long time ago. She closed her eyes. "He's really done it to you, hasn't he?"

Andrew looked at her and raised one eyebrow, a trait inherited from Lee.

"He's infected you with the same damn sickness he has," she said bitterly. "His insane love affair with a piece of ground." Her eyes opened, showing splinters of light and darkness framed by long lashes. "You poor little bastard," she whispered, staring through him as though she were talking to herself. "Dirt doesn't love anybody. I learned that when I was nine years old."

"It doesn't betray anyone, either."

"Are you saying that I do?"

"Only yourself," said Andrew sadly. He hesitated, but felt compelled to continue even though he knew it would probably infuriate her. "Lee wants to see you."

Maggie said nothing.

"He almost died two summers ago," said Andrew, his throat tight. "He's finally getting old, Maggie."

"We're all getting old," she said harshly. Then, reluctantly, "Why does he want to see me? It's too late to make up for—"

Maggie stopped abruptly and looked away, afraid that she had told Andrew more than she herself wanted to know. When Andrew was sure that she would not continue, he reached out and touched her cheek.

"He loves you."

Maggie turned on Andrew, her face twisted by rage.

"Like bloody hell! He traded me for a fucking piece of dirt!"

"Maggie—"

"Ask him," challenged Maggie. "Make him tell you how he was offered a choice—me or the ranch—and you know what he chose!" She stopped, as though suddenly aware of the ugliness of her voice. Her hands trembled as she pushed hair away from her face. "I don't blame him. I would have done the same . . . and it was so long ago, anyway," she said more calmly. "But I don't delude myself, either. He made his choice based on what was good for him, the same way we all make our choices."

"And sometimes," said Lee's voice from the darkness of the house, "what seem to be choices are just other sides of the same box."

In the shocked silence that followed his words, Lee stepped noiselessly out onto the porch. He saw Maggie turn on Andrew, her mouth hard with accusation.

"No, Maggie," Lee said. "He didn't know I was here any more than I knew either one of you was."

Maggie turned slowly toward the tall man whose voice had not changed, a voice out of her memories. Slowly, Lee walked over to the daughter he had not seen for nearly twenty years. Maggie had to tilt her head back to see Lee's eyes, but they told her nothing. The touch of his fingers on her cheek shocked her as much as his words coming out of darkness. She did not resist the gentle pressure that turned her face toward the brightness of the moon.

"You are like her . . . beautiful," murmured Lee.

Lee turned Maggie's head slowly, watching cool light and dense shadows slide over the face of his memories. Like Cira, yes, but also different. Harder.

"You're unhappy, *niña.*"

Maggie jerked away from his hand and said harshly, "Don't call me that. I'm not your little girl—remember?"

Andrew saw pain tighten Lee's features. But when Andrew would have spoken, a look from Lee froze the words in Andrew's throat.

"I've often wondered if you came back that night for

298

Jaime's jacket," said Lee, nothing more than curiosity apparent on his face.

Maggie did not have to ask which night Lee meant. "Yes," she said. "And yes, I heard."

"I see. That explains . . . much." Lee sighed for a past he could not change. "Then what would you like to be called?"

Lee's voice was controlled, almost without inflection. Andrew knew that Lee was concealing a great many emotions, but Maggie did not. She laughed strangely, looking at the eyes of her childhood, eyes that were never the same, even in memory.

"A long time ago I wanted to be called your daughter."

Lee reached out to her, but she stepped back. His hand dropped to his side.

"And now?" he asked neutrally.

"Now? Maggie will do. Just Maggie. Not Pico. Not McCartney. Not Vasconcellos. And," she added bitterly, "certainly not Buckles!"

"That's enough," said Andrew angrily. "You're acting as though everything that went wrong in your life was Lee's fault. You—"

"Andrew."

Lee's soft voice stopped Andrew more effectively than a shout. With an inarticulate sound of frustration, Andrew turned his back on both of them. He spoke with a cool neutrality that was an unconscious echo of his father.

"You're wrong, Lee," said Andrew. "I knew you would be here. You come here whenever you're tired or hurt or lonely. I thought if Maggie knew that, if she saw you here, she'd realize that you've had your share of grief. And then some." Andrew paused, and anger crept into his voice. "I was wrong. She's spent her life looking backward. She can't see a damn thing."

Andrew turned around in a single, swift movement. He looked at Maggie with eyes that were pale and cold.

"Come on, 'Just Maggie.' We're leaving. Lee has earned whatever peace this place can give him."

Lee watched his two angry children facing each other on a dark porch that held so many peaceful memories.

For a moment he wanted very much to let them walk out into the yard, let them vanish beyond the jacaranda tree, leaving him with memories of Cira that grew more real as his body grew more weak. But he could not let go yet; there was a debt to the future he must try to pay.

"Come inside, children."

The exhaustion in Lee's voice made Maggie forget the hot words she wanted to throw at her brother. With a face that held more concern than she realized, Maggie turned toward the man she thought she hated. Wordlessly, she followed Lee into the house she had not entered since her mother died almost two decades ago. Andrew hesitated, then followed with a grimace; nothing was going as he had planned.

Quietly, almost afraid to speak, Maggie and Andrew waited while Lee lit the oil lamp hanging above the kitchen table. The wick caught fire, burning incandescently. Rich gold light flooded the kitchen like a silent benediction.

"I wanted to put in electricity for her," said Lee, dropping the spent match into an ashtray, "but she wouldn't hear of it. She said it was ugly. She was right, of course. She was right about so many things."

Lee stood quietly, remembering. Memories and light transformed him, gold light pouring down, smoothing out lines and wrinkles, stiffness and hesitation. His hair was no long white, but the color of the sun. When he turned toward Maggie she saw him not as her father, but as a man in his prime, strong and sensual, intensely alive. Then the moment was gone and she was a woman nearly forty, watching an old man in a kitchen crowded with too many ghosts . . . Cira's and Lee's and a child who would always be too young to understand. Maggie closed her eyes, wanting to cry, but she had lost the habit of tears long ago.

"Sit down, Maggie. We have to talk about choices and consequences. Maybe you can choose better than I did, better than you have so far."

Lee pulled out a chair and sat down with a weariness he could not conceal. Andrew sat next to Lee. Maggie hesitated, then chose the chair next to Andrew. As they sat down, Lee changed, gathering his will and his strength to measure the dimensions of one more box.

"You," said Lee, looking at his daughter, "carry the past into the future like a burro staggering under the weight of too much firewood. You bray and kick and bite, but—sit down!—you never try to lighten the load. In fact, you try to run away when anyone suggests taking off a few sticks.

"And that's understandable, I suppose," he said softly. "You have selected each twig, each branch, with great care. You've chosen your load, but like a silly burro you blame others for the weight that bends your proud back."

"I suppose I chose to be a bastard," said Maggie, her lips pale and tight.

"You chose to think of yourself as a bastard."

"How else could I think of myself?"

"As a child of love rather than duty. As a daughter. *Niña.* Or even as Maggie, Just Maggie. A beautiful woman with no past and an unhappy present."

"And no future," said Maggie, looking beyond Lee.

"Is that the choice you want to make?" Lee said, leaning toward her, his eyes reflecting yellow light. "I want better than that for you. I love you, *niña.*"

"Not enough to—" Maggie bit off her words and looked away from his compelling eyes.

"To what, *niña?*" asked Lee gently, though he knew the answer. "Say it."

"To give up your land!"

Lee nodded almost absently, his eyes never leaving her face.

"Always the land . . ." murmured Lee. "Is that the biggest stick in your load, *niña?* Or do you still blame me for her death?"

Maggie struggled against the force Lee radiated, the soft voice like a net drawing her closer and closer to feelings she did not want to acknowledge, choices she thought she had already made or had been made for her. But it was too late for evasion; she was caught.

"Yes," she said leaning forward. "Yes, I blame you! If she had lived in a fine, big house with fireplaces and servants, a house without drafts and dampness, she would never have caught pneumonia. But my mother lived in a crummy old house on the edge of the barrio.

"If you loved your *whore* so much, why didn't you keep her in better style!"

The lamp hissed, filling a silence that expanded, engulfing them until Andrew moved and Maggie was able to look away from her father's white eyes.

"I'm sorry," she said, her voice ragged. "Neither one of us deserved that." Maggie held the heels of her hands pressed against her temples in a gesture that recalled her mother. "Why am I here? Why did I ever come back?"

"Because hate is as strong as love," Lee said quietly. "But hate is so much heavier than love, *niña*. Hate will break you."

"I don't think I hate . . . you," she said in a strained whisper. "Not anymore. My God, it all happened half a lifetime ago."

"Yes, *niña*. So leave it where it belongs, in the past. Leave it behind. Leave it now. Tonight. Before you're hurt any more. Before you tear this county apart."

Maggie's head came up with a snap and her hazel eyes glittered like glass. "So that's what all this was about—a nice little chat and send her on her way. And then back to the really important thing, the only thing that matters. The land." Maggie laughed coldly. "You almost fooled me, Mr. Buckles. Almost."

Andrew looked at her angrily. "The ranch will survive if every last orange turns to shit on the trees."

"Then it doesn't matter what I do, does it?" challenged Maggie. "Go. Stay. No difference."

Andrew slammed a fist on the table, but it was Lee who held Maggie's attention.

"Maggie," said Lee softly, "Maggie. You aren't the only person who has a burden of hatred from the past. Reggie Heer is our sheriff."

"I know," she said with a carelessness she did not feel.

"You know?" said Lee. "Yet you're staying. My God, Maggie, what are you trying to do?"

"It was a long time ago, like everything else. I know him. He won't do—"

"You don't know anyone," said Lee, "least of all yourself!"

With a feeling of desperation and futility, Lee tried to find words to explain two generations of hatred, the sins of the fathers coiling around children who grew in anger as their fathers shrank with age.

"Reggie Heer would enjoy hurting me, but he doesn't know how," said Lee simply. "When he recognizes you, he will know how."

Maggie looked away, her face hard and closed.

"What did you do to Reggie?" asked Andrew finally.

"Besides seeing that he was expelled from high school?" said Lee.

"There must have been more," said Andrew. "Even Reggie isn't stupid enough to hate you for that—not to the point of wanting revenge twenty years later."

Lee sighed, wondering how much of the truth he could tell without fanning old coals into flames that would burn everyone within reach. After a few moments, he spoke, choosing his words with great care.

"I systematically ruined Reggie's father. Wherever Roger Heer went, whatever he did, I was there before him. And I left nothing behind." Lee paused. "Ruining him was one of the greatest satisfactions of my life."

Maggie looked at Lee, shocked by the violence seething beneath his words.

"Then it's true," said Andrew. "I've heard more than once that you drove Heer to suicide just because he tried to build a railroad on your land."

Lee smiled grimly, and said nothing. Cira's rape was one side of the box that he did not want his children to have to explore.

Maggie turned suddenly, looking at her brother and then at Lee. She moved with restless impatience.

"Reggie's father died when I was wearing braids.

303

Whatever you did to him died with him. What I did to Reggie is between us—assuming he remembers. None of it has anything to do with the strike." Maggie stood up with a speed that made her chair grate on the floor. "I'm leading the march tomorrow night. If I'm recognized, so be it."

"Your choice," said Lee softly.

"Yes. My choice." She turned to Andrew; her mouth curved with rueful affection. "Smile, little brother. In a few days I'll be out of your hair—until the next time you send me jacaranda leaves."

Before either man could stand, Maggie was gone. Her voice floated back from the darkness of the living room.

"I've thought of you often, Lee. Not always unkindly."

The front door closed, leaving both men with silence and the memory of her smile.

Twelve hours later, after little sleep and less rest, Lee sat behind his desk in a chair that creaked comfortably when he shifted his weight. That creaking, and the occasional, surprising snap of glass expanding as the morning sun warmed the windows, were the only sounds in the grove house as dawn swept silently over the land. In another hour the sunlight would be brutally hot, but now Lee enjoyed it.

Beyond the windows were hundreds of acres of groves where orange fruit glowed as sun penetrated the dark-green foliage. Beyond the groves were several hundred acres of row crops reaching to the edge of the hills, where the ground pitched up sharply to meet the mountains.

The cultivated lands were the heart of the ranch, its economic strength and its future, but Lee found little solace in them. The mountains were his peace. He watched them rising out of darkness as though summoned by his silent need, mountains bringing Cira back to him in a blaze of light. Now he could see the notch and rock shelf that rose above a spring whose water was flecked with gold light.

For years after Cira had died, Lee had avoided the places, the sights, even the tastes and smells that brought her flooding back to him. In time, he had adjusted; not to her death, but to living without her. Though he no longer turned to talk with her, or reached out for her in his sleep, he had never stopped wanting her to be there. Like a tumor that his body had encapsulated but would never absorb, her loss was always with him.

The sun was above Cira's mountain when Lee roused himself to pour another cup of coffee from the pot that Elena had set out on a hot plate for him. As he replaced the pot, the tall, black phone on the corner of his desk rang harshly. He picked up the receiver.

"Buckles here."

There was a long pause. Lee heard ambiguous sounds, as though the caller were fumbling with the phone, unsure whether to speak up or hang up.

"Buckles," repeated Lee.

"We know who it is." The voice was louder than necessary. "And we also know who is behind this fucking strike. You, Buckles."

Lee's mind raced, trying to match the voice with a face. He could feel the tension that vibrated in the caller's voice, the barely leashed violence that distorted the voice beyond recognition.

"You sicced your communist bastard on our pickers," continued the voice. "You're trying to ruin us just like you ruined Roger Heer."

The voice paused, but Lee had nothing to say; he was concentrating on a voice that was both familiar and strange.

"Call her off or she'll get hurt bad."

There was a harsh click followed by the sound of static. Lee was left holding a dead line. Slowly he hung the receiver on its chrome-plated hook and turned to face the window again. He sat without moving, his eyes fixed on a bleak horizon only he could see.

Christina opened the door noiselessly. She had heard the office phone ring and had known that Lee must have answered it. She had gone to the kitchen, stolen a handful of croissants and a pot of jam, and tiptoed up the stairs to her grandfather's office. Now she walked soundlessly across the thick carpet to his desk. When she was able to see his profile she stopped abruptly. Her involuntary exclamation made Lee spin around toward her.

"Grandfather?"

The expression on Christina's face told Lee what his own must be like. With an effort, he dragged his mind away from weighing the past and the future.

"I'm s-sorry," said Christina, putting the croissants and jam on the desk with a clatter.

"You've done nothing to be sorry for."

"But you looked so—so sad—and so angry."

"I'm just an old man watching a new day," said Lee smiling as gently as he could. He reached for a croissant. "Thank you, Christina. It's been a long time since you stole breakfast for the two of us. You even remembered that I like blueberry jam."

Christina watched her grandfather put a bit of dark jam on a golden croissant. The long fingers which held the knife trembled slightly. Christina looked away, remembering a time when his hands had been steady, a time when he had been the solid center of her life. Without him, there was nothing for her to hold on to.

Something in Christina's silence made Lee look closely at her. Where he usually saw the beautiful, heedless expression of youth, he now saw an expression that was almost fear. He set aside the croissant without tasting it.

"I didn't mean to frighten you, child," he said, holding his hands out to her.

"You didn't. Not really." Her violet eyes met his, searching for something she had lost. She knelt suddenly, burying her face in his lap as though she were ten once more.

"Oh, Grandfather," she whispered, "why do things have to change?"

"I don't know, Sunshine." He stroked her hair with a hand that was no longer steady. "I don't know."

After a long time, Christina got to her feet, leaving as silently as she had come. Lee seemed almost unaware of her absence; the hand that had touched her hair lay limply in his lap. Then with a deep sigh, he reached for the phone. He told Andrew about the threat to Maggie's life in short, almost abrupt sentences.

Within minutes after hanging up, Andrew was dressed and driving toward Frenchman's Cove, once known as Blue Lagoon. The name was not all that had changed. The old Victorian hotel had burned down in 1910, to be replaced by a structure that was much less elegant. Even the shoreline had changed. A long jetty stretched between the horns of the crescent beach, holding the surf at bay, creating a harbor that was slowly being engulfed by sand.

After the hotel fire, Roger Heer had bought the land before Lee Buckles could make an offer to the Frenchman. It was Heer's last victory over Lee. Heer built the jetty, planning to turn the area into a resort. He drained the two sections of salt marsh that had come with the hotel. His dredging created several islands surrounded by channels wide enough for pleasure craft. He cut the muddy islands into tiny lots and sold the lots to speculators to repay the cost of the jetty and of rebuilding the hotel.

In celebration of completing the new hotel, Heer commissioned a painting by a local artist who had more enthusiasm than training and less talent than either. The resulting canvas, titled *Blue Nude,* was promptly renamed the *Blue Turtle* by patrons of the hotel bar. In time, the name came to refer to the hotel as well as to the painting.

Several other hotels, many saloons and numerous bordellos grew up around the Blue Turtle. The hundred acres of dry land and the two sections of dredged marsh became a sleazy resort area where traditional vices were openly bought and sold. Through the years, a small town congealed around the amusements, a town ignored by Moreno County citizens and controlled by Roger Heer, who had not lost his ability to analyze and satisfy the weaknesses of men.

In spite of the hotel, poker rooms and bars, land sales and development, Roger Heer died a bitter man, with neither the respect nor the wealth nor the power he had always believed were his due. Heer blamed Lee Buckles for everything that went wrong, from the ocean currents that undermined the ill-designed jetty to the wild fluctuations in land prices which forced Heer to sell lots for less than the cost of reclaiming them from the marsh.

Fortunes were made as Frenchman's Cove grew, but none of those fortunes belonged to Roger Heer.

Heer brought his sons up in an alcoholic brutality that made Lee Buckles's name a curse. Reggie Heer was the older son, child of a bruised woman whose fear of her husband's fists was never great enough to overcome her fear of leaving him. She drank herself to death with a silent determination that would have been frightening . . . if anyone had noticed.

Jason Heer, as dark and slender as his half-brother was blond and thick, was the son of a smoky cabaret singer whose skills extended beyond, and behind, the stage. She had died of tuberculosis when Jason was five, leaving her son little more than memories of fights, wracking coughs and napkins bright with blood.

When Roger Heer died, Jason quietly stepped in and took over the operation of the rundown hotel that was all that remained of his father's dreams. With a calculation that the elder Heer would have admired, Jason cultivated the weaknesses of powerful men, collected their IOUs from nightlong card games and then called in all debts to make his older brother sheriff of Moreno County.

Much to everyone's surprise, Reggie Heer became a good sheriff. He had the size and the temperament to be effective against petty criminals, and the common sense to be respectful of power. He even kept his notorious temper leashed, except for the beautiful, half-Mexican woman he beat so badly that she died. Jason had paid off the woman's pimp and then casually informed his older brother that if it happened again, Jason would smash Reggie's hands so that they would be unable to close into fists. Wisely, Reggie believed his brother.

In the decade since Roger Heer's death, Jason had paid his father's debts; but no matter how Jason tried, the profits from his poker games were never enough to finance the construction of the restaurant-*cum*-casino he dreamed of, a luxurious place where men in rich clothes would bow to him before they sat down to games where there was neither limit nor mercy. For the moment, Jason's dreams were merely that. He was nothing more than a gambler with cotton cuffs and silk ambitions.

It was to this man that Andrew mentally addressed various ploys while he drove along the bluffs to Frenchman's Cove. Lee's call had crystallized the foreboding in Andrew's gut; he knew that Maggie would lead the march no matter what threats were made. Nor would it be wise to approach Sheriff Heer. If the sheriff did not know Maggie's identity by now, Andrew did not want to enlighten him. The only thing left to do was to approach Jason Heer, a man Andrew had never met, a man Andrew had instinctively avoided meeting.

Andrew drove down the narrow streets of Frenchman's Cove with a speed that would have been reckless were it not for his skill. With no unnecessary motions, he brought the car to a clean stop in front of the Blue Turtle. Though it was barely eight o'clock, the sun had already burned through the fog that lay along most of the coastline. Through a gap in the row of cheap cafés, bars and shuttered sporting houses, Andrew caught the blue glint of water.

Andrew got out of his car, stepped over a sidewalk drunk curled protectively around a brown paper bag, and went into the Blue Turtle's street-front café. The smell of stale grease replaced the crisp smell of salt air. Several people straggled along the lunch counter, eating eggs that had congealed before they were served. A few secretaries and shopgirls sat in the high-backed booths, smoking white cigarettes and drinking coffee the color of tar.

Without looking either way, Andrew strode down the length of the chipped linoleum counter, turned left and opened a door marked "Employees only." Neither the cashier nor the cook looked up when the door banged shut behind Andrew. He took the dingy stairs two at a time, hardly pausing as he pushed open the heavy wooden door at the top of the stairway.

The upstairs room was as big as the café and saloon combined. The entire second floor of the hotel was given over to three gaming rooms separated by warped partitions. In the summer and on most weekends, the rooms were crowded with tourists who had few dollars and unlimited enthusiasm. This morning, only one room was open, a narrow room crowded with gambling apparatus—crap tables and roulette wheels, slot machines and round tables covered with green felt.

Whatever windows there might have been were hidden, suggested only by the faded bands of red twisting down cheap drapes that hung from ceiling to floor. There were flickering overhead lights and a rash of cigarette butts covered the floor. The air stank of smoke and alcohol and the greed of small men.

Only one of the tables was occupied. Five people sat in round-backed chairs, playing cards with the blank intensity of men who neither knew nor cared what hour it was. The one closest to Andrew was hunched, gaunt, a man in his late fifties who sucked on a cigarette with a one-inch ash. There were two men in their thirties, professional musicians who knew more about cards than scales. The fourth was a black man with a heavy face and prominent eyes.

The fifth man at the table was Jason Heer. He was the youngest, Andrew's age. Like Andrew, he was handsome and self-assured. He dealt the last card and tossed five silver dollars into the center of the table. The money rang as it fell, making a small silver pile.

"Ante's five," said Jason.

His voice was noncommittal. The most that it conveyed was a vaguely pleasant invitation. More money rang into the center of the table. Crumpled green bills were added with a sound that was almost secretive after the chime of silver.

The table was surrounded by kibitzers, three of them women dressed in the cheap finery they had worn the night before when they went out with their men. Like their clothes, their faces were tired and creased. Their men looked no better. They had eyes that were dark hollows surrounded by skin the color of greasy butcher paper. Their faces were exhausted, almost tortured.

310

Jason was the exception. He looked neither starched nor wilted, triumphant nor tormented. He showed neither fatigue nor pleasure nor anything else. His pale hands were blunt and incredibly deft, white blurs distributing cards as precisely now as he had at the start of the game sixteen hours ago.

Jason finished the deal and picked up his own cards, shielding them. He took a quick look and replaced the cards face down on the felt. He was so fast that none of the kibitzers saw his cards. It was not so much that he distrusted the kibitzers as that he played the game for himself rather than for the entertainment of others.

"Bets?" inquired Jason in a voice that neither encouraged nor discouraged.

Andrew stood with the kibitzers, staring intently, trying to catch a hint of Jason's mind and personality. But after a few moments, Andrew realized that Jason was opaque; neither his face nor his voice nor his posture gave away information. He might as well have been a slot machine.

The thin man with the cigarette pitched two silver dollars into the kitty. Then he lounged back in his chair, his posture oddly aggressive, almost a challenge. The musicians and the black man put in their money. Without saying a word, Jason dropped two cartwheels onto the growing pile and followed with two more. The gaunt man shot a sideways look at Jason, raised two dollars and leaned back again. The other three men folded with varying degrees of reluctance.

"Cards?"

Jason's voice was low and without inflection. The gaunt man's cigarette ash landed soundlessly on the burn-scarred felt. The man hesitated, then eased two cards toward Jason. In a blur of motion, Jason snicked two cards off the deck and across the table. The cards landed precisely at the man's fingertips.

The gaunt man picked up the cards, glanced once, then gathered his hand face down on the felt. His eyes flicked from the cards to Jason. The man inhaled deeply. He slipped his thumb beneath the tight fan of cards on the table before him, looked once more, then let the cards flatten with a snap. Slowly the man pulled the remains of the cigarette from the corner of his mouth. He dropped the burning butt on the floor.

Jason slipped the top two cards off the deck, laid them out in front of himself and removed the top two cards from his hand. Without looking, he discarded the old cards and with the same motion picked up the two new cards. He cupped the new cards in his hand for an instant, then placed them face down on the felt. He sat silently, waiting for the other man to bet.

The gaunt man's posture had changed subtly—less challenging, more sure. He lit another cigarette, coughed, shifted position. Then he tossed a ten-dollar bill onto the pile.

Jason slowly reached down and stacked up two piles of five silver dollars each. He added two more stacks of five and pushed the money across the felt.

The man's mouth moved in what could have been a smile. He took another bill from the small pile in front of him. With a snap of his wrist, he showed the bill to Jason. Twenty dollars. The bill fluttered into the kitty. The kibitzers seemed to sigh and lean closer, drawn toward money like moths toward fire.

"Twenty—and twenty more," said Jason.

"Done."

The man's voice was as gaunt as his face. His mouth was an odd, small curl as he tossed another twenty dollars into the kitty. The silence was so complete that Andrew could hear the rhythmic growl of the rising tide. Jason broke the spell with a faint, short laugh.

"You always get this funny look when you're bluffing, Harry."

Harry stared while a flush of anger spread up his face. Jason met the glare with amusement. Harry straightened in his chair.

"Damn you, Heer." He fumbled over his cards until they were face up. "Let's just see who was bluffing who. Beat those three deuces!"

Andrew's glance swept between the two men. He suspected that Harry had indeed been bluffing up until the moment he was dealt a third deuce. Which meant that Jason had taken a single reading off of Harry early in the hand and then had been so sure of victory that he had not bothered to look closely at his opponent again. Jason's confidence bordered on carelessness.

Jason turned over his own cards one by one, his dark eyes never leaving Harry's flushed face. With each card turned, Jason's smile increased. The smile was all the more cruel for its easy dominance.

"Why, Harry," Jason said, his voice echoing with hints of mockery. Three cards showed—a nine, a four, another nine. "For once you have something." Jason flipped over the last two cards, the cards he had dealt to himself. "But so do I."

A trey and a nine showed on the table in front of Jason.

"Three nines." Jason smiled. "You lose, old man. Again."

"Damn you, Heer," snarled Harry, more angered by Jason's words than by losing. "You take all the fun out of playing cards."

"Two things, Harry. Card-playing is business, not fun." Jason's smile became overtly cruel. "And second . . . you keep coming back, Harry."

Andrew knew then that he had discovered Jason's weakness; the gambler was so unsure of his own strength that he had to crow over his victories. Jason had not yet learned that it was foolish, sometimes even dangerous, to bait a man you have just beaten.

And Jason had misread Harry, a man Jason often played cards with. Jason was not nearly as seamless as his careful exterior led others to believe.

Jason's expressionless black eyes moved from face to face, almost as though he were checking to see whether he had successfully covered the humiliation of having called a bluff that was more than it seemed to be. His glance settled for a moment on Andrew, who cocked his eyebrow and moved his head toward the door. Jason's face did not change as his glance moved on. Then he picked up his money, pushed back his chair and stood up.

"Deal me out."

Without looking right or left, Jason turned and went out of the room. His abrupt departure caused no comment. The black man had picked up the cards and was already dealing a new hand. Andrew turned and left the room as inconspicuously as he had arrived. He caught up with Jason on the sidewalk outside the front door of the Blue Turtle. Jason glanced over his shoulder, then set off through a trash-strewn alley that opened onto a beach swept clean by wind and water. When he reached an overturned rowboat he sat and waited for Andrew.

"McCartney, isn't it?" said Jason, extending a dry, warm hand. His grip was like his voice, firm but without character. "We don't see you here in the fleshpots. At least," he smiled slightly, "we don't see you as often as we see your half-brother."

For a moment, Andrew was confused. He never thought of himself as having any blood relatives beyond Maggie—and Lee. When Andrew realized that Jason was referring to Champ, he became angry. Neither Andrew's confusion nor his subsequent anger showed. Like a gambler, a bastard learns to hide his feelings.

"I'm a working man," said Andrew, his eyes pale and opaque, his smile wide enough to include even Jason. "I can't afford the Blue Turtle's . . . pleasures."

By his very lack of inflection, Andrew made it clear that the Blue Turtle was a cesspool in which Andrew did not care to swim.

"Your half-brother has different tastes," said Jason, ignoring both the words Andrew had spoken and the ones he had not. "Seems to run in that half of the family."

Andrew waited, his face as blankly polite as the gambler's.

"Teeny. Champ brought her here last week. Lovely thing. She seemed to share her father's thirst for . . . action." Jason's smile changed as he stretched. His fingers moved as though caressing a woman's body. "Lovely."

"Yes," agreed Andrew indifferently, measuring Jason with eyes that were wholly white. "And so young. Even

314

friends, official friends, could not save a man from the kind of trouble a sixteen-year-old girl would bring."

Though casually spoken, the warning was clear. Jason watched the tumbling surf as though for the first time. In daylight, the nights of tension and alcohol and smoke showed clearly. Already the smooth planes of his face had begun to sag. With an impatience that was almost anger, Jason stood and faced Andrew.

"Anything else I can do for you, McCartney?"

"You have the reputation of being a smart, careful man." Andrew paused, studying Jason's reaction. There was none. Andrew decided to continue being blunt. "This strike could destroy the county's economy. Bad for me. Very bad for you. Ruin for a lot of people. Apparently, some of those people believe that my sister—the woman known as the 'Workers' Magdalene'—is acting in behalf of Lee Buckles."

Jason's cold eyes had not left Andrew's face. When Andrew stopped, Jason nodded once, almost imperceptibly, to indicate that he had followed the thread of the conversation. If he was surprised by Maggie's identity, he did not show it.

"My sister is acting only for herself," continued Andrew. "She is no more responsive to Lee Buckles than she is to you. Nor are the Buckles's interests served by this strike."

Jason nodded again, a movement so slight as to be nonexistent. "Just why are you telling me this, McCartney?"

Andrew paused. When he spoke, he chose his words carefully.

"There have been death threats in connection with the strike. Lee Buckles believes that everyone in a position of influence in the county should be enlisted to prevent violence. Martyrs are expensive, Heer. The county can't afford them."

"I'm a gambler, not a politician."

"In a county where gambling is illegal," said Andrew dryly, "a gambler must be politically astute, not to say powerful. Your brother, for instance. He could be a deciding force against violence from the growers."

"Who was threatened?"

"Maggie."

"So that's why you came to me instead of Reggie."

Jason laughed softly, a sound with no meaning. Andrew watched his face, but saw nothing to indicate what the man was thinking.

"You've carved yourself a profitable niche," said Andrew, pushing for a reaction both with his hard tone and his words. "If Maggie dies there will be one hell of a housecleaning. Your brother would be the first to get the broom shoved up his ass."

There was a long silence. Then Jason smiled oddly.

"You think you can make things happen or not happen just like that." Jason moved his thumb and middle finger together, making a hollow pop. "You and the great Lee Buckles. But you're wrong. What will happen . . . will happen. And there's damn all you can do to stop it. How does it feel to be a peon, McCartney?"

Andrew studied the handsome, closed face that mocked him.

"You're betting a lot, gambling man," said Andrew softly. "Can you pay up when you lose?"

Jason laughed, a sound that made the skin tighten on the back of Andrew's neck. For an instant Andrew looked into black eyes that were less than sane.

"No, McCartney. But that doesn't matter. I'll just do what my daddy did—die and let my children pay for my sins."

Jason turned and walked back to the Blue Turtle, leaving Andrew with the relentless beat of surf in his ears and a feeling of emptiness in his gut.

Ranks of men walked silently along the dusty roadway, torches swaying above faces shadowed with fear. Fading light transformed the men and oily smoke into a slow, sinewy dragon with restless eyes of fire. The heavy sweetness of orange blossoms mingled uneasily with smoke. As darkness fed the torches their flames licked high and bright.

Maggie walked at the head of the dragon, her body moving with the easy grace of torchlight. Ahead of her was the first barricade, two dark sedans with headlights and red roof lights blazing out of the engulfing darkness. The rotating scarlet beams swept over her and the black citrus groves and the men clustered on the far side of the barricade, waiting for the dragon they had helped to spawn.

As she walked, Maggie's full white dress clung and floated in a paradox of sensuality and innocence. She was careful to stay framed in torchlight, knowing her impact on the men who waited behind steel cars. Her white teeth glimmered in a smile for the men on either side of her. Faustiano and Jorge straightened, smiling in return. She held out her hands to them and her laughter rose with the smoke.

Concealed in the darkness of an orange grove, Andrew watched Maggie and the marchers approach the barricade. He had never seen her so vivid, so complete. Like a woman responding to a lover, sexuality radiated from her with a heat even her brother could not deny. And if it were so for him, what must it be like for other men?

"Score one for you, pretty sister," muttered Andrew, taking a drag on his cigarette, careful to shield the glow. "But it's not enough. Your strike threatens their God, their country and their bank accounts."

He leaned against the smooth-barked valencia tree, watching Maggie as though she were a stranger. And she was; the aroused woman, the Workers' Magdalene, was someone he neither knew nor particularly liked. When her torchlit figure stopped a few yards short of the barricade, he killed his cigarette and slipped to the edge of the growing clot of men who waited behind Sheriff Heer.

Beacons of red light swept across faces taut with anger and fear, across hands knotted into fists and shoulders bunched with impatience. But for all their coiled violence, the men behind the sheriff were motionless, pinned by the

317

beauty of the woman who faced them. There was no sound but muffled steps as the two hundred men behind Maggie closed up their ranks.

Maggie stepped forward, flanked on either side by men carrying flaming torches.

"That's far enough, Maggie."

Sheriff Heer's voice was ragged. His neck muscles were corded as he struggled to control his response to her.

Maggie's eyes flicked over the sheriff, lingering around his sagging torso long enough to tell him that she had once again measured him as a man and once again found him lacking. She took a step forward. So did the two deputies, armed with shotguns, gun muzzles held waist high. Maggie stopped.

"Turn around," said Sheriff Heer hoarsely. "Maggie." He swallowed and said loudly, "There won't be any goddamned May Day marches in my county."

One of Maggie's eyebrows arched slightly.

"Your county?" she asked softly. "My mother's family has lived here for one hundred and fifty-three years. When did your parents get off the boat?"

Torchlight rippled over her unbound black hair as she swayed forward one step, then two, then three. A smile played over her full, slightly parted lips. Sheriff Heer made no move to stop her; he could only stare with a hunger that increased every time she moved. The men behind him stirred and muttered angrily.

"No further," he said hoarsely.

"We have a right to walk on public roads."

The red beams circled relentlessly. Shouts rose, voices harsh with ugly words and fear.

"Bust some heads, sheriff!"

"Shoot them!"

"Teach that slut some manners!"

The men flanking Maggie stiffened like seconds at a duel, but the moment for ritual or civility was past.

"Shoot the goddamn Mex whore!"

Maggie appeared to waver in the uneven light, but

318

when she spoke her voice was hard and clear and carried far beyond the sheriff.

"These people are not your slaves! They have the right to organize, the right to a decent wage, the right—"

"Like hell they do!"

"Fucking greasers!"

The hated epithet galvanized the field workers. Torches jerked as men surged closer to Maggie until they were a wall of smoke and anger and fire behind her.

"Fun's over," snapped the sheriff. "Go back to the colonia and sleep it off."

"We're not—"

Sheriff Heer's voice overrode hers. "Lots of oranges to pick tomorrow, boys. Fancy words—and fancy ladies—don't fill empty field boxes or bellies."

"We aren't working tomorrow!" said Maggie. "We aren't working at all until the growers raise the box fee five cents."

Maggie's statement rang above the rising anger of men on both sides of the barricade. Raw, inarticulate shouts answered her. Sheriff Heer stepped closer to her and spoke in low, urgent tones that reached only her ears.

"Stop it, Maggie. You don't know what—"

"Five cents!" she shouted, tossing her head, making torchlight flash in her wide hazel eyes. "Five cents or you can watch your damned oranges rot on the ground!"

Sheriff Heer shouted over her shoulder at the field workers. "Go home or go to jail!"

"You can't arrest—" she began, her smile a cruel parody of sensual invitation.

"Can't arrest one of Buckles's bastards?" The sheriff laughed shortly. "Watch me, bitch."

Sheriff Heer reached out and his fingers dug into her smooth, bare shoulder. Field workers surged forward to protect their Magdalene, but hesitated when they heard the distinctive sound of shotgun shells snapping into chambers. Their uncertainty gave Sheriff Heer the moment he needed. He handcuffed Maggie and dragged her toward the rotating beacons.

When a car door finally slammed behind Maggie, the

dragon shook itself and roared—and was answered by a barrage of abuse. Growers and townspeople snarled across the barricade like unleashed hounds.

Andrew cursed quietly, tonelessly, as he saw the deadly gleam of new ax handles swinging in the red light, saw a torrent of faces contorted by anger, fists and boots and searing torches, rocks and bottles and polished wood smashing into men, savage dances choreographed by rage. And there was nothing he could do to stop it.

Andrew turned away from the cover of the grove and ran toward the patrol car which was slowly edging free of the battle. Sheriff Heer was not going to make even the smallest attempt to stop the mayhem. Andrew stepped into the headlight beams as the car eased free of the last fighting men.

Sheriff Heer jammed down both the brake pedal and the horn. The sound was an insignificant bleat against the shouts and screams rising from the fight. Andrew did not move. Sheriff Heer stuck his head out of the window. On his left cheek, parallel scratch marks gleamed wetly.

"Get the hell out of my way!"

Andrew moved just enough to confront the sheriff through the open window.

"Leaving so soon, sheriff? Or have riots been legalized?"

"Damn greasers asked for it, and they're getting it. My deputies will make the arrests that need to be made after it quiets down."

Sheriff Heer squinted, then recognized Andrew. "Should have guessed it would be you, McCartney."

Andrew looked past the sheriff to Maggie, face-down in the back seat. She struggled to sit upright. Her white dress was torn at the shoulder, revealing a swell of breast and bands of bruises that could only have come from a man's hand. Her hair was a tangled fall of black that did not conceal the bruise puffing up on her right cheek. She watched Sheriff Heer with the brilliant eyes of anger. Anger—and something more, a wildness her brother had never seen. She did not realize Andrew was there until he spoke.

320

"That's your free one, Heer," Andrew said, pointing toward his sister's bruised face. His gray eyes shone like mercury in the reflected glare of headlights. "Any more and you'll pay."

"She resisted arrest."

"Bullshit."

"Listen, boy. I—"

"You listen, Heer. I was fifty feet away. She did not resist."

"She incited a riot."

"So you knocked her around."

"A rock hit her."

"You're lying."

Sheriff Heer's big, blunt hands clamped around the steering wheel in a grip that whitened his skin. His blue eyes reflected light like broken glass. He spoke distinctly, as though if each word were unnaturally clear, Andrew would understand.

"Maggie has had it coming for a long time. She's my prisoner now. Mine. Got that? Now get the hell out of my way."

Sheriff Heer stamped on the accelerator. The car leaped forward. Only Andrew's reflexes saved him from injury. He spun away into the darkness while the back wheels spat streams of gravel. Before the siren wailed up to its peak, Andrew was up and running through the grove toward his car.

For a time there was no sound but the siren, then Sheriff Heer's hand moved over a switch and the siren died. Maggie looked around, her hazel eyes wide and intense. It was as though she were seeing for the first time.

"This isn't the way to the jail," she said.

Sheriff Heer ignored her.

Maggie raised her hands to wipe a trickle of blood from her cheek. Steel handcuffs glimmered in the dim light. She looked at the broken fingernails on her right hand. For a moment she was puzzled, then she remembered the soft, tearing feel of Heer's cheek beneath her nails.

The car raced through darkness. There were no other

cars on the rough, narrow road Sheriff Heer had turned onto, a road that led across the plains to Buckles's land. The last of the orange groves fell away. As the road humped up toward moonlight and mountains, the car thundered across a cattle guard buried in the pavement. Heer's hand moved again. Headlights died, leaving only moonlight as a guide to the twisting, climbing road.

"Where are we going."

Maggie's voice was flat, more demand than question.

"I'm taking you to the county line."

The paved road ended, dropping the car into deep ruts with a jolt that cracked Maggie's head against the window. She cried out as much from surprise as from pain. Heer laughed. His foot slammed down on the gas pedal and the car leaped forward, skidding and shaking around tight curves. Maggie was thrown against the window again and again, but she made no other sound.

"I'm taking you to the county line," repeated the sheriff. "But first I'm going to beat some manners into you."

He looked quickly over his shoulder, but could see nothing more than the white of her dress. He laughed again, a sound too high for a man of his bulk.

Maggie neither moved nor spoke. The car jerked like a wild animal as the sheriff fought the wheel with more strength than skill. Once, below and to the right, Maggie caught the distant gleam of San Ignacio's lights.

The car slowed to a stop between two steep hills, scattering dust in a wide arc. Silence and moonlight flooded the small clearing that Heer had chosen. All around, brittle brush reached toward the stars. The sharp, resinous odor of chaparral cut through dust rising on a dry swirl of night wind.

Sheriff Heer climbed out of the car, turned, and opened the back door.

"Out, bitch."

Maggie moved in the opposite direction until her back was pressed against the far door. When Heer leaned in after her, she pulled her legs up against her body.

Heer swore and leaned in further. Maggie lashed out with both feet, narrowly missing his face. Her sandals clipped his outstretched hand and thudded into his shoulder. His blunt hands locked around her ankles and jerked, pulling her off-balance. Her head hit the window. With a grunt, Heer yanked again, his shoulder muscles humping up as he pulled. He dragged her feet-first into the moonlight. She cried out once when her head bounced off of the side of the car.

Maggie twisted as she fell, instinctively trying to get her feet under her, but Heer had both of her ankles firmly imprisoned in one big hand. Her white dress was dragged up to her waist as she struggled; her long legs gleamed in the pale light. Heer's eyes followed the curving line of calf and thigh. He was suddenly aware of the warmth of her skin against his hand.

"Maggie . . ."

If Maggie heard the hoarse, unconscious plea in his voice, it served only to enrage her. She thrashed violently, helplessly, against the almost casual strength which held her ankles immobile. When she realized the extent of her helplessness, she began to curse Heer in three languages, ridiculing and reviling him. He did not understand her French, but he understood enough of her Spanish and too much of her English. He dropped her ankles, wrapped his fingers in her dark hair and yanked her to her feet.

"It's time you learned your place," said the sheriff grimly, slapping her across the mouth with a hard, open hand.

Maggie's torrent of abusive words ended in a gasp of pain. She brought her manacled hands up in a reflexive gesture of self-defense, but it did no good. His hand descended relentlessly. Blood welled from her mouth, black in the moonlight. She twisted wildly, trying to escape the cruel hand tangled in her hair, holding her upright while his other hand descended again and again, as monotonous as his curses.

Maggie's hands came up again, but this time she attacked, fingers arched like claws, seeking Heer's eyes. Nails raked down the right side of his face in the instant before he released her. Off-balance, Maggie staggered back against the car and slid down the rear fender, snagging the back of her loose dress on the bumper as she fell. She lunged up again, trying to run away, but the dress held her like a leash.

Heer laughed. His blunt hand closed around the chain linking the handcuffs. With contemptuous ease, he pulled Maggie toward him. Her dress tore away, leaving her wearing little more than bruises and streaks of blood. She saw his face change when he saw her body, more beautiful than his dreams.

"No," she said hoarsely. "No!"

She threw herself against the handcuffs until her wrists bled as freely as her face, but his grip never slackened. Then, as though impatient with her struggle, Heer moved suddenly, slamming her against the fender, driving the breath from her body. He released her long enough to unfasten his gunbelt and pants.

Maggie's foot lashed out. Heer grunted, turning aside to take the force of her heel on his thigh. He swore viciously, grabbed her foot and yanked her off-balance. Before she could get up he was on top of her. She writhed, clawing and biting until he pressed his forearm across her throat, cutting off her air.

When Maggie's struggles slowed, Heer lifted the pressure slightly, wanting her to be conscious while he punished her. He dragged her legs apart with careless strength. She screamed, raking her fingernails across his unprotected eyes. He leaned on her throat again, his lips by her ear, telling her in obscene detail how he was going to humiliate her, whispering as he jerked against her, whispering, forcing, until he had breath only for a final, brutal spasm.

"There," he panted, "there, you bitch."

Maggie lay slackly beneath Heer's weight. Slowly, he realized that his forearm was still across her throat. He shifted his body, rolling off of her. The only sound in the clearing was his own breath, hoarse and rapid. He looked down at her, pale and utterly still, lying in a pool of thin light. He had seen too much death not to recognize its presence now.

Slowly, Sheriff Heer got to his feet, wiping his hands on

his thighs. With automatic motions, he hitched his pants into place and picked up his gunbelt. His hands were shaking too much to fasten the belt buckle. With a strangled curse, he threw gun and belt into the front seat of the squad car. He looked around, his eyes showing whitely. Behind him, foothills climbed toward mountains and transparent silver light. In front of him, a hundred yards beyond the car, a steep, anonymous canyon plunged toward the plains.

Sheriff Heer tugged until the shreds of Maggie's white dress were freed from the car bumper. He shifted a large rock and stuffed the fabric beneath. When the rock settled back into place, no cloth showed. He returned to Maggie and unfastened the handcuffs from her bloody wrists, trying not to look into the eyes that were no longer brilliant. He moved jerkily, like a man unused to his own body. His own eyes were too wide, focusing only when he concentrated.

With an odd, hoarse sound, Sheriff Heer pulled Maggie's body up and over his shoulder. A hundred yards away, in a canyon with no name, he buried Maggie beneath an angular pile of brush.

Scented beeswax candles marched down the length of the formal table, shedding golden light on crystal goblets and Haviland china and heavy, gleaming silver. Though the table was set for twelve, only six were present.

Lee picked absently at his veal Oscar, looking at the elegant display without seeing it. His eyes, like his thoughts, were focused inward. He shivered with a chill born of unease. Without realizing it, he cursed very softly, damning the ugly box he sensed closing around him.

"Yes, Leander?" said Joy with subtle sharpness. "I did not hear you clearly."

"Nothing, Marjorie," said Lee in the neutral voice he habitually used with her.

Joy's eyes, faded with age, narrowed as her irritation mounted. Her dinner party was a disaster. Due to the rumors of violence between strikers and growers, three couples had phoned in their last-minute regrets. And Lee was here only because it was a duty to her that was easier fulfilled than denied or delayed. It angered her that he showed his indifference to her in front of guests.

Lee speared a morsel of crab, forcing his thoughts away from their futile circling around the past and an angry Maggie he could not claim as his daughter. As he chewed the crab, he recognized the flavor of the cook's revenge. Elena had ruined the meat; Elena who could create flawless meals when she and Marjorie did not argue over the menu. He sighed and his fork clinked against the bone china. After forty years, Marjorie had not learned that she could not bully Elena.

"Leander, you're ignoring our guests."

Joy's voice was light, warm and biting in a way only Lee would recognize and understand. He looked up from his congealing veal. His penetrating gray eyes ignored Joy, concentrating instead on Harold Snelling, the gifted and civilized pianist Joy had imported to fill one of Moreno County's many cultural gaps.

"Tell me, Mr. Snelling," said Lee softly. "What do you think the growers ought to do about the Farm Workers' League?"

Joy stiffened, but only Lee knew, as he also knew that his question was unfair; Snelling was an excellent pianist whose interests went no further than the keyboard. Snelling dabbed at his lips with a fine linen napkin.

"I'm sure I don't know," he said, lowering his napkin and spreading his long, smooth fingers in a gesture of helpless resignation. "Politics . . . so very messy, don't you know? So unsatisfactory."

Snelling's wife accepted another glass of wine and took a long swallow of the light, nearly transparent liquid. Lee's glance dismissed her and passed on to Champ. Champ was looking everywhere but at his father, a fact that did not surprise Lee. Champ had not looked him in the eye since he had brought a seventeen-year-old bride home—four months' pregnant. The marriage, to no one's surprise, was a disaster. Cynthia was the spoiled daughter of Eastern wealth. Her only interest in life was breeding

326

and showing horses. Her pregnancy was the result of her ignorance and Champ's carelessness. The former, if not the latter, was promptly cured. She never became pregnant again. Nor was she particularly interested in being a mother. Between shows and foaling season, Cynthia sometimes managed to see Christina, but tonight did not coincide with one of Cynthia's rare visits. Champ's wife lived in the East as though she had neither married nor borne a child.

Lee's eyes moved on around the table, passing over the Snellings again; both were suddenly fascinated by their inedible veal. Joy looked at a spot just to the right and above Lee's ear. Only Christina returned his steady glance. In the muted light her eyes were a deep violet lit by intelligence and shadowed by the tension she sensed coiling around the glittering dinner table. Lee smiled with a warmth and gentleness that he gave only to her.

"Field workers," said Joy, exhibiting a coldness she rarely displayed in front of others, "are hardly a topic for civilized discourse. Dear."

"Granted," said Lee, sipping his wine. "But I'm not a civilized man, as you know." He smiled coolly in her direction. "My lack entirely. I can't hope to equal your example."

Christina coughed quietly into her napkin, drawing a waspish look from Joy. But before Joy could rebuke her granddaughter, Lee resumed speaking as though he had never been interrupted.

"Civilized or not, the strike is crucial to our ranch and therefore, tangentially, to this delightful dinner. What would you do, Marjorie, if the decision were yours to make?"

Joy shrugged, a graceful gesture learned after many seasons in Paris.

"I leave such matters to you, Leander. You get on so well with Mexicans. But I must say that our Mexicans should be grateful for whatever work we give them. They are slovenly drunkards with morals that . . . ." she paused delicately. "Especially the women. What we really need

327

are some decent, clean, sober Chinamen." Joy smiled serenely. "More wine, Mrs. Snelling?"

Only Christina knew the extent of Lee's rage. Her sixteen-year-old face took on a sweetness that was a warning to anyone who knew her well. Joy did not.

"Grandmother, the Chinese smoke opium, which is a lot worse than whiskey."

"Nonsense."

Christina's large violet eyes fixed on Joy. "Grandfather Lee has seen the opium dens of San Francisco."

"San Francisco has no such things! Your grandfather has an unnatural aversion to the city," said Joy crisply. "He is always finding fault with San Francisco, though it is the most refined city in the world, with the exception of Paris. Now eat your veal."

"Christina," said Lee, before she could respond to Joy, "every race and every place has its own virtues. And vices. That's something your grandmother would rather not face. But she is right about eating your veal."

Christina sensed that Lee's gentleness went no further than his voice. She picked up her fork, took a small bite and wrinkled her nose.

"Ugh. Did you fight with Elena again, Grandmother?" she asked, setting her fork down with finality.

Lee said nothing; considering the quality of the meal, Christina's response was polite enough.

"Champion," said Joy in a low, sweet voice.

Champ dragged his eyes away from the kaleidoscopic shadows cast by crystal chandeliers.

"Yes, Mother?"

"Your daughter is disrupting our meal. Again."

"Oh." He glanced at Christina with a total lack of interest. "Do behave, Teeny."

The desultory command and the despised nickname made Christina's lips thin into the sullen line that Lee hated. His anger showed, but only in the paleness of his eyes. Though he was not looking at Christina, she picked up her fork and began to eat.

Silver clicked lightly on china for a few moments. Just

328

as Joy had revived the conversation with an adroit reference to Snelling's favorite conductor, the sound of door chimes resonated through the dining room.

Conversation paused while Joy waited for Elena to answer the door. Chimes rang again in the silence. Elena had chosen to forget that the houseboy was ill. Joy measured the seconds, then dropped her napkin in the middle of her plate and rose. Her movement caught Lee halfway out of his chair. With a cutting motion of her hand, she halted him and marched out of the room.

The solid oak door swung inward easily on its massive hinges. Andrew stood on the veranda, looking both angry and uneasy.

"Would you please tell Mr. Buckles that Andrew McCartney—"

Before Andrew could finish, Joy closed the door with a force that was felt throughout the house. When the echo died, Joy was standing by Lee's chair. Her body was rigid and her fine-boned face was as white as her hair. Her voice shook.

"I told you I never wanted any of *them* near my house!"

Lee was out of his chair before she finished her sentence.

"David promised me!" she shouted after his retreating back. "Never!"

Lee walked out of the front door without a word or backward look. Andrew came quickly toward him across the moonlit veranda.

"How bad?" said Lee, closing the door quietly behind him.

"Ax handles. Rocks. Blood."

"Where?"

"A mile east of the colonia."

"Sheriff Heer?"

"That's just it. He's got Maggie."

Lee closed his eyes as the vague malaise he had felt all evening condensed into cold bands around his heart.

"Is she hurt?" he asked, his voice subtly ragged.

Andrew moved as though caged. "Not yet. But Heer got a whiff of blood and is baying at the moon. Said that Maggie was his. Nearly ran me down when I tried to talk to him. I went to the county jail, but couldn't get in. That's when I came for you." He hesitated, looking reflexively at the house. "Sorry about—"

Lee dismissed Joy's anger with a curt gesture of his hand.

"Did Heer slap Maggie around?"

"How did you know?" said Andrew, opening the car door for Lee.

Lee said nothing; passing on rumors of Heer's brutality would serve no purpose. Lee eased himself into the car. Andrew closed the door and quickly circled around to the driver's seat.

"Is he likely to do her real harm?" Andrew asked as his quick hands brought the car to life.

Lee did not answer.

"I hope not," Andrew said, as though Lee had spoken. "I don't particularly want to kill a sheriff."

Andrew's voice was soft, passionless, as though he were discussing the best location for a new well or the merits of tenant farmers versus hired help. Lee looked at his unacknowledged son for a long moment, measuring the depth of Andrew's rage and control.

"Andrew," began Lee, then tiredness and a sense of futility overwhelmed him. Who was he to tell his son to kill or not to kill? None of this would have happened if he himself had killed the right man more than half a century ago.

With a silent, ragged breath, Lee leaned back against the seat, trying to let the orange-scented darkness relax the bands tightening around his heart. Air flowed in through the open window, drying the almost invisible mist of sweat on his face, air as smooth and as fine as silk.

Andrew studied Lee covertly in the moonlight pouring through the window. The lines of age and exhaustion and pain on Lee's face weighed as heavily on Andrew as his fear for Maggie.

330

Andrew's foot came down hard on the accelerator. Lee opened his eyes to glance at the speedometer, but said nothing. Andrew's urgency answered a gnawing need in both men. Tires whined as the car leaned into a tight curve. Both men were silent on the drive to town. The miles seemed slow and unnaturally long; with each minute, the tension shared by the two men built until it was all but tangible.

As the car approached Colonia Juarez, it was forced to detour again and again. Roads were closed off by deputies bent on controlling the spread of the riot. Both Andrew and Lee realized that they were gradually being forced away from an area that included both the colonia and the section of San Ignacio that held the jail.

"Shit," hissed Andrew between his teeth when he spotted yet another barricade.

"The field," said Lee. "Right."

Without even looking, Andrew pulled hard on the wheel. The car lurched, swung to the right, then bumped across an open field and into a colonia alley. From there, Andrew drove the car hard but carefully, dividing his attention between the road and random clots of fighting men. When he finally reached the outskirts of San Ignacio, he found a paved road that led to the county jail. He slowed as the car approached the jail. The red sandstone facing of the building was black in the moonlight. Men jammed the sidewalk and spilled over into the gutter. The streetlight in front of the jail was smashed, but both Andrew and Lee could see the thin shine of varnished ax handles in the moonlight.

"Guess they ran out of Mexicans," said Andrew bitterly.

He swung the car into an alley. The passage was dark, deserted but for a lean cat that leaped across the white glare of headlights. At the end of the alley, two deputies armed with riot guns guarded the rear door of the jail. Their badges glinted like widely spaced eyes. As Andrew shut off the engine, the angry muttering of the crowd swirled in through the open windows. Lee got out and

331

stood beneath the unshaded lightbulb outside the jail until the deputies recognized him. In no way did Lee reveal the pain and tightness radiating through his chest.

"Good evening, gentlemen," Lee said quietly.

The deputies straightened unconsciously as Lee walked closer.

"Evening, Mr. Buckles."

"Evening, sir."

Lee and Andrew were up the steps before it occurred to either deputy that their orders were to allow no one near the back door. As one they shrugged and returned to their cigarettes; if the sheriff wanted Leander Buckles kept out, the sheriff would have to do it himself.

The boiler-plate door rang with the authority of Andrew's knuckles. A slide in the middle of the door hissed open and two red-rimmed eyes peered out. The eyes widened as they recognized Lee.

"Mr. Buckles! What—"

"The sheriff is waiting for me, Jackson."

The eyes blinked, then the slide snapped shut. A lock clicked and the steel door swung open.

"Uh, Sheriff Heer isn't in his office. He said he don't want to see no one. But, uh, I'll tell him you're here."

"I'd appreciate that," said Lee, brushing past the indecisive jailer with a strength that came from will alone.

"But—"

"Thank you, Jackson."

Lee's tone dismissed the jailer. Andrew followed Lee inside before Jackson thought to object. The door shut heavily behind them.

The thick stone walls held out most of the sounds of the crowd, but held in the odor of sweat and urine and disinfectant. Behind a barred gate, men were packed into the main holding cell, strikers streaked with dirt and caked with blood. Their complaints and curses were vicious; as with the townspeople outside, the riot had only whetted the strikers' hatred.

Sheriff Heer was not in his office, but they heard his harsh voice back in the cell blocks. As Lee waited, he looked at FBI and local wanted posters that covered one side of the sheriff's office like bizarre wallpaper. From the posters, men of all ages and races stared out, glassy-eyed, frozen at the moment of capture, a black-and-white graphic of failure.

From the rear of the building came other voices, angry or frightened or merely despairing, words without meaning, sounds out of a nightmare. For an instant Lee saw again a leather book enclosing hell and Roger Heer doubled over the barrel of a shotgun and this time Lee pulled the trigger, blowing apart a man and a world. The instant passed, leaving Lee with an inner despair that showed only in his eyes, a despair echoed by the voices seeping through the jailhouse.

"We can't be as stupid as they are," whispered Lee to himself. "No matter what, we must be smarter. Or they will win."

Sheriff Heer strode into the office, his thick body nearly blocking the doorway, dominating the small room. The harsh light of the bare, overhead bulb filled his face with unsettling shadows and highlights. Blotches of sweat were black against his dirt-streaked uniform. His gunbelt was fastened in the wrong notch. He put one hand on his hip and rested the other on the butt of the gun. Both hands trembled very slightly, the hands of a man who was sick or afraid. But his voice was without weakness, cruel.

"I've got better things to do than waste time on rich old farts and their bastards. What do you want that can't wait until morning."

"Maggie. Now."

As he spoke, Lee turned to face the sheriff. He saw a face shattered into angular shadows and glaring triangles of skin bleached white by naked light. Lee felt like he was falling, turning, time peeling away, but there was no shotgun in his hands now and Maggie had not been born then.

The sheriff's tongue flicked out, but the motion was futile, his mouth was as dry as his lips.

"Tough," he rasped. "You can't have her."

Though the sheriff's voice was steady, the tremor in his hands increased. Lee closed his eyes, weary almost beyond words.

"Do you want me to call a judge and have bail set for her?"

"I want you to get out of here."

The sheriff stepped closer, trying to intimidate Lee by size alone. But Lee was too tall and too old to be impressed by bluster. And he had seen the marks on the sheriff's face.

"Get her, Heer," said Lee softly, his eyes white. "Bring her to me. Now."

The sheriff jerked and the cruel light made each scratch on his cheeks leap out. Andrew stared, trying to remember if Heer had had so many marks earlier. Andrew's eyes, and the sweat that ran into the scratches, made Heer rub his right cheek. His fingers came away glistening with a mixture of sweat and fresh blood. He flinched suddenly, then balled his hand into a fist to conceal his stained, shaking fingers.

"She's not here," said the sheriff slowly, staring at his fist. "I turned her loose at the county line."

"I'll have the jail searched," said Lee.

"Search away." The sheriff laughed, too high, almost a cry. "I turned her loose, I tell you," he said, eyes unfocused as he tried to picture his own lies, to believe in them. "She's gone. She was scared. Yeah. God, was she scared. She'll never come back. You'll never see her again."

Both Lee and Andrew sensed Heer was telling some truth, and a vast lie, and finally neither man believed anything but the bright lines of blood drawn on the sheriff's cheeks by Maggie's hand.

"You're a dead man, Heer," whispered Andrew.

The sheriff's hand closed convulsively around the butt of his gun. He looked once at Andrew, but could not meet the white truth of his eyes.

"Get out," Heer said to Lee. The sheriff's voice was

334

higher now, more constricted. "Get out of here and take your other bastard with you. You ruined my old man, made him kill himself and now you're trying to do the same to me." He wanted to draw his gun, but his hand was shaking too hard. "I'll kill you right now."

"Dead man."

Lee walked toward the door as though the sheriff did not exist. Heer moved aside slowly, his eyes turned inward, looking for the death that the other two men saw so clearly. Andrew stood for a moment longer, watching Heer with clear, measuring eyes. Then Andrew turned and followed Lee out into a night seething with unspent violence.

Neither man spoke through the long drive back to the ranch; neither man wanted to be the first to say what each believed: Maggie was dead.

Lee stared out through the windshield at the night rushing by. Emotions moved over his face like winds over water as he saw old friends and enemies, children and the woman he loved, Cira who grew more alive with each breath he took.

Andrew stopped the car in front of the grove house, but Lee did not seem to notice. His eyes were pale, almost dazed. Even when Andrew got out of the car and opened Lee's door, Lee did not move. Andrew touched Lee's shoulder, feeling the bone too close beneath a thin layer of muscle.

"Lee," said Andrew softly. "You're home."

"Home . . . ?"

Lee blinked and his eyes slowly focused on Joy's house. The bands around his heart squeezed, dragging him into a present that offered only anguish and regret. His shoulders slowly sagged beneath Andrew's hand and Andrew felt Lee's strength draining away. Then, before Andrew could react, Lee straightened and pulled himself out of the car. He stood close to Andrew, his hands on Andrew's strong shoulders in a grip that was painful.

"I've lived too long," said Lee, looking into and beyond the eyes that were almost a mirror of his own. "Maggie is dead. Your mother is dead. I am dying. You're all that I have." Lee drew a slow, painful breath. "I'm sorry, son, that I could do no better for you."

Slowly, Andrew nodded, unable to speak.

For a moment they held one another, then Lee moved away from his son's support. With the slow steps of an old man, Lee walked across the driveway and vanished into the dense shadows of the grove house.

The strike ended quickly. Men on both sides were spent after two days in the devastating embrace of violence. Torpor settled over the land, a listlessness disturbed only by three events that rose like huge bubbles from the depths of the county's viscous peace.

The first event was the disappearance of the Workers' Magdalene on the eve of her greatest victory. Informal and formal searches were launched, to no conclusion. Though Sheriff Heer searched with a dedication that bordered on frenzy, he found no tangible sign of Maggie McCartney.

Rumor, however, was not restricted to the tangible; witnesses came forward who, since the riot, had seen Maggie in every Western state and three foreign countries. But no one could find her now, at that moment.

No rumor mentioned an anonymous canyon where chaparral grew.

The second event was Sheriff Heer's death. He had been chasing Maggie's ghost through the first rainstorm of the season. He was alone, refusing the company of other officers though his hands shook continually and he had not slept since the riot; and he drank one beer after another, as though there was an emptiness inside him that was greater than his bulk. He drove hard and fast, depending on strength rather than skill to keep the car on the road. But strength could not make a wet road dry, nor concrete soft.

The sheriff's car was found telescoped against a bridge abutment. He was still inside, and his hands no longer shook. Rumor said that he must have been wild with drink, or grief, or fear for his job, or any and all of those reasons in every combination.

No rumor whispered of a canyon with no name, where chaparral bent over a body in angular supplication.

The third event was Leander Buckles's illness. The morning after the riot, Gil Zavala found Lee slumped over a kitchen table in a small house on the edge of Colonia Juarez. No one knew how Lee had gotten there, until the next day when an aging Tennessee Walker was discovered tied in the garage that had once been a stable.

On Joy's unbending demands, and over a doctor's angry protests, the unconscious Lee Buckles was taken to the grove house. There, Joy sat by his bedside, saying no more than he, waiting. When Andrew arrived he was turned away with a brutality that Christina witnessed and never forgot. In those instants she learned to loathe the old woman who had been pressed between heavy volumes of experience until she was as faded and fragile as a dried flower.

Andrew went back to the house at the edge of the colonia. Gil was there, rocking in the sunshine on the porch, waiting for Lee's death, and his own. Beyond the graceful sweep of the winter jacaranda tree, at the other end of the path worn by Cira and Maggie and Andrew, the children of Gil's grandchildren played.

"She refused even you?" asked Andrew, climbing up the steps to his mother's house.

"*Si,*" said Gil, his voice dry and old. Then he smiled, showing long ivory teeth. "*Ni modo, hijo.* I knew a Lee Buckles that the gringa bitch could not imagine. Aaiieee," he said softly, "the times we had. I shared his life . . . she is welcome to his death."

Andrew looked away, eyes and throat aching with something deeper than anger. He lowered himself into the broad rocking chair next to Gil. Gil's dark, gnarled hand reached out, touching Andrew in silent comfort. Andrew glanced at Gil's seamed face. There was sorrow in the sunken eyes, but there was also serenity. He was an old man who had made peace with his own death. And, more difficult in many ways, with the deaths of his friends.

"Seguro," said Gil, as though he knew Andrew's thoughts. "I have lived about long enough, I think. Lee is the last one who knew me long ago. When he dies, there will be no one to look at me and see a young man."

Gil breathed shallowly and shifted his weight, easing the hip that had never quite healed after he had broken it in an irrigation ditch five years ago. He began to speak again, hesitated, then shrugged; if Andrew was not old enough to understand now, he never would be.

"Your father," said Gil deliberately, "probably never told you why he didn't divorce the gringa bitch."

Andrew's surprise showed only in the slight widening of his gray eyes; it was the first time Gil had ever referred to Lee as Andrew's father.

"That never mattered to me like it did to Maggie," said Andrew finally. "Besides, I know the ranch better than anyone but you and Lee. Marjorie had him by the balls. And when Marjorie's money no longer mattered to the ranch, my mother was dead."

There was more to it, of course, human emotions less substantial and more powerful than Byrd Todhunter's legacy to a vengeful daughter; but Gilberto Zavala was too weary to explain how the past resonated through the present and echoed into a future that he would never see. So he sighed and said what was simple to say.

"You will not be named as an heir in Lee's will."

Andrew's hands bunched on his knees as he leaned toward the old man who had given him a home when Lee could not.

"I don't give a shit about Lee's will. I've always known that the land would never be mine. Lee is all I have—and he's more than most sons ever have!"

Gil nodded, rocking slowly, unruffled by a young man's anger. "I know, *hijo.* I know. But you underestimate him, a common fault of sons. You will have your land, *hijo.* Somehow, he found a way to keep his word and still give the land to you."

Gil stood, descended the steps stiffly and shuffled across the yard toward the sound of his great-grandchildren's laughter. Andrew sat staring after him, stunned. Before he could gather himself to follow, a bright yellow convertible flashed by on the narrow dirt road that skirted the colonia. The car skidded, fishtailed, then clawed its way up the twisting lane that led to Cira's house. The car slid to a stop beneath the leafless jacaranda tree. Christina climbed out, stumbling toward the porch, her eyes deep and staring, dry and almost wild as she approached Andrew.

"He's dead," said Christina, her voice as dry and strange as her eyes. "He's dead and you know what she did? She laughed. She laughed and said, 'I've won, David. I've won. I outlived his whore and I outlived him. Haven't I won, David? David?' And then she made a funny noise and put her face in her hands."

Like an eerie human echo with violet eyes and nearly white hair, Christina imitated her grandmother's fragile movements.

"Who did she mean, Andrew? Who's David?"

"Mr. Carrington," he said softly. "David Carrington."

"But she acted like he was there and he died years and years ago."

"Yes."

"My father is drunk."

"Yes."

Christina paced the porch in front of Andrew, her eyes as restless as the rising wind. She stopped in front of him, then knelt suddenly, bringing their eyes almost level.

"Nobody cares that Lee is dead. Nobody but me. And you, Andrew. You care, don't you? You have caring eyes, like his. Eyes that see everything, even me. You care, don't you?"

Andrew reached out and touched her cheek with fingers as gentle as his voice. "Yes, Sunshine. I care."

Christina shuddered suddenly, violently. "Oh, my God. He's really dead, isn't he?"

"Yes," whispered Andrew, pulling her shaking body onto his lap, "yes."

Christina's arms went around him as she buried her face against his chest. Huge, dry sobs shook her body. He held her close, rocking her and whispering words with no meaning except the reassurance that he was there. At last tears came to her and to him and they wept for the death of the man who had loved them.

1941

The red sandstone exterior of San Ignacio's county court-house was spartan, radiating the heat of an unusually sunny, sultry autumn. The interior of the building was cooler, more inviting, thanks to some forgotten architect's love of high ceilings, wide rooms and mellow oak pan-eling. Tall windows admitted a lazy breeze and light tinted a cool green by passage through sycamore trees that stood more than two stories high. The light streaming in was like a halo around Christina Buckles's thick, pale hair, giving her a lambent aura of life just stirring, barely awakened.

The same light that caressed Christina stripped Joy of all but age. Her faded lavender eyes squinted against the unwanted brilliance, making her eyelids almost vanish in the myriad colorless wrinkles that were her face.

Nor was the light kind to or welcomed by Champ. He had his back to the windows, his eyes almost shut in an attempt to mitigate the hammer blows of light against his bloodshot eyes. His hair was wan and thin, the color of winter butter. Like his grandfather Todhunter, Champ would be bald before he was gray.

Joy leaned toward her only child. The hand she put on

341

his sleeve was graceful despite the dark spots mottling the skin that had once glowed like fine white jade.

"I still don't understand why the judge couldn't come to the house," she said in a dry, querulous voice. "After all Leander did for the county, and especially for Judge Prufrock's uncle—"

"Great-uncle," corrected Champ, rubbing his eyes with hands as delicate as Joy's. "Or was it his great-great uncle?"

"—you would think I would be entitled to a small amount of consideration," finished Joy, oblivious to her son's interruption.

Champ glanced away from his mother. He sighed and shifted on the oak bench that was more uncomfortable than a church pew.

"Yes, Mother," Champ said with a total lack of interest.

In the nearly four years since Lee had died, Joy had taken less and less interest in the details of daily living. She had begun to ignore the present in favor of a past which she reshaped to suit her needs. As a result, her reasoning had become less accessible to others, and her memory had failed her on a number of significant points.

Champ sighed and closed his eyes against the cruel light, wishing he could as easily shut out the frail woman whose bony hand held his wrist.

"Champion, I still don't under—"

"Mother. I've told you a hundred times, there is a little problem with the will." At the understatement, Champ made a high, short sound that was meant to be a laugh. He moved his thick tongue over his lips, wishing he had the flask he had left in the car. Scotch would cut the sludge that coated his mouth. "A little problem. So here we are, waiting for Judge Prufrock to give me what is already mine. And then, my dear mother, I'm going to sell my father's fucking land and live in Monaco."

"Problem," repeated Joy slowly in her dry, husky voice, ignoring most of what Champ had said because it did not coincide with the reality she desired. "There can be no problem, Champion. David promised me, as did

Leander. And whatever your father's other moral failings, he always kept his word."

Champ rubbed his forehead with shaking hands. His mother and the will were like separate knives behind his eyes. Cheap cigars, bad liquor and worse cards in the Blue Turtle's airless upstairs room had left him with a hangover that was shattering his brain and twisting his stomach into a knot that threatened to push his breakfast back up his throat. He tuned out his mother's futile words and studied the tall, cut-glass pitcher that waited on the bench at arm's length from where Judge Prufrock would sit. The pitcher only increased Champ's thirst. He needed a drink, badly.

"Champion, are you feeling well?" asked Joy, her eyes and voice suddenly aware. "Your hands are not steady."

Champ balled his betraying hands into his suit pockets and wished for a drink with a passion he had never felt for anything else.

"I'm fine, Mother."

"But—"

"Shut up, Mother," he said quietly, brutally, ignoring Christina's shocked look. "Just shut up."

Joy's expression faded into countless anonymous wrinkles. As Champ had intended, his unpleasantness drove his mother into her own world where people were unfailingly polite, unfailingly kind. Champ knew he would loathe himself for hurting her, but the loathing would not come until the final maudlin stage of drunkenness. At the moment, he had no emotion to spare for any pain but his own.

The tall swinging doors that opened onto the corridor pivoted on their brass supports. Champ looked up long enough to see three of his lawyers. Two lawyers were from Los Angeles and the third had been imported—at the urgent advice of the first two—from New York. All three men were laden with briefcases and portfolios and law books, ammunition enough for an interminable legal battle. All three men had the controlled, yet subtly desperate look of generals who were seeing their campaign collapse in the face of a superior enemy.

343

Just as the doors swung silently shut behind the lawyers, Champ glimpsed something through the frosted glass panels, an impression of a clean profile that belonged to a man four years dead. Champ shuddered, wondering if he was going to experience another horror-filled siege of delusions and waking nightmares. He bit the inside of his lip, hoping that pain would sidetrack his nerves until he had time to get his flask from the car. He tried to get to his feet, but so long as that dark ghost waited beyond the door, even the certainty of liquor could not give Champ the strength to walk.

The silhouette behind frosted glass moved, pushing the door open. Champ jerked, then realized that the figure who was clothed in a dark suit and confidence, the figure who moved and spoke and even gestured like a man four years dead, that figure was not a dark ghost conjured by alcohol-deprived nerves. With a feeling of mingled relief and hatred, Champ recognized Andrew McCartney standing four feet away.

Champ stared beyond Andrew's shoulder, pretending he had seen no more than the shadow of leaves sliding across a window. Joy, however, was shocked out of her carefully constructed world by Andrew's presence.

"What is that—that *Mexican* doing here?"

Joy's hissing whisper was audible in every corner of the large courtroom. Her groping choice of insult brought a fleeting smile to Andrew's face. In that instant Andrew looked so much like Lee that Champ's stomach twisted, spreading a sour feeling throughout his body. Andrew nodded in the direction of the three Buckleses, acknowledging their presence with a politeness that Joy should have appreciated.

"What is he doing here?" she demanded again. "This is private. For family."

Then, as though Joy remembered something she had given most of her world to forget, her mouth clamped in a thin line. She glanced from Champ's sagging, sweating face to Andrew's clean profile. Then she carefully looked nowhere but at the scented lace handkerchief peeping out of the long sleeve of her silk dress.

344

Slowly, Champ moved his head until even Andrew's shadow was beyond his bloodshot vision. Though Champ was taller, broader and more socially acceptable than Andrew, Champ always felt diminished in Andrew's presence. Diminished, and angry. No one needed to tell Champ that he lacked his father's compelling personality. That a bastard son had Lee's presence was a source of corrosive resentment to Champ.

Champ closed his eyes fully, retreating into soothing dimness. Effortlessly, his thoughts clicked into a familiar track that led back nearly two decades to the time when his mother had given him more money than even a dedicated playboy could spend. But that had ended when Cynthia had become a too obviously pregnant bride. Joy's reaction had been swift. Champ's allowance was reduced drastically, and even that remainder depended on Champ living at the grove house with his mother.

Champ had complained, argued, sulked . . . and moved his pregnant, sixteen-year-old wife back to California on the assumption that he could cajole his mother into changing her mind. Joy, however, proved to be adamant. When Champ finally demanded that his father "do something," Lee had immediately offered Champ a job with the Buckles Company. Champ had been so incensed that he had not spoken to his father for weeks. Or to anyone else. It had been the first of Champ's many monumental drunks.

The memory of that sweet oblivion made Champ's lips twist into a smile. Without realizing it, he made a sound between a sigh and a groan.

"Daddy," said Christina.

Champ either did not hear her or chose to ignore her. Christina gave him one last look, then decided that his face—sweaty and vaguely yellow beneath a thin tan—looked no worse than it had many times in the past. With an impatient movement of her shoulders, Christina returned her attention to Andrew, who was talking with the bailiff no more than six feet away.

It was as close to Andrew as Christina had been since the night Lee died. Even now, the memory made her throat tighten. No one, before or since, had given her such a feeling of comfort. On that porch at the edge of the colonia, she had discovered what it was like to be accepted, wholly, with neither disguise nor artifice. It had been an experience both precious and shattering. That night she had sensed the bonds from the past flowing between Andrew and herself like a river sunk so deeply into the earth that it was hidden from all but itself.

With a feeling that was part longing, part fear, Christina looked at the face that had smiled over her childhood, at the man who had not been afraid to share her grief. Andrew had not changed, except to become even more handsome, more assured, radiating strength as inevitably as fire radiated heat. She could not help comparing his calm assurance to her father's queasy withdrawal. The comparison made her uncomfortable, defensive; was it Champ's fault that Lee had had an unreasonable affection for a boy raised by a Mexican ranch hand?

Andrew murmured something that made the bailiff grin. When Andrew turned away, smiling, his clear gray eyes rested briefly on Christina. His smile went through her defenses, sinking into her, one more current added to their unknown river. She smiled at him, a quick curve of warmth in a face framed by hair like pale fire.

Sunshine.

Though Andrew did not speak, they both heard the word as clearly as they heard the bee that was quartering the transparent barrier of a nearby window. Suddenly the bee landed on the glass, making the courtroom's silence complete.

"I don't want him here."

Joy's dry whisper seemed to galvanize everyone. The attorneys began conferring in low tones, Champ opened his eyes, and Christina realized that she was smiling at the man her father said was no better than a thief trying to steal what by right belonged to the Buckles family. Feeling confused and helpless and more than a little angry at a life that grew more complicated as she grew older, Christina looked away from Andrew's translucent gray eyes.

"Hush, Grandmother Joy," said Christina. "It will be over soon."

As though to prove Christina correct, the doors swung open again. A group of lawyers, as laden as the first three attorneys had been, pushed into the room. All the men were grim, apparently restraining themselves only out of deference to the traditions of the courtroom.

The lawyers passed through the swinging gate separating the empty spectator seats from the tables which faced the bench. In silence, three of the attorneys went to sit with Andrew at one table. The remaining four lawyers joined the other three at the table where three generations of Buckleses sat.

The bailiff took his position at a side desk. The court clerk entered. Just behind him was the white-haired judge. Everyone stood up, except Joy. No one presumed to ask her to stand. Judge Prufrock mounted the steps to the bench so quickly that his black robe belled out behind him. The bailiff hesitated, eyeing the empty rows of seats. After a moment of indecision, he cut his customary spiel to a single, succinct statement.

"This court is now in session."

While everyone sat down again, Judge Prufrock examined the papers that had been placed in front of him. The judge was both nervous and guarded as he nodded to each member of the Buckles family, to the assembled lawyers, and, almost as an afterthought, to Andrew.

"Yes," said the judge, rearranging the papers in front of him. "Well . . ." He cleared his throat, obviously reluctant to speak. "We may as well begin." He focused his darting brown eyes on the attorneys. "Have you gentlemen been able to come to any agreement?"

All seven Buckles attorneys stood as one, anxious to show their respect, as there was little else they could do to affect their situation.

"I'm afraid I would have to say that we have not yet reached any agreement," said the senior Buckles attorney in the accents of New York. "I am afraid that the attorneys representing Andrew McCartney and the Buckles Trust have not been inclined to reach an equitable settlement." He cast a disparaging, sidelong glance directly at Andrew, who cocked an eyebrow in cool amusement.

"Your honor," said one of Andrew's lawyers, "as usual, Mr. Hart is being less than forthcoming. He had yet to offer anything that a fair man would recognize as equitable. He certainly has not offered any settlement that is even tangential to the desires of the late Leander Buckles. If the attorneys for the Buckles family had seen fit to offer a settlement that even began to approach propriety, we would have been more than willing to entertain it."

Judge Prufrock frowned. "In other words, there is neither settlement nor prospect of one."

"Yes, your honor," responded the lawyers at both tables. It was the one thing they could agree on.

"What a shame." Judge Prufrock folded his hands. As though drawn by the bee's futile buzzing, the judge addressed his remark to the high window. "I had hoped to avoid this."

The judge picked up the sheaf of papers on the bar before him, tapped the sheaf into an even stack and set it precisely in a line with the edge of the wood. He glanced once more at the two parties, as though trying to find the one approach that would resolve what four years of strenuous litigation had not.

"Well," began Judge Prufrock finally, "I suppose that the first thing I must say is that this disagreement must be settled, both for the good of the parties and the property involved.

"Now, I have read the extensive briefs from both sides, and I can assure both parties that they have had able representation. There can be no question of that."

Judge Prufrock nodded again to the Buckles family and, belatedly, to Andrew. In return, the judge received a noncommittal look from the latter and an angry stare from Joy. With a brittle movement, she inclined her head toward her son.

"What is he running on for?" Joy asked in a voice that could be understood on the bench. "Can't he make up his mind?"

Judge Prufrock flushed. The color of his face seemed more pronounced for the whiteness of his hair and the blackness of his robes. The remark, however, did goad him into an arena he had no wish to enter.

"Yes, Mrs. Buckles," said the judge with remarkable aplomb. "I've made up my mind. I'm afraid you won't be pleased with the result. Be that as it may, I'm not going to abrogate your late husband's will. There is neither legal nor moral reason to do so. The worldly goods itemized in that will are now and will remain under the control of the Buckles Trust as stipulated in Leander Buckles's will."

"What kind of nonsense is this?" asked Joy, straightening and fixing Judge Prufrock with eyes where a shadow of lavender fire flickered once again. She turned toward her son, whose disappointment was as plain as the cold sweat on his face. "Champ, what kind of fiddle-faddle is he talking?"

Champ did not reply. His eyes had closed and he was living only for the moment that he could go to the car and take his cool silver flask out of the glove compartment.

"Grandmother Joy," said Christina softly, putting an arm lightly around Joy's shoulders, "please let the judge finish."

Startled more by the touch than by the gentle admonishment, Joy looked up into her granddaughter's unlined face. It was like looking back fifty years into a mirror. With a small sound, Joy closed her eyes.

"To repeat," sighed Judge Prufrock, "there is no legal reason to abrogate this will. When Mr. Buckles drew up this document in 1910, he obviously had the benefit of extremely able legal advisers. The will and the articles of incorporation of the Buckles Trust are seamless legal documents." The judge sighed. "Seamless. The late Mr. Buckles periodically reviewed and ratified them with additions and amendments, each one signed and witnessed. He was definitely of sound mind. He knew precisely what he was doing."

"But we're his family—not the Trust," wailed Joy softly. "What about us? He promised. David promised."

Christina touched her grandmother again, but Joy drew

349

away. Her distaste for being touched had increased as she grew older.

"Mrs. Buckles," said the judge, looking everywhere but at her, his voice a mixture of reason and embarrassment, "your husband's will provides for you, and very handsomely." He shuffled the papers in front of him until he found the passage he wanted. He began to read aloud, paraphrasing into common English as he did so. The ease with which he spoke showed that it was not the first time he had had the experience of explaining complex legal documents to laymen.

"My lovely and devoted wife, Marjorie, shall never want for anything so long as I live . . . and . . . should I precede her in death, the Buckles Trust . . . will be ever mindful of her needs. I intend . . . fifteen percent of the shares in the ranch to her, ten percent to Champion, and twenty-four percent to my beloved granddaughter, Christina. The proceeds from the operation of the Trust . . . divided accordingly on an annual basis"—the judge turned to a new sheet—"should that income ever fail their fundamental needs . . . the Trust will . . . make up the difference."

Judge Prufrock paused, looking up. He saw that Joy was not in the least mollified. Before she could speak, he continued reading aloud, summarizing and simplifying in a way that made the attorneys wince.

"Both my wife and Champion have made clear to me their desire . . . to be free from . . . direct control of any aspect of my business. I respect those wishes in death as I did in life. The control of the ranch and of all my holdings will be lodged with the . . . fifty-one percent share of stock . . . to the Buckles Trust. The Trust will be controlled and administered by Andrew Pico McCartney, a man trained by myself to operate my holdings in a profitable manner . . . benefit to those who bear my name and those who do not. . . ."

The judge looked up and met Joy's eyes without flinching. "Mrs. Buckles, I have to say that this document is an expression of the love your husband had for you. Your feelings of betrayal are . . . misguided. Your husband made every effort to respect your wishes and your welfare. In my opinion, he succeeded admirably, as even the most cursory perusal of the balance sheets of the Buckles Trust profit-and-loss statements would show. Though of course," he said hastily, "as a charitable Trust, the word profit is a misnomer." He cleared his throat. "Granted, Mr. McCartney's salary might seem generous for a man so young, but he is also an extremely able—"

Joy stood up before Christina could restrain her. The old woman faced the judge and pointed dramatically at Andrew.

"If my husband loved me so well, why did he leave control of what is mine to that Mexican bastard!"

With a calm, small smile that infuriated Joy almost as much as his opaque gray eyes, Andrew nodded toward Joy as though acknowledging a compliment. Rather than face those eyes—Lee's eyes—Joy turned and bent over Champ, who was pressed against his seat as though pinned by the weight of his own helplessness.

"Do something, Champion. Stop them. I'm only a woman, but you, you are a man. You can't let a Mexican take away all that is ours. Stop him!"

Champ stood and said clearly, "I left something in the car."

Joy watched her son vanish through the swinging doors. Then she turned and looked at each face in the courtroom, searching for someone who was not there.

"David?" she asked softly as her eyes went from face to face. "Where are you? Don't tease, David, I need you."

No one spoke. No one could face the faded eyes and the plea on Joy's wrinkled face. And then she stood looking at no one and nothing.

"I didn't win after all, David, did I?"

The last pale flicker died behind Joy's eyes. She smiled brightly, meaninglessly. Christina bent her head, fighting against a sadness she could not explain. When she finally looked up, she saw her grandmother swaying slightly. Christina stood and touched the frail, white-haired woman.

"It's time to go home, Grandmother Joy."

Joy turned toward her granddaughter with an utter lack of recognition, but she did not pull away when Christina led her from the courtroom. As the doors swung back and forth behind them, their voices floated back into the courtroom.

"Is David waiting for me at home?"

"David Carrington is dead, Grandmother Joy."

"Dead? Oh, no, that can't be," said Joy lightly, reasonably. "If he is dead, why am I alive?"

The courtroom doors closed, shutting out Christina's answer.

Bayshore Road wound across the shore bluffs like a dusty snake. As the sultry yellow light of day deepened into late afternoon, the sun-cured grass and brush took on a golden glow. At times the road ran along the ragged edge of the bluffs, close enough for a clear view of the dark Pacific stretching to a horizon as distinct as it was distant.

Andrew drove south along the bluffs, enjoying the almost steamy ocean vista. From the corner of his eye he watched a seiner working a school of anchovies a few miles offshore. The ocean was one of the few things in Andrew's world that he neither wished to nor had to affect. He was too caught up with the land-locked interests of the Buckles Trust for the ranch to offer him much relaxation. The ocean was different. He could watch it, speculate about its source and nature and purpose, and not feel required to produce results from his splendidly idle thoughts. The ocean brought him peace and asked nothing in return.

Late afternoon sun poured over the land like lava, hot, thick, and orange. The air coming in the windows of the Ford was rich with moisture and brine, almost as tangible a presence as earth and water. Andrew drove without a hat, resisting fashion in favor of comfort, allowing the heavy air to rumple his dark hair and bring at least an illusion of coolness. He drove the car with one hand and tried to assess the texture of the air outside with the other. He had never felt air quite so thick, so steamy, so . . . full. Like a fluid weight over the land.

The road to Frenchman's Cove was newly graveled. Pebbles sang against metal as they snapped off of the underside of the car and bounced away into the dry grass. A thin banner of dust trailed behind, no higher than the car, as though the air was too full to digest even the lightest snack of dust.

When Andrew glanced in the rear-view mirror, he saw that the car that had been following him for the last four miles was still there, keeping station four hundred yards behind him as though being towed at the end of a long line. All of his attempts to shorten the line by slowing down had been unsuccessful. He was not particularly concerned about his belated shadow, merely curious. After yesterday's scene in the courtroom, he wondered why a member of the Buckles family would choose to come close to him.

The road swung away from the ocean edge of the half-mile-wide bluff top and turned inland as though heading toward the low, rugged hills that rose beyond the flat land of the bluff top. The road zigzagged around a steep, short ravine and returned to the edge of the bluffs as though reluctant to leave the sound and sight of waves breaking over black rock cliffs.

After several miles, the road dropped into a crease in the bluff line. At the bottom of the crease lay a place called Smugglers' Beach. The road cut across a narrow mud flat, rose over a rib of slate, dropped again, then began the final climb back to the top of the bluffs. Just before the road rose to the bluffs, two twisting ruts headed off for the sandy beach. The height of the slate rib hid the turn-off to the beach. When Andrew pulled off the main road, he effectively vanished.

Andrew sat for almost a minute with his engine still running, watching the main road in his rear-view mirror, waiting for the car that had been following him. If the other car's presence was mere coincidence, the car would simply drive on by. But the other driver saw Andrew's car, braked to a sharp stop and sat for a moment in the

353

middle of the main road as though trying to decide what to do.

Andrew stuck his left arm out the window and waved the other car to come around. A moment later, Christina Buckles's scarlet Chrysler convertible came to a stop beside his car. Christina's face was flushed with more than the sultry afternoon. She hesitated again, then turned off the ignition and slid across the seat until she was no more than two feet away from the black Ford.

"Hello, Andrew. How have you been?"

There was little left in Christina's voice of either child or schoolgirl. In the years since Lee had died, Christina had grown up. And, if rumors were to be believed, she had grown up wild. With Lee gone, there was no one Christina respected, no one strong enough to curb her impulses. Marriage had been one of those impulses, an arrangement so unimportant to her that she had ordered the contract dissolved after only a few months. She had become bored with the East and had returned to a family that could neither understand nor handle her. She was a sexually confident woman, accustomed to controlling men through their desires, desires she neither understood nor really shared.

"I've been all right, Christina," Andrew said.

There was a distinct gap in the conversation that was subtly dominated by the iridescent beauty who sat within reach of Andrew's left hand. He was vaguely uncomfortable, though a moment ago he had been sure how he would treat her. But that sureness had vanished with her slow smile. For an instant he was nothing more than the bastard offspring of a dead man. Then the instant passed without causing even a ripple across the face of his control.

"Why were you following me?" asked Andrew in the neutral tone he had learned from Lee.

Christina studied Andrew with violet eyes that were confused and wary, searching for the man who had comforted her four years ago. "I wanted to talk to you," she said slowly, "but I couldn't think of how to approach you."

The remark had a candor that could have been a remnant of youthfulness or a warning of new maturity. Andrew had lost his own youth long ago, but he still used candor—as a weapon. He sensed that Christina used truth in a similar way.

"Why do you want to talk to me?"

Christina's hand moved as though to reach out to him, to ask for help. The mute plea went through Andrew like a knife, as did the fact that she had grown up enough to control her impulses. Once she would have touched him without thinking, but that was in the past and they were caught in the present.

"You're not very popular around our house," said Christina, looking away from Andrew's watchful gray eyes. Then, as though compelled against her judgment, she faced him again and her hands gripped the side of the car as though it were his arm. "I need you—to talk. No one else—" She stopped and began all over again. "I can't get straight answers from anyone else."

"What makes you think you can get them from a Mexican bastard?"

"From a—" Christina shook her head as though waking from a dream. "I don't think of you like that," she said in a small voice. "You're Andrew. You're Andrew and you've never lied to me and I need you. Answers. Grandmother is no help and Daddy is drunk." Christina stared out at the ocean with sightless violet eyes. "You and me and Lee. Funny, but sometimes I think we three are—were—more alike than anyone else in the family. On the ranch, I mean. That's sort of a family, isn't it?"

Andrew studied Christina's face for a long time, seeking some signal that she was taunting him, but there was nothing in her expression except a confused groping toward some kind of truth.

"You really don't know, do you?" he said.

Christina looked at him, confused and somehow fearful, as if she suspected that the things she did not know could hurt her very deeply.

"Let's drive down to the beach," said Andrew. "That way no one will see your car and run to tell your daddy."

Andrew drove down the twin ruts toward the headlands that were 'the Buckles horn of the crescent around Frenchman's Cove. Christina followed more slowly. She parked beside his car on a rocky edge of the road. Andrew was already out of his car, sitting on the front fender of the Ford with an assurance that was as much a part of him as his eyes.

Even in the relative cool of the late afternoon ocean breeze, Andrew's blue shirt clung to his body, held against each swell of muscle by heat and sweat. Christina hesitated for a moment, staring, surprised by his unexpected power and silence. She had seen Andrew as many things, but never simply as a man. And as a man, he was a primal presence, nearly overwhelming.

As though Andrew sensed Christina's fear, if not its source, he turned toward her, smiling crookedly. "Hey, you've come too far to chicken out now."

Christina's answering smile was tentative, but the teasing voice out of her past banished the flash of fear. Her natural confidence reasserted itself. She got out of her bright convertible and leaned gracefully against its fender, facing Andrew, determined to hold her own with him, not to crumble in his presence as her father did.

"Thank you for talking to me. I know my family has been . . . unpleasant . . . to you in the past."

Christina avoided Andrew's probing gray eyes by staring out over the oily heave of the ocean. The waves were small, as though the sultry weight of the air was pressing even the ocean flat.

Andrew watched Christina without seeming to, measuring the changes four years had made. Four years containing one husband, one divorce, and no children. But there was nothing to show for the experience, except that her expression had lost the soft curves of childish innocence. The triangular shape of her face was striking, intelligent, and oddly vulnerable. She wore little makeup. The translucent blush across her high cheekbones was as natural as the unlacquered toenails peeking out of her sandals. Her body was slim and yet rounded, promising both strength and softness.

As Andrew looked, he realized that Christina had irrevocably crossed the boundary into womanhood. She was in that time of her life when women learn the sweet power of their bodies. The thick sunlight touched every aspect of her with a freedom he suddenly envied. He had never seen her as a woman before; his response was too potent to be comfortable.

Christina turned toward Andrew, searching his face as she had searched the distant horizon. In the orange light her eyes were incredibly violet, shadowed by emotions Andrew wanted to explore. But he kept his arms crossed tightly against his chest, unsure of his own reactions for the first time in many years.

"Why is all this happening?" she asked, her voice streaked with pain and confusion. But before he could say anything, she spoke quickly, as though afraid that if she did not speak now she would lose the chance forever. "I don't understand. I always thought my family was just a family. Like everyone else, only richer. Then Lee died and there was his will. Why did Lee hate his family so much?"

The simple hurt in Christina's question convinced Andrew that somehow Christina had remained innocent of the truth and gossip surrounding the Buckles family. Innocent, yet not invulnerable.

"Lee didn't hate you," said Andrew, his voice gentle, certain. For a second his hand rested on her arm, but he was too conscious of the smooth heat of her body. He lifted his hand almost before she realized he had touched her. "Lee loved you very much. Have you forgotten so quickly?"

Christina shook her head, then lifted her eyes to meet his. "I know. I remember. That's why I wanted the land. I thought he understood that. My need. Without him there was no center, no—" She shrugged and her face suddenly looked harder. "Everything changed when Lee died. He said he loved me but he gave everything he cared about to a—to a damn piece of paper, to—" She dropped her eyes suddenly.

357

"To me, you mean," said Andrew quietly, no longer smiling.

"Yes, I guess so." She glanced at him in a flash of violet. "But I don't mean it like Grandmother Joy means it." She touched Andrew's arm as quickly as he had touched her. "I don't hate you, Andrew."

"Thank you," said Andrew softly, and was surprised to realize how deeply he meant it.

Andrew looked away from Christina, toward the ocean where a freighter was hull-down on the horizon, headed north from San Diego. Just behind the freighter, deep purple against the blaze of the falling sun, was the ragged shape of a Channel Island. The air between island and mainland turned and shimmered, alive with light.

"The ranch was all that Lee Buckles had," Andrew said finally, choosing each word, trying to reveal no more than she needed to know, knowing just how powerful a weapon truth could be. "The ranch was pretty much his whole life from the time he came here when he was twenty-one until the day he died. It was all that separated him from other men, and he made the most of it."

Andrew paused and glanced over at Christina. She was watching him intently. Her eyes were almost as dark as the island, but clearer in color, deeper. He pulled his glance back to the sunset twisting over the face of the sea.

"All of Lee's life was spent trying to keep this ranch intact, to make it produce so that he wouldn't have to sell it off a piece at a time. He wanted the ranch to be whole, a gift from the past to the future.

"But your grandmother and father . . ." Andrew shrugged. "They never shared Lee's love of the land. I have it. So do you, in many ways." Andrew paused, picking his way through thickets of near-truths, half-truths and gentle lies. "But he could not leave the land to you. He did what he could, divided what he had to and put the rest into the Trust. And he told me before he died that he would have left more of it to you, except that you were too young to understand what to do with that kind of power."

358

"He loved you."

". . . Yes," said Andrew simply, feeling a loss that was no less painful for its familiarity.

Christina read the emotions that shadowed Andrew's face and realized what she had only suspected before: Andrew had loved Lee better than anyone in the Buckles family, even Lee's own son. Especially his son.

"Is that why Grandmother Joy hates you?" said Christina, thinking aloud. "And Daddy?"

"Probably," Andrew said with a casualness he did not feel.

Christina sighed. "Well, I suppose Lee did what he believed was best. That's what he was always telling me to do." She smiled, remembering the tall, silver-haired man with the deceptively soft voice. "He said I had a good head for business, except when I dug in and demanded my own way 'come hell or high water.'"

"He said the same thing to me. Told me I could out-stubborn a mule." Andrew smiled and looked over at Christina. "I suppose that means our partnership in the Trust will be a little difficult."

"I suppose. And," added Christina with an ironic edge to her voice, "I also suppose you'll enjoy it more than I will, if only because you'll have more of the partnership than I do."

"I doubt that I'll have twice as much fun," said Andrew dryly, "even if I have twice the stock at my disposal."

"Twice, plus one percent," she corrected, her eyes once again measuring infinity. "Don't forget that crucial one percent."

"I won't forget it, partner," drawled Andrew, inviting her to smile at his expense. He held out his hand for a ritual shake and added, "We'll have to hold business meetings like this more often."

Christina laughed lightly as she extended her own hand. When she felt the firm pressure of his fingers around her own, his palm over hers, warmth moving over warmth, her laughter died. The woman in her rose up to

359

measure the man who was so close. For an instant she saw the deep river flowing between them, past and future; and she knew she could drown. She pulled back against the fender of her bright convertible, forgetting all the questions she had wanted to ask, forgetting everything but the answering blaze of gray eyes measuring the woman in her.

"I'd better go now," Christina said hurriedly.

She turned and walked around her car without looking back. The door slammed behind her and she started the engine up quickly. As the convertible sped away, Andrew found himself willing her to look back at him. And at the last moment, she did. Then she was gone in a flash of chrome and scarlet paint, leaving him alone in the sultry evening, watching the road where she had disappeared, knowing he should not see her alone again. And knowing he would.

The electric cars of the Pacific Coast Railroad clacked and whirred into the Frenchman's Cove depot and disgorged the first weekend crowds of inlanders. In spite of almost daily headlines hinting at the ramifications of European battles—or perhaps because of them—the tourists seemed determined on buying, drinking and blustering their way to a memorable time. Their flushed, sweating faces were almost grim, their laughter erratic and unconvincing.

The sun was hot. The humidity was brutal. Southern California was struggling in the twentieth straight day of a tropical pressure cooker. Even though every window of the rail cars had been thrown open, the long, slow trip from the steamy San Gabriel Valley to the steamy vices of Frenchman's Cove had been enervating.

Once the rail cars stopped moving, still air wrapped around the passengers like an unwelcome blanket. By the time the crowds peeled sticky limbs off of uncomfortable seats, the collective temper was a silent snarl. The depot, only a dozen blocks from the water, was almost as hot as the stifling farmlands across which the tourists had fled.

The air was so still that the ocean's influence went no further than the high tide mark. Even there, with a water temperature of seventy-two degrees, there was no solace except in the surf. As a result, most people crowded into bars, drinking whatever was tall and cold and quick, anesthetizing themselves against the relentless heat.

Andrew watched the Friday-evening people flow away from the small depot. Frenchman's Cove had always been an attractive place to visit, but the people who were now drawn to the seaside town were different from those Andrew remembered in his youth. There had been a geniality in the past years. People had known one another, had stopped to socialize on the streets and along the sun-brilliant shore. But now the crowds were larger, more anonymous and less affable. There were textures of aggression, of general predation.

Though Andrew did not like it, he knew that the changing composition of the crowds in Frenchman's Cove reflected an era and a country in turmoil. Whole populations were on the move, headed West out of the dust bowl or out of the carnivorous cities of the East, people pouring into the small cities and smaller towns of California, swelling them until the gracious traditions of another era burst apart, leaving only tattered scraps of custom to restrain the restless newcomers.

San Ignacio had doubled, then tripled in population in less than a decade. Frenchman's Cove had a permanent population of 1,500 and a weekend population of at least four times that number. Cheap cottages and stucco duplexes crowded the beach and the margins of the bay. The islands that had been created when the bay was dredged were paved over with narrow lanes and tacky weekend houses. And for those who could not afford a room, there was always the sand, dirtier every season.

With an insight that Lee would have admired, Andrew watched the tidal wave of people engulfing the town and knew that he was seeing the future. The last great migration West, a migration that would both invite and force change; and the greatest change would be in the use of the land. Agriculture was the mainstay of the Buckles

Trust, but that would change. People who visited today would want to buy homes tomorrow. The price of land would double, triple, quadruple and then soar. Land was taxed at its market value rather than at its rate of production; Andrew could foresee a time when even the best harvests would fail to cover taxes, much less complex agricultural costs. Profit would be only a memory.

And then the land would have to be sold.

It was not a thought that comforted Andrew McCartney. But it was not simply growth and its inevitable dislocations that were disturbing to him, it was the type of people who were crowding up to the edges of Buckles land.

Frenchman's Cove had once been a respectable fishing village. The old wooden pier still marched out five-hundred feet into the ocean. The pier had provided an outlet for agricultural products as well as a convenience for fishermen. From the pier, fresh fruit and vegetables from the Buckles Ranch were shipped north along the coast as far as Seattle. To fishermen and farmers alike, the pier symbolized hard work and expanding markets.

But fancy lights and easy living also had been a part of Frenchman's Cove for almost all of its history. When the Buckles Ranch was little more than Lee's determination to hold onto the land, the Frenchman had built his elegant hotel just a few hundred yards for fishermen's shacks. After the shacks and hotel had burned down, encouraged by a fierce exhalation of a Santa Ana wind, Roger Heer had built a new, much less elegant hotel-*cum*-whorehouse. The lack of elegance was intensified by time, poverty and Reggie Heer's management. Nonetheless, the seamy pretensions of both Heers had crowded out all but a few stubborn fishermen.

There had been another aspect of the Heer operation in Frenchman's Cove. During the years of Prohibition, whiskey ships anchored beyond the three-mile limit and sent ashore swift boats crammed with high-proof contraband. Before the harbor had been dredged—opening up dozens of small docks to smugglers—Heer's men had unloaded onto the long pier. Lee had attempted to prevent use of the pier by Heer's smugglers, but Southern California's thirst proved more potent than Lee's influence.

Lee's antipathy to smuggling had been pragmatic rather than dogmatic. He wanted to prevent Roger Heer from expanding his base of power. When Roger Heer died, his son Reggie had continued the family business—hotels and whorehouses and casinos. Reggie Heer was an inept businessman. By the time younger brother Jason was eighteen, Jason knew much more about the economics of whores, barrooms and poker than Reggie would ever learn. So it was Jason who operated their father's rundown legacy, living by scavenging the edges of society.

As Andrew saw it, the problem was not that Jason Heer's fleshpots existed, but that—unchecked—they inevitably would take over the character of the community. Already, Frenchman's Cove was losing its reputation as a decent, small resort and gaining notoriety as a town of ill repute, a place where "Heer's Hell" meant more than just the casino.

To Andrew, the town's slide into illegitimacy was not only personally distasteful, but commercially appalling as well. He had visions of Frenchman's Cove as a Gold Coast, not a Barbary Coast. The visions were part of Lee's legacy to his unacknowledged son, and to the future. Lee had often talked about the day when the coastline rather than the fertile inland plain would be the richest resource of the Buckles Ranch.

Lee's prediction had been partly realized. The dredged harbor at Frenchman's Cove had quickly become the site of a cluster of expensive homes owned by Angelenos who were too busy to go to the French Riviera every time they wanted to relax in the sun. Motion picture directors, actors, lawyers and other assorted professionals were the leading edge of a gradual migration of fame and wealth to the beautiful place once known as Blue Lagoon. The homes that such immigrants built were large, luxurious and private. Many of them were built on land leased from the Buckles Company, Lee's way of encouraging the carriage trade to settle in Moreno County.

For a time, Lee's plan had worked. Frenchman's Cove

had been as prestigious as Beverly Hills or Miami Beach. But then the other migration had begun, that of rootless young men flushed with their first steady paychecks as America went from Depression through various Deals and finally to the profitable work of producing war materials. The character of Frenchman's Cove had become flashier, less substantial, attracting people who rarely lifted their eyes from the stained green baize of the Blue Turtle's poker tables. Lately, Frenchman's Cove had become synonymous with tawdry entertainments; or as one Los Angeles columnist put it, "Frenchman's Cove is a place where Lot's wife would have felt right at home." Unless the trend was reversed, Moreno County was on its way to becoming a magnet for every sleazy operator west of Chicago.

Andrew frowned and shifted slightly against the sticky seat of his car. The thin shade of the coconut palm he had parked under was more cooling in thought than in practice, but it was preferable to facing the torrid afternoon with no shade at all. He shifted again and his clear eyes raked through the crowds walking away from the depot. Nowhere did he see a flash of champagne hair or the slim, assured figure of Christina Babcock-Buckles.

The crowds thinned, flowed into gloomy bars like water into cracks, and vanished. Andrew swore silently. The next train was not due for half an hour. He wondered if Christina's early-morning telephone call had been a childish joke. But she had not sounded like a child. Her soft, husky voice had been as provocative as the controlled swing of her tight bottom.

"I can't talk much now," she had said, her voice intimate, almost a whisper. "But I have to see you. Can you meet me in Frenchman's Cove?"

Andrew considered his reply for a moment, weighing the potential costs against the sudden race of his blood.

"What's wrong?" he had asked finally, compromising.

"Do I really have to have a reason to want to see you?"

There was impatience in her voice, a clear sense that

she was not accustomed to being questioned by anyone, especially a man.

"Considering the kind of trouble it would be for both of us—yes."

"Where's your bloody sense of adventure?"

"Firmly in hand," he said dryly. "But I'm more worried about what would happen to your reputation if you were seen with a Mexican bastard."

"Andrew—!" Her voice was half angry, half anguished.

Andrew had laughed then, not knowing that the sound of his laughter did to her what her intimate tone had done to him.

"They're trying to send me away," she said hurriedly, her voice husky, thick with emotions she could not put in words. "They say they want me to finish college back East and then go to some goddamned ladies school in Switzerland. And before I go, they want me to join with them in a stockholders' suit that would force you to sell off the ranch. Can they do that? I mean, you have fifty-one percent and even with me, they only have forty-nine percent."

"American law is kind to minorities, particularly if their name is Buckles," said Andrew, his mind racing with the implications of her words. Fifty-one percent of the stock in the Buckles Trust was no guarantee against the kind of trouble that could come from forty-nine opposition. "Are they trying to get you to sign over your interests to them before you go?"

"The land matters more to you than my being shipped off to what our papers call a 'troubled Europe,'" said Christina coolly. "I understand, of course. Lee taught me."

"That's not what I said," began Andrew.

"You didn't have to." Christina's voice was precise, almost Eastern in its accents. "Yes, they want me to sign over my interests. Apparently their chances of winning a suit against you are much better with my twenty-four percent under their control." She waited, but Andrew said nothing. "Is that correct?" she asked, her voice clipped.

"Yes."

"Then do you think you could spare a bit of your precious time to discuss business with me?" said Christina, not bothering to soften the hostility in her voice.

"Christina," began Andrew, then abandoned the attempt to make her understand. "All right, when and where do I meet you?"

"Grandmother Joy thinks I'm taking the train to Los Angeles for a three-day holiday with some friends. I'll double back to the Cove on the five o'clock train."

The confidence in Christina's voice told Andrew that it was not the first time she had used this particular ruse to sneak away from the grove house. But Andrew agreed without comment. "Fine. Then you can take the eight o'clock train to LA."

"Why? My friends aren't expecting me. See you at five."

Christina had hung up quickly, leaving him with a host of double-edged questions and no answers. From the look of the empty depot platform, the answers had not arrived on the five o'clock train.

Andrew got out of his car, stretched with animal grace, and walked across the street to a small grocery store. He bought several bottles of very cold beer, opened one and carried out the rest in a paper bag.

By the time he walked back across the street, the long-necked bottle was covered with a patina of icy sweat—and Christina Buckles was sitting in the front seat of his car. Andrew said nothing, merely cocked an eyebrow as he opened the door.

"Did you drive after all?" he said, sliding into the welcome shade next to her.

"No." Christina smiled a faint, superior smile. "I came in on the four-thirty. I've been watching you for the past fifteen minutes from the restaurant over there. I couldn't decide if I really wanted to see you."

"You called me, remember?" Andrew said, looking at her with eyes that were harder than they had been a moment ago.

"I can change my mind, can't I?" snapped Christina.

"Any time." He shrugged. "You know where the door is," he added with an indifference he did not feel.

Andrew studied the neck of the beer bottle for a moment, then took a long drink. When he finished, he neither looked at Christina nor spoke to her. It was as though she had already gone.

"May I?" Christina's voice was soft, unsure, her eyes were on the frosty beer bottle.

"You're too young," said Andrew under his breath.

But Andrew handed her the dark bottle. Christina took a grateful drink, put both hands around the icy, dark glass and rolled it across her forehead. Then she pressed the cold bottle against her throat and caressed each cheek, sighing with pleasure. Andrew watched, then looked away, realizing he had been on the verge of reaching out and touching her. Instead, he reached for the ignition key.

"Did you bring a swimsuit?" he said abruptly.

Christina gave him a sideways smile. "I knew that you weren't as slow as you sometimes seem."

"I'm going to ignore that," said Andrew, smiling and easing the car into traffic. "Just tell me where you're going to change your clothes."

"In the street, of course. Wouldn't that be——"

"Quite a show," finished Andrew with no inflection in his voice. "But why don't we see how discreet we can be, rather than how wild. Be just folks, for once."

Christina's lips curved down, then she sighed. "I can't even tease you anymore, can I? If it makes you any happier, you clam, I have a suit on underneath this oh-so-goddamn-plain dress."

Andrew glanced at the sleek, beautifully filled dress. "Plain?"

"When a man doesn't notice my dress, it's plain," said Christina emphatically.

"You're spoiled."

"Not by you."

"I'm not a man," Andrew said, more than half seriously. "I'm just a hangover from your childhood."

"Ye gods and little fishes," Christina muttered. "I haven't heard such crap since pledge week."

Andrew laughed, full and rich. "You're beautiful, Sunshine. It's a shame you already know it."

"Sunshine . . ." she said softly. "You're the only one who calls me that now."

Neither spoke again until Andrew parked the car near the beach. For a moment, both sat and watched head-high waves turning over, hissing up onto the golden sand, spending their force in foam and slow withdrawal beneath the molten afternoon sun. The wide beach was rumpled by countless feet, its sand hollows filled with velvet shadows pushed out by the slanting light. The beach was less crowded than it had been a few hours ago, but there were still many bodies sprawled in various positions of sunburned abandon. Andrew and Christina melted between groups and individuals without being recognized or even particularly noticed.

As one, Andrew and Christina stopped long enough to peel down to their bathing suits. Christina wore a black, one-piece suit that would have been wasted on a less well-proportioned figure. She stuffed her dress into her beach bag, lifted her hair off of her neck and stretched unselfconsciously, arching her back and enjoying every vagrant wisp of breeze on her flushed skin.

"Ahhh, that's so much better," she said, shaking her head until bright hair tumbled back to her shoulders.

Andrew folded his pants and tucked them into the beach bag. When he looked up and saw her arched against the bronze light, he felt something tighten deep inside him. It was as though he had never seen a woman before. Her skin was like honey, fine and smooth, demanding to be touched, savored, tasted.

With an effort, Andrew forced himself to look away from the body that moved so invitingly beneath the thin black suit. His own bathing suit was in the brief style he had discovered on the French Riviera and had worn ever since in preference to the clumsy American suits. By French standards it was almost excessively modest. By American standards, it was not.

Christina glanced over at Andrew. Her eyes swept down, widened and jerked back up to his chest. Then, as though unable to stop, she looked at him again before assuming a blank inattention that would have been appropriate for an inexperienced girl. Andrew was silently amused by her reaction. He wondered if she and her husband had spent their marriage with their eyes closed; it would explain the brevity of their match, if nothing else. But Andrew neither did nor said anything to point out the inconsistencies of her behavior.

With a folded blanket under one arm, two towels under the other and the bag containing cold bottles of beer in his left hand, Andrew led Christina across the hot sand to an open stretch of beach north of the pier. There they stood and watched the long swell of warm water.

Christina stared out over the brilliant sea into the hot, orange sun, a sun close enough to burn her and yet impossibly distant. Even near the water, the air was heavy and too hot. But soon the astringent smell of brine and the rhythmic crash of waves drugged the senses, dimming even the ability to perceive heat. Andrew felt a sensual release, like soaring, as his body succumbed to the primal rhythms of the rising tide.

Christina reached for the cotton blanket underneath his arm, touching his ribs with a sliding pressure of smooth fingertips as she freed the blanket. She shook out the colorful red cloth and spread it on the sand, offering a generous view of her breasts when she bent over. There was a knowing but uncertain air to her movements, as though she were trying on a dress whose style was unusual. She would have to look carefully, turning and posing, before she decided whether the cloth had been cut for her.

Unlike Christina, Andrew did not avert his eyes from the nearly nude body moving so gracefully just beyond his reach. He admired the resilient swell of breast and hip, the sinuous line of waist and leg. The nine years that once had separated Andrew and Christina like an unbridgeable chasm had shrunk to a tiny crease not deep enough to hold a shadow.

At twenty, Christina was smooth and firm, warm, like sweet fruit ripening in the sun, and waiting. Only a certain carelessness of action betrayed her youth. She had not yet learned that tomorrow always came, bringing reward and retribution for yesterday. But he did not hold that carelessness against her. He knew many people twice her age who had not learned the elementary relation between today and tomorrow.

"I guess this is for common folks," Christina said, sinking to her knees on the blanket and straightening a corner. "Grandmother Joy detests suntans almost as much as bathing suits. Both are not ladylike." Christina laughed in her throat and threw her arms out toward the sea. "But I love the sun!"

"I can see Joy's point," said Andrew, still standing. "That suit leaves a lot to be tanned."

Christina glanced up at him quickly, then away, unable to keep her eyes from following the strong lines of his body. For an instant Andrew was angry at himself and at her. Neither of them was being very honest, and honesty was the least that they owed each other. He looked at her openly, his gray eyes measuring her with neither insult nor invitation.

"You've become a beautiful woman, Christina," he said evenly. "One of the few who could wear that suit and not look ridiculous."

"Thank you," she said after a long pause.

Christina did not meet his eyes as a surprising flush spread over her cheeks. The slow growl of surf failed to fill the silence that pooled between them. The silence grew and deepened until it was as much a presence as water and sand and sun. Andrew looked down at her again. She was lying on her back in a provocation that was part accident, part intent, wholly inevitable. He flipped the towel off of his neck onto the blanket and lay on his side, facing her. He waited, looking at her with deliberate appreciation until she blushed over her whole body, mutely acknowledging his presence less than a foot away from her.

"We're messing around, Christina," he said, his voice

deep and hard. "Ask your questions and then shag your lovely ass onto that LA train."

"What do you mean?" she asked faintly.

"Shit," breathed Andrew. "We're acting like a couple of thirteen-year-old virgins."

Christina's head snapped over toward him. "I'm not a virgin," she said, suddenly angry and tired of being made to feel gawky and foolish. "And I hope to hell you aren't!"

"Hardly." Andrew's answer was slow and amused. "And yes, I find you attractive. Too damned attractive. What are your intentions, Miss Christina Babcock-Buckles—tease or pleasure?"

"What are my—that's not a very romantic thing to say."

"Jesus. You're younger than you look." Andrew levered himself up on one elbow and leaned across Christina. With complete disregard for the contact of their two bodies, he fished out two bottles of beer from the paper bag and then rummaged until he found an opener in her beach bag. He popped the metal-ridged caps from the bottles and handed her a beer. She carefully took it in such a way that their hands did not touch. The very deliberation of her movements told him that his closeness burned her skin as it burned his. He set his beer down, screwing it into the sand until the bottle was secure.

"You're a big girl now," he said carefully, "and if you don't know the kind of signals you're putting out, you'd better learn before you end up on a deserted beach with someone who's even less a gentleman than I am."

Christina looked away, her expression almost guilty. Very gently Andrew placed his fingers along her chin and turned her face toward him. Her eyes were troubled, turbulent, a violet so deep that he could feel himself sinking into them, turning, drowning.

"What signals do you mean?" she said faintly, looking over his shoulder.

"Be honest, Christina. Look at me. All of me."

"Damn you," she said, her voice ragged. "I didn't expect you to be so—so goddamned *male!*"

"And you so goddamned female," Andrew said softly.

Without warning, without thinking, Andrew lowered his head the few inches it took to cover her mouth with his. With a gentleness that left her weak, the tip of his tongue traced her lips. Then his fingers dropped from her chin and brushed the top of her thigh like silk drawn across her skin. In the same motion he picked up the bottle he had set aside and took a long, cold drink. Then, as though he had just remembered how, he took a deep breath and slowly expelled it.

"That wasn't supposed to happen," Andrew said, his voice neutral again. "I'm sorry."

Christina looked at him, still too surprised by his caress to do more than regret that it had ended. She wondered what she had done to deserve the grim look he was giving her.

"I'm not sorry," Christina said suddenly, her voice husky, her violet eyes no longer sliding away. "Andrew—"

He shook his head regretfully, "No, Sunshine."

"Why not?" she demanded, exasperated by the man who always seemed to have her at a disadvantage. "What's wrong with it? I'm not a virgin, as you so tactlessly pointed out. So why can't we?"

"You know as well as I do."

The wind shifted for an instant, bringing to Andrew a wisp of her scent, warm and rich and somehow secret. He closed his eyes, struggling with a desire as fierce as it was unexpected. Christina watched his face. He looked hard and withdrawn, almost cruel, and she felt very young, unsure. He had always had that effect on her.

"Do I? I know some things," she said, her voice tentative, almost wistful. "A few."

The wave of desire that had almost overwhelmed Andrew evaporated at the uncertainty and youth in her voice. Suddenly he doubted that she knew about the tenuous ties of blood uniting them. The relationship did not bother him, but he had no way of knowing how it would affect her. And he did not want to—could not—risk losing her to disillusionment and scorn. Yet he knew he should tell her. He must, or he would always feel he had tricked her.

Andrew was pulled between the conflicting imperatives, torn by an indecision that was as painful as it was unusual. For once he did not know what he was going to do. He opened his eyes and saw her, child and woman, vulnerable and secure, troubled and serene and totally desirable, trusting him as she had always trusted him. He spoke quickly then, before he could change his mind.

"You know some things," he said harshly. "Do you know that I am Lee's son?"

Christina looked at Andrew while waves rose and swelled and broke into curling ribbons of foam. She saw Andrew's eyes, as changing as the sea, Lee's eyes looking at her, waiting. She saw Andrew's face, the familiar slant of cheekbones over lips that were fuller than Lee's, more sensual, yet the same, waiting. She saw Andrew's body, shorter than Lee's, stronger, more perfect, graceful even in repose, waiting. But most of all she saw Andrew, intelligence and power and stillness, waiting.

"Poor Daddy," she whispered, thinking aloud. "He didn't have a chance against you. No one would. Not even me."

"Christina—"

"No," she said quickly, sitting up, hugging her knees against her chest, staring at the restless ocean. "I feel like a fool. I've heard gossip about it—you and Lee—since I was old enough to understand. But I never believed it." She laughed oddly. "I should apologize to Marcia. I pulled out a handful of her hair in sixth grade, but it didn't change the truth, did it?" Christina closed her eyes for the space of three heartbeats, but when her eyes opened, there were no tears. "There's another one, isn't there? A girl." She rocked slightly, comforting herself. "Is she Lee's too?"

"Yes. My sister," said Andrew tonelessly, wanting to gather Christina's huddled body against his. "Her name was Magdalena. Maggie."

"Was?"

"She died four years ago."

Christina looked blank. It was obvious that gossip had not stretched to connect Maggie with the disappearance of the Workers' Magdalene.

"Was she like Lee too?"

"No." Andrew turned away from her, toward the darkening sea. "Maggie was like my mother. Too beautiful. Much too beautiful."

"Maggie, or your mother?"

"Both. But Mom had Lee. Maggie had only herself. It wasn't enough. It never is." Andrew stood in a controlled surge of strength. "I'll take you to the depot now."

Christina seemed not to have heard. She put her chin on her knees and stared at waves dissolving into foam and thunder.

"Are you my uncle?" Christina asked, not looking at Andrew.

"Almost," said Andrew flippantly, but his voice was strained. "Get up, Christina. It's time to go."

Christina took a breath so deep that she shuddered. She tilted her head back and looked directly into eyes the color of rain. "My name is Sunshine. I don't want to leave."

Andrew stared down at Christina for a moment, then bent and lifted her to her feet with an ease that should not have surprised her, but did. When he sensed the tremor that went through her, he dropped his hands immediately, afraid that he had misunderstood, afraid that the touch repelled her. Then he felt her lips brush across the muscles of his upper arm, a touch as hot and light as flame.

"Sunshine . . ." whispered Andrew.

But she was already gone, walking toward the waves as though hypnotized. He followed slowly, until he stood next to her. They let warm water rise up their legs until the wave's force was spent and water slid away, only to return again in a rush of warmth rising. After many waves, Christina spoke without taking her eyes from the carnelian blaze of the setting sun.

374

"I need time . . . like this. Don't send me away. Please."

Andrew's fingertips touched the corner of Christina's mouth in an answer that was both intimate and undemanding.

"I've had a lifetime to get used to being Lee's bastard," said Andrew softly. "Take as much time as you need."

They stood motionless, surrounded by the surge and retreat of water, not touching, closer than they had ever been before. They watched the falling sun pull red-hot streamers of cloud into an ocean turned indigo. The water burned, a silent explosion of incandescence. The eye of the sun slowly closed, taking light and leaving behind dusk like a velvet exhalation.

When Andrew and Christina could no longer see the horizon, they turned and walked through sand to the crowded streets of Frenchman's Cove. Doors and windows were open, a futile gesture against the heat that clung like a bad reputation. As with Andrew and Christina, most people wore swimsuits barely covered by an unbuttoned shirt or dress. Even the concession to civility seemed too much.

Outside the Sundowner Ballroom, the sidewalks were thronged with couples and small groups of dancers sucking in fresh air before plunging back into the steamy maelstrom of the dance hall. The band was playing loudly, a fast tune that was a challenge flung at the sultry night and the sweating dancers jammed together on the big parquet floor.

Andrew raised his eyebrow in a silent query as he turned to Christina. She nodded. He took her hand and led her through untidy groups of sidewalk people to the open door of the Sundowner. There, a silent pressure of her fingers stopped him. Christina stood on tiptoe by his side, leaning lightly against him when people pushed by her. Heat from the ballroom rolled out onto the sidewalk like an invisible tide.

"You don't really want to go in there," said Andrew, putting his lips close to her ear in order to be heard over

375

the band. "Or do you have an overwhelming yen for a secondhand steam bath?"

Christina did not look away or answer. Her face was frozen in an expression of distaste and shame. Andrew looked back into the ballroom, sweeping the area with quick, penetrating glances, trying to see what had upset Christina. Just at the edge of the crowded dance floor, he caught a glimpse of a familiar face. Then the dancers shifted and the face vanished.

Within moments, the face emerged again—Champ Buckles, his skin streaked with sweat. He was moving ungracefully to the music, staggering more than dancing, obviously drunk. He was shirtless, his skin blotchy beneath a thin tan, his stomach loose over swim shorts that were too tight and too bright.

Champ's partner was a short redhead who had been luscious at fifteen, but she was nineteen now, a whore with features that were blurred, as though drawn onto her face with a blunt pencil. She was dressed in a bikini that looked more like a stripper's penultimate costume than a bathing suit. Her breasts were big and soft, bouncing independently. She stood almost on Champ's feet, pumping her hips against his. When he staggered, she reasserted his balance with a twist that popped one breast out of its flimsy restraint.

A passing dancer grabbed at the bouncing breast. Champ whooped loudly, hauled the man out of the crowd and pressed him close until the three of them were a sweating, heaving triangle of flesh.

Christina turned and slipped back through the crowd. Andrew followed, using her pale hair as a beacon. She walked with quick grace, moving rapidly away from the Sundowner and toward the north part of town, where cottages spilled down to the sea.

When Andrew caught up with Christina, people had given way to silence and shadows. He stopped her beneath a streetlight, wanting to see her expression, afraid that she was too young to accept what she had seen. With careful eyes he searched her face, finding repugnance and withdrawal . . . and a sadness that came from understanding too much. She moved away and light flowed off of her into darkness.

"I'm sorry I had to see that," she said tightly, throwing the beach bag aside as though she could not bear to touch anything. "But then, you never know which illusions you have until they're gone, do you?" Her laughter was a brittle warning of how hard she was fighting to control herself. "Christ, he's not much, is he? And that bargain-basement cunt he was—"

"Stop," Andrew said, grabbing her shoulders. "Don't hurt yourself over things you can't control."

"Was your mother like that?"

"No," Andrew said, his voice breaking between anger and pain as he let go of Christina. "No."

Christina reached blindly toward him. "I'm sorry, I'm sorry." She held on to Andrew as though she would fall if she let go. "Please, Andrew. Hold me."

Slowly, Andrew's arms came up, then wrapped around Christina with a strength that held her together until she could hold on for herself. After a long time she stirred against his chest and looked up into his eyes.

"Lee's descendants—legitimate or not—have paid," Christina said slowly. "You, me, Daddy. All of us."

Andrew said nothing, remembering Maggie, who had paid more than anyone. Christina's hands slowly moved from Andrew's back to his face, making a warm pressure on his cheeks. "But I'm not going to go on paying. I'm not going to let my bloodlines rule my life."

"You can't help it," said Andrew tiredly.

"Can't I?"

Christina pulled Andrew's face down to hers, kissing the corners of his mouth and then his lips, savoring their softness as much as she enjoyed the feel of his body against her breasts. She sensed his desire in the instant before he denied it.

"Don't use me for revenge, Christina."

"Revenge?" Her voice and her expression were baffled. "But—" she shook her head and then became very still. She spoke with extreme care, sensing that she had used up most of her chances with Andrew. "For me to use you for revenge," she said softly, "I would have to believe that what we would do is ugly. But there's nothing that we can do, you and I, that is nearly as . . . unpleasant . . . as what I just saw. In fact," she hesitated, wanting a response but getting only silence, "I don't think there's anything we could do that's either unpleasant or wrong. Andrew?" she searched his eyes in the cold illumination of the streetlight. "Please believe me."

Andrew studied Christina's face for a long time. His eyes were white, measuring. Then his mouth curved in an easy smile that melted the ice in his eyes.

"I never said that there was anything we could do that would be ugly, Sunshine. But you had to make up your own mind."

Andrew lifted Christina's hand and kissed her palm. His teeth closed gently on the flesh at the base of her thumb. She tilted her head back and closed her eyes, smiling. She felt his breath on her cheek, his arms hard around her. She waited for his lips, but they did not come to soothe the need in her own. She opened her eyes, saw his face close and his eyes watching her.

"Andrew . . . ?"

Andrew's mouth closed over hers in a kiss more penetrating, more hungry than any Christina had known. He drew her up against him, shifting their bodies subtly until they met with an intimacy that made a mockery of their clothing. Christina made a sound halfway between shock and desire, then moved against him with a sensual demand that surprised her as much as his kiss.

"If you do that again," said Andrew, holding her away from him firmly, "I'm going to put you on your back right here in the sand."

Christina's eyes blazed with a sudden desire that matched his. "Yes."

Andrew abruptly pulled her against him. His hands slid over her back and hips, holding her closer, moving against her with a strength and hunger that answered the recklessness he had seen in her violet eyes. Then he heard people coming toward them, across the sand.

"Damn!"

Andrew stepped back from Christina, grabbed her and the beach bag and all but dragged her back to the sidewalk. They moved quickly, leaving the people behind. Christina said nothing, following him down short streets crowded with cottage homes. The houses became larger, not so crowded together, and each lot was walled away from its neighbor in the Spanish style.

Andrew pulled his keys out of the beach bag, unlocked a high, wooden gate separating a white house from the street, and led Christina into the walled garden. He locked the gate behind him before he turned to Christina. She was standing very still, transfixed by the beauty of hidden lights embracing a young jacaranda tree that lifted its graceful arms to the night.

"What a lovely tree," she sighed. "What kind is it?"

"Jacaranda. My mother's family believed that they brought luck to whoever lived near one."

"Do you believe it?" Christina asked in a husky voice.

Andrew smiled. His finger traced a line from Christina's forehead to her shoulder to her breast. "I believe the tree is very beautiful. Like you."

Andrew's hand finished tracing the length of her body, with a light caress. He led her through the inner garden, through shadows that were inviting rather than frightening, to the front door of his home. When he unlocked it, she seemed to shake herself out of her sensual daze.

"I thought you lived in San Ignacio."

"I do," said Andrew as he ushered her into a room with a high ceiling, a cool tile floor and a sense of peace. "This is my retreat."

"Oh," she said, suddenly seeing Andrew differently, as a man who controlled a multimillion-dollar empire that demanded his time and thought and strength until nothing was left but a need to be alone. Retreat. "I didn't know."

"Almost no one does," said Andrew wryly. "That's what makes it a retreat."

Andrew led her through the house without bothering to turn on any lights. His bedroom was at the back of the house. With a casual motion, Andrew opened the French doors that led from the bedroom onto a patio. The patio was closed on three sides and open to the ocean on the fourth.

The sound of waves tumbling beneath a moonless light flowed through the doors. Lights from the patio garden gave illumination without disturbing the hushed sense of privacy and peace. Andrew stood behind Christina on the patio, almost afraid to touch her. She was withdrawn, locked inside herself in a place where he could not reach.

"What is it, Sunshine?" he said finally, resting his lips on her neck just above the collar of her unbuttoned dress. "Would you really prefer making love in the sand?"

Andrew's hands moved over the warm flesh of her arms, then beneath her arms to her ribs.

"I just realized—I don't know you, Andrew," Christina said, her voice husky. But in spite of her words she did not move away from the strong hands stroking her stomach and her breasts. "I thought I did. I thought I knew Daddy. And I—ahhh." Her breath caught when his fingers slid beneath her bathing suit in a caress that made her involuntarily arch against him. "—I thought I knew—myself."

Before Christina could say any more, Andrew turned her in his arms. He kissed her while his hands moved down her back and cupped beneath her hips. She was lifted toward him, his tongue sliding between her lips, touching her teeth and exploring the soft warmth of her mouth. His hands moved beneath her suit again, supporting her and at the same time discovering another texture of her softness.

Christina was motionless, as though shocked by his intimacy. She twisted against him almost helplessly, increasing the depth of the pleasure he gave her. Andrew bent over her, whispering her name, feeling her slow surrender to their mutual sensuality. His hand found the zipper of her bathing suit, tugged. She moved away from him suddenly and he felt empty, angry. Then he realized that she had only wanted to get out of her suit, not to evade him. Slowly he eased the straps of her swimming suit off her shoulders.

With a supple twist, Christina stepped out of her suit

and kicked it aside, watching Andrew's face as he discovered her beauty again. His hands followed his eyes, and his mouth tasted her as he had longed to do.

When Andrew finally lifted his head, Christina smiled up at him with eyes that were as dark and enigmatic as a distant island. She ran her hands up beneath his shirt in a silent demand. Smiling, Andrew pulled off his shirt. This time her eyes did not turn aside, even when it was obvious that his bathing suit was not able to cover, much less conceal, the extent of his desire.

Christina stepped close to Andrew again. Her hips moved once, slowly, a repetition of the invitation she had given on the beach. But this time the movement was calculated rather than spontaneous. Andrew sensed the difference and wished he had taken her in the sand when her eyes had been half closed, brilliant with desire.

"Come on," Andrew said lightly. "My feet are tired."

Andrew led Christina toward the bed, where covers were turned down invitingly. After her pointed look at his bathing suit, he shrugged and discarded the scrap of cloth that had given up the unequal contest with his body.

"Much better," said Christina, but her voice lacked conviction and she made no move toward him.

"Don't look, and for God's sake don't touch, is that it?" asked Andrew, smiling yet serious.

Christina did not answer. She lay down as though it was something expected of her rather than her own desire. Her body was tight rather than relaxed, withdrawn rather than inviting. Andrew wondered what he had done to turn her off.

"What's wrong, Sunshine?" he said, lying down on the bed without touching her.

Christina looked at him, her eyes wide with surprise. "Nothing."

"I don't call it nothing when you close up like a tight little clam."

Christina blushed, surprising him. Then her eyes narrowed in the beginning of an anger that sprang as much from frustration as embarrassment.

"Look," Christina said coolly, "I've had my fun and

now it's your turn. So I'm not a very good actress. So what? I'm not planning on backing out and—"

"Hold it," said Andrew. "Let me be sure I've got it straight."

"It looks straight enough from here," she said sarcastically. "So let's get it over with, okay?"

For an instant Andrew was tempted to mount her, pump until he came and then kick her all the way back to the grove house. But the violet shadows behind her eyes stopped him. He could not discard years of trust for an instant of anger and physical release.

"Is it something I've done?" asked Andrew.

Christina looked away. Her voice crackled with resentment. "The rest of them were goddamn happy just to climb on and—" She made an impatient gesture. "What more do you want?"

"You."

"Well, here I am," she said acidly.

"No," said Andrew. "You were here, but you've gone away. Why?"

"I told you. I like the—the play—but the rest of it leaves me cold."

Andrew remembered her instant of abandon on the beach, when her body had demanded his more clearly than words. He remembered, and wondered if she even knew what she had done.

"No problem, then," Andrew said casually, running a fingertip down Christina's cheek and neck and breast. "I like to play too," he continued, his fingers teasing her nipple until it was hard, "so let's just play," his hand slid down to the bright triangle of hair and moved until she shivered involuntarily, "and we'll worry about the rest of it later."

Christina lay without answering. Long before she murmured her agreement, Andrew had read her answer in the subtle movement of her hips. When the lift of her hips became demanding, he smiled and went back to stroking her breasts and stomach and thighs while his tongue moved inside her mouth. Soon her tongue was answering his and her hands were kneading down his arms and back.

With a restraint Andrew had not known he had, he caressed and retreated, returned and withdrew until Christina was twisting and murmuring words with no meaning, unaware even that she spoke. In a last, slow assault his mouth moved over her body, biting gently, tongue exploring. His hands stroked her thighs until she moaned and shifted, asking for a caress she had never felt. When his lips finally touched her she began to tremble, a trembling that increased until she called his name again and again.

Andrew laughed against her. His teeth and tongue closed softly until she wanted to scream but did not have the breath. Her eyes opened suddenly, holding surprise and intense pleasure at the slow, fiery tide rising in her.

Andrew kissed her once more and this time she did cry aloud. He entered her as gently as though she were a virgin and moved slowly, until she closed around him in rhythms as old and as new as transcendent pleasure. And when she thought she could feel no greater ecstasy, he began to move quickly, deeply, ruthlessly until she cried out and held him against her, moving with him until both of them sensed nothing but the rhythms of need, felt nothing but the tide of pleasure swelling, overwhelming, until they knew nothing but the luminous sea of their passion.

Slowly, Andrew and Christina came back to a sense of common reality, of sultry air and distant surf and their bodies close with heat and love. Andrew kissed Christina gently, telling her by touch what he had no words to describe. Her eyes half opened, dazed, purple, unbelieving.

"Andrew . . . ?" she whispered.

Christina's fingers trembled over his lips. Afraid that he might be too heavy against her, Andrew shifted his weight. Her legs tightened around him and she moaned softly. He felt the pleasure that rippled through her again. Smiling, he moved slowly, watching her face, enjoying even her nails digging into his buttocks as she pressed hard against him.

When Christina was still once more, her body boneless, sated, Andrew started to roll over onto his side.

383

"Don't leave me," Christina sighed, her arms tightening around his body.

Andrew laughed against her neck. He slid his arms around her and rolled both of them onto their sides, still joined. "Sunshine, you couldn't get rid of me with a gun."

Christina stretched languidly against him, her muscles tightening to hold him inside her. When she realized what she had done, her eyes snapped open.

"You must think I'm—"

"—hot, sticky, slippery and sexy," he said, nibbling on the corner of her mouth. "All but the last can be cured by a shower."

Christina moved slowly, reluctant to disentangle herself from him.

"No hurry," said Andrew, moving his tongue lightly over her lips. "I like you the way you are. Close."

Christina smiled and caught his lower lip between her teeth. "Now I've really got you."

Andrew's tongue flicked out, tickling her upper lip. She giggled and let go, but he did not move away. Instead, his strong hands moved over her back and hips, pressing her against him. She heard and felt her name breathed against her hair. They lay for many minutes, holding each other tightly. At last they sighed, succumbing to the sultry night wrapped around them like a hot towel.

"About that shower . . ." Christina said, kissing Andrew's neck and moving slowly against his body.

Andrew's hands slid down until they held her hips. "A shower is not what you're asking for."

"But you feel so good," Christina murmured, her hands stroking the muscles of his back and buttocks, then sliding between his legs, touching him.

Andrew groaned softly.

"Did I hurt you?" Christina asked, quickly removing her hands.

"No," Andrew said, realizing in that instant that Christina had not touched a man with her hands before.

"I've never touched a man," she said, echoing his thoughts. "I mean—" She looked away in sudden confusion.

384

"I know what you mean." Andrew's hand captured her chin, forcing her to meet his eyes. "Touch me whenever you want, Sunshine. Wherever you want."

"I never wanted to, before."

Christina looked at Andrew for a long moment, then bent her head. He felt the unique texture of her tongue sliding across his shoulder. When she lifted her head her eyes were closed. She licked her lips.

"You taste . . . salty." She smiled. "I like it."

"That's good," Andrew said, his hand closing over her breast, "because I don't want you out of reach long enough to wash the salt off."

"Then we'll just have to shower together," she said reasonably.

Andrew gently bit her nipple. "Sold."

But when the moment came to separate completely, Christina and Andrew moved with a reluctance that almost undid their resolve. Slowly they walked into the shower. They stood side-by-side beneath warm water pouring down. Andrew washed her completely, building a fragrant lather over her skin, touching all of her until she could hardly breathe for wanting him.

Even after Christina had rinsed off every bubble of lather, her breasts were still aching, her eyes still brilliant. She held out her hands for the soap. She began on Andrew's back, enjoying the muscles that slid and coiled beneath her fingers. The strong muscles of his legs and buttocks brought a remembering smile to her lips.

Without speaking, Christina turned Andrew around and began to lather his arms and the broad muscles of his chest. He watched her face as she worked, smiling, almost dreamy. Her hands stroked down his flat stomach, then she knelt and began to wash his legs, disappointing him. She seemed oblivious both to his disappointment and to the warm water pouring over her while she massaged his calves and thighs with hands that were surprisingly strong.

Andrew closed his eyes, enjoying her hands, forgetting his disappointment that she still did not want to touch the part of him that gave them both so much pleasure. Then

385

her hands were suddenly, gently, around him, exploring him with a sensual curiosity that made him ache.

Andrew opened his eyes and watched her, saw her smile with pride and anticipation as he changed beneath her hands. She had dropped the soap sometime ago, but neither noticed. He reached out, turning off the water, and lifted her to her feet. He felt her shiver of pleasure when their bodies touched.

Before Andrew realized what was happening, Christina slipped through the circle of his arms and knelt once more in front of him. He felt her hands again, more sure, more knowing. He looked down at her, her hair wet against her head. Both of them were sleek and dripping, two creatures riding waves on a sea of pleasure, laughing. Then she caressed him, lips and teeth and tongue speaking in the shattering language of sensuality that he had taught her, a language that she now taught him.

The Sunday morning sky was slate gray and threatening, oppressively hot. Christina awoke at dawn, not sure what day it was, knowing only that she and Andrew had made love, showered, loved, slept, raided the kitchen, made love and showered and then had begun all over again in an enthralling cycle of passion and release.

Christina stretched, then rolled over onto her side to look at the man who could take her outside of herself and at the same time unite her with her own deepest impulses. She was amazed by the sensuality he had tapped in her, and equally amazed by the pleasure it gave him. The other men she had known were always in a hurry, interested only in getting into and then out of her with the greatest possible speed. But Andrew delighted in every aspect of their lovemaking.

Smiling, Christina watched Andrew, asleep on his back, beside her, his arm flung back over his head, a white cotton sheet rumpled over his hips. The line of his profile fascinated her. There was the unmistakable reflection of Lee in Andrew's cheekbones and nose and lips, especially now, in repose. But there was another influence too. The springy dark hair she loved to feel between her fingers and the compact, well-muscled body were tantalizing hints of a woman Christina had never seen. All that she knew of Cira was her name, her death, and that she had held Lee's love beyond all custom or reason for more years than Christina had even been alive. She wondered what kind of woman Cira had been to have had such a lover ... and such a son.

With delicate fingers, Christina traced the line of Andrew's profile, her fingertips barely touching his warm skin. The whisper of contact did not seem to disturb his sleep, nor did the increased pressure of her fingers brushing over the hair on his chest. What had begun as an impulsive touching of the past became a delightful sensual exercise in the present. She slowly traced side paths on his torso, lightly touching the swell of muscles beneath skin that was warm and smooth, browned by the sun.

Andrew had awakened as he always did, completely, between one heartbeat and the next. But he neither moved nor opened his eyes, for he felt Christina's fingers like gentle flames on his face. He lay perfectly still, relaxed, savoring the intimacy and pleasure implicit in her touch. He was reluctant to move, even to open his eyes. Unlike Christina, he knew that it was Sunday, that they had lived and loved and laughed together for thirty-six hours, and that tomorrow would come, bringing the rest of the world with it, demands and requirements, past and future, dividing him from her. But until he opened his eyes there was no world, no others, no time, nothing but Christina's slow caress and her breath warm against his skin.

When Christina's fingers had traced and retraced the side paths of his chest, the rumpled barrier of the sheet became more irksome to her. After an instant of hesitation, her hand slipped beneath the sheet and her fingers resumed their blind journey down his body. It was then that she discovered that Andrew was not asleep, that he had submitted to her delicate assault without moving a single part of his body, save the one that now pulsed beneath her hand.

With a sudden, indrawn breath, Christina pulled the

cover off of Andrew's hips, substituting her body for the cotton sheet. She settled over him with a low murmur of pleasure. Andrew's eyes stayed closed, his expression unchanged but for the faintest suggestion of a smile. Except for his hands locked on her hips and the driving force between her legs, he could have been asleep. The climax came sharply to both of them, a sensual explosion that made both cry aloud. She collapsed on his chest with a breathless, satisfied laugh.

"I thought you were asleep," Christina said, when she had regained some of her breath.

Andrew's eyes stayed closed. "I am." His lips curved in a smile that made fire twist through Christina all over again. His voice was heavy, lazy, and his hands were stroking her with slow, sure motions. "And I just had the most vivid dream—"

The shrill sound of a telephone ringing stopped Andrew's voice and hands. His face changed as Christina watched, sensuality evaporating, replaced by a hard alertness. His eyes snapped open, clear and cold as winter rain. He gently lifted her off of his body.

"Excuse me, Sunshine," he said, kissing her.

The phone rang again, knifing through the silence.

"I thought no one knew about your retreat," said Christina, trying for a light tone, but achieving only wistfulness.

'Nothing's perfect," Andrew said, smiling crookedly.

"It's bad news, isn't it?"

"Probably."

Andrew walked quickly out of the bedroom. After a fourth ring, the phone was quiet. Christina lay alone in the bed for a few moments, then followed. The tile floor felt smooth and cool beneath her bare feet. The murmur of Andrew's voice led her to a second-floor suite that overlooked an ocean luminous with dawn.

Christina hesitated in the doorway. Andrew stood with his back to her, his muscular nudity incongruous amid the office furniture. He began to pace the front of the desk, his steps limited by the black telephone cord.

As though pulled against her will, Christina came into

388

the room one slow step at a time. Though she made no sound on the thick wool rug, Andrew sensed her presence. Without turning around, he held out his hand to her.

". . . understand perfectly. Put him through." Pause. "Yes." Pause. "Yes." A long pause. "No. Keep only the Hawaiian cane fields. Sell the Asian holdings." Pause. "I don't care who promised what to the Philippines. Christ Himself couldn't hold those islands if the Japs move in. Sell or gut everything east of Hawaii. If Hawaii isn't safe, nothing is." Pause. "Yes, I could be wrong," said Andrew softly. "Keep the cane and sell the rest. Discreetly, of course."

Christina took Andrew's hand almost tentatively, watching his face. He was relaxed, yet frighteningly intense. He smiled briefly at her and pulled her against him with one arm, but his mind was focused wholly on the man who was at the other end of the conversation.

"—yes, yes." Andrew allowed impatience to creep into his voice. "Yes, what about them? You received a letter to that effect nine months ago. Didn't you stockpile as per orders?"

Andrew's voice became very soft. Christina stirred uneasily, remembering Lee.

"Why not?" asked Andrew. He waited without moving during a lengthy pause. "Allow me to rephrase that," he said finally. "You did not stockpile because you believed there was no reason to do so. Correct?" Short pause. "And your estimate of the situation was reinforced by the belief that my stockpiling order was just one more of my attempts to bankrupt the Trust." Pause. "Thank you, Mr. Wainwright," said Andrew, interrupting coldly. "Unfortunately, your education has cost the Trust more than half a million dollars." Pause. "Oh, yes," said Andrew softly. "I, too, am quite sure it won't happen again. Good-bye, Mr. Wainwright."

Andrew hung up. He glanced at a complex desk clock that marked every time zone in the world. He frowned, then shrugged. He gave the operator a number, waited, then had to talk loudly. The connection was hollow, static-filled and the man who answered was slightly deaf.

"Jeff? McCartney here. Yeah, all the way from California. Listen, we're unloading everything east of Hawaii. No, no special information," said Andrew, lying easily. "The Trust is just a bit widespread to handle. Like the British Empire—Sun never sets on us and all that." Andrew smiled. "But we're going to be short a few items now . . . yes, exactly. I knew you would understand. Get on it right away. Good. Call me if it gets to the short ones. Right. And one more thing. We're going to need a replacement for Wainwright. Immediately. Yes." Pause. "Sounds like a live one. Telex the file to me." Pause. "Right. Sorry to interrupt your dinner, Jeff. Give Julie my love."

Andrew disconnected and stood for a moment, staring at the desk clock, his arm around Christina and his mind thousands of miles away.

"He'll still be asleep," muttered Andrew to the clock, "and he couldn't do anything for ten hours anyway. Damn."

Without letting go of Christina, Andrew wrote on a blank pad with quick, clean strokes. She glanced over but could not decode the cryptic message. She looked at his face, equally enigmatic. His pale eyes seemed to burn behind heavy black lashes.

"Was that Ted Wainwright?" she asked finally.

". . . mmm . . ."

"He's a good friend of ours. Daddy, especially."

Andrew's pen paused, then he continued writing quickly. "Yes. I know."

"You're firing Ted?"

"Yes."

"You'd better ask the other forty-nine percent how we—"

"No."

Andrew put his pen aside, removed his arm from Christina's waist and faced the woman who was, among other things, the daughter of a man who hated him.

"What would happen if I went to my father?" said Christina coldly, resenting the way Andrew had dismissed her, angry that he refused even to consider consulting

390

with her about the Trust which, after all, bore her family name.

"I'll tell you what would happen. You go to your daddy. Champ goes to Wainwright. Wainwright does his best to sink our holdings in Malaysia. Depending on his skill—negligible—and his desire for revenge—considerable—the result would be between four and twelve percent less earnings this year for the Trust. That's a minimum of $400,000 out of your pocket." Andrew moved abruptly away from the desk. "There's the phone. Call your father."

"Ted has a wife and three kids—"

"Four," corrected Andrew in a bored tone. "Also two dogs, a cat and a tankful of tropical fish."

"In spite of Lee's will," said Christina angrily, "you are not a Buckles. Lee's legitimate family has the right to protect their friends from your arbitrary decisions."

"Not when those friends threaten the Trust," said Andrew, his body tight and his voice empty of emotion.

"*Your* Trust," she said bitterly.

"All right. *My* Trust."

"Your Trust. Your land. It should have been ours," said Christina, her voice low and passionate. "And the ranch should have been mine. Joy and Daddy may hate the land, but I don't. The ranch is all that's left for me. I thought Lee understood. The land is always there. If you let it alone, the land will always be the same. It won't get old and sick and then die and leave you with nothing to stand on." Christina stopped suddenly, aware of how much she had revealed to a man who was already too strong. "But Lee made the ranch a part of the Buckles—no, the *McCartney*—Trust. You control everything, don't you?"

The anger that Andrew was too controlled to reveal showed clearly on Christina's translucent skin. She was abruptly conscious of her nakedness and his. Every instant they had shared went through her like fire.

"Bastard," she hissed, fighting a hunger that threatened to overwhelm her.

"Yes," Andrew said tonelessly. "Bastard. But this

391

bastard knows something that your dear, legitimate daddy never had to learn. Business is like war—they don't give prizes for second place."

Christina looked at Andrew, seeing a stranger, opaque and subtly dangerous, compellingly male. She thought of her father as she had last seen him. She pitied her father again, so weak and Andrew so strong. And again, she hated herself for seeing her father too clearly.

"It isn't fair," whispered Christina.

"Fair? Jesus Christ!" Andrew laughed shortly. "Was it fair that I was born Lee's bastard instead of his legal son? Was it fair that I was treated like shit because Lee loved a woman he could not marry, a woman who loved him so much she had his children in spite of the cost to her and to them? Was it fair that your grandmother wouldn't let me say good-bye to the man who was my father, the man I loved more than that cold bitch could ever love anything?"

"No," Christina whispered, suddenly remembering Joy's cruel triumph as Lee lay dying alone. "Please don't. I saw you that night—in the hall—I'm sorry," she said, reaching blindly for him. "I'm sorry."

Andrew struggled silently with himself, trying not to show the sadness that made him feel hollow, the hunger for Christina that had grown beyond simple sensuality, the agony he felt as he sensed her pull away from him by events he was powerless to change. The same past that bound them also would inevitably separate them; he had known it would be this way, but he had not known how much it would hurt. Silently, helplessly, he cursed Lee's will, bastard legacy to a bastard son.

Christina shook her head, dazed by memories and unshed tears and a tangle of emotions she could neither name nor control. Andrew seemed cold, distant, far beyond her reach.

"We didn't have much time together, did we?" she said, her voice thin with the effort of withholding tears.

Andrew closed his eyes and leaned against the desk, trying not to go to her, to hold her, to love her and then to have her turn on him again, punishing him for a past that could not be changed.

"Tomorrow always comes," Andrew said, his voice empty. "Some days it comes sooner than others."

Andrew felt Christina's warmth very close to him. His response was involuntary, total. He kept his eyes closed, afraid to see her too clearly, afraid to see himself reflected in her eyes.

"Andrew," breathed Christina, her lips barely touching his, "I can make tomorrow go away, Andrew. Please, let me make it go away."

Andrew groaned softly, deeply, as she stood on tiptoe, clinging to his body, moving slowly over him in a caress that left both of them trembling. His hands raked suddenly down her back, demanding.

"Yes," said Christina, arching against him. She sank down onto the thick rug.

Andrew looked at Christina, her hair and body glowing against the indigo rug. She smiled up at him, passion and promise on her lips, her eyes brilliant with desire. Her hand reached up and touched him intimately.

"Now is the only time there is," Christina whispered. "Love me, Andrew. Love me."

Andrew lowered himself over her, felt her warmth surround him. He gave himself to her belief that if they explored each other totally the past would be vanquished, never again to come roaring at them out of the future, smashing them. They sank endlessly into one another, each seeking rather than denying the fathomless currents that flowed between them, each finding the other and themselves. For a timeless moment they knew a sharing so profound that it left them shaken, feeling as though they had dissolved and then coalesced once more, differently, for nothing could be the same again.

Andrew and Christina drew apart slowly. They showered and dressed in silence. Both were withdrawn, nearly frightened, trying to regain the sense of self that each had known. They had been prepared for physical pleasure, had been delighted to discover a deep sensual compatibility, but nothing in their essentially solitary lives had prepared them for such complete sharing. By tacit agreement they left the house, afraid that if they stayed alone together their bodies would dissolve one into the other, never to be separate again.

Christina and Andrew stepped into a day that was sluggish with heat and moisture. The sky overhead was all that moved. There were high, thin smears of gray cloud with lower, darker clouds beneath, all coming in from the south. The air was heavy with a diffuse threat of rain and something worse, something more violent. Christina hesitated, then broke the long silence.

"What is it?" she asked, turning to Andrew.

Andrew stood just beyond the gate on the sidewalk. His head was up, his eyes searching the sky as though the clouds were a language he could read. His intense alertness was that of a wild animal testing the wind, and waiting.

"*Chubasco,*" said Andrew.

Christina laughed shakily and turned away from the intensity in his eyes.

"Is that some kind of hot sauce?" she asked, her voice light in spite of her nerves tightening.

"*Chubasco* is another name for hurricane." Andrew turned and locked the gate. "My uncles used to look for a *chubasco* everytime the ocean stayed warm for more than ten days in a row. Most *chubascos* never get beyond the Gulf, but it looks like we might catch the edge of one."

"I still think it sounds like hot sauce."

Andrew smiled and said nothing. By the time they reached the commercial district, the streets were full. It was nearly noon, but Frenchman's Cove was not the kind of town where people spent Sunday in church; and even if it were, the sticky atmosphere would have made sermons unbearable. Both the tourists who had ridden through a steamy morning to the debatable relief of the beach, and those who had spent a restless night beneath a blanket of heat, were prowling the streets, looking for action and relief in the honky-tonks and taverns along Ocean Way.

Andrew led Christina down sidewalks that reflected heat back into the slowly seething sky. The first café they

394

came to was the Blue Turtle's coffee shop. Andrew chose a booth close to a large, desultory four-bladed fan. The walk had raised a thin sheen of sweat on both him and Christina. They talked little, on edge with themselves and the sultry, insufferable day and each other.

Champ's redheaded companion walked toward them. Her pink cotton waitress uniform was already stained with the sweat of more than one day. She sauntered down the counter, swinging her ample hips and the pot of coffee she held in one hand. She poured cups full and then some, leaving a trail of slopping saucers. Her face was sullen, blunt, almost ugly in the light of day. She wiped her forehead, pushed a dyed curl underneath her black hairnet and grunted a greeting to a customer. She stopped beside Christina's and Andrew's booth. Without asking, she poured Andrew a cup of coffee and reached for Christina's cup. Christina's hand snaked out, covering the cup. The idea of drinking anything the redheaded whore had touched made Christina's skin crawl.

"No," Christina said. "I don't want any."

The redhead took her eyes off of Andrew's body and her hips away from the general area of his shoulder. She gave Christina a long glance. The waitress was not pleased by Christina's beauty, luminous in spite of the muggy heat.

"Suit yourself, girlie," she said in a voice that was as coarse as Andrew had expected.

Christina's eyes narrowed at the redhead's patronizing tone. Christina said something Andrew could not hear, but the redhead could. She started pouring coffee into Christina's cup, spilling hot liquid over Christina's hand. Andrew grabbed the coffeepot so quickly that the waitress gasped. Before she could say anything, a hard voice cut through the café's clatter.

"Rita, you clumsy bitch, I told you what would happen the next time you spilled something."

Andrew set the coffeepot on the table with a sharp sound. Rita turned to face the voice.

"I'm sorry, Mr. Heer," she said slowly, not meeting anyone's eyes. "Someone bumped me."

"Go back to the counter," said Jason, stepping forward, smiling when she stepped hastily away. "Now." There was an almost subliminal flash of cruelty in Jason's voice. It was underlined by the look on his face, a look that intensified in the instant that he recognized Andrew.

"Well, well. If it isn't McCartney," Jason said slowly.

A faint gambler's smile removed any trace of emotion from Jason's face. Andrew looked at Jason, nodded minutely.

"Heer," said Andrew in an absolutely neutral voice.

The tone was so like Lee that Christina felt her throat close. Jason's smile widened, but became no more meaningful.

"Lot of water under the bridge since the last time, right?" Jason said. "Hope there's no hard feeling left over."

For the murder of my sister. But Andrew had not spoken except with his eyes, white and feral.

"You're a prick, Heer," said Andrew indifferently, picking up the full cup and sipping at the bitter coffee. "And your brother was a murderer."

Jason's eyes narrowed. "Prove it, you bastard."

"I don't have to. A concrete bridge saved me the trouble of killing him."

Andrew smiled while Jason's face seemed to thin and flatten.

"You bastard," said Jason, "you think—"

"You're repeating yourself," said Andrew in a bored voice. "But what you expect from a Heer?" He threw some change on the table and glanced at Christina. "Ready?"

Jason turned, realizing for the first time that the booth held more than Andrew.

"Well, I'll be a son of a bitch. Chrissy." Jason's arched eyebrows could have been a reaction to Christina's face, a combination of natural beauty and recently satisfied sexuality; or his look could have come from acquiring a bit of new and potentially important information.

"Champ said you wouldn't be here this weekend. Something about friends in LA . . . ?"

When Jason's gentle inquiry drew no response, he looked slowly from her to Andrew and then back again to her. Anger tightened Jason's face, but his smile remained wide, a professional shill's invitation to camaraderie. Only Andrew noticed the change, and the smile that did not reach the gambler's eyes. With an anger of his own, Andrew realized that Christina and Jason knew each other better than he had suspected.

Christina looked at both men, her eyes alight with curiosity. She had missed neither the reference to murder nor Andrew's deadly rage.

"Let's begin all over again," murmured Jason, taking Christina's hand and bowing over it. "Jason Heer, humble proprietor of the Blue Turtle and sundry other establishments, at your exquisite service."

Jason smiled in smooth self-deprecation, inviting her to share the game of being introduced to someone she knew well. He lifted her hand to his lips, held it there for several seconds, and did not release her fingers even after he lifted his mouth. Christina gave him the slow, practiced smile that had brought more than one man to flash point.

"Why, thank you, Mr. Heer," drawled Christina in a husky voice. "But there's no need to make a fuss over me. I'm simply a small-town girl who came to Frenchman's Cove for a good time."

Andrew leaned back tensely, watching Christina flirt. He felt jealousy twisting through him, but he did nothing. There was nothing he could do. Christina was reacting in her own way to the unnerving closeness she had shared with Andrew. If he tried to stop her, to bring her close again, she would pull even further away. In any event, he had no intention of letting Jason know the depth of his feelings for Christina.

"You've come to the right place for a good time," said Jason, squeezing her fingers. "The Blue Turtle may look like a tame reptile, but despite our restrained shell, we're wonderfully amusing inside."

Christina raised one pale, sleek eyebrow in a silent

query that somehow managed to encompass the scarred tables, grubby floor and coarse waitresses.

"Ah, yes," murmured Jason, "but you forget the private rooms upstairs. Would you like to come back this evening, as my guest?" When Christina hesitated, looking at Andrew, Jason said, "Your friend is of course included in the invitation, though I'm told he has little love of gambling." When Christina still said nothing, Jason added lightly, "There won't be any inconvenient inquiries about LA. Champ is spending the weekend on his yacht and won't be back until tomorrow. Catalina or some such island. He took an interesting group of young people along. And," he said, caressing her fingers, "we could always take another tour of the most private parts of the bay, *n'est-ce pas?*"

"Heer," said Andrew coolly to Christina, "works very hard to see that people are entertained. Especially if they're rich. The women he hires serve coffee in the morning and men at night."

Jason's smile flattened as he turned toward Andrew. "Service is an old profession, although perhaps not as grand as the work you do with the Buckles Trust. But then, not all of us are born with a silver spoon in our mouth. Even if the spoon in your case was, shall we say, tarnished?"

Turning again to Christina, Jason bowed slightly. "Please do come tonight. We're not so grand as Monaco, but we're ever so much closer. Seven o'clock?"

Christina looked at the slight, handsome man who subtly inclined his body toward her in wordless invitation. There was desire in Jason's voice and eyes, a reaction that was hardly new or surprising to Christina. She was aware of her effect on men, but she was never sure whether that effect came from her beauty, her wealth, from both or from neither. She was also aware of the intense animosity between Jason and Andrew, an enmity that predated whatever present jealousy either man might feel. She sensed that she was or could be a pawn in their private war.

Most of all, Christina was aware of her need to assert her separateness from the man who could overwhelm her with a touch or a smile or a single, swift look. Christina squeezed Jason's hand, still holding hers. "We'll see you at seven."

Jason hid his disappointment that Andrew was included in the assignation. "Until then, mademoiselle," Jason said lightly, releasing her hand as he turned away.

Andrew picked up his coffee cup, sipped, and studied Christina. When she finally met his glance, there was defiance in her eyes.

"We can't spend all our time in bed," she said crisply. "We have to live in the real world too."

Andrew set down his cup carefully and looked at Christina with eyes that had no color.

"Which reality, Christina? His? Mine? Yours? Or, perhaps there might be a reality called . . . ours. Did you think of that?"

Christina did not answer, because she could not. She suddenly wished that Jason had not left. He was safe, like the Blue Turtle's swimming pool, a known quantity with all depths clearly marked and none of them over her head. Andrew was like the sea, unbounded, unknowable, overwhelming in his power. Did he ever drown in her as she did in him? She did not know, was afraid to guess wrong and find herself drowning alone. She felt defenseless; beyond their shared past with Lee, she knew so little of Andrew.

"Is there some reason why we shouldn't take advantage of Jason's invitation?" Christina asked, knowing there must be, wanting to know just what it was.

Andrew looked at Christina narrowly, then realized that if she had managed to ignore the gossip connecting him with Lee, she had undoubtedly ignored other rumors. He started to answer, but suddenly he was too tired, too emotionally raw to explain the tangled past and present of the Buckles, McCartneys and Heers. How could he sit and speak of murder and Lee's bent body, death and revenge, concrete and rain? The agony and rage caused by Maggie's murder was still too close, too naked to be shared across a greasy table owned by the brother of Maggie's murderer.

With an immense effort, Andrew stepped back from all emotion, and in doing so inevitably stepped back from Christina.

"Heer and I are just on opposite sides of the same box," said Andrew finally. "It goes back a long time. I'm not sure where it began or where it will end. If it will end."

"That's hardly a reason not to go out tonight," said Christina, her voice almost hard as she sensed his withdrawal. Then, "Forget it. I'll go by myself."

"Come hell or high water," said Andrew softly. "Right, baby?"

"Right. Especially high water. I'm one hell of a swimmer."

"So am I." Andrew smiled faintly. "So let's go swimming. It beats drowning alone."

Christina sensed the renewal of passion in him and her eyes blazed with sudden, sensual fire. The slow smile she gave to him was almost enough to bring color back to his white eyes.

The tinny sound of coronet, clarinet and snare drums cut through the torpid night air and carried into the street outside the Blue Turtle. The windows in the second-floor gaming rooms were thrown open in hope of a breeze, but all that moved was the metallic music.

Andrew and Christina walked silently, side by side, watching the crowds that clotted in surly community on the sidewalks. The people were limp from the heat and the humidity and two nights of revelry. Grim-faced, they searched for the money and energy to spend on one more round of drinking, dancing and damnation before they had to leave Frenchman's Cove and face the world at the other end of PacCo's silver rails.

There was a finality in the air that pressed down like an invisible steamy weight. Off to the south, snake tongues of lightning flickered repeatedly, illuminating masses of clouds boiling silently, incredibly, forewarning of deep storms and thunder that would shake the earth. But the flaccid breeze belied the clouds' warning. It was as though the air had never moved and would never move again.

Andrew and Christina walked without talking, caught in separate webs of thought. They walked without touching, for the night was simply too close. The atmosphere and distant lightning gave them a sense of endings rather than beginnings, or of both unhappily mingled.

Tinny music penetrated their mutual withdrawal. Andrew looked up at the second floor of the Blue Turtle and then at Christina's luminous face. The relentless heat had flushed her skin, making it glow.

"It will be like the last circle of hell in there," said Andrew, looking at the shabby hotel.

"Stop trying to talk me out of this," Christina answered with a determination that equaled the heat.

"For the love of God. What is so hypnotizing about an evening in a third-rate poker dive?"

"You don't have to come," Christina said, cutting across his objections. Andrew's face assumed the closed expression that made her want to lash out. "But I'm going in. After all, there's no point in being rich and powerful unless you can have your own way, is there? And I'm told that I'm both. Rich and powerful."

"So am I," replied Andrew. "So what?"

"So we're well matched, you stubborn son of a bitch. Now do we go in or do I gamble alone?" Christina looked into his eyes, suddenly feeling a bit more separate than she wanted to be. "Andrew . . . I'd rather go with you."

Andrew allowed Christina to take his hand and lead him through the door to the lobby of the Blue Turtle Hotel. A few moments later he stopped her in front of the bullet-headed bouncer who guarded one of the four stairways to the second floor.

"McCartney and guest," said Andrew blandly.

The bouncer immediately did his best to metamorphose from thug to polite doorman. He stepped aside with a slight bow.

"Right this way, Mr. McCartney. Lady Luck is waiting

401

for you. And if she's unkind, Mr. Heer has set up a free credit line for both of you."

"How nice," said Andrew. "We'll play for cash."

Andrew brushed past the bouncer, leading Christina by the elbow. When they mounted the stair and the door closed behind them, Christina turned to him sharply.

"Why were you rude? It was thoughtful of Jason to arrange that we have a good time."

Andrew stopped on the stairway and swung Christina around so that she faced him. His fingers tightened painfully on her arm.

"With a shit like Heer," said Andrew, "there's no such thing as free. You pay for it sooner or later. In spades. Don't trust him."

Christina smiled coolly. "But I do. Jason's a close friend. I've known him for several seasons. Is that what's bothering you? Could it be that the great Andrew McCartney is jealous?"

When Andrew spoke, his voice was so controlled that it revealed neither his pain nor his fear. "If you play Heer's game, everyone will lose."

Christina saw Andrew's eyes measuring her, gray eyes that were pale and opaque, the eyes of a stranger. She saw his stillness and strength, but not his fear and his pain. She felt terribly alone, unable to touch or influence him. She wondered if anyone could if a man that strong ever needed anyone. She turned away, going upstairs to the casino, seeking an ally to support her.

"Sunshine . . ."

Andrew's whisper was as subtly despairing as her feeling of helplessness. She leaned against the wall, suddenly weak. He was beside her in a single stride, kissing her forehead and her eyelids with a gentleness that made her tremble.

"My God," she said, her lips blindly seeking his. "I—you make me—almost afraid."

Andrew held Christina tightly, but before he could reassure her, the door at the bottom of the stair opened, allowing more gamblers access to the second floor. An-

402

drew stepped back from her, but he kept her hand, running his thumb lightly over her fingertips in a hidden caress that was both a plea for understanding and a promise for which he had no words.

Christina and Andrew slowly climbed the length of the stairs. The big room at the top was seething with people and smoke and the noise and a fever that had nothing to do with the heat. Andrew noticed that Jason had managed a considerable upgrading in the past four years. The room had changed from a sleazy collection of cigarette-scarred tables into a small casino with pretensions of elegance, where the dealers and the croupiers moved deftly and the cards were clean and crisp.

There were a dozen blackjack tables, a pair of roulette wheels, a dice table and a local variation of a keno wheel called The Flasher. The dealers and pitmen were shaved, clipped and dressed in cheap tuxedos. There was a patina of excitement, of glamor and long shots coming home, hope and greed and the end of the rainbow. The lights were subdued enough so that only a knowing eye could detect the desperation and frenetic need that lined some faces, the despair and the hands that shook when a stack of chips moved across the table.

Christina turned toward Andrew with an impish grin. "Tell me again how gambling is illegal in Moreno County." She laughed at Andrew's sour look. "I don't believe it—you can't be a Puritan."

Christina slid her hand out of his and merged with the crowds before Andrew could say a word. When he found her, she was standing in back of a table that was four-deep with kibitzers and blackjack players. With the aid of a few sharp nudges and several melting smiles, Christina made her way to the rim of the table. There she stood for a moment, watching the snap of cards and the play of light over markers and cash. Andrew moved in behind her, watching her face with growing impatience and unease. But Christina did not notice him. She was immersed in the turn of cards that raised and crushed human emotions with Olympian indifference. After several rounds, one of the players who had lost all but one white chip vacated a tall stool.

"It's all yours, lady," said the player, flipping the chip to the dealer.

Christina slid onto the stool.

"What do you intend to play with?" said Andrew quietly.

"Your money. Just like you play with my land. Partner."

Christina held out her hand for money without taking her eyes off of the deal. Andrew stifled his anger and took out his money clip; he would rather she play with his money than with Jason's. Andrew peeled off several bills and gave them to the dealer. The man changed paper into chips and skillfully stacked them in front of Christina. Andrew waited until the dealer was done.

"Make sure she only plays with cash," said Andrew, flipping a bill to the dealer.

The dealer looked up and nodded once, knowing that Andrew meant exactly what he had said.

Christina frowned, but Andrew faded into the crowd of kibitzers before she could think of a suitable reply. Shrugging, she gave her attention to the cards, forgetting everything, even the heat.

Andrew moved away from the table and began to quarter the room, estimating the crowd and the action. He did not spot Jason Heer, but he saw several people drifting purposefully around the room, watching the tables or the crowd in the same way Andrew was, although for different reasons.

An efficient bartender with an old-style walrus moustache and watery eyes drew Andrew a beer that was remarkably cold. Andrew leaned against the bar, out of the crush of the crowd, sensing at some primitive level that coming here with Christina was the biggest gamble he had ever taken.

Across the room a pair of thick-necked bouncers picked up a drunk who was slumped in an obscure corner. The drunk put up a slow-motion resistance that would have been amusing if it were not so pathetic. One

404

bouncer quickly pinned the drunk's wrist up near his shoulder blades. The second bouncer delivered an unnecessary blow to the drunk's solar plexus. The drunk would have doubled over, had the first bouncer not held him upright. The drunk's mouth was wide open, twisted in a helpless grimace of pain. Together the two bouncers propelled the drunk toward a side door.

Andrew turned away, his face showing the marked lack of expression that was a warning of anger. No one else in the crowd appeared to have seen what happened. And if any of the players had seen, they had not cared. There was a manic urgency in the room, an invisible current that hummed like high-tension power lines.

Andrew faced toward the windows that overlooked the ocean. They were thrown fully open, but the curtains that surrounded them were limp, unmoving. Tongues of lightning flickered and spat, giving fitful illumination to distant, swelling clouds. Andrew remembered the high, oily surf and was glad that he was not at sea. The menace of the night was tangible.

"Why so grim, McCartney?" said Jason's voice. "I thought you'd particularly enjoy the action, what with the sporting blood you have in your veins."

Andrew turned to face the voice. Jason Heer was standing very close, dressed in a lightweight white summer suit that shone like silk. He was almost too elegant for his surroundings, as slim and supple as lightning. His smile was measured, caustic, but it took all of his gambler's control not to flinch when he met Andrew's white eyes.

Andrew smiled and raised his beer glass. "To concrete bridges," he said softly, and finished the beer to the last golden drop.

Jason stopped smiling. "Touché, McCartney. But the evening is young, *n'est-ce pas?*"

Jason turned and signaled the bartender who quickly brought two more beers, setting one in front of Jason and the other beside Andrew's empty Pilsner glass. Andrew turned to leave as though the second beer did not exist.

"What's your hurry, McCartney?" said Jason, moving quickly. "You know, we really must stop circling each other like street dogs."

"Why?" said Andrew in a totally indifferent voice, waiting for Jason to step out of the way.

"Bad for business."

Andrew studied the gambler for a long moment. There was an odd confidence in the gambler that Andrew knew he should investigate. He turned slowly back toward the bar.

"You like my place?" asked Jason, motioning negligently toward the crowded room.

Andrew looked around briefly and said nothing. His face was impassive, waiting for the thing that Jason had not yet said.

"Well, it may be a little ragged around the edges," conceded Jason, "but it has a great future. Even if those jerks out there tonight are only worth a nickel or a dime, I'm going to turn more than a half million through my books alone."

Andrew's surprise did not show on his face. He remained impassive, waiting. He did not reach for the fresh beer bottle that beaded so temptingly just beyond his fingertips.

"And that's just the beginning," Jason continued, trying and failing to read Andrew's face. "More people every day, and more money than even my pop saw in the boom times. Military money, mostly." Jason drank slowly, giving Andrew an opportunity to talk. Andrew did not. "Some people think we'll be at war soon," added Jason casually. "They think we'll need a lot of planes and pilots. And air bases."

Andrew turned and fixed Jason with a penetrating gray stare.

"Let's be frank with one another," Jason said, grinning, knowing that candor was unlikely unless it was used as a weapon, as he was using it now. "I know about your deal with the government. Ten thousand acres of Trust land for the biggest military air base on the West Coast."

Andrew made a quick note to himself to investigate the source of Jason's information. The sale to the government was contingent on several other very lucrative land swaps; it was the type of secret he could ill afford to reveal until the deals were concluded.

"Go on," said Andrew softly.

"I keep myself well informed," said Jason with a small smile. "I have to. Unlike you, I don't have powerful allies. Just me."

"And the people you can blackmail," replied Andrew absently, his mind quickly sorting through the ramifications of Jason's conversation.

"Such an ugly word—blackmail," said Jason. He touched the corners of his silky moustache. "I prefer to call it a commonality of interests. Friendship, perhaps?"

"Call it what you like," said Andrew indifferently. "I find neither friends nor common interest here."

"But you will, you bastard. You already have. I'm not going to tell everyone what the government is giving away for that air base. Eighty thousand acres of federal land. Sweet, McCartney. Really sweet. If the public knew—poof!—no deal."

"Don't do me any favors. The Trust can live without the air base."

Jason gestured elegantly, palms up. "Would I be so unpatriotic? Those fifteen or twenty thousand flyboys have to be based somewhere. Why not within reach of my establishments?"

Andrew shrugged almost imperceptibly. "People have to get their vice somewhere, I suppose."

"There's another ugly word," said Jason. "Vice. But I'll overlook that slur, just like the Heers have always overlooked the Buckles's insults."

There was a cold edge to Jason's voice. Andrew sensed the sudden surge in Jason's intensity. Then, almost immediately, the gambler's eyes went flat again.

"I'll ignore your crap because you and I need one another, McCartney. I can make real trouble for you over that air base, if I want to."

Andrew said nothing. He knew that Jason owned pieces of several powerful men. But so did Andrew.

Jason nodded slightly. "You're beginning to understand, bastard. You go ahead with your deals, and I'll go ahead with mine. I'm going to turn this place into a real casino, not a shabby imitation. I'm going to build a place where people of wealth and class, people like Chris, can come to play in the atmosphere they enjoy. A place with style and elegance, as well as pleasure of the more human sort."

Andrew sensed Christina standing close behind him and made no reply.

"I think that's a wonderful idea," said Christina slowly. "When the war comes, no one will go to Monaco and gambling in Mexico is so tawdry that none of us really enjoy it."

Andrew looked at her, hearing more than he wanted to in her quick assessment of a local casino's chances for profit. She displayed a business acumen that he had not suspected. Or looked for, he admitted silently.

"A well-appointed casino," continued Christina, "should be quite profitable, as well as amusing."

"Precisely," said Jason, examining Christina with new interest.

"The Blue Turtle has a good location," mused Christina, looking at the people thronging the second floor, "but it could be just a little less . . ." she searched for a gentle description.

"Common?" suggested Jason, smiling wryly.

"Crowded," said Christina tactfully. "It makes it rather warm," she added, touching her moist forehead.

Jason lifted his hand slightly. The bartender appeared at Jason's elbow with impressive speed.

"Champagne," Jason said, "champagne the color of the young lady's beautiful hair."

Jason bowed slightly without taking his eyes from Christina's. For a moment his slim elegance overwhelmed the reality of the Blue Turtle. Heat and noise and discomfort receded, banished by a magician in a white silk suit and an enigmatic white smile.

"There you are, Chrissy," Jason murmured, handing her a glass of champagne.

"Christina," she corrected softly.

"Christina," Jason said, his eyes and his smile making the name a caress.

Christina handed a glass of champagne to Andrew. When he did not accept it, she gave him an impatient look and thrust the glass into his hand. Andrew could either take the glass or create a scene by dropping it. He accepted the thin-stemmed crystal with the feeling of having been finessed.

"What shall we drink to?" said Christina in a husky voice, facing both men at once, her glass held just below the line of her amethyst eyes.

"To friendship and common interests, of course," said Jason smoothly, smiling in humorless victory at the man who was holding a glass of champagne he did not want.

Christina lifted her glass slightly to Jason, then again to Andrew. "To friendship, common interests . . . and an elegant casino."

Andrew looked into Christina's eyes, violet, mocking, filled with the excitement of gambling with human emotions, including her own. Money meant little to her. Feelings were the only valuable currency, the only wager that brought the excitement that came with risk. Andrew could not help responding to that blaze of feeling, to the intensely alive woman who had sunk into him until she was as much a part of him as his skin. Yet even as he responded, he knew that her recklessness could ruin both of them. She was too young to know about tomorrow's inevitability. Deliberately, he set the glass down on the bar without taking a sip.

"Surely you aren't going to be so crude as to ignore a toast?" Christina demanded, deflated and angry.

Andrew looked at her. "What do you expect from a Mexican bastard?"

Andrew's cool question shocked even Jason. The gambler tried to regain his feeling of victory by making Christina turn away from Andrew's colorless eyes.

"I heard that your father left Catalina early. Bit of ruckus with the local police. He'll be in soon," added Jason casually, as though he did not know that Christina would rather not see Champ.

The excitement drained from Christina's eyes. She had no desire to encounter her father, with or without Andrew. Andrew, for his part, suddenly cared very little. He was more angry than he had realized. He turned away from Jason and Christina and the bar.

Jason smiled at Christina. "I left word that I was to be told when the *Silver Buckles* reaches the breakwater."

Andrew glanced out of the window just as lightning lanced across the southern horizon. Slowly the curtains began to stir, twisting like red-black shadows in a hot, invisible breeze. Distant thunder rumbled hoarsely.

"I hope they make it before the squall line," said Andrew. "That looks like a nasty piece of weather."

Jason looked out, then shrugged with the confident ignorance of a man who had never fought the sea. "The bay will stay calm."

Andrew gave him a single, contemptuous glance. "The trick is to get into the bay," he said cuttingly. "The gap between breakwater and headland is damn small even in good weather."

"Daddy will be all right," snapped Christina. "He bought a crew with the boat. He hates being seasick," she added, as though that explained everything.

In the pause that followed her words, Andrew suddenly realized that he could hear the surf clearly, even above the hum of gamblers.

"Hear that?" said Andrew.

"So what?" said Jason after listening for a moment. His fingers slid across Christina's hand as he took her glass to refill it. "I hear a lot of surf."

"Not like that." Andrew looked at Christina and saw from the subtle tightening of her mouth that she understood. "Your daddy's in for one hell of a ride. I hope he

410

bought a good crew, one with enough sense to run for the open sea."

As if to underline Andrew's statement, the night air took on a new dimension of heaviness, a presence like death but without any odor, without anything at all except stillness. Activity at the tables faltered as the players looked up, trying to isolate the reason for their sudden, acute malaise.

The night split into soundless, incandescence, blinding light that shattered man and land alike. The Blue Turtle cowered beneath a twin onslaught of wind and thunder. Before anyone could recover, the sky shattered again, a primal explosion of light and sound and mindless fury. Andrew reached out to Christina, pulling her inside the protection of his arms.

"Chubasco," Andrew whispered, but no one heard.

Then the rain came as though the world had been turned inside out and oceans were pouring down, drowning the land. Air went from dead-still to forty miles per hour in a single howl that climbed, increasing, and rain slashing through open windows, drenching the scarlet curtains and the tuxedos of the dealers who rushed to close out the storm. The temperature went from ninety to seventy degrees so quickly that people shivered from fear as much as from the chill of unleashed storm. Lightning and thunder came as one, a single violence consuming everything.

"My God," said Christina when the fury subsided for a moment.

"I doubt if this is His night," said Jason cheerfully. His voice slid above the drumming rain and his eyes glittered with inner excitement. He glanced around the room in quick assessment. People were suspended in the moment, caught between the outer storm and their inner needs. "Drinks on the house," called Jason clearly. His smile was an echo of lightning. He radiated charm and a contagious excitement. "You only get a night like this once in a lifetime." he called out to the room. "Enjoy it!"

The gamblers cheered and turned away from the dripping curtains and the windows where rain beat like thousands of anonymous fists. People crowded in toward the bar, pressing close in a restive exhalation of smoke and sweat, alcohol and unease. Andrew tried to guide Christina away from the bar and the people, but she resisted.

"I want more champagne. We can't go anywhere in this, anyway."

"I'm not sitting out a *chubasco* with a crowd of drunken, small-time gamblers," said Andrew. "And that most particularly includes our so-called host."

Andrew was nearly yelling to be heard over the storm and the forced revelry. Christina's fingers tightened around her champagne glass in a gesture of stubbornness that was repeated in the tilt of her chin. Andrew pulled her even closer, until his lips were touching her ear. He spoke coldly, precisely, like a machine punching out metal pieces.

"Look, baby. Heer is a bookie and a pimp and a black-mailer. What he wants to do to this county is about 180 degrees from what your best interests are."

"Just what are my best interests?" Christina said with a coldness that matched his.

"The same as mine and your father's and everybody else who has a stake in the Buckles Ranch. Heer and his kind corrupt everything they touch. Look around you, baby. Do you like what you see?"

The fact that she did not only made Christina more angry.

"What do I care about that?" she said, dismissing the casino with a contemptuous toss of pale hair. "We're ranchers. What do orange trees and cattle and crops have to do with Frenchman's Cove?"

"Everything. The ranch that your grandfather and my father worked so hard to keep together is potentially the most valuable land in California, perhaps in the whole country. But the land won't be worth the shit to fertilize it unless good people want to raise families here."

"What are you talking about?" demanded Christina, torn between anger and the compelling light in Andrew's eyes.

412

"I'm talking about the future. Something that you've obviously never bothered to think about. Lee was right not to leave you any more of the land than—"

A frantic shout cut across Andrew's anger.

"Hey, Jason! They're bringing in the *Silver Buckles!*"

"Nobody's that crazy," yelled one of the gamblers.

Andrew grabbed Christina's hand and started shoving through the crowd toward the back.

"My car's in back," Jason said, appearing at Andrew's elbow. "This way."

Jason led them through an unobtrusive door, down a narrow stairway and into the alley. His big, black Chevrolet was parked in a shed guarded by another thick-necked man. Christina and Andrew climbed quickly into the front seat next to Jason. Although they had been exposed to the storm for only a few seconds, all three of them were wet to the skin.

With screeching, spinning tires, Jason backed out and turned onto Ocean Way, heading to the breakwater and the narrow neck of the bay. Sheets of water overwhelmed the windshield wipers, making driving both difficult and dangerous. Driven by a wind, water forced through cracks to ooze down the inside of the windows and trickled down onto the seats. The car staggered, wallowing and tipping as the wind engulfed it. Claws of wind raked over the car, threatening to overturn it. The people inside felt like mice trapped by a malevolent cat.

In the ten minutes since the *chubasco* had slammed into the coast, the wind had increased to hurricane force, blowing in erratic gusts that would eventually even out into a relentless force battering everything it met. The cacaphony of wind, water and thunder made inaudible anything less than a full scream. Jason, Andrew and Christina sat silently, separated from each other by cages of noise.

A few other cars were on the street, wipers flailing, windshields drowned. Jason fought the Chevrolet through the flooding streets to a small park at the base of the

413

breakwater. They sensed the *chubasco* pause, as though drawing in breath for another attack.

"Look!" called Christina, pointing through the windshield toward the churning water a quarter mile beyond the tips of the rock groins that formed the breakwater. A beautiful ship was silhouetted against curtains of lightning and rain. "It's the *Silver Buckles*."

"Turn off the lights," snapped Andrew.

Without the headlights glaring, the three people could more clearly see the lights of the power cruiser. The red and green running lights and a pair of searchlights at either corner of the bridge turned rain into fragments of color. The lights in the large salon were a vague lemon glow atop the invisible black surface of the sea. The yacht leaped and dove, fighting for headway, fighting away from land yet sliding toward the continuous thunder of white water that heaped up and over the three-hundred-yard length of the black rock groins.

Andrew watched the yacht's slow surrender to a superior force. In spite of power and sleek lines, the ship could not seem to hold a straight course out to sea; it pulled to port as though on a leash.

"Oh, Christ," said Andrew. "He's only got one engine."

Christina looked at Andrew and quickly looked away, unable to bear the intensity of his face. She heard something thump against the car and looked toward Jason. Jason rolled his window down two inches, just enough to hear the man who was huddled outside, the man who had been assigned to watch for Champ's boat.

"They were a half mile out when the storm hit," shouted the man. "They kept coming and then at the last minute they turned back out to sea. Damn good thing too. They would have piled up sure. One engine's gone."

Jason nodded curtly and rolled up the window. His face was wet, glistening from wind-blown rain.

"Are they going to stay out there?" Christina asked, her voice tight.

"They will if they know what's good for them—oh, shit," said Andrew. "The fools!"

414

The *Silver Buckles* turned in the heaving black sea, showing white flanks to the waves. The yacht began sliding toward the hundred-yard-wide gap between the twin daggers of the breakwater.

"They'll make it," said Jason confidently, squeezing Christina's hand. "The gap is a lot bigger than the boat."

Andrew's lips thinned with unspoken contempt. Christina saw, and pulled away from him, not wanting to see or hear her own fears reflected in him.

"They can't stay out with just one engine," Christina said unconvincingly. "It's smarter to come in."

"Crap! You know better than that," said Andrew, not looking away from the ship. "Their best chance is at sea."

Andrew's eyes measured the *Silver Buckles*'s crabwise progress toward safety. He sensed Christina draw in her breath as she realized that he was right.

"It would be too rough," said Christina tonelessly. "Daddy will make them come in. He hates being seasick." Her hand clamped on Andrew's arm and her fingernails dug into his wrist. "Stop him, Andrew. Stop him!"

"I can't," he said softly, but she heard.

Christina's answer was lost in lightning and rolling thunder. For an instant the ship hung black against an incandescent sky, then both sky and ship were engulfed by dark water streaked with foam. The lights of the *Silver Buckles* reappeared, closer. The ship closed to within two-hundred yards of the tip of the jetty.

Huge walls of water rolled toward the boat from the invisible black sea. Some waves were nearly three times the height of the bridge. One of those waves caught the *Silver Buckles* while it was still struggling to right itself from the previous wave. White water crashed over the fantail, threatening to drive the ship beneath the surface of the sea. That wave alone dragged the *Silver Buckles* almost fifty yards to one side before the helmsman regained control and brought the ship back to its original heading, toward the bay.

"Daddy, don't do it!" Christina cried. "You can't make it!"

Jason glanced at Christina's white face. He took her hand and rubbed it against his cheek, comforting himself as much as her. "Quiet, honey. He can't hear you."

Christina buried her face against Andrew's shoulder. Her fist beat against his leg. He caught her hand gently, knowing the sense of horror and helplessness that was overwhelming her, the guilty inner cry that she should be able to do something. Then she raised her face and Andrew saw a flash of Lee in the hard line of her lips.

The *Silver Buckles* was less than a hundred yards off of the breakwater when the *chubasco* relented again for a moment, an instant of suspended force. The ship's remaining engine spun the propeller on the port side, and for a moment the screw equalized the drag on the storm. The *Silver Buckles* shot forward, racing toward the foamy gap between the black groins.

As one, Andrew, Christina and Jason abandoned the car and ran toward the water. The *chubasco* flexed and returned, roaring. They were instantly drenched, barely able to stand against the wind and lashing rain. During the worst gusts it was difficult even to breathe. Christina hugged herself out of fear as well as sudden cold. Andrew put an arm around her, but there was nothing he could do to shelter her from the ramifications of the storm.

The renewed fury of the wind forced the *Silver Buckles* off course again. The ship was close enough that Andrew could see the bow come around in an attempt to correct. At that instant another wave humped up, black and massive, breaking like liquid glass over the stern of the ship.

Only Andrew heard Christina's high scream, and only because her lips were barely an inch from his ear. She went rigid until she saw the sleek white shape of the ship come shooting out from beneath the wave like a ghostly surfboard propelled by hundreds of tons of water. But the helmsman was no longer silhouetted against rain and lightning. He had been swept away by the black wave. The *Silver Buckles* turned sideways into another wave and began to roll over just as it passed the end of the breakwater.

416

Christina's long scream was subsumed by thunder. With a soundless sob she ran toward the groin where the black water churned. Andrew caught her in two steps and held her while she screamed and struggled and watched her father's yacht slide closer to destruction on the far side of the passage into the bay.

"Do something!" shrieked Christina.

Andrew did not answer. There was nothing he or anyone else could do to interrupt the death of the *Silver Buckles*. Christina wrenched around, trying to run out onto the breakwater toward the doomed yacht.

"No," Andrew said, holding her with gentle, implacable hands. "You can't help him now. No one can."

Christina trembled between Andrew's hands and her breath came in jerks. Above the wind came the metallic scream of an overrevved diesel engine. The last wave had snapped the shaft and the engine was racing without a load, screaming futilely, until something snapped. The night was almost quiet as the storm flung the *Silver Buckles* toward the black rocks.

The ship smashed into the breakwater with a sound like a falling tree. Wooden planks and ribs literally exploded. The *Silver Buckles* screeched along the rocks until it was hammered by another wave that all but broke the ship into pieces. Black rocks and ship and even the wave itself seemed to flash into foam as dark water thundered the length of the groin.

When the foam subsided and the water receded, the bay was empty. In the space of a few seconds, the *Silver Buckles* and her crew had been destroyed.

"Oh, God—no!" screamed Christina. "No!"

Christina turned on Andrew, her face a mask of horror and guilt.

"He was so weak——not like Lee—not like you!" she screamed in his face. "Why didn't you help him? Why didn't Lee help him? Daddy was weak but he didn't deserve that! Nobody ever gave him a chance! Especially you!"

"Sunshine—"

Christina's screams were ragged, raw, like the wind-torn waves spewing over the rocks. "You killed him! You took away his father and his pride and even his land!" Lightning came, blinding everyone but Christina, already blinded by death. "Now you're trying to do the same to me!"

Christina wrenched savagely away from Andrew and ran through the bruising rain toward Jason Heer's car. Andrew watched her disappear as surely as Champ, leaving him alone, chaos wheeling like thunder, surrounding him. He turned as lightning stabbed across the sky, turned and saw Jason Heer very close. The gambler's face was twisted in a strange smile.

"You shouldn't be strong," Jason said in a voice that slid between the spaces of the storm. "No one is strong enough all the time, so you always end up with people hating you. You disappoint them, you see. Be like me and you'll never disappoint anybody."

Jason's smile dissolved into laughter as he turned toward his car, and Christina waiting for him. Andrew stood beneath lightning, blinded, felt the ground shake with thunder, deafening, but still he heard Jason Heer's laughter, the sound of the past mocking him out of the future. He listened and knew that she was gone and tomorrow had come.

1951

The 1951 Moreno County Grand Jury was sworn in with more than the customary fanfare. The nineteen-member panel was virtually a *Who's Who* of the county. No one could recall a more prominent body of citizen jurors, nor one that had a more potent foreman. There was much speculation among reporters and regulars around San Ignacio's red sandstone courthouse, but no one really knew why Andrew McCartney had been willing to undertake the public and time-consuming task of being foreman of the Grand Jury. It was an unusual concession for a man who was politely, tenaciously committed to privacy.

On the morning following the Grand Jury's first session, Andrew and two other members of the jury appeared in the courtroom basement, the haunt of the courthouse's small press corps. Andrew McCartney's smiling accessibility was almost as much news as the Grand Jury itself. For many people, it was the first time they had seen Andrew in the flesh. At forty, Andrew had lost none of his muscular grace or the sheer presence that made him the focus of any room he entered. Out of deference to the public requirements of the occasion, he wore a dark-gray business suit and handmade black shoes. The two men with him said very little, apparently feeling that grim silence was the proper manner for Grand Jurors in the presence of their foreman.

Five reporters, each representing a different county paper and each stringing for another paper in Los Angeles, quietly gathered around Andrew. Usually the reporters were an unruly pack, driven by personal and professional imperatives to heights of rudeness rarely scaled by common man. But even reporters were not immune to Andrew's subtle charm, a combination of strength and intelligence and reserve. Nonetheless, the reporters were slightly hostile; an important man who made a career out of privacy could not expect to be well loved by the press. The most hostile reporter was the one whom Andrew needed the most: Ed Hennegan, a chestnut-headed Irishman noted for his caustic tongue and stubborn pursuit of unpopular stories.

"You must finally want to see your name in print," said Hennegan when he recognized the man who had walked into the basement.

Andrew gave Hennegan a quick, cool look and a distant smile. Andrew settled onto a straight-backed chair, and looked at each reporter. The other two jury members sat more slowly, reluctant to become too friendly with men who were adversaries by temperament and training.

"We've come to ask your advice on a few matters," Andrew said without preliminary greetings. His voice was soft enough to require the reporters' close attention. "But, for the moment, I must request that what I say be off the record. Agreed?"

Andrew smiled as he made his request, and the smile transformed him from a formidable executive to a handsome, warm presence. The reporters put pencils back into binders, coat pockets and behind ears. Even Hennegan found it difficult to refuse without appearing foolish. With a new appreciation for the chairman of the Buckles Trust, Hennegan softly set his pencil on the table.

"Thank you," Andrew's smile faded. "I need to know

420

if there are any good . . . honest . . . investigators in this county," Andrew said slowly.

Andrew emphasized the qualifications by letting his voice linger on each one. There was silence while the reporters looked thoughtful. Andrew glanced at each man in turn, finding four men who did not understand and one who did.

One of the reporters who did not understand asked, "Do you mean honest cops or what?"

"I have no difficulty finding an honest policeman," said Andrew smoothly, ignoring Hennegan's cynical smile. "But I had in mind a private citizen who has the intelligence to investigate sometimes obscure and delicate relationships, and the integrity not to be amenable to bribes."

"You and Diogenes," said Hennegan dryly. "Good luck. Or have you forgotten that in this county most people break the law three times a week and four times on Saturday?"

One of the reporters sitting next to Hennegan sighed and shifted his weight. "Knock it off, Ed. Mr. McCartney's not interested in your hobbyhorse."

Andrew raised an encouraging eyebrow at Hennegan. "Hobbyhorse?"

"Gambling," said Hennegan succinctly. "I don't like those little games of chance that draw thousands of tourists a day from Los Angeles."

Andrew smiled thinly. "I've heard rumors to that effect." Andrew glanced again at the reporters. "I don't expect an answer right now, but I would appreciate one as quickly as possible."

"Why?" said Hennegan bluntly.

Andrew turned his gray eyes on the reporter, wondering if Hennegan could be trusted not to rush into print. Then Andrew made a small, impatient movement. Soon he hoped to be trusting Hennegan with more important facts than whatever was said here. If Hennegan could not be trusted, now was the time to find out.

"On my recommendation, the Grand Jury has agreed

421

to hire its own investigator, rather than use the ones available through the sheriff and prosecutor's office."

"Are you implying that the official investigators can't be trusted?" said a reporter quickly.

Andrew managed to look surprised. "Of course not. But they are very busy."

"Yeah," muttered Hennegan. "Picking up all those bribes really keeps them hopping."

Andrew seemed to hear neither that comment nor the mixed groans and laughter that followed it. The two jurors sitting behind Andrew stirred, but said nothing. It was Andrew's show and they knew it. Andrew waited until the laughter changed into silence and the silence became uncomfortable as each man realized just what he had been laughing about. Satisfied, Andrew began the carefully platitudinous speech he had prepared.

"The rest of this is on the record," said Andrew with a faint smile. "What we, the Grand Jury, want to say is that this session will be one of the most important in the history of Moreno County. The county is at a crossroads. The decisions we make now will affect our future and our children's future."

Andrew paused, allowing pencils to catch up with his speech. When he continued, he spoke slowly, making it easier for the reporters. It was more courtesy than they received from most people, and the reporters were grateful.

"One of the responsibilities of the Grand Jury," continued Andrew, "is to insure that those decisions are not made in secret by people acting out of selfish interests rather than out of the interests of the people of Moreno County. That's why the Grand Jury will be holding a number of public sessions this year, as well as our usual closed hearings.

"We expect that this Grand Jury will issue an unusual number of indictments. We intend to serve this county as it should be served, without fear or favor."

The reporters had been writing quickly, intent only on recording key phrases rather than meaning. But as the import of Andrew's words sank in, the reporters' pencils slowed, as though their minds could not digest words and write them at the same time. When Andrew paused, all of the reporters sat forward, questions poised like knives in their hands.

"Do you believe that county officials are going to be indicted?" asked one reporter quickly.

"Only if they deserve to be indicted."

"Do you think any of them deserve to be indicted?" Hennegan asked.

"No comment," said Andrew coolly, but he allowed a small smile to move across his face like a cloud shadow over water.

"Why now?" pressed Hennegan. "We had elections last fall, and the voters returned damn near every incumbent. That hardly sounds like a mandate for the Grand Jury to clean house."

"Excellent question," murmured Andrew, more sure than ever that Hennegan was the right man for the Grand Jury's needs. "Without an informed citizenry, elections can be a farce. The Grand Jury feels that it's time that the citizens were informed. If they then wish to return incumbents to office, so be it."

Andrew stood with fluid grace. He had answered enough questions to interest the reporters and he had left enough questions unanswered to keep them interested.

"That's all that I'm free to say right now. Thank you for your attention."

Andrew smiled, turned and walked swiftly out of the door, leaving the reporters with more questions than answers. Andrew stepped from the building into an August sun that was pleasant under the lacy shade of elm and sycamore trees, but uncomfortably intense out on the sidewalk where heat welled, surrounding him. He peeled off his coat, pulled upon the knot on his dark tie and unbuttoned his collar while he stood on the sidewalk waiting for the traffic light to change. San Ignacio had become a city with all the congestion, frustrations and pleasures that accrue to metropolitan areas. Andrew eyed the traffic, gaug-

423

ing his chance of crossing against the light. With a sigh, he decided to wait.

"Mr. McCartney," called a voice from the direction of the courthouse. "Hold on a minute."

Andrew recognized the voice even before he saw Hennegan's medium-sized figure jogging toward him across the courthouse lawn. With an expression of polite curiosity, Andrew waited until Hennegan caught up.

"About that investigator," began Hennegan, searching Andrew's face for encouragement.

"Yes?" said Andrew.

"Have you considered an ex-reporter?" said Hennegan bluntly.

Andrew managed to look thoughtful rather than triumphant. "Not until this moment, but . . . yes. Depending on the reporter, of course."

"How about one Ed Hennegan?" said the reporter dryly. "He's dedicated, usually sober and spent five years in military intelligence."

"What happened?"

"A misunderstanding," said Hennegan. "Mine. I thought that the rules applied to a general's nephew."

Andrew laughed in spite of himself. "What about your job at the *Vindicator?*"

"I'm tired of working for a man who couldn't find his pecker with both hands in full daylight."

Andrew smiled crookedly. "Oh, Tom's not a bad guy."

"Loves small children and dogs," agreed Hennegan. "And gamblers."

Andrew's smile vanished.

"Not that there's anything wrong with that," continued Hennegan sarcastically. "After all, the very best people meet in Heer's silver-plated hell for a little bit of genteel lawbreaking."

Andrew watched Hennegan with colorless, intent eyes.

"Or were you just planning on rousting the cheapest sluts, dollar bookies and bingo parlors?" said Hennegan. "Saving the lower classes from themselves, as it were."

There were several moments of silence while Andrew measured Hennegan. Then Andrew spoke slowly, clearly.

"I want them all. Every last son of a bitch from Heer to the penny-pitching shoeshine boy."

Hennegan blinked, surprised by the quality of hate in Andrew's soft voice. The reporter's lips stretched into a predatory smile that he revealed to few people.

"McCartney, I'm beginning to like you."

"That's not a job qualification."

"It wasn't meant to be."

Andrew weighed the reporter for the last time, then smiled and held out his hand. "The job is yours."

Hennegan took Andrew's hand in a firm grip. "Who do I report to?"

"Me."

"Who's paying me?"

Andrew hesitated, then shrugged. "If I don't tell you, you'll just waste time finding out."

Hennegan nodded, smiling.

"Officially the Grand Jury pays you," said Andrew. "Unofficially, the Buckles Trust."

"You."

"Yes."

"You seem pretty sure you can trust me. All my griping about gamblers might just be an act."

Though it was not quite a question, Andrew answered. "Each time you've tried to do stories on local gambling, you've been offered various sums of money to forget the whole thing. You refused."

Hennegan's eyes narrowed and he looked at Andrew with real speculation. "You've got good sources."

"It's become a personal thing with you," continued Andrew blandly. "Also, you're in a dead end at the paper, unless Tom suddenly forgets his prejudice against Irishmen."

Hennegan's laugh was almost a bark. "No chance."

"All in all," said Andrew softly, "I think you're a damn good risk, Mr. Hennegan."

"I think you're right, Mr. McCartney."

"I know I am." Andrew smiled to take the bite out of his words. "I also know a bar where they make more drinks than bets. Thirsty?"

"I'm Irish."

Andrew laughed and led the Grand Jury's new investigator to one of the few honest bars in Moreno County.

The night was cool and dry, a fine wine decanted over the land. The last indigo twilight had merged into moonrise. As though held in a silver net of moonlight, the ocean was quiescent, almost unmoved by slow waves curling and sighing into foam. Pleasure craft gliding into Frenchman's Cove left silver wakes that widened until they lapped gently against moorings glittering with lights.

Several large, luxurious ships were tied up at the guest moorings in front of the bay's most elegant resort, a seven-year-old hotel and casino called the Silver Buckles. The hotel was reasonably legitimate. Anyone with the price of a room could stay the night. Prostitutes were discouraged to the point of persecution. The third floor and rooftop of the Silver Buckles, as well as several of the outlying cottages, were reserved for group use. Those rooms were always booked up. Large, polite and immovable doormen checked "invitations" before allowing people to enter.

The private "parties" were so successful that they were given every night and well into most days. Nor were invitations difficult to procure. All that was required was wealth, a few social graces and an appetite for games of chance. Nonetheless, the stiff, silver cards that admitted one into the Silver Buckles's private rooms had an undeniable social cachet in the county, the state and among the knowledgeable in the rest of the country.

The interior of the Silver Buckles's private rooms were done in shades of champagne and silver, lavender and amethyst, a décor that extended even to the gambling equipment. The traditional green baize and red velvet and gilt were nowhere to be found. The employees wore

426

white, right down to pearl pinky rings, cufflinks and smiles.

There were echoes of the old Blue Turtle in the frenetic undercurrents of despair and hope, risk and betrayal that were endemic to every gambling house, whether grand or tawdry. Players still drank too much, sweated too much, lost too much and returned too often. The doormen were not merely decorative. The bank required payment. Despite the silk and champagne trappings, tomorrow came to patrons of the Silver Buckles with the customary frequency.

Christina Babcock Buckles Heer walked slowly through the hotel's biggest gambling room. Her strapless, floor-length gown of heavy silk was the precise shade of her violet eyes. Her skin glowed as richly as her smile, and she wore a scent redolent of sensuality and desire. Dark amethysts circled her throat, a necklace inherited from Joy along with the grove house and twenty-five percent of the Buckles Trust.

Christina paused at a blackjack table populated only by a bored dealer. By the time three hands had been dealt, the table was crowded. Christina smiled at the people who had come to be within touching distance of her beauty, and then she left. Her eyes moved ceaselessly while she walked, checking the action, seeing that nothing was out of place. She knew instinctively that a casino was like a silk stocking—a single snag would reveal the mundane flesh beneath the smooth illusion.

Inevitably, Christina's thoughts and eyes went to her husband, at this moment seated at the bar, sharing bourbon and lies with whoever had the taste for either. His white silk suit was too elaborate for Christina's taste—lace and pearl buttons, pleats and vents. But Jason brought it off well enough, in spite of the extra flesh that blurred his jawline and pushed his waist out beyond the ability of even a skilled tailor to disguise.

As though Jason sensed his wife's penetrating glance, he looked up from the bar. Smiling, he raised his drink to her. She saw the flash of a tall, sterling silver mint julep

427

glass and felt impatience curdle her smile. Jason's clothes, his preferred drink and his incessant French phrases irritated her to the point of unreason.

The casino itself, the dream she had built for a husband who could not equal it, also irritated her. She had inherited Joy's gift for organizing and sustaining a gracious environment, but unlike her grandmother, Christina was bored by the niceties of décor, dress and demeanor that made the casino so attractive to its wealthy clients. Worse than boredom was the fact that in the years since she had married Jason, she had lost even her taste for gambling.

Unfortunately, gambling and a marriage license were all she had in common with Jason. Her love for roaming Buckles land on foot or horseback was a source of sarcastic jokes for Jason. His drinking buddies were an equally fertile source of scorn on her part. She had tried to interest Jason in her lengthy and often futile battles with the Buckles Trust, but Jason cared only that her quarterly checks were large and negotiable. For his part, Jason had tried to interest Christina in his own pastimes, but her instinctive, appalled reaction excluded her from sharing—or even wanting to know about—his unusual pleasures.

Christina turned her back on the bar where Jason sat and made her way to the roof garden, feeling a sudden need for the sight and clean scent of the ocean. She crossed the roof and stood between flowering trees lining the rail. For a long time she looked out over the deep, silent ocean, trying not to think about the past, about the decisions made on impulse that had brought her to this moment of solitary darkness. Most particularly she did not think about the night her father had died, the night of anger and sheet lightning and fear when she had left Andrew.

Christina put her hands on the wrought-iron rail and squeezed until her fingers ached. Each year it was getting more difficult to believe or even to pretend that she had made the right choice; each month it was harder to bury her unhappiness under layers of thoughtlessness; and some nights, like tonight, it was almost impossible not to scream.

For an instant Christina wanted to change the past with a yearning that was as irrational as it was fierce. But no matter the depth of her need, yesterday never came—just tomorrow and tomorrow again, an infinity of bleakness relieved only by the moments when she walked out into the golden silence of the land, sensing Lee and her childhood in every curve of hill and cropland. In the early years of her marriage she had wanted a child of her own to share the land with, but between running the casino and fighting the Trust, she had had no time for a baby. Now, when she would gladly abandon the casino, she had absolutely no desire to have Jason's child.

Sensing that she was no longer alone, Christina loosened her grip on the cold railing. Even as she turned, she smelled the flowery cologne that Jason wore in spite of her protests. Or because of them.

Jason stood silently, watching Christina and almost smiling. Like his father, Jason had an intuitive grasp of human weakness, a nearly infallible sense of just how much he could corrupt a given human being at any one moment. But unlike his father, Jason partook of human weaknesses in full measure, especially after he had found himself unable to live up to his own more meager dream—the casino. Buckles wealth had given him the means to forget, to discover how many and enthralling were the roads to hell. He had never forgiven Christina for building the casino, and then for not sharing his almost imperceptible slide into decadence. Nor had he given up trying to erode her to a point where she would welcome the diversions of hell.

With an inward shrinking that Christina did not admit even to herself, she measured Jason's mood. She knew from his tight, faintly amused expression that he had something unpleasant to tell her. There was a subtle aura of tension around him. At one time she had thought that the tension came from fear of her anger. Eventually she realized that his tension was like a child's before a present was opened—anticipation rather than anxiety. The realization had infuriated her, but only in the last few months had she been able to control her feelings to the point of not responding to his deft baiting.

"What do you want?" said Christina, turning back to the silver sea.

"I just wanted to share a minute with the most *très belle femme*—"

Christina jerked around impatiently. "Get to the point."

"The point, my Chrissy, is that your bastard uncle or cousin or whatever the hell he is has made a lot of trouble for us with his tame Grand Jury."

"Are you referring to Andrew McCartney?" she said coolly.

"Do you have other bastard uncles I don't know about? Or is he more your bastard lover?"

"He is not my lover," said Christina, biting off each word in a manner that revealed her anger.

Jason smiled. "Are you sure, Chrissy? The way you two look at each other sometimes is positively indecent."

With a control that cost more strength than she had to spare, Christina said quietly, "I'll take your word for that. You have a much greater knowledge of the indecent than I do."

Jason's smile widened and he moved very close to Christina. "There's no need to be jealous, *ma chérie*. I'd be more than happy to teach you all about indecency."

"Thanks, but no thanks," said Christina with a smile that was as narrow as her eyes. "Unlike you, I prefer my lovers one at a time, using only the equipment they were born with."

"Touché," murmured Jason, clapping his hands silently. "I must have been indiscreet, *n'est-ce pas?*"

Jason's transparent pleasure told Christina more than she wanted to know; he had arranged for her to discover his extra-marital perversities. It was a way of punishing himself, which he enjoyed, and of punishing her for his

430

inadequacies, which she did not enjoy. She felt suddenly weary, almost cold.

"Is there anything else you want to tell me?" said Christina tonelessly.

"Wasn't that enough? Or are you getting as jaded as I am?"

"Good night, Jason," Christina said, stepping around him.

"What about McCartney and the Grand Jury?"

"What about it?" said Christina. "The Grand Jury does only what the sheriff and district attorney let it do. The last time I checked, both Sheriff Johnston and District Attorney Mayhaw were downstairs at the crap tables, losing with our money and winning with theirs."

"I don't trust that Mexican bastard."

Christina shrugged and changed the subject with a skill born of long practice. "I saw two more of those hoods downstairs. They came in on Senator Barkham's card."

"Perhaps we aren't paying the honorable senator enough."

"We're paying him more than he's worth," said Christina curtly. "I arranged for the local cops to give the hoods a toss."

Jason's face suddenly showed strain beneath the careful tan. "When?"

"A few hours ago." Christina saw the sweat and tightness on his face. "Oh, come on, Jason. They're just two-bit LA thugs."

"They're New York, expensive and dangerous." Jason saw that she did not believe him. "Listen, Chrissy. You're great at shilling the carriage trade, but I'm the gutter-snipe of the family. I know Dago trouble when I see it."

"They haven't bothered us before."

"We haven't made enough money before." Jason smiled almost sadly and touched Christina just above the edge of her low-cut gown. "In some ways we're a very successful partnership. Too successful. We've attracted the wrong kind of attention."

Christina stepped aside slowly but definitely, moving beyond Jason's reach. Jason tried to smile, but failed.

"Are you mad at me, Chrissy? I promise I won't do the group thing again. And I won't ask you to dress up in—"

"Jason," said Christina clearly, painfully, understanding more than she wanted to about the man she had married. "Jason, I'm not going to fight and scream at you anymore. You'll have to find another way to get it up."

"Chrissy—"

"No."

"You hate me, don't you? Just like McCartney. It's always been like that, Buckles against Heers."

"What I feel or don't feel toward you," said Christina, "has nothing to do with what my grandfather felt or did not feel toward your father."

Jason smiled. Christina looked at him and felt the skin on her arms shrink and move.

"Doesn't it?" Jason asked, his voice strained. "You don't know much about the Buckleses and Heers do you? I didn't marry you just for your money and your platinum ass. I married you to get the Buckleses off my back."

Christina edged away from the dark intensity of Jason's eyes.

"You're not making sense," Christina said, her voice steady in spite of her unease.

Jason grabbed Christina's arm, cutting off her retreat.

"Aren't I? Listen, dear wife. For once, just listen to me. A long time ago my father worked for a man called Franklin Kaiser."

"I know," Christina said, trying and failing to slip out of Jason's grasp. "He built railroads."

"My father," continued Jason, ignoring both Christina's words and her subtle struggle to be free, "was to have been Kaiser's successor. But Lee Buckles, goddamn his soul, hated Pop. He bullied and beat him and bought a judge to throw Pop and Kaiser's railroad off the Buckles Ranch."

"I've heard it all before," said Christina impatiently.

"Not quite all," said Jason, smiling in a way that made

Christina even more uneasy. "Pop got even. Do you know how?"

Christina shook her head, as much in denial of Jason as in answer to his question.

"Lee had an uppity Mexican bitch he liked to ride. My father arranged for three men to ride her instead. She didn't like the idea much. They had to beat her a long time before she let them fuck her." Jason's smile widened. "Her name was Cira McCartney."

"No . . ." whispered Christina.

"Oh, yes, Chrissy. Pop would have done the job himself, but he was too smart. Somebody killed one of the men, but Pop was in the clear."

Christina shuddered helplessly. "Was it Lee?"

"No. Lee didn't even find out about it for ten years. She went to Mexico and hid, I guess." Jason laughed softly. "Pop loved that story, loved telling how the great Lee Buckles turned two countries inside out searching for a Mex whore and never even knowing why she ran off."

Christina remembered Lee's eyes when he spoke of Cira, remembered the hints of Cira that she had seen in Andrew's body nine years ago. With another shudder, Christina suppressed memories of Andrew, willed herself to forget the past just as she had willed herself not to look ahead into the future.

"Are you listening Chrissy?"

Jason's fingers were like metal bands squeezing Christina's flesh. She longed to shake him off and flee to the ranch, to wake in the morning and ride abandoned trails until peace seeped into her, an inarticulate recapitulation of childhood where tomorrow never came.

"Listen to me!" Jason's eyes were dark slits and he no longer pretended to smile. "You always thought you were in control, didn't you? Doing just what you wanted when you wanted. It's time you learned that you don't control a fucking thing. The past owns everything, Chrissy. The past is all that matters."

Christina tried to jerk away, but Jason had expected

433

that. He shoved until Christina was pinned against the cold railing.

"Listen to me," he snarled. "Lee found out about what Pop did to his whore. Lee hounded Pop then, ruined every deal, every plan, every chance, sucked Pop dry and then sent flowers when Pop killed himself."

Jason's eyes became wide and blank, staring beyond Christina's white face into a past that was more compelling than any present he had ever found.

"It didn't end there," he said in a low, jerky voice. "Lee's bastard girl, Maggie. She looked like her mother. My brother Reggie wanted Maggie. She wouldn't have a bit of him. She teased him until he went crazy. He half killed her greaser boyfriend. It wasn't Reggie's fault, she made him do it. But Lee made sure that my brother was kicked out of school. He lost his football scholarship to UCLA, and no one else would have him. He would have killed her then, but she was gone." Jason smiled. "She came back, though. It was during the League Riots. She was their leader. And Reggie was our sheriff."

Jason's staccato words stopped suddenly. His eyes focused on Christina. "Are you still listening, Chrissy?" he asked, his voice a whisper.

Christina nodded her head, never taking her eyes off Jason. She shivered repeatedly, but neither of them noticed.

"Reggie took Lee's bastard out into the hills and gave her what her mother got." Jason laughed. "Maggie's still out there, but I don't suppose she's very pretty anymore."

Christina made a low sound of revulsion and struggled weakly against Jason's grip. He did not notice her.

"It didn't end there. Lee and Andrew killed Reggie. It looked like an accident, but it was their fault. Reggie was crazy with fear. He knew Andrew was waiting in every shadow. Waiting to kill him." Jason's fingers ground into Christina's arm until she could not help but cry out. "Are you listening, Chrissy!"

"Yes," she said faintly, but she was hearing only the past, Andrew's voice cold with hatred as he told her not to play Jason's game. But she had. She wanted to scream and run and lash out, wanted to do anything but stand in a garden and hear about a past that would not stay buried but instead curled around and broke over her todays in a long, black wave. "Yes, I'm listening."

"I looked around—Pop dead, Reggie dead and Andrew waiting for his chance at me. I figured the only way to beat the Buckleses was to join them. Lee died quick enough after Maggie, but Champ and Andrew were still around. And you, but you were too young then to count for much. Champ was easy to corrupt. He always needed money. And did you know that he had an occasional taste for boys? *Mais oui, ma chérie.* And I was a most handsome boy."

Waves of sickness washed over Christina like a clammy tide. "I don't believe you."

"I know," Jason said. "That's your greatest weakness—you believe only what comforts you. I'm grateful for that Chrissy, damned grateful. If it weren't for that determined blindness, you'd have walked out on me by now."

Jason smiled down on her and drew a finger across her lips.

"Andrew's weakness was much more difficult to find," he said relentlessly. "I'd about given up until I saw you two in my café the morning of the hurricane. Jesus God, but you were beautiful! You never looked like that for me or for any of your other lovers. But I knew you even then, Chrissy-bitch. I knew you were too arrogant to bend your neck for anyone, even him. The whip hand had to be yours. He loved you, but he was strong. I needed you, and I—I was wonderfully weak, *n'est-ce pas?*"

Jason bowed mockingly. "It was a marriage made in heaven, *ma chérie.* And consummated in hell."

"Why are you telling me this?" whispered Christina.

"Weren't you listening?" demanded Jason between his teeth. "I want the Buckleses off my back. Especially that bastard. I won't be railroaded to death like my father and brother!"

Jason waited, trying to read Christina's answer on her face, but she was as expressionless as moonlight.

"Listen, Chrissy. Those hoods you tossed out are here to make sure that nothing happens to the Silver Buckles. No. No questions. Just shut up and listen, my dear wife. If McCartney's Grand Jury closes me down, those hoods are going to lose money. When they lose money, people get hurt. People like me, Chrissy. I'll be the first."

"I don't believe you."

"For God's sake," Jason said, his voice grating with desperation, "just for once in your life believe something you don't want to. Those hoods are killers. You've got to get McCartney off my back!"

Christina looked into Jason's eyes and saw nothing, not even her own reflection.

"How?"

"The usual way." Jason smiled sardonically. "Suck his cock."

Christina's hand smashed against Jason's smile with enough force to snap back his head. A thin line of blood darkened his lips. After an instant of silence, he licked his lips slowly, as though savoring the taste of blood.

"Do it again, Chrissy," he murmured. "You must know by now that I like it."

"You're disgusting," Christina said in a voice that shook uncontrollably.

"I thought you'd never notice."

"This time you've gone too far. I'm leaving you."

Jason licked his lips and laughed indulgently. "You still don't understand, do you? You're strong, but not ruthless enough to let those hoods kill me when you could stop them. Could you let them kill me, Chrissy?"

Christina dropped her eyes, unable to meet the certainty in his.

"That's right, Chrissy. Weakness always wins against simple strength. Pity corrupts you and feeds me, but you can't believe that, because then you would have to believe that you're weaker than the husband you despise." He laughed, enjoying the expressions crossing her face. "I

436

need you, my sweet silver bitch. I'll always need you. So you'll stay with me and we'll keep on eating each other alive. Too bad you can't lay back and enjoy it like I do."

Jason turned away and sauntered across the roof garden. Unable to speak, Christina watched him vanish down the winding stairway. She leaned against the railing, hanging on until she could control her shaking body. Finally she walked slowly across the garden and through a private entrance to her suite. She moved as though stunned, measuring the extent of her misjudgment of Jason in the waves of nausea rising in her.

Once inside the safety of her suite, Christina locked the door, went into the bathroom and was wretchedly sick. When she could throw up no more, she turned on the shower and washed herself repeatedly, standing in steam and lather, scrubbing and rinsing until her body was nearly raw. She dried herself, wrapped up in a violet robe and sat in front of the mirror, brushing her breast-length hair. The heavy silver brush that had once belonged to Joy turned and flashed with each stroke.

After a long time, Christina set the brush aside and went to bed. She lay between silk sheets, wide-eyed and tense, trying to comprehend all that Jason had told her, but all that she really understood was horror and revulsion for Jason's father, for Jason's brother, for Jason and for herself. She had become a part of the Heers' revenge even after Andrew had warned her. She had been young, but did that excuse such stupidity? It certainly did not excuse her stubborn refusal to face what Jason had become during their years of marriage.

Christina's throat convulsed around screams she could not release. She tried to sleep but found that was as impossible as going back ten years and this time not blaming Andrew for Champ's death, this time not hating Andrew for being what he could not help being—Lee's son. If only she had realized then that she was not as weak as Champ, that she would not fade into insignificance next to Andrew as her father had, as Joy had next to Lee.

But then Christina wondered if she really was stronger

than her father and grandmother, or if Jason was right, that she was weak and willfully blind.

With a low sound, Christina turned over and tried to think of nothing at all, an ability she had nearly perfected in her years of marriage to Jason Heer. The cold sweat on her skin soaked into the sheets, making them clammy. She rolled over again, shivering, remembering against her will what Jason had told her, remembering lives spent, lives ruined, lives given for the land. Rape and murder, revenge and heartbreak and the land, always the land, the still center of their wheeling lives.

Christina sat up, hugging her knees against herself, rocking slowly, comforting herself because there was no one else to comfort her. She felt a strong kinship with Cira and Maggie, women who had paid too much for a land they had never owned. Especially Maggie, knowing the lust of many men and the love of none, never secure in the land, having little present beyond calumny and disdain, and no future, not even the vicarious future of a child. Nothing enduring. Nothing to leave behind but memories that would grow more tenuous with each passing day until finally they vanished.

Blindly, Christina got up and walked over to the window, but even the moonlit sea could not calm her. It looked cold, indifferent. Shivering, she left the window and paced the room, wishing it were light so she could ride horseback over the land. She felt stifled in the hotel, trapped.

Christina went to the closet and pulled out the worn jeans and jacket she used for riding. After she dressed she studied herself in the mirror as she would a stranger, seeing a woman neither young nor yet old, a woman whose beauty had always concealed her fears and loneliness. Shorn of makeup she looked both stronger and more vulnerable. She was surprised that the night had left no marks on her face; she felt drained, hollow, used up and thrown away.

Christina left the room just as the first vague promise of dawn began to dim the stars. She drove north quickly along the Shoreline Highway, thinking of many things, fragments. On her right a row of rugged coastal hills began to condense out of the waning night, black on darkest gray. The trace of light revealed the ocean without illuminating it.

Though Christina could not see the unobtrusive road that led toward the sea, she knew the road was there. Impulsively, she turned onto it, driving toward a rugged black headland that thrust into the sea. She was on Buckles land now, the northern horn that curved protectingly around Frenchman's Cove.

There was only one house on the headland, a house of wood and glass and native stone, Andrew's home, where he sat alone and watched the supple transformations of the sea. At dawn a Santa Ana wind would begin to blow, turning the sea to indigo crystal below a cerulean sky, but now the sea he watched was dark, silent, poised in its waiting for light.

Andrew sat as he usually did at sunrise, wearing only jeans, his bare feet propped up on a leather hassock that matched his favorite chair. His hands were wrapped around a fresh cup of coffee. The room surrounding him was almost all glass, slanted out over the surf. He sat in darkness, preferring to watch dawn with eyes that were not dulled by artificial light.

When Andrew saw the headlights of a car turning off of Shoreline Highway, he set aside his coffee and rose in a single motion. Without turning on any lights, he went into the hall and lifted a shotgun off its wall pegs. He opened the gun, checking by touch that both barrels were loaded. The sound of the breech closing was cold and distinct. It was the only sound Andrew made on his way to the front of the house.

Andrew stood back from the front windows, watching headlights flash and vanish like a cryptic message as the car followed the twisting road toward his home. When he recognized the white Mercedes, he moved to return the gun to the hallway, then decided against it. Jason sometimes drove Christina's car, and Jason was smart enough to be desperate.

The car door opened. Moonlight and a pale prelude to dawn washed over Christina's hair, making it lambent silver against the midnight of her clothes. Without moving, Andrew watched the woman who changed as she grew older, changed like the sea, never diminishing in her fascination for him. It had been a long time since he had talked to Christina alone. Too long . . . and not nearly long enough. He wondered if it would ever be long enough, if he would ever see her without wanting her.

Andrew controlled his thoughts as carefully as he controlled his face. Emotion drained from his expression, leaving behind a mask of polite attention that was habitual, if not effortless. Silently, he opened the front door of his home. Though barefoot and shirtless, he was comfortable in the silky dawn. Christina shut the car door and walked up the steps to where Andrew waited, the shotgun forgotten in the crook of his arm.

"That's a helluva greeting," said Christina, her voice not as light as she wanted it to be.

Andrew looked down at the gun and smiled slightly. "Yeah, I suppose it is."

Silently, Andrew turned and led Christina into his house. He did not bother to switch on the lights. He paused in the hallway long enough to replace the shotgun on its pegs. Then he led Christina to the room where glass walls invisibly separated the house from the sky. Casually, Andrew swung a heavy leather chair close to his own chair and hassock. Christina watched the muscular grace of his movements and remembered the weekend of the hurricane as though it had been yesterday.

"Are you cold?" said Andrew, sensing as much as seeing the quiver that went through Christina.

Christina shook her head.

"Sit down," said Andrew, gesturing to the chair he had drawn up opposite his. "Coffee?"

Christina shook her head again, then sat quickly, before her body could betray her. She kicked off her sandals

440

and put her feet up on the hassock, letting silence fill the room like a second, colorless dawn.

Instead of sitting down, Andrew walked over to the huge window that framed the coastal hills. The sky turned to pale rose as sunrise divided the hills from each other and the night. Andrew's gray eyes slid away from the hills to the woman who leaned back in her deep chair without relaxing, without talking. He was tempted to ignore her until she told him what she was doing alone in his home in the dawn and silence after ten years, but she looked too wan to question, too defenseless.

Emotion stirred painfully beneath Andrew's control. He told himself that what he felt was pity for her, for memories of a child and a woman too beautiful for the harsh usages of this world. But Andrew did not have Christina's gift for self-deception. He knew, even as he wanted to deny it, that whatever he felt for Christina was not pity. He sighed soundlessly and turned to face her, his tormentor. His expression was distant, relentlessly polite.

"How are you, Christina?" he asked, as though it were perfectly normal for him to stand half naked, sharing sunrise and conversation with her.

"All right, I guess," Christina said, her voice thinner than she wanted it to be, more frightened. Absently, she pulled her fingers through her thick, pale hair, trying not to stare at Andrew as he stood lit by a dawn that made each line of his body seem sculpted, perfect. "You look good." she said softly. "But then, you always do."

Christina looked quickly away from him. The sudden movement pulled Andrew's eyes off of the dawn. The increasing light in the room made Christina's hair and skin pale gold, luminous, but the tightness in her body and the shadows surrounding her eyes told him that she was either ill or unhappy or both.

"You don't look well." Andrew said. his voice flat, emotionless. "When was the last time you slept?"

"Thanks." snapped Christina. "you really know how to make me feel good." Then she realized that she could not remember the last time she had slept for more than four

441

hours without the aid of alcohol or pills or both. "I'm sorry," she said huskily. "I didn't come here to fight with you. I get enough of that at Trust meetings."

Christina tried to smile, but could not. She looked at Andrew's eyes watching her, Lee's eyes, and felt lost, nearly helpless. He was so polite, so indifferent to her. But could she honestly expect anything else? She should ask him about the Grand Jury and then leave, quickly, before she made a fool of herself by crawling into his lap and crying as though she were six again and he sixteen. She bit her lip, gathering her courage, but courage ran like water through her shaking hands. She closed her eyes and fought for self-control. "I wish to God I had your strength. No, your ruthlessness. I need that more than strength."

She laughed brittlely, remembering Jason's words, his certainty. The laughter ended in a barely controlled sob. Andrew was at her side in three swift steps, his concern obvious only in the darkening of his clear eyes. He reached to stroke her shining hair, then stopped, burned by memories of its cool softness sliding over his bare skin. He moved back until she was beyond his reach, then sat down across from her. As his legs stretched out on the hassock, his bare feet accidentally brushed against hers.

The touch was electric, but did not pierce the mask of Andrew's control. He could not afford to have feelings where Christina was concerned, a lesson she had taught him the night Champ died. Yet the bonds remained, inevitable, invisible ties of blood and memory, love and desire.

Andrew spoke, because he saw that Christina could not.

"I'm glad you came here," said Andrew quietly. "There's something you should know. I should have told you a long time ago, but I never found the right moment."

Christina opened her eyes and brought her knees up against her chest. "Please, it's not ugly, is it?" she asked in a small voice. "I've heard too many ugly things tonight."

The anguish in Christina's shadowed eyes made Andrew want to pull her onto his lap and comfort her as he had done so many years ago; though she had hurt him as no one else could, he did not enjoy seeing her pain. He slid from chair to hassock and put his hands over Christina's cold fingers, feeling her continuous inner trembling. He waited, but she said nothing about what had happened that night, what had driven her to him.

"Look at the hills, Christina."

Christina turned her head, letting sunrise pour over her drawn features. Andrew's breath caught at the sadness and beauty he saw in her face. He spoke very softly, never looking away from her.

"See the hill just to the left of Baja Creek? It's the highest in the row."

The silky whisper of Christina's hair as she nodded her head was Andrew's only answer.

"My mother is buried there," said Andrew.

Christina became utterly still. She made no sound, no move that might betray her knowledge of Cira's rape.

"Lee is also buried there," continued Andrew quietly.

Christina stared at the hill that was gaining depth and texture with every expanding instant of light. She remembered the hill now, with its crown of wind-worn stone. From the coastal side, the shape of the hill was subtly altered, but it was the same hill. Three years ago she had gone riding during one of her many flights from Jason. She had found a dim trail leading to a fenced hilltop. Though it seemed to be a cemetery, the two weathered wooden markers bore no names. There was only native stone thrusting like a barricade protecting the graves from the cold wind off of the sea.

"Lee is in the middle of Fairhaven Memorial Park," said Christina automatically, "with Joy and Daddy and David Carrington."

"No," said Andrew gently. "He's up there with my mother. It was the last order he gave. Only three people knew—Lee's lawyer, Gil and myself."

"Why are you telling me now?" Christina asked faintly.

Andrew smiled, but his eyes were white. "Gil and the

lawyer are dead, and I"—he shrugged—"I'm making a lot of enemies lately. Some of them are professional killers." Andrew's eyes lifted from Christina's profile to the hills. "Someone else should know about Lee and my mother. You loved him. You have a right to know what happens on Buckles land. So now you know."

Andrew turned back to Christina, watching her with haunted eyes. "Was that an ugly thing to tell you?"

"No," Christina whispered.

Christina held her legs more tightly against her chest, as though the feel of her own body was all that was real to her. Nothing was what it had seemed to be, nothing was what it should be, what she tried to make it be. Things she did not know until too late mocked her efforts to transform the future. Worse, things she refused to know had made her present unendurable.

Christina watched Buckles land being renewed by sunrise, land as fresh as hope and as old as despair. She watched, and did not know whether to love or loathe the land that should have been hers. The land that had divided her from Andrew.

"Why don't we hate the land?" whispered Christina, staring at the hills growing out of the dawn, curving and flowing with a timeless beauty that made her eyes burn. "It controls us, it always did—Lee and Joy, my father, your mother and sister. You and me. You and me most of all."

"The ranch is part of me," said Andrew quietly. "Hating it would be like hating my own hands."

Christina stared at Andrew, drawn by his changing eyes and his soft, compelling voice. She let his presence sink into her, warming her.

"You," continued Andrew, "can afford to hate the ranch. You have Lee's name, a husband, the possibility of children . . . but the ranch is all that I have left of yesterday, and all that will be left of me tomorrow."

"Is that why you're trying to destroy Jason—a way of punishing me for all the times I've fought with you over the land?"

444

Andrew stood swiftly and went to the window where sunlight poured over him, replacing the warmth that he had felt touching Christina's hands. He did not speak until anger no longer licked at the edges of his control.

"I despise your husband," said Andrew calmly, "but that's not the reason I will ruin him. I won't even ruin him because of what he has done to you, though that would be reason enough for most men."

"Then why? Because I married him?" whispered Christina.

"No. Because of the land. I'm going to make something of it, something unique that will live after I'm dead."

Christina looked into Andrew's clear eyes. "You talk as though the land is your child," she said softly.

Andrew's smile was a reflection of sorrow, like looking in a mirror.

"It's the only child I'm likely to have." He shrugged. "I've made my choices with my eyes open. No hard feelings and few regrets. That's enough. It has to be." He faced her again. "The land is my life. Whatever threatens the land threatens me. Can you understand that?"

"Yes . . . but what does that have to do with Jason?"

Anger returned, making Andrew's voice polished and polite, as though she were a stranger. "Jason Heer corrupts everything he touches. He and his backers are like gangrene, spreading quietly, destroying this county. Your brains and your name and your money made his casino respectable, but what is a wife for if not to help her husband? That's why you're here, isn't it?"

Christina did not answer. Andrew looked away from the violet eyes watching him, eyes that had haunted his silences for as long as he could remember.

"For the love of Christ," Andrew said harshly, "don't look at me like that! If it were just the casino, I could live with it. But it's a lot more. Whores, drugs, bookmaking, loan-sharking, leg-breaking."

"No," said Christina loudly. Then, more softly, frightened by the hysteria she had heard in her voice.

"No. That's not true. He's just a gambler, and not a very good one at that."

Andrew measured Christina for a long moment. Then he sighed. "Hennegan was right. You don't know the first thing about your husband's hobbies. Sweet God."

"Whoever Hennegan is," Christina said tightly, "he's wrong. Jason is weak, but he's not a criminal. You're just saying he is so that you'll have an excuse to destroy him."

"That's bullshit, baby. Just plain bull *shit*. Why do you think that Jason has systematically bought senators and police chiefs, the sheriff and the prosecutor and too many cops to count? Do you think that Jason corrupted an entire county just to protect the Silver Buckles?"

The skin on Christina's arms shrank and crawled, responding to her inner certainty that Andrew was telling the truth. But she could not accept it, for if Andrew were right, she was as weak and as blind as Jason had taunted her with being. It simply could not be true.

"You sound like a member of Christian Women Against Gambling, or whatever you call the group that's been picketing the Silver Buckles," said Christina thinly.

"Maybe that's because I've spent a lot of money getting them out on the sidewalk every Sunday."

"My God. I wondered who had invented them."

"I'm behind them, but I didn't invent them."

"Who the hell cares if adults gamble?" snapped Christina.

"I do, Christina. I can't build the kind of city I want in a county so corrupt that decent people wouldn't use it for a toilet, much less a home."

Andrew turned his back on her and looked out at the hills with eyes that were opaque.

"If you care about your husband, Mrs. Heer," said Andrew coldly, "get him the hell out of Moreno County before I drive him out. And then run, baby, run. Jason's friends are killers."

"That's what he said," Christina whispered, her eyes blank, incredulous. "I didn't believe him, not really. I mean, those things don't happen to . . ." her voice died.

"Nice people?" finished Andrew sardonically. "Jason isn't 'nice people.' He's scum. And he's promised things he can't deliver to his gangster playmates. If he's lucky, they'll just break his legs."

"I don't believe it," repeated Christina mechanically.

"Suit yourself," Andrew said in a savage voice. "You always do, don't you?"

Christina heard echoes of Jason's smug accusation in Andrew's angry words: she believed only what comforted her; she did only what suited her. They were right. They were both right and she had been so wrong. Her arms strained around her knees, pulling her legs closer to her body, but it was not enough to comfort her. Nothing was enough. Nothing had been since Lee . . . and Andrew, of course, Andrew who now looked at her with such contempt.

Without realizing it, Christina bit her lips and moaned so softly that Andrew was not sure he had heard anything more than the wind lifting with the heat of the sun. Then he saw that Christina was unnaturally pale in the golden aftermath of dawn. He heard the low sound again, saw her white teeth biting into bloodless lips, sensed the wildness waiting behind her unseeing violet eyes. She was on the brink of flying apart in an orgy of self-destruction, and he had helped to push her there. No matter what she had done or not done, believed or not believed or misbelieved, he could not bear to see her hurt like that.

"Christina," said Andrew gently, sitting across from her and touching the cold hands that were clenched around her knees.

Christina looked through Andrew with eyes that were too dark in a face that was too white.

"I tried to cry tonight," Christina said in a stranger's voice, flat, colorless, "but I haven't cried since Lee . . . not even for my own father."

Andrew was appalled by her voice and her eyes and her transparent, cold skin. He sensed her control thinning in each small shudder of her body, as she tried to subdue

447

each failure, each separate anguish. But there were too many.

"Christina," murmured Andrew, rubbing his hands over her arms as though he could bring warmth and control back to her shaking body, "Christina."

"Then I tried to scream," continued Christina, her voice almost conversational. Almost, but the difference made Andrew's skin crawl. "I've done a lot of that since Daddy died, so it shouldn't have been hard, should it? But I couldn't even scream. So I came here like I've wanted to for . . ." Her voice thinned until it broke. "I waited too long. So many, many years. Poor Andrew. Poor Christina. They're dead now, aren't they?"

She shuddered, but her eyes were dry, blind, staring at a past that mocked her and a future she did not even want to face.

"Don't," said Andrew, his voice hard, his hands very gentle. "Don't tear yourself apart over things you can't change."

"Why not?" asked a stranger's reasonable voice. "Everyone else does."

The muscles along Christina's neck and jaw stood out against her pale flesh as she strained against the random shudders that threatened to break the grip of her arms around her knees. Andrew's hands moved up her arms to her shoulders, kneading rigid muscles, trying to ease the tension that was pulling her apart.

"Cold," said Christina suddenly between clenched teeth, "sweet Jesus it's so cold."

Andrew reached beneath Christina's denim jacket. Her thin blouse was damp, and her skin was roughened by goose flesh. He stood abruptly and went with long strides to his bedroom. Before she realized that he had gone, he was back, carrying a shot glass of brandy and a goose-down comforter.

Christina tried to drink, but her teeth were chattering so hard that most of the brandy spilled down her jacket. Andrew lifted her to her feet, wrapped the quilt around her and sat down, pulling her onto his lap. He held her against his body, held her so hard that she no longer had to hold onto herself.

"Whatever happened," Andrew said against Christina's cheek, kneading his strong fingers through her hair, "whatever it was it's not worth what you're doing to yourself now. You're too strong, too good to waste yourself like this, especially for him." And then he added almost helplessly, "For him, oh my God, for *him!*" He felt her shuddering increase and held her even more fiercely. "Sunshine," he said, bending his head to her pale hair, "Sunshine . . ."

When Christina heard Andrew call to her, her breath caught in a wracking sob that could have been his name. She tried to speak but could not. She was choking. With a hoarse sound, she abandoned herself to the tears that were strangling her.

Andrew held Christina for a long time, stroking her, comforting her wordlessly until her shudders came further and further apart and finally died to distant tremors, aftershocks of grief. Though her tears still fell, she was no longer out of control. She stirred, and Andrew reluctantly loosened his arms to release her. She shifted so that her own arms were freed from the comforter he had wrapped around her. With a ragged sigh she put her arms around him and laid her forehead against his neck.

Andrew closed his eyes as he felt the warmth of Christina's tears sliding down his chest. His arms went around her again, pulling her closer. His lips brushed against her incandescent hair, lingered, brushed again and stayed. Christina pressed against him, subtly changing until she seemed to flow over him like warm water, matching every contour of his body. Her hands slid up to his face, then lost themselves in his thick, dark hair. She kissed him softly, asking nothing for the moment but to feel the reassuring warmth of his mouth against hers. Then she sighed and opened her lips, kissing him slowly, fully, savoring every texture of his mouth.

Andrew's arms tightened around Christina, returning her kiss with a hungry searching that made her tremble all over again. Abruptly, his arms loosened and he lifted his head.

Christina sat up, her eyes searching the face that was so close to her own. She shivered, a resonance of the deep currents stirring within her, stirring and turning, awakening the sensuality that only Andrew had ever tapped. With dreamlike grace she slipped free of the thick comforter and the jacket.

"You'll get chilled again," Andrew said in a strained voice.

"Not if you hold me." She leaned forward until her lips were pressed against Andrew's neck where his pulse made a deep, hard beat of life. "Hold me, Andrew."

"Are you sure?" whispered Andrew. He tilted her face up until his tongue could trace her lips. "Are you sure, Sunshine?" Then, fiercely, "No, no, don't answer. I can't let go of you now."

Christina returned Andrew's kiss with a need as deep as his own. Her hands touched his face, rubbed through his hair, slid over the warmth of his naked chest. Andrew unfastened her blouse with quick, sure motions, and she smiled with each look, every touch, his mouth on her breasts, caressing her with his tongue until she moaned. She let her head tilt back until her hair drifted over his bare arm like cool fire. He lifted his head and as he looked at her something close to fear moved deep in his eyes.

"Sunshine," he whispered raggedly, "my God, Sunshine . . . I worked so long to forget how beautiful you are."

So long, and so many women, but none of them like her, sinking into him until leaving her was like tearing off his own skin. With a groan he buried his face between her breasts, wondering if she knew what she was doing to him. Then her hands slid down his body until he wondered nothing at all but that it was possible to feel such need and not explode.

Andrew's hands and lips surrounded Christina until reality shrank to a timeless present where nothing existed but her warmth turning slowly along his body in a

450

wordless plea. He looked up from her and fought for control so that he would not take her right there.

"Don't stop," said Christina against his ear, her tongue and teeth caressing him until he shivered. "Touch me, Andrew. I need you. I've always needed you."

Christina's hands stroked the strong muscles of Andrew's thighs, moving upward until she cupped the flesh straining against his jeans. His hands moved quickly, urgently, and she felt her clothes slipping off of her body.

With a soft laugh, Christina twisted until she could straddle Andrew's legs. She reached for his belt buckle, but before she could do more than unfasten it, his fingers were touching her, sliding, driving out everything but the concentric rings of ecstasy that were claiming her.

"Is that what you wanted, Sunshine?" said Andrew, smiling, enjoying her pleasure as though it were his own.

"Yes," said Christina. "Yes." Her fingers slid down his chest until they caught against his jeans. "You have on too many clothes," she said. Her hands moved and Andrew's jeans were suddenly loose. "How can I touch you with so many clothes between us?"

Christina's hands slid blindly inside his jeans, seeking, finding and she closed around him while her body slid down, lips following her hands until her hair was like a second dawn shimmering across his lap. His fingers twisted through her hair while he was swept away by hard currents of pleasure, trying not to drown.

Christina's mouth returned to Andrew's lips in a salt-sweet mingling that left him shaken. Her hands sought him again, and again tangled in his jeans. She tugged at the cloth impatiently.

"Until a moment ago," Andrew said, standing and kicking aside his jeans, "I was going to offer you the comforts of my bed." He smiled and pulled her down onto the rug. "But the bed is just too damn far away."

Andrew's hands and mouth moved over Christina's body, returning the fiery pleasure she had given him, adding to the deep currents of passion that flowed between them, joining them. They sank into each other, drowning.

451

For a time it was as though yesterday had revoked natural law and come in place of tomorrow. Andrew and Christina lived only for the other, rediscovering and exploring the deep, almost clandestine currents that bound them one to the other, a river flowing out of their past to engulf their present with its irresistible power.

They laughed and slept and ate and made love and tried not to think about tomorrow. There was no sultry heat to oppress them this time, no random churning crowds seeking relief, no *chubasco* to explode, grinding flesh off of men and dreams alike. There was only a strong Santa Ana wind and an incandescent sun, drawing water from hills and plains, chaparral and crops crackling beneath a blue-white sky.

Andrew stood in the glass room, looking out at hills that had gone from green to gold in less than three days. His eyes measured the land's dryness and he remembered things that needed to be done. He must check that cattle and sheep had been moved out of the most inaccessible chaparral canyons; check that fire breaks and fire roads to those canyons were cleared; check that wells and stock tanks and irrigation equipment operated properly; check the thousand things that made farming an arid land not only possible, but profitable. His ranch manager, Esteban Zavala, could and would do what was required, but Andrew knew that if he showed a direct interest, the ranch hands would feel the importance of their jobs. This week he would have to ride out over the land with Esteban.

Noiselessly, Christina entered the room with a cup of coffee steaming in each hand. She had walked slowly from the kitchen, as much to enjoy the house as to carry the coffee without spilling. She had come to love the clean lines of Andrew's home, the furnishings which combined richness with restraint. The total effect was Spanish in its understanding of masculine luxury and Oriental in its pervasive reserve. The sole concentration of color in the home was deep vermilion where tile replaced thick carpets the exact shade of sand under a late afternoon sun.

Christina walked soundlessly across the room until she was close to Andrew. For long moments she admired her lover, naked but for the sunrise and the grace he had inherited from Lee. Yet even Andrew's male beauty could not keep her eyes from the sight of hills condensing out of the dawn.

"The land changes so quickly," said Christina, her voice soft as she watched the glory of hills bronzed by sunrise and dry winds. "And yet the land never really changes . . . just cycles turning and returning, always the same."

Andrew turned to look at Christina, caught by the emotion in her voice. She was as naked as the sun, more beautiful than the dawn.

"They were the same a year ago, ten years ago," Christina continued, her violet eyes never leaving the hills. "They were the same when I was a child, and you, and Lee, and for thousands of years before. They'll be the same a year from now, ten years, a hundred, a thousand. They are the only perfection in the wreckage we call life."

"Everything changes, Sunshine," said Andrew, stroking the brightness of her hair, "even the hills."

"No."

The word was polished, rounded, leaving no purchase for argument. Andrew shook his head slowly, but she did not see. She saw only the hills. Andrew understood, and even shared, her desire to have the land remain unchanged, but he knew that was impossible. After today's Trust meeting, she would know it too. But the meeting was hours and miles distant, and she was here and now, incredibly beautiful, floating in the soundless cataract of dawn.

Andrew's fingertips traced the line of Christina's back to the swelling hips divided by a soft curve of shadow. She turned toward him, smiling, so close to him that he felt her breasts tighten at the touch of his skin.

"About that omelette you promised me . . ." said Christina, taking a sip from one of the coffee cups she still held.

Andrew's hands touched Christina lightly, stroking her until she shivered with pleasure. He kissed her slowly, completely, while his hands held her lovely hips close to him.

"No fair," she said breathlessly, unable to touch him because of the cups of hot coffee.

Andrew's laugh was like another kind of caress, as warm and exciting as his lips. Christina stood helplessly, feeling even her bones melt at the teasing intimacy of his tongue roaming over her body.

"Andrew . . ."

The name was almost a plea. For a moment longer, Andrew's teeth closed lightly on Christina, then he relented with slow reluctance. He took the coffee cups and set them on a table.

"I've changed my mind about breakfast," said Christina, her face flushed and her eyes brilliant in the growing light.

Andrew smiled while Christina's hands stalked down his chest and pounced lightly. "Good," murmured Andrew, his hands alive with her warmth. "I'd rather have you than any breakfast on earth."

"You can have both," pointed out Christina, holding him with gentle hands.

"Not today. Trust meeting at nine."

Andrew did not need to ask her if she were going to attend. She always did.

"Is it Monday already?" asked Christina, stiffening for an instant.

"Yes."

"Screw Monday," said Christina distinctly.

Andrew laughed. "I have a better idea, Sunshine."

"Mmmmm, let me guess. Is it this . . . ?"

Christina kissed Andrew while her hands kneaded the resilient muscles of his back and hips.

"That's part of it," Andrew said, nibbling on her lips.

"And this . . . ?" murmured Christina, putting his hand on her breast while her own hand traveled down his body.

454

Andrew drew in a slow breath of pleasure. "That's definitely part of it."

Laughing, Christina slid through Andrew's arms until she was kneeling on the soft rug. Before she could move he caught her face between his strong hands. Christina smiled, aroused by the desire that made Andrew's eyes burn like crystal in sunlight. He knelt in a single, swift movement and buried his long fingers in her hair. His eyes searched her face, found an answering blaze in her violet eyes. She felt the subtle trembling of his fingers and heard the huskiness of his voice.

"I want to be part of you, Sunshine."

Andrew bent his head and kissed Christina so gently that she began to tremble in response. She whispered his name again and again in a soft litany of love. They touched each other slowly, giving and receiving without urgency, shaping their ecstasy with exquisite care until ecstasy shaped them, transforming them.

Andrew was nearly late for the monthly Trust meeting. Christina almost missed it altogether. She had been afraid of encountering Jason at the hotel, so she had gone out and bought clothes to wear to the meeting. When she came into the boardroom, Andrew was just wrapping up his monthly presentation to the advisory board. The five men who listened to him were grave and attentive. From time to time they referred to the thick reports in front of them for the particulars pertaining to Andrew's verbal summary.

As Christina slid into her seat, Andrew looked up and gave her a smile that was as intimate as a kiss. Then he pulled his eyes away from her and concentrated on his speech, one of the most important he would ever make to the Trust's advisory board. He spoke easily, explaining what he felt and what he knew.

"The land was whole before man wandered down from Siberia and began to grub a living out of a nameless continent. Tribes of men came and went, responding to cycles of drought and plenty. Then the Spanish missionaries

455

came. They stayed, and named the land. Enormous pieces of country that had never been owned were claimed or granted to men, and then passed from fathers through sons down to our own time."

Christina stared at Andrew, her expression drawn, uneasy. She watched Andrew's changing eyes, Lee's eyes, and she was held by the sad voice speaking so gently, so relentlessly, of the past.

"Leander Champion Buckles came into the twentieth century riding on a dinosaur," said Andrew. "The other tracts and grants of land were gone, divided among sons and thieves and then divided again and again until nothing was left but memories—and the Buckles Ranch. The last dinosaur." Andrew paused. "It's been a great ride, but it's over."

"What are you saying?" Christina whispered, feeling the world falling away beneath her feet. She held tightly onto the table's edge. The land could not change. "What do you mean?" she asked, her voice harsh.

"Lee bought us time with the Trust," answered Andrew, speaking to everyone, holding Christina with his eyes and his voice, "but not even the Trust can stand against a land boom that has increased taxes to the point that it's flatly impossible to hold onto the Buckles Ranch."

Andrew's voice caught, suspended by the emotions shadowing Christina's face.

"I know you wanted to keep the land undeveloped, Christina, but it just can't be done. I'm sorry."

Christina's throat closed around all the words she wanted to hurl at Andrew. Screaming would only diminish her in the eyes of men she needed, men whose patience she exceeded at every monthly meeting. At the very least, before she argued with Andrew she had to know precisely what she was fighting. Christina looked away from Andrew to the thick report in front of her chair. The title page said: The Inevitable Development of the Buckles Ranch.

"As the report shows, we have three choices," continued Andrew, barely able to take his eyes from Christina's drawn face. "We can hold onto the land and go bankrupt. We can sell the land piecemeal. We can develop the land as a whole. Bankruptcy doesn't appeal to me," he said smiling humorlessly. "Neither does piecemeal selling—raffling off chunks of our future until we create a new Los Angeles to sprawl over the land like warm cowshit." Andrew shook his head decisively. "Not that way. We owe the past and the future more than that.

"But there is a way, a good way." Andrew looked again at Christina, his eyes alight with the dream that Lee had shared with him, the dream that Andrew had transformed and made his own. "If we develop the land as a whole, we can build the first city of the twenty-first century." Andrew held Christina with his eyes and his body leaning toward her, trying to share his vision with her, to replace her futile dream of an untouched land. "We could achieve a city that is both rational and poetic, functional and fanciful. The most successful community in the world. It will take years to plan, decades to build, but it can be done. And it will be done."

Christina's hand slammed down on the report.

"No! Never!"

For long moments they stared at one another across the old oak table. The five other board members showed varying reactions, but impatience was uppermost; Christina Buckles Heer was well known for opposing whatever Andrew Pico McCartney proposed.

"Christina," said Andrew reasonably, "you haven't read the report yet. You can't reject something before you even look at it. It will be a beautiful city, clean and bright. Read the report," he urged, "particularly the population growth estimates on page twelve and the property tax curve on—"

"No," Christina repeated. "You have no right to—to desecrate what Lee left. If he had wanted the land made into a city he would have done it himself."

"It wasn't the time, then. It is now," Andrew said evenly. "The land is no more than what we make of it,

457

Christina. That was the first thing Lee taught me and he made damn sure I'd never forget it. You see, the city I describe is Lee's dream too."

"I don't believe you."

Christina's voice was flat, scornful. Andrew's eyes went pale in a suddenly expressionless face. He turned toward the other five board members who were toying with pencils and pads, ties and ashtrays, and any other handy objects.

"There's no reason to bore you while I explain the facts of land and taxes to Mrs. Heer," said Andrew smoothly. "After you have had time to read the report, I look forward to your questions and advice. Of course, if any of you feels you have anything to contribute to my discussion with Mrs. Heer, you are welcome to stay."

There was a subdued rush of men toward the door. They had heard enough Heer vs. McCartney arguments to last them a lifetime. Andrew shook hands with the men as they left, then shut the door to the conference room. The building was old, its walls thick enough to subdue everything short of a determined scream.

Slowly, Andrew walked over to Christina. He stood behind her and put his hands on her shoulders. She made no response. His hands gently kneaded her rigid back.

"I know it's hard for you, Sunshine, but I have no choice. Development won't start tomorrow or even next year. Probably not for ten years. But we have to plan now, or the time will come when the land will be too expensive for agricultural use. If we're not ready, we'll be forced to sell land right and left just to pay taxes. After a few years there would be nothing left. I'm not going to let that happen."

"Lee would never develop the land."

Christina pushed back her chair and stood with her back to Andrew. His hands dropped to his sides.

"The hell he wouldn't," said Andrew harshly. "You didn't know your grandfather very well. Lee used the land—he didn't worship it. He changed the land. He developed groves and row crops, pastures and packing houses. The land was dry, so he built dams and cisterns, dug wells and ditches and canals, and then he stole water from a river four hundred miles away and brought it here. The reason he never had to sell off chunks of his ranch like other men was that he made the land produce as a single, integrated unit.

"That's what that report is about—how to keep the land intact by making it produce as a unit. Things change, Christina. We have to develop communities instead of tomatoes."

"No."

Andrew swore silently and tried again. "Saying no doesn't lower wages or taxes. Saying no doesn't raise the price of crops or—"

"—or lower the price of water, transportation, fertilizer and all the rest of it," finished Christina, turning to confront Andrew's eyes. "I know what it costs to run the ranch, Mr. McCartney. I know that land prices are irrationally high. I know that the land is taxed as though it were already developed." Christina stared up at him, her violet eyes hard. "I know all that, but I don't believe that the only alternative is to ruin the land."

"Development doesn't equal ruin," Andrew stopped, forcing the anger out of his voice. "I love the land, too, Sunshine. It's all I have to give to the future."

"There has to be another way," insisted Christina, both anger and pleading in her voice.

"Read that," Andrew said, pointing to the report on the table. "Read that and then tell me about alternatives. Development is the only game in town for the Buckles Ranch."

"Then widen the game," snapped Christina. "Isn't that what Lee always told us to do?"

"I tried. I even changed the town by swapping acreage here for government land in Wyoming, but that only delayed the reckoning. Short of changing California's property tax structure—and I tried, Sunshine, I tried!—there isn't one damn thing I can do but develop the Buckles Ranch."

"No." Christina's voice was cold. "Not my land."

"The land belongs to the Trust," said Andrew tightly.

"And the Trust belongs to you. That's not good enough. I own forty-nine percent and I want my forty-nine percent left just the way it is now!"

"Don't be childish. There's no such thing as your forty-nine percent. There's only the Buckles Trust which owns, among other things, fifty-one percent of the Buckles Company, which owns one-hundred percent of the Buckles Ranch. I thought you understood that, or are you so used to having your own way that you just ignore whatever doesn't fit with your cozy view of reality?"

Christina flinched at the tone of Andrew's voice, but then flushed with an anger equal to his. "I'm going to fight you. I'm going to tie up the ranch in so many stockholder suits and legal snarls that no one will be able to build so much as an adobe hut on my land. And then I'm going to take the land away from you." Her voice rose and her eyes darkened. "You won't be able to sell my heritage, chop up my hills and flatlands, grow tracts instead of oranges, rip out crops and bury my land under asphalt and garbage."

Christina closed her eyes suddenly, remembering all of the times that her dream of showing the land to her child had comforted her when there was nothing and no one else to comfort her. "What would I show my child, then?" she whispered. "What—"

"Your child?"

Christina's eyes snapped open. The rage in Andrew's voice was so complete, so final, that she was stunned.

"You came to me carrying his child!"

There was no question in Andrew's voice, no chance for her to answer. The rage consuming him ripped apart her stuttered objections.

"That explains a lot, Mrs. Heer. I don't have to wonder anymore why you came to me. It doesn't surprise me that you were shaky—it must have been quite a shock to realize that your child would have to visit his father in prison! Unless you could get me to let him off the hook, of course. Was it your idea or Jason's? It sounds more like him, but if you love him enough to have his child, you love him enough to go whoring for him, right, baby?"

"No," said Christina, shaking her head, trying to shout but her throat was too tight. "No. I didn't—I'm not—"

"I'll tell him you were very good, Mrs. Heer," said Andrew, interrupting her contemptuously. "The best I've ever fucked. But even that isn't good enough to make me give up the land." Andrew's lips were flat, white. His hands were balled into fists but still they shook very slightly. He leaned toward her, smiling coldly. "Jason Heer will be indicted, arrested, tried and convicted. The Buckles Ranch will become a city, rather than a silver-plated cesspool." He paused, then added very softly, "I hope your husband's playmates strangle him on his own guts . . . slowly."

Christina stared at a man utterly transformed by rage. He had reached the door and opened it before she could force her throat to work.

"Andrew," Christina said desperately, "I'm not—"

The door shut, cutting off her words as effectively as a blow.

"—pregnant."

Christina felt her world sliding away, spinning around her. She leaned over the table, fighting for control. Eventually she realized that her fingers were clutching the report. With a cry she flung the report across the room.

"You're wrong!" Christina faced the door and screamed. "Do you hear me, Mr. Andrew Pico McCartney, Chairman of the Trust? You're wrong, you bastard! You're wrong!"

❧

Christina awoke in the grove house, hearing only the special silence which told her she was alone in the east wing. It was a silence she had gotten used to. Sometimes she enjoyed it. Other times it made her long for Andrew. Those were the worst days.

With a supple twist of her body, Christina rolled over. Nausea rippled through her, then faded. Christina smiled

461

and felt less alone. Barely eleven weeks after conception, her child was already company for her. Still smiling, she stretched, then snuggled further into the pillow. Lately she had slept a lot more. Slept, and wandered through the grove house and over the land.

She had fled to the grove house simply to be alone. It was not the first time she had done that, but it was the first time she had stayed so long. She spent most of her time walking and riding horseback, thinking about the land. The land, and the people whose lives were influenced by it. She compared Jason's view of the past with her own . . . and Andrew's.

Although she tried not to think about Andrew at all, it was like trying not to breathe; Andrew was the father of her unborn child.

Christina's mind sheered away from thinking of Andrew, and settled on the child. Would it be a boy or girl, large or small? Would it resemble Lee Buckles, tall and strong with hair the color of the sun? Or would it be like Joy, like Champ, white and frail. Or dark and beautiful like its aunt Maggie, dead in a nameless canyon somewhere on Buckles land. . . .

Whatever the child looked like, its very birth would knit up the ragged histories of Cira and Maggie, Champ and Joy, Andrew and herself. Her child and his, the present at last healing the past and making the future whole. A child for her to share her memories with, and to share the land.

Somehow, she promised herself, somehow she would take the land from Andrew's control, take the land and give it unchanged to the child whose ancestors had bled dreams and strength and life itself into the land.

The land would belong to Christina's child, not to an alien paper construct called the Buckles Trust.

Christina pulled open the French doors and walked out into early morning sunlight that poured over her like wine, fragrant and warm, pale gold. She felt as though she were floating on a sea of incandescence. She became acutely aware of every breath, every heartbeat, the warm rush of blood. She sensed subliminal movement within her body, as though she were slowly revolving around a tiny, still center deep inside her.

Smiling, Christina put her hands on her abdomen, sure that she carried within her both consummation of the past and consolation for the future. She stretched her arms out in silent embrace, looking west to where the sky met the honey-colored hills lifting toward the sun. Beyond the hills lay Frenchman's Cove, where white cottages broke over chaparral canyons like angular surf. Behind her leaped mountains, purple in the clear light. And beyond all, the sea, restless and alive.

Christina was part of it, ocean and land, past and future all turning around the life within her, the next level of time's spiral. Smiling, she went back inside and was soon asleep again. She did not sleep long before Jason found her.

"Wake up!" shouted Jason, digging his fingers into her shoulder and shaking her hard. "Wake up!"

Christina's hand lashed out in the direction of Jason's high voice. He straightened quickly, stepping back. When he saw her eyes open, he shoved a newspaper under her nose and began shouting phrases that were as jumbled as they were obscene. Christina saw that Jason's eyes were wide with an animal panic that was echoed by his pale lips. Through a haze of sleep, Christina managed to sort out his meaning.

"—thought you had taken care of that bastard! Thought you were going to fuck him until—"

"Shut up," Christina said coldly. "Stop raving and rattling that newspaper at me." Christina sat up, gathering the sheet over her breasts as she did so. "Did the maid let you in? I told her that I didn't want to see anyone. Period."

"Fuck the maid," snarled Jason. "What about McCartney?"

Jason threw the paper at Christina. She caught it with the lightning reflexes that always startled him. Without changing her indifferent expression, she read the banner headline.

GRAND JURY INDICTS TOP COUNTY OFFICIALS

"We're going to lose a few politicians, aren't we?" said Christina, skimming the article. "Looks like you'll have to go somewhere else to gamble."

"We're going to lose the Silver Buckles."

Christina shrugged. "I think you'd be grateful to see the last of the casino. You'll never have to try to measure up to the Silver Buckles again . . . and fail."

Jason looked more closely at Christina, sensing a difference that went beyond her tone of voice. She had changed. She was more distant, harder. More ruthless.

"Hey, I'm sorry for storming in like this," Jason said hesitantly. "But I need you, Chrissy. You know I do. When are you coming back?"

Christina looked up at Jason with a total lack of interest. She realized that at one time she had needed Jason, too, needed his weakness as a safe way to measure her own strength. But no longer. She was sure now, past and future fused in her womb.

"I'm not coming back. But if you want my advice," she said indifferently, "sell your other businesses. Take the money and build something in—where is it, Las Vegas?—yes, Las Vegas."

"My other businesses?" repeated Jason.

"Whores, loan-sharking and leg-breaking," Christina said succinctly."

"How—how long have you known?"

"It doesn't matter."

"Nothing matters to you anymore, is that it? Even me?"

"Especially you," said Christina, idly flipping through the newspaper, pausing over various headlines or advertisements.

The thin rattle of pages turning was the only sound in the room until Jason made a noise halfway between a laugh and a cry.

"I tried to sell," Jason said thickly, "but no one wants to buy the kind of trouble McCartney is handing out. What with that bastard pushing and Las Vegas pulling, you can stand at the county line and watch the crooks streaming out."

Jason laughed, a strangled noise that put Christina's nerves on edge. His eyes were wet, indistinct, as shapeless as the sweat stains on his shirt.

"It's over," Jason said. "Even the whores. The pimps have been stealing me poor, taking me over one trick at a time. I offered to sell out to them, but why should they pay for what they can steal? If I go there today, I'll bet they won't even let me touch the girls. And they'd kill me if I came around a second time. It's gone. All of it. Gone."

Christina watched silently while Jason's speech blurred into plaintive sounds and ragged breathing. Never had she been so acutely aware of the thin boundary separating legitimate and criminal enterprise. Except for the literal death Jason feared, he could have been describing the takeover of a poor corporation by a rich one—and the subsequent ouster of the poor corporation's owner. Jason understood the power struggle in which he was involved—he understood, but he no longer had the strength or the desire to affect the outcome.

"Is that the best you can do?" asked Christina, simple curiosity in her voice.

The look on Jason's face said that he did not understand her question, or did not want to understand.

"I've given a lot of thought to the conversation we had a few months ago," said Christina. "You kept ranting about the curse of the Buckles family, and how it has controlled your life and your brother's death and your father and God knows what else." She looked at him, her violet eyes unshadowed, penetrating. "That simply isn't true, you know."

Jason stood silently, held by the certainty and serenity in her lovely eyes.

"What is true," continued Christina, "is that you're weak, like your brother and your father. You give up, Jason. Is it a family trait in the Heers—give up and then whine about bad luck and revenge? You quit just about

465

the time you married me. I gave you your dream casino and it frightened you to death."

Christina looked back to the newspaper. "Get your gangster friends to back you in Las Vegas. Or have they left already?"

"Left?" Jason's laugh rasped across Christina's nerves almost as badly as his fingers on her bare shoulder. "I wish to God they had. I owe them money, Chrissy. I've lost a lot, since you don't come to the casino anymore. I need you."

Christina struggled to keep her newfound serenity, trying not to show her abhorrence of Jason's fingers on her bare flesh. When his hand dropped to the soft curve of her breast, she got up swiftly and went to the closet for a robe.

"They'll hurt me, Chrissy," said Jason, his voice high and childlike. "They could even kill me."

"I doubt it," said Christina matter-of-factly. "You're not worth killing."

Christina tied the soft violet robe around her hips, realizing that she had lost her tolerance for weakness, whether Jason's or her own. The realization swept through her like a shock wave, freeing her. With each second that passed, Jason seemed weaker, smaller, fading. He was watching her with eyes that overflowed with hurt . . . and a calculation she recognized from former fights. Only this time it would not work. His tears no longer moved her to pity and protect him like a child.

"Chrissy—?"

"Excuse me," Christina said, brushing by her husband.

The bathroom door clicked as Christina locked it behind her.

"You're tired, Chrissy," said Jason hollowly. "I'll come back when you've had time to wake up."

If Christina answered, the words were lost in the noisy rush of water from the shower. Jason hesitated, then left. Christina neither knew nor cared that he had gone. She washed herself, humming quietly, fascinated by the body that was subtly changing as Andrew's and her child grew.

When she finished, she put on the robe again and walked to the window that overlooked the land.

Christina stood drinking in the golden invitation of the sun, so far away and yet so fierce. She felt a sudden desire to shed her robe, find a sheltered spot and stretch out beneath the sun, losing herself in the incandescent light, sun surrounding her, heat shimmering, sinking into her, light shining . . . sunshine. Sunshine.

Longing swept Christina, shaking her. She closed her eyes but that did not help, it only made her see Andrew's eyes, clear and compelling, binding her to him in spite of all her efforts to forget. She opened her eyes and looked blindly over the land. Then she remembered her unborn child and slowly her control returned.

Standing in the grove house built by Joy, Christina planned how to save the land for her child.

Six days later, Jason Heer was found dead, his .45 automatic still in his hand, his body torn apart by five bullets from his gun. Jason's death was ruled a suicide, in spite of testimony by a hotel maid who had heard shouts, shots, a car leaving at high speed—and then silence. Within hours of the coroner's verdict of suicide, Christina stepped onto an airplane and vanished as though she had never existed. When she reappeared, she had a child with her.

Though Christina Buckles Heer never again attended a Trust meeting, her lawyers were always in evidence. The bitter struggle for control of the Buckles Ranch had begun.

1960

The Buckles Tower and the Seacoast Country Club stared at one another across the toast-colored bluffs. The former building had been erected for sober commerce and the latter for genteel diversion. Echoing the powerful, unbending personalities behind them, the two institutions dominated the land that had become the center of life, wealth and power in Moreno County.

To the uninitiated, both institutions seemed part of a unity, the unity of control. But the people who had more than a casual understanding of the subterranean relationships of Moreno County's power structure knew that the Towers and the Club were engaged in a quiet, lethal battle over leadership of the richest county in the richest state in the richest country of the world.

Over the seven years that the bitter contest had raged, the people who were both adept and cautious had managed to stay in the good graces of both the Towers and the tennis courts, both Andrew McCartney, chairman of the Buckles Trust, and Christina Buckles Heer, minority stockholder in the Buckles Ranch, widow and mother of an eight-year-old boy called Leander Champion Buckles

Heer. It was a joining of names in historic irony that Andrew, for one, found less than amusing.

The child was as impressive as his name, tall, well made, having a confident manner that was precocious without being impudent. He had the gray eyes and disturbing grace of his father and of the man who had been both his grandfather and great-grandfather. Because his mother used her maiden name in all business dealings, and because she called her son Buck, Andrew was one of the few people who remembered that Buck's legal name was Heer. The boy's arresting gray eyes, rarely the same color twice, so resembled those in the oil portrait of Leander Champion Buckles III, that no one thought to connect Buck with the equally gray-eyed Andrew.

Christina took care that son and father never stood close enough together to elicit comparisons, particularly by Andrew. Yet Buck was also his mother's son in so many ways—quick intelligence, quick temper, a social ease based on a native shrewdness in assessing people—that the hidden portion of Buck's lineage was never seriously questioned, least of all by Andrew McCartney.

Andrew had seen photographs of Buck in the local newspaper and had even seen the boy once or twice, in the distance, at Buckles Ranch family barbeques. Christina, of course, Andrew spoke to rarely, if at all, though their business interests were as interwoven as the flowering bougainvillea vines that covered the Seacoast Country Club's older buildings.

Whatever Andrew felt toward Christina Buckles Heer was concealed beneath his unbending, polite exterior. It was a façade that sometimes tested the limits of Andrew's control. Christina's allure had increased rather than decreased over the years, and Andrew had a memory that was too good for his own comfort. The fact that Christina sometimes shimmered with sensuality when she watched him did little to shorten his memory—or hers.

Christina's feelings were usually as well-hidden as Andrew's. After she had returned from the Bahamas, where she had given birth to Buck, Christina divided her time

469

between Washington, D.C. and Moreno County. Wherever she lived, there was no division of her energy; she worked unceasingly to remove Buckles Ranch from control of the Trust, of Andrew. Her plan and her son had grown up together. Both son and plan would have pleased Lee Buckles, for both were the result of her instinctive appreciation of the fact that she would lose the game unless she widened the arena. Today, Christina would find out if she had succeeded in expanding the arena to include the U.S. Senate.

The black Cadillac limousine carrying Christina Buckles Heer went through the guarded gates of the Club without stopping. The car followed a winding road along bluff-tops overlooking the bay and ocean until the heavy auto whispered to a halt precisely at the top of a semicircular drive lined by colorful flowers. Rudy, major domo of all the workers at the Club, opened the limousine's rear door at the exact moment that the car came to a full stop.

"Señora, I'm glad you are early," said Rudy, flashing a smile that was both appreciative of her beauty and respectful of her position. "All the arrangements are complete."

Christina touched Rudy's arm and smiled. "I knew I could count on you, Rudy. Today you'll earn another piece of that avocado grove down in Vista."

Rudy's face showed an instant of surprise that Christina knew so much of his private affairs. Before he could say anything, she was gone, walking quickly through the open doors of the fieldstone clubhouse, her hips swinging beneath the black sheath dress and the sharp heels of her shoes rapping confidently on the clean tile floor.

Christina made a quick, thorough tour of the facilities and found everything as she had ordered, right down to the prestigious labels lining the mirrored shelves behind the bar. The substitution of the most expensive for the merely expensive was typical of her preparations for this gala. In no way did she want Senator George Thomas James of Georgia to feel slighted.

After Christina checked the bar, she toured the kitchen, her violet eyes comparing what she saw against her mental list. The kitchen was a subdued chaos of odors and Spanish dialects as the chef's minions washed, peeled, sliced, diced, stuffed and otherwise prepared the feast Christina had decreed. Satisfied, she went into the ballroom, checking the floral displays at the tables and at strategic points around the room. She had spent thousands of dollars and had personally approved each of the floral designs. Her selection of the floral sculptures had been prominently displayed in the society sections of major newspapers.

As Christina had hoped, the effect of the vapid feature stories was to convince almost everyone that the affair Christina had so carefully contrived was nothing more than a social function masquerading as a benefit for California's newest U.S. senator. Even Harley Foss, the senator in question, was convinced that the party was for him. He was particularly pleased, not to say surprised, that several of his Senate colleagues—including the powerful George Thomas James—had come thousands of miles merely to attend a party in honor of a very junior senator.

By the time the first guests began to gather around the five champagne fountains, Christina was finished with her tour of inspection. Everything had been as per her instructions, including the recent manicuring of the gently rolling fairways and incredibly perfect greens. Although it was several hours from sunset on a pleasant day, none of Christina's guests had to contend with stray wood shots. Seacoast Country Club, down to the last crystal cup and velvet blade of grass, had been preempted by Christina or her guests. Even the weather seemed to be at her command; the slanting sunlight, turned golden by moisture from the sea, gave depth and richness to everything it touched.

Senator James arrived with Senator Foss, the putative guest of honor. More than one hundred of the guests were assembled on the lawn, sipping champagne. The junior senator moved into the crowd, immediately recognized by

471

friends and strangers alike. Senator James, whose face and real power were known only within the closed club of the nation's most powerful men, went unrecognized by all but one businessman who greeted the senator with quiet speculation.

Later, when all the guests had arrived, Rudy moved through the elegant throngs and spoke unobtrusively to Senator James. After a few minutes, the senator quietly went to the waiting Rudy and followed him. The senator was silently ushered across a spectacular garden and through a discreet gate into the Oriental garden surrounding Mrs. Buckles Heer's personal cabana.

The cabana stood on the crest of a small rise off the fifteenth fairway. Christina's privacy was insured by a screen of camellias and sheltered by three graceful pines. Senator James stopped on the path just before he reached the front door of the cabana. Instinctively, he looked over his shoulder. The rise of a few feet of elevation was enough to afford a view of the emerald golf course, a segment of the rough gold bay bluffs and a small, shadowed canyon that opened into the silent blue sea at the northern edge of Frenchman's Cove.

The view was an unusual mixture of open land and artfully designed homes scattered along blufflines and bay and sandy beaches. The senator stood motionless, struck by the view and the quality of the air, the undeniable Mediterranean aspects of the land and climate.

"Magnificent," said the senator quietly.

"Yes," said Christina, walking noiselessly out of the cabana. "Well worth fighting for, isn't it?"

The senator turned toward his hostess, a pleasant, professional smile on his face. They had met several times in Washington, but he had yet to decide exactly what the beautiful widow Heer wanted from him—or rather, what she would give to get what she wanted. Christina studied the impersonal smile, returning it with one of her own. Her face was a flawless mask concealing the woman beneath. Only her eyes were alive, intelligent, scrutinizing him as he was scrutinizing her.

"Won't you come in, Senator?" said Christina, extending her right hand in a gesture of hospitality rather than in the more businesslike gesture of a handshake.

"Could it be that you don't want to be seen with me?" the senator asked, watching Christina carefully.

Christina concealed her flash of irritation at being subtly baited. She had learned that the senator liked his women soft, pliant and safely married. As she was none of the three, she had to walk carefully around his prickly Southern dignity. Nonetheless, her controlled sensuality had intrigued the senator at least as much as her proven ability to support political candidates.

"I'm always glad to be seen with a handsome man," said Christina in a husky voice. "If you prefer, you may escort me back to the party."

Senator James looked into Christina's clear violet eyes and sighed soundlessly, wishing Christina's attention was as simple as it was compelling. But it was not, and he knew it; she represented his sole exception to the rule about mixing business with pleasure.

"After you, ma'am."

The senator bowed slightly as he gestured to the cabana rather than the clubhouse. Christina allowed her pleasure to show in the lingering pressure of her hand against his.

"Thank you, Senator," Christina said, smiling up at him through long, dark lashes.

Christina crossed the small, elegantly furnished sitting room and stopped by a cart stocked with glasses and several bottles. When she heard the door quietly close, she turned toward the senator.

"May I get you a drink?"

"Yes, thank you. A touch of . . ." Senator James stopped when he saw that her hand was on a tall, dusty bottle.

"I trust Glenfiddich is an acceptable Scotch?" murmured Christina.

The senator smiled in spite of himself, amused and flattered. "You know that it is, or it would not be on that

473

cart." His dark eyes sharpened a bit. "Do you always treat your guests so cordially, and privately?"

Christina finished preparing the drink and handed it to Senator James, smiling directly into his eyes. "Only when they are very appealing, very powerful men."

Senator James suddenly found himself succumbing to Christina's un-Southern directness. He accepted the drink with a light pressure of his fingers across hers.

"You'll teach me to appreciate honesty," he said, sipping at the pale, potent Scotch.

"I'm known for my candor," replied Christina, slightly emphasizing the last word.

"A fine distinction, but vital," agreed the senator, more than ever intrigued by her.

Christina turned away and walked slowly, gracefully across the room to a couch covered with amethyst plush. She sat and crossed her legs, knowing that Senator James had watched her hips with his fullest attention.

"Won't you sit?" asked Christina with a cool civility that was in direct contrast to the message sent by her body. When the senator sat next to her, she said, "Please do smoke. I love the smell of Havanas."

Senator James produced a silver case and took from it a full, blunt cigar which he clipped and lit with a minimum of ritual. He exhaled fragrant smoke and leaned back, shoulder touching hers. Christina sniffed, remembering the cigars Lee had smoked. She was on the verge of telling the senator that the scent of Havanas brought back her grandfather's memory, but did not. She doubted that being compared with her grandfather would flatter the fifty-five-year-old politician.

The memory of Lee softened the outline of Christina's mouth, making her look younger, more vulnerable. The crack in her façade was more alluring than her experienced preludes to seduction. Senator James puffed on his cigar and decided to be as direct with her as she was with him.

"My staff has reviewed the papers your lawyer de-

474

livered a few weeks ago. I've spent several hours with the material myself."

The shadow of a frown subtly altered Christina's face. "Your staff has been impressed with the fact that the material is highly confidential?" she asked, her voice soft, husky, covering the demand beneath the warmth.

"Mrs. Buckles Heer," began the senator, irritated at her reminder.

"Christina. Please."

The senator's voice softened. "Christina. You must understand that what you're proposing necessitates passing legislation through the U.S. Senate and the House of Representatives. That can't be done by keeping the bill a secret."

"It's just a rider," countered Christina with a small smile. "Not a real bill. And I certainly didn't mean to imply that I expected any special, secret treatment. It's simply that the rider has a very limited impact. If Andr— anyone learned of my proposal prematurely, attempts would certainly be made to kill it."

Senator James turned toward her and watched her eyes as he slowly drew on the cigar, letting scented smoke drift up from his fingertips.

"If I put that rider on, it will pass. You may be certain of that."

"You say 'if.' Is there a problem?"

"Yes," said the senator, deciding it was time for her to remember the fact, as blunt as the tip of his cigar, that he could give or withhold his power as he saw fit. The beautiful widow seemed to promise much, but so far had given nothing other than smiles and a lavish party he had barely begun to enjoy before he was called away to her cabana.

"Tell me about it," Christina invited, leaning toward him, shifting her body until she sensed a response he could not conceal behind his politician's façade.

"You mentioned the limited effect of this proposed rider," said the senator, deftly answering the pressure of her leg along his. "Is there any charitable trust which would be affected—other than the Buckles Trust, of course?"

"The document has been very carefully drawn to exclude all but the Buckles Trust," said Christina, her voice so soft that the senator had to lean forward slightly to hear her. "You see, the Trust was constructed to take advantage of certain loopholes in the tax laws, as well as other legal considerations. Your legislation would merely plug the major loophole pertaining to this particular trust. If you wish," she added, smiling cynically, "you could use this as the first step in a larger campaign to close loopholes that grant unfair tax advantages to the wealthy."

"You're very experienced, aren't you?" said the senator, looking down into his pale Scotch.

Christina's smile changed from invitation to simple, shallow convention. She suddenly had little patience for the game. It was becoming clear to her that the senator found it difficult to accept her as both sexy and intelligent. She could probably convince him to accept the rider on the basis of pragmatism instead of pleasure, but she regretted the necessity. Other than his unease around women who did not act frail or foolish, the senator rather reminded her of Andrew. Both men were the same age, height and build. Both wore an indefinable, fascinating aura of power. Though she doubted that the senator could either rouse or satisfy her as Andrew had, she would find the senator a pleasant change from most of the men she had seduced on her way to power.

With abrupt grace, Christina stood and walked across the room to the liquor cart. She poured herself a small amount of Scotch and swirled the liquid slowly over ice as clear as the crystal glass. She watched the pale pink whirlpool while she decided how to handle the senator. She took a cigarette from a rosewood box she had inherited from her grandfather. Her movements were clean and efficient, no longer redolent of sexuality. Senator James recognized the difference immediately, and regretted the change.

"There are, of course, a great many considerations that

go into making the law of the land," said Senator James slowly, watching Christina's back as she sipped her drink, an unlit cigarette held between her long, elegant fingers.

Christina considered the senator's ambiguous statement. It had the easy flow of a line he had used before. It conveyed nothing and everything about the process in which they were at the moment involved. She turned toward him, smiling, and her words left little room for comforting ambiguities.

"There are, of course, a great many considerations that go into making a political winner," said Christina coolly. "Money is the most significant one, as I'm sure even our Mr. Foss knows. He also knows who financed and arranged his campaign, as well as this little victory celebration.

"Mr.—*Senator*—Foss is not the only beneficiary of my, shall we say, patriotism?" continued Christina blandly. "Several of your colleagues are pleased to number me among their supporters. As is one of your potential colleagues, a certain charismatic younger son of a poor preacher—oh, yes, I almost forgot," said Christina lightly. "If the preacher's son becomes a senator, you won't be colleagues after all. There's some dreary law limiting the number of senators each state can have, I believe."

Christina sipped her Scotch idly, letting Senator James consider the fact that Georgia's other senator had been elected so many times that it was obvious that only death would remove him from office. Not that Senator James was particularly insecure in his own position, but a sustained challenge from an appealing, well-financed candidate would force the senator to spend more time mending rural fences in Georgia and less time building empires in Washington, D.C. It would be an inconvenience that could range from annoying to crippling.

Senator James looked at Christina's delicate profile and felt a distinct sense of disbelief as he realized that she was as hard as any man he had ever faced. She could be a generous ally or a dangerous adversary. She was offering him the choice.

With a feeling of disorientation, the senator stared at

the black silk dress that followed the curves of Christina's tanned body. The neckline was low, giving occasional, tantalizing glimpses of breasts untouched by the sun. For an instant the senator could not conceive of such femininity coupled with a ruthlessness he had always thought of as masculine. Then Christina turned away from him with a supple movement that made him forget a lifetime of certainties about what women were and were not.

"Your rider will be on the next bill out of my committee," said Senator James, his Southern drawl noticeably thicker.

Christina looked at the senator over her shoulder, searching his face to see if she had made an enemy she would have to watch carefully or a business partner who would respect her strength. What she saw was a handsome, sophisticated senator who wanted her.

The senator's dark eyes moved over the lines of Christina's body with unmistakable intimacy. As he looked, he realized that power and the exercise of power carried a sexual content that he had never before understood, much less defined. Christina set her drink aside and walked toward the senator. Once again, her body radiated sexual invitation. He was aware of her subtle female scent as she slid onto the couch, the unlit cigarette still in her hand. Her violet eyes were soft, her lips moist and full, waiting. With an economy of motion, the senator laid aside his cigar and produced a gold lighter. A tiny flame leaped out, close to but not touching her cigarette.

"You don't have to," said the senator softly, intimately. "Your . . . patriotism . . . is more than enough reward for such a simple request." The flame twisted and danced silently. "Besides, I'm not accustomed to mixing business and pleasure."

Christina, her unlit cigarette poised halfway to her lips, studied the senator over his gold lighter. His dark eyes were no longer hooded with calculations. They reflected naked flame in twin points of gold.

"I've rarely separated business and pleasure," said Christina, a slow, languid smile spreading across her lips.

"You really should," murmured the senator, "while you can still distinguish between them. They're quite different, you know."

Senator James smiled and snapped the lighter shut. He took the unlit cigarette from Christina's hand as he kissed the smooth flesh of her shoulder.

"You're amazingly beautiful," said the senator, lifting his head, "in spite of your—"

Christina's lips and tongue moved skillfully across the senator's mouth, making him forget his reservations about her ruthlessness.

Andrew McCartney turned slowly in his swivel chair, stopping when he could gaze down the coastline toward the Club. In his hands was a two-page, single-spaced typewritten report. The document was unsigned, a private report from an ex-reporter called Hennegan, a man who was as valuable to Andrew as Gil had once been to Lee.

Hennegan had proved to be an ideal investigator. He had no memorable physical characteristics—medium height, weight, build and coloring. He had a shrewd sense of the larger world and a pragmatic view of man and society. He was concerned utterly, completely and exclusively with facts rather than opinions. He was not particularly fastidious about how he obtained those facts, only that he did obtain them. Finally, he maintained an enduring discretion about the affairs of Andrew McCartney and the Buckles Trust. The relationship between the two men was so confidential that the report Andrew had just read had been typed and delivered by Hennegan.

Andrew's eyes shifted from the distant hills to the report. He reread the final paragraphs, the latest episode of a long, long investigation into the affairs of Christina Buckles Heer.

"The subject then met with Senator James in a cabana at the Seacoast Country Club. The meeting lasted more than forty minutes. Its purpose could not be learned. The cabana was checked later. No documents or notes were found. The bed had been used for sex. The subject and

479

the senator left separately. They did not speak again during that evening.

"The senator's room at the Silver Buckles was checked, but little of value was found, except a discarded photocopy of a section of the Internal Revenue Service regulations dealing with charitable trusts. (Photocopy enclosed.)

"Sources are now being developed on the senator's staff, through contacts we already have in Washington."

Andrew snapped his finger against the report, annoyed for several reasons, not the least of which was the irrational jealousy that he always felt when he learned that Christina had added another name to her lengthy list of conquests.

Andrew was also irked by the knowledge that he had underestimated the honorable senator from Georgia. They had met privately for lunch the day of Christina's party, and Andrew had come away with a reasonably positive impression of the senator. That impression was favorable enough that the following day Andrew had contributed five thousand dollars to a Georgia campaign committee representing some unknown congressman. Senator George Thomas James had turned out to be a smooth double-dealer. The important information was not his duplicity—Andrew had come to expect that of most people—but the smoothness with which the senator operated.

The intercom light on Andrew's desk flashed, followed by a discreet buzz. Automatically, Andrew flipped the switch.

"Yes?"

"The group from Frenchman's Cove is here, Mr. McCartney," said the voice of his secretary.

Andrew felt a warning tightness in his body as he considered the prospect of yet another in a long line of futile, acrimonious sessions with the Friends of Frenchman's Cove. Christina's generous sponsorship of the group was one more source of sustained irritation. Worse, local and state sentiment had begun to respond to Christina's lavish environmental campaigns. The Friends of Frenchman's Cove had passed from an irritant to a danger. Unfortunately, it was a danger he could do little about.

"Thank you," Andrew said after a pause. "I'll be out in a moment."

Andrew put the report and the accompanying photocopy into a wall safe only he could open. He had no intention of being as careless with his own secrets as others were with theirs. He would read the report once more and then he would destroy it. He particularly wanted to inspect the photocopy of the IRS regulations, for he sensed that was the meat in the sandwich of facts. The tax-exempt status of the trust fund he administered was the key to control of the Buckles Ranch, as both he and Christina knew very well.

Andrew also knew that control was more tenuous every day, despite the complex legal infrastructure of the trust. There were times, especially when he watched sunrise spread light across the land he loved, that he admitted to himself just how thin the lines of his control were, how eroded by time and circumstances he could not control. At those moments he envied Christina, for she was not bound by considerations of consequence. She could seek to unhorse him without facing the ramifications of a world that changed while their dreams and the land did not.

Andrew turned away from the wall safe and the image of Christina that haunted his silences more than he admitted even to himself. He had another problem to deal with now, a problem that made all the rest of his worries merely academic, a problem that waited for him just down the hall.

Andrew stood and lifted his jacket from the back of a chair. Almost automatically, he straightened his tie and the shirt that had pulled out a bit at his waist. Glancing toward a mirror that reflected the coastal hills, Andrew ran a hand through his hair, a gesture that echoed a man who had been dead for more than twenty years.

Andrew's hand paused as he was struck by his own reflection. His hair was still full, but it was more silver than

481

dark now. His body was still strong, his skin still taut, but there was unmistakable age around his eyes and at the corners of his mouth. He moved less freely, as though he were being cautious for the first time in his life.

Smiling, Andrew turned away, comforted by the marks of age reflected in the mirror. It had been a long time since he had wanted to live forever.

The boardroom of the Towers was paneled in tawny, open-grained wood that was echoed by the long, broad table. The room was glass on two sides, affording a sweeping view of hills green with spring rain, an ocean flecked by a white wind and caressed by sunlight the color of champagne. The colors of the room echoed those of the land in all of its seasons. The effect was serene and exhilarating at the same time, subdued and magnificent. Yet the eyes of the dozen men and women at the table were drawn immediately to the man who walked in as quietly as a cat.

"Good afternoon," said Andrew in a calm, even voice. "Thank you for agreeing to meet here. I hope it didn't inconvenience you too much."

Andrew paused, carefully making eye contact with each one of the people. Over the two years he had dealt with the delegation, its composition had varied little, as though it was set by fiat rather than circumstance. There was a bookstore owner in a rumpled suit, a local writer with wary eyes, three housewives intent and intensely uncomfortable in dresses that the women lacked the native style to wear, dresses made tasteless by the simple elegance of the boardroom. There was also a relentlessly bourgeois husband and wife, as well as a male couple whose combination of defiance and apology irritated Andrew far more than their militant homosexuality. The last member of the delegation was a tall, hawk-faced man whose fingers lovingly stroked the grain of the table. His hands showed the scars of a lifetime spent handling sharp tools.

"Magnificent wood, isn't it?" said Andrew softly, moving his hand over the table that had once belonged to Lee Buckles. "Oak like this is almost impossible to find now."

482

The man scowled and jammed his hands into his pockets. "Yeah. I know. Bastards like you chopped down all the good trees."

Only Andrew seemed to find that an odd remark for a woodcarver to make. It was typical of the responses that Andrew had come to expect from the Friends of Frenchman's Cove. He did not let his irritation show. What he wanted was too important to be lost in an instant of unguarded anger.

"In the past two years," said Andrew coolly, "you have met with me and various members of the Buckles Ranch Company to discuss the future of the ranch. We were not required by either law or custom to share with you our plans for the land. But we did, because what happens to the Buckles Ranch will inevitably affect your lives."

Andrew looked at each of them again, hearing the echo of his words in their tight faces. His voice was too smooth, too hard, too uncompromising. With an effort he injected softer resonances into his tone.

"The Buckles Ranch is the largest undeveloped parcel of land in the most rapidly developing area of the world. Not just the state," Andrew repeated softly, "but the world."

In a low, intense voice, Andrew described the land as it had been and as it was, dry and brittle, green and fertile, unyielding and infinitely promising. He spoke of the low, steep mountains at the inland boundary, the quiet canyons where chaparral whispered, the flatlands crisscrossed by dirt roads joining groves and row crops, the bluffs and coastal hills sliding down to meet the endless sea.

With no pause, no hesitation, as though there were no difference between the reality and the dream, Andrew went to the wall map with its clear plastic overlays. As he spoke, he shifted the sheets, magically creating the civilization of his dreams, a civilization surrounded by hillside agriculture and mountains left untouched, for they were both too unforgiving and too fragile to sustain development. Industrial parks replaced groves, self-supporting communities supplanted bean and tomato fields. The coastline was transformed into an exquisite Riviera, a cosmopolitan city and resort that was as beautiful as its setting, as unique as the opportunity to build a city where one was needed instead of just letting a city happen with no informing principle other than greed.

Andrew let the last transparent sheet drift into place and turned back to face the group.

"You'll notice that there has been a thirty-two percent reduction in residential density, a seventeen percent reduction in commercial density and a ten percent reduction in industrial density, as well as a two hundred percent increase in land set aside for regional parks. That's as much as we can change and still have self-supporting communities. Frankly, it's much more than the planners wanted, but I insisted.

"Are there any questions?"

The silence spread while Andrew looked around a table where the faces ranged from confused to hostile. Thomas Peel, one-half of the male couple, was the most hostile. He was also the spokesman for the group. He straightened in his chair and looked past Andrew's shoulder.

"It won't do, Mr. McCartney. It just won't do at all."

Peel's voice was deep and his hands moved quickly, almost uncontrollably, straightening his pant leg or collar or glasses in a ceaseless round. His eyes flickered as restlessly as his hands, but he never seemed to look directly at Andrew. It was apparent that most things made Peel nervous, especially Andrew McCartney.

Andrew, as he had done so often in the past, suppressed his urge to challenge the deep-voiced man with the frightened eyes. Instead, Andrew nodded slightly, encouraging Peel to speak.

"Perhaps you could explain," said Andrew softly.

"Why bother?" said Peel, throwing up his hands. "You never listen to me."

Andrew waited, his eyes pale and cold.

"I agree with Tom," said the writer.

"So do I," said the woodcarver.

484

Murmurs of assent passed around the table, leaving Andrew with the feeling that the decision had been reached before he arrived.

"It's possible," Andrew said, "that I would also agree—if I knew what you were talking about."

Though Andrew's voice was gentle, several of the people stirred uncomfortably. Peel smoothed his pant leg and jabbed at his glasses. He spoke with a speed that made his unusually deep voice difficult to understand.

"We discussed this matter before you got here. We discussed it at length. We all agreed that it just won't do. The plans, that is. Much too grandiose."

"The plan I described," said Andrew, "is the result of seven years and nearly a million dollars' worth of work by teams of professional urban planners."

"I can't help that," snapped Peel. "They're wrong. Development is wrong. It would destroy the character of this area. We won't allow it."

"You won't allow it," repeated Andrew, his eyes white. "Aren't you forgetting something, Mr. Peel?"

"What?"

"You don't own the land."

The woodcarver leaned forward suddenly. "We have a right to life, liberty and the pursuit of happiness and that land is a part of all three for us. No one has any right to that much land. The old man must have been an out-and-out thief, because there's no honest way to get that much land. But that's all changed, because now we the people are finally going to assert our rights. You can't develop the land because we won't let you. We have our constitutional rights."

The woodcarver sat back and stopped speaking as abruptly as he had begun. The illogic of the man's tangled outburst left Andrew torn between rage and laughter.

"Title to the land," said Andrew finally, "resides with the Buckles Trust, not with the Friends of Frenchman's Cove. The Constitution and Bill of Rights that you paraphrase so freely guarantee my rights as well as yours. Or have you never heard of property rights and private ownership?"

The woodcarver frowned and looked at Peel. Peel straightened his cuffs and spoke again.

"Title doesn't mean much these days. In order to do that," Peel said, gesturing carelessly toward the scale models and transparent land use maps, "you need permission from the county planning board, the cities whose sphere of influence includes the ranch, the state shoreline people and a bunch of others." Peel smiled triumphantly. "Keep your precious title, Mr. McCartney. We have all that matters—control over land use."

Andrew could not help but smile, hearing Lee's words coming back at him out of the future. Peel moved uneasily.

"What's so funny?" demanded Peel suddenly. "I won't be laughed at, you know."

"The joke," said Andrew, "is on me. Or should I say, the joke is on all of us."

Andrew leaned forward, his hands flat on the old oak table. His pale eyes examined each closed face, each closed mind. He knew that he had lost, knew that there was nothing he could do, but he had to try once more . . . if only as a foretaste of the bitter revenge time would bring as it proved him right.

"Development will come to this ranch within ten years, no matter what you do. The days of sheep and cattle, citrus and row crops belongs to the past. Nothing you or I can do will bring back that past."

"No," said Peel emphatically. "No no no no. The ranch is a natural park. It must stay that way."

"Then buy the land and turn it into a park," said Andrew reasonably. "Lobby the county and the state. I'll make you a price on the ranch that will get me fired as chairman of the trust, but it would be worth it."

"I don't believe you," said Peel. "Besides, why should we buy the land? We can keep things just like they are without going to all that trouble."

Andrew's body tightened and his voice became very soft, very cold, like frost.

"Peel, pull your head out of your ass and look at the real world. The land is being taxed as though it was already developed—'highest and best use' is the phrase, I believe. The entire output of the ranch does not pay one-twelfth of the tax burden."

Peel shrugged impatiently.

"That's two sides of the box," said Andrew. "Taxes and profit. Another side is of my own creation. I wanted to keep the land intact, to be developed as sanely and beautifully as possible."

"Dammit," said Peel, slapping his hand against the table. "You weren't listening. We don't want any more people living in this area!"

"That's the fourth side," agreed Andrew with deceptive calm. "But you can't force me to keep the land as it is and at the same time have me pay taxes as though the land were already developed."

"We won't let you go ahead with that abomination you call a plan. We can stop you, you know."

"I know," said Andrew, his voice neutral once again. "You'll force delay after delay while land value rises and the tax burden becomes so great that I have to sell off chunks of the ranch just to survive."

Peel blinked. "Sell off what?"

"The land, Peel. Pieces of the dream."

Peel looked at Andrew, then looked away quickly, unable to confront the certainty in Andrew's white eyes.

"You didn't think that far ahead, did you?" continued Andrew softly. "You didn't think beyond the pretty view out of your bedroom window. Well, I'm tired of paying for your view, Peel. That's the first piece of land I'm going to sell."

Peel blinked again, rapidly. "I won't let—"

Andrew's hard laugh cut across Peel's words. "You can stop me from building a dream, but you can't stop me from selling a nightmare. One piece at a time. Fast-buck housing where oranges used to grow. No rhyme, no reason, no symmetry or beauty. Nothing but the slums of to-morrow built on the most beautiful land God ever made."

"I don't believe you," said Peel faintly.

"What you believe is no longer my problem," Andrew said with a thin smile. "Now if you will excuse me, I have some land to sell."

Andrew left the boardroom so swiftly that it was a moment before anyone realized he was gone. He walked quickly back to his office, knowing what he must do. He would sell off enough land to pay taxes while he cajoled, bribed and fought his dream through a hundred faceless committees. He could buy several years before the integrity of his dream would be hopelessly compromised by piecemeal sale.

Andrew stood at the glass wall of his office, looking out over the land he loved too much. He could fight, and he would, but he no longer believed he would win. Slowly, Andrew sat and reached for his telephone. As he dialed, he felt the land slipping away, the dream fading, everything vanishing into the cracks of time.

"Fred? This is Andrew. Just fine, and you? Good. A few years ago you said to call if I had any land for sale. . . ."

Andrew stared sightlessly out of the window as he sold the first piece of his dream.

The ending came more quickly than the beginning. Christina's rider slid through Senator James's committee and a small law was born, a few densely legal lines whose effect was to force the Buckles Trust to sell the Buckles Ranch. Andrew fought what came to be known as "Christina's Revenge" through federal courts, and at the same time he fought the Friends of Frenchman's Cove through local and state courts. He fought for three years, until the break-point came, when what was left of the land could no longer sustain his dream of a gracious future.

The land was given over to men who did not respect it, who had paid for it with money alone, not with their lives.

The break-point came months before anyone but Andrew knew. Local newspapers were still filled with vituperative arguments over the pros and cons of developing the Buckles Ranch. National newspapers were still running articles on the battle between the trust and Christina Buckles Heer over control of the remaining 120,000 acres of the ranch.

But Andrew knew it was over, knew it as surely as he knew the sunrise pouring over the hilltop where Lee and Cira were buried. With that knowledge of defeat came an odd feeling, like an immense burden lifting. All of his life the land had come first, preceding everything, even his own needs.

Andrew watched dawn strengthen into day, illuminating and flattening the hills. He felt a sudden, overwhelming need to be outside, to know the land as he once had, personally, intimately, to see the land as it had been and was, not as it could have been.

An hour later Andrew parked his car near the old Buckles Ranch Store and began to walk between the fragrant green rows of orange and lemon groves. He crossed dusty roads between fields of beans and peppers, asparagus and strawberries. He walked the wet furrows between all the different row crops, kicking stones out of narrow irrigation ditches with practiced skill, pulling tall Johnson grass from the mouths of culverts and furrows, watching water sparkle in the warm golden light.

Day after day he dressed in jeans, blue shirt and muddy boots, his only sign of authority a ring of keys that admitted him to the silent, locked confines of the past, phased-out packing houses and bean sheds whose machinery was coated with neglect. He left his fingerprints in the dust, remembering the day he had helped install a machine whose inner workings he understood as well as he understood the ramifications of Christina's Revenge.

There were days when Andrew's peace was broken, when necessity or carelessness brought him to a road that went to the edge of land he had sold, showing him pieces of a broken dream where earthmovers peeled away the

489

soil in great thick strips and the smell of subsoil and diesel mingled uneasily. It was then that Andrew decided the time had come to ride the coastal hills and inland mountains. He went to the ranch stables and saddled the Tennessee Walker he had bought for the infrequent days when he had time to ride.

The tall, dust-colored horse took him over the land, ghostly echo of another horse, another man, another time. The horse found old trails winding through gray-green chaparral canyons, taking Andrew to places he had forgotten existed, secret places where wind keened between black rock walls, where coyotes and eagles pursued their solitary ways, where mountain lions still moved like tawny shadows over the land.

It was the horse that led Andrew up a game trail, through a canyon that twisted and narrowed until it clawed toward a huge outcrop of rock almost at the top of the highest mountain. At the base of the massive rock was a spring surrounded by maple trees and knee-high grass, a silent place where leaves divided sunlight into luminous shades of green and gold.

Andrew dismounted and stood for a long, long time, remembering Lee's description of a hidden spring whose water was flecked with the same gold that haunted Cira's eyes.

The tall horse pulled impatiently at the reins, eager for the water whose scent had lured him up the rugged canyon trail. Andrew let the horse drink, then mounted and rode down out of the mountains, seeing nothing but gold, hearing nothing but the past whispering in every piece of chaparral lining the canyon with no name.

In those last months, Andrew was almost entirely alone. He attended no meetings, went to no luncheons, took few calls, spoke to no one he did not have to.

Christina's life was almost as solitary, for many of the same reasons. Like Andrew, from the moment the rider went through Congress, Christina was wholly caught up in the struggle for the land. Like Andrew, she saw no friends and took no lovers. But unlike Andrew, she believed she would win. And she had the comfort of a son.

Buck had watched his mother's lengthy, often angry telephone calls to potential business partners and he had been in the background of a hundred business meetings that masqueraded as dinner parties. He had become a tall, silent, intense boy who understood too much to stay a child and not enough to become a man. Nor could Christina help her son; she was too driven by circumstances and dreams to help even herself.

In desperation, Buck turned to the land, slipping out of the house into hills where cattle grazed. The challenges of the land were direct and comprehensible—a crumbling trail, the warning quiver of a rattlesnake, cold rain or wind, hunger, his own inexperience. Buck met the challenges and was comforted. Each time he returned to the land he was a little stronger, a little more resilient. The coastal hills and bluffs overlooking the sea became his second home, his only family.

As the months passed, bringing Christina closer and closer to her goal of owning the land, Buck became tougher, quicker, as supple as the mountain lions he fervently hoped to see one day. He had heard two old ranch hands talking about cougar tracks in a sandy canyon north of his home. It was a canyon he had never explored because of its distance from the house, but today he was determined to go there.

The canyon was almost in the center of the wide stretch of coastland that was still intact. Buck walked quickly, his sack lunch and canteen knocking comfortably against his hip, his clear gray eyes alert for snakes as he scrambled up a winding sandy chute to the blufftop. But the sounds he made masked those of the tall, dust-colored horse that was descending the same narrow chute.

The horse saw Buck and shied violently, sitting back on its hocks, sending sand and pebbles flying. Even as Buck leaped off of the trail, he saw the rider yank up on the reins, holding the horse upright with a combination of sheer strength and skill. The horse scrambled frantically,

491

hooves flailing, until it found balance again. The rider dismounted in a swift, smooth motion. He stood by the frightened horse's head and spoke in soft, low tones.

Andrew looked around quickly as he calmed his horse. He saw the boy standing very still, well off of the trail. Andrew nodded, approving the boy's quick action; few children would have been either smart or fast enough to get out of the way. Andrew found himself wishing that Thomas Peel had showed just a fraction of the boy's intelligence and pragmatism. Then he put the thought out of his head, keeping a promise to himself not to curse what he could not change.

Andrew looked up again, making sure that the boy had not moved.

"It's all right, sir," said the boy distinctly, but softly. "There's plenty of room now."

Andrew led the horse down the rest of the chute. The boy did not move until Andrew looked back and gestured for him to follow. When Andrew reached the bottom, he turned and waited. After a few moments of watching the boy's uncanny balance as he descended the scrambling chute, Andrew knew that the child must be Lee's great-grandson, Christina's child, the boy known as Buck.

When the boy slid to a graceful halt at the bottom of the chute, Andrew felt separate, almost physical shocks as he recognized Christina in Buck's triangular face, sensed Champ in the boy's smile and Joy's presence in the boy's beautiful skin. But most of all Andrew saw Lee, the past echoing out of the future, changed and yet the same. Buck moved with Lee's grace, waited with Lee's quiet confidence and most of all he watched with Lee's unflinching gray eyes.

"For a moment up there, I thought you were a trespasser," Andrew said. "I can see I was mistaken."

The irony and sadness in Andrew's voice confused Buck. Andrew sensed it and explained softly, "You're very like your great-grandfather. If your hair weren't brown. . . ." Andrew smiled and said no more, knowing that the boy could not understand what it was like to see the past returning, changed and yet the same, separate levels in an endless spiral. "Do you know who I am, Buck?"

Andrew took off his hat and ran his fingers through hair more silver than dark. Buck nodded, then spoke with a voice that was surprisingly deep for a boy not yet twelve.

"Yes, sir. Mom pointed you out to me at the barbeque last year. I recognized you right away when you came off that horse so fast. You don't move like other people."

Andrew smiled crookedly, surprised and a bit flattered. "You're no slouch yourself." Andrew paused, reluctant to mount and ride away from the boy with Lee's eyes. "What brings you out here?" Andrew said casually. "You're five miles from home."

"Cougars," said Buck eagerly.

Andrew's left eyebrow arched in silent query.

"Mountain lions," Buck said. "You know. Cats."

"I know," said Andrew, smiling.

"I heard two of the ranch hands talking about cougar sign in September canyon."

"And you want to see a live cougar."

"Yes, Mr. McCartney. I sure do."

"Call me Andrew," he said, and was rewarded with a wide smile from Buck. "Does your mother know you're here?"

"She knows I like to walk in the hills. She doesn't mind."

"She might," said Andrew, watching the boy closely, "if she knew who you were with right now."

"Oh, no, sir—Andrew. She talks about you a lot."

"In front of you?" said Andrew wryly. "I'd think she would be more careful of her language."

Buck's left eyebrow arched in surprise and confusion. "She gets angry with you, sure, but I've never heard her say anything really bad. She told me once that—"

Buck stopped abruptly, caught between his child's sense of candor and his adult sense that he might be tell-

493

ing family secrets. But he instinctively trusted the soft voiced man.

"Go ahead," said Andrew, smiling. "I'm sure she's said worse to my face."

"She said you're a good man, a strong man," Buck said, his eyes clear and unshadowed as he searched his memory for the exact words his mother had used. "She said I could do a lot worse than to grow up like you."

Only Andrew's long experience in hiding his feelings kept his shock from showing. Even so, Buck sensed that something had changed. Andrew's face was suddenly unreadable and his eyes were distant, seething with emotions lying just beneath a veneer of control.

"I better go," said Buck miserably, wondering what he had done wrong. "I'm sorry."

"Wait." Andrew held out his hand, touching Buck lightly on the arm, asking him to stay rather than demanding. Andrew took a deep breath and smiled down at the boy whose troubled gray eyes were a mirror of his own. "Do you ride, Buck?"

Buck shook his head.

"Would you like to?"

"Oh, wow, sure!" said Buck excitedly, looking at the big, dust-colored horse waiting near Andrew.

Andrew nodded, pleased that Buck had neither fear nor hesitation about the big animal.

"Good," said Andrew.

With a single motion, Andrew mounted the tall horse. He set his feet in the stirrups, leaned down and swung Buck up behind the saddle. The boy was more solid than he looked, and surprisingly strong. He settled lightly behind Andrew. Other than a delighted grin, there was nothing in Buck's manner to suggest that he had never been on a horse.

Andrew moved the horse into a slow walk. Buck balanced instinctively, adjusting himself to the horse's rhythms with the ease of a natural rider. After a few minutes, Andrew urged the horse into the marvelously smooth, fast gait the animal had been bred for. Buck's reaction was a soft whoop of pleasure when the ground began gliding by at a rapid rate.

"Still want to find a cougar?" asked Andrew over his shoulder.

"Oh, boy!"

Andrew grinned, feeling younger with every minute. "Then hang on."

Andrew turned the dust-colored horse back toward the narrow, sandy chute. When he felt Buck's wiry arms wrap around his waist, Andrew smiled. Horse and riders took the steep climb with ease. Andrew looked over his shoulder into gray eyes that were brilliant with excitement.

"You're a natural rider, Buck."

"Anybody could ride this horse," said Buck, patting the animal's rump. "He's as smooth as a bike. Is he like the horse great-grandfather Lee used to ride?"

The question sank into Andrew, catching him unaware. He had never defined his reason for choosing to ride the tall horse. "I guess it is," he said slowly. "There's an old picture of Lee on a horse this color. A big horse."

"Mother has a picture like that on her dresser. She said Lee was the most handsome man she'd ever seen, except for you. Was he really a great man?"

There was a quality in Buck's voice that told Andrew the boy's question was not as casual as it seemed. "What makes you ask?" said Andrew, wanting to turn around but sensing that Buck would find it easier to talk to his back.

"Well, Mom practically worships him, but other people and kids, and the newspapers, make it sound like he was awful. A crook and a thief and . . . robber baron seems to be the favorite."

Andrew considered all of the easy answers and rejected them. Buck needed and deserved more. Anything less than the best Andrew could give would be as bad as a slap in the face.

"That's a hard one," said Andrew quietly. "Lee was not like everybody else," Andrew said, groping for words and concepts a child could understand. "Lee was stronger, smarter, quicker. He was also gentle and funny and sad. He wanted to do things that most people simply didn't understand. And what people don't understand, they suspect. What they don't have, they envy.

"They envied Lee for what he had and for what he was, and they never understood him. He was a great man," finished Andrew softly.

"But how did he get all this land and keep it?" said Buck, asking the same question that had been thrown at him many times.

"Lee's father, your great-great-grandfather, bought the land from the Picos, among others. Lee inherited the land from his father, and then Lee spent his life fighting to keep it. He learned, and I learned, that you don't own land—land owns you." Andrew stared ahead, remembering too many things, trying to explain two lifetimes to Buck, and to himself. "Lee's best friend all of his life was Gilberto Zavala, a cowboy. No, he was more. Gil was a vaquero. Do you know what that means?" Andrew asked, glancing over his shoulder as though he needed reassurance that he was not talking to himself.

Buck nodded.

"I can remember Lee saying to Gil, many times, that he wished they could trade places so that Lee would be the vaquero and Gil the ranchero."

"Why didn't they?" Buck said quickly. Then, more slowly, "I guess I know why. You are what you are."

"That's right, Buck," said Andrew softly. "You can't escape your heritage. It isn't all of you, but it's always a part of whatever you are."

Andrew was suddenly silent, remembering what he wanted to ignore—Buck's father, weak, cruel, not entirely sane. Even as Andrew had recognized the Buckles heritage in the boy, Andrew had searched for that part of Buck that was, inevitably, Heer.

They did not see a cougar that day, but neither seemed to notice. Almost in spite of himself, Andrew's reservations melted before the obvious pleasure Buck took in his company. When, in the late afternoon, Andrew brought

Buck within half a mile of his mother's hillside home, the boy was reluctant to leave.

"I wonder if Mom would let me get a horse," he said wistfully.

"Not if she knows who you'll go riding with," said Andrew wryly. He stretched, feeling the warmth of the sun across his shoulders. "But I'll bet I can find a horse for you to ride."

"Really?" said Buck eagerly. "When?"

"Tomorrow. I'll meet you here at nine o'clock. Okay?" Andrew hesitated, struck by a thought. "Aren't you playing hooky?"

"School was out two weeks ago," responded Buck indignantly.

Something in Buck's protest told Andrew that the boy had played hooky more than once. Laughing silently, Andrew swung the boy to the ground, and then held onto him while Buck's legs adjusted to carrying weight again.

"You'll be sore tomorrow," warned Andrew.

"I don't care. See you at nine."

Buck turned and walked toward the elegant, multilevel home one hillside away. He looked back several times, as if to reassure himself that Andrew was real. He waved to the man who sat so easily on the tall horse. Then, with a last look, Buck went over, wriggled through the barbed-wire pasture fence and ran toward his house.

Andrew was half an hour early the following day, but Buck was there, waiting as patiently as he could. The sun was already hot and a dry wind was blowing, a Santa Ana wind sweeping from the mountains to the sea.

A long-legged sorrel mare followed Andrew's tall horse. The mare had a disposition that was unruffled by wind or noise or birds that flew up beneath her feet. For all her even temperament, the mare was spirited. Buck quickly learned that the mare was a living creature not entirely unlike himself. Treated well, she responded well; treated abruptly, she turned stubborn. After half an hour of work that was more demonstration than instruction,

Andrew decided that Buck could handle the mare about as easily as a duck handled water.

"Hey," said Andrew. "Let's go take a look at the ranch."

Buck's response was a wide grin that made Andrew feel twenty years younger. Buck happily fell in beside Andrew as the dust-colored horse headed out onto the coastal plateau that gently rose toward the coastal hills. They rode with dry wind blowing over their shoulders, a wind from the distance, redolent of sun and dust and chaparral. Sometimes they dismounted, walking side by side through golden grass while hawks turned and cried overhead.

Andrew and Buck followed game and cattle trails into coastal canyons that cut deeply into the hills, through canyon bottoms where the wind spent itself among sycamores and thickets of wild grape. They rode in companionable silence broken by Buck's questions about the shape of the land or the growth of plants or the lives of the animals that moved like ghosts through the underbrush.

Once they surprised a doe and two fawns grazing in the shadows flowing out of a canyon mouth. Buck and Andrew sat motionlessly on their horses, watching the elegant wild creatures feed. Then the doe sensed an alien presence. Deer and fawns vanished like smoke into a tangle of grape vines and sycamore.

"I've never seen a wild deer," said the boy, whispering even though the deer had gone.

Suddenly unable to speak, Andrew nodded. He had a dizzy feeling of time turning, uncoiling the spiral until he was forty years younger, seeing a wild deer for the first time all over again. Past and present fused and he was unsure whether he was the man or the boy.

Andrew stared at Buck while the hair on the back of his neck moved. Andrew sensed an unconscious knowledge within himself, a realization that eluded articulation, a ghost seen out of the corner of his eye.

Like a wild creature, Buck sensed Andrew's scrutiny.

The boy turned, looking at Andrew with Lee's eyes, his own eyes, child and man.

"It's getting late," said Andrew. "We should start back."

Buck frowned. "I suppose," he said reluctantly.

"Does Christina—does your mother know where you are?"

Buck hesitated, then shook his head. "No," he said softly, his voice an unconscious imitation of Andrew. "I don't . . ."

Buck's voice faded. Andrew saw confusion rather than guilt on the boy's face. Whatever was bothering Buck was not as simple as slipping away from his mother without permission.

"Do you want to talk?" said Andrew.

"I don't know if I should," Buck answered seriously. "It's business, and Mom and you are—" He shrugged unhappily and said no more.

Andrew lifted his hat, running his hand through his hair, giving himself time to think. "I understand, Buck. If it helps any, your mother and I want the same things. It's just that our ways are separate."

Buck nodded several times, then spoke in a rush. "Mom's not home because she's at a meeting with some of the people who will be her partners. Maybe her partners. She's been worried about this meeting for months. She won't be back until late. She's been so worried," repeated Buck, as though it was a relief to admit it to somebody.

"Did she say why she was worried?" asked Andrew, before he thought how the question might appear to the boy. "You don't have to answer that," he said quickly. "I don't want you to say or do anything that would put you in the wrong with your mother."

Buck searched Andrew's eyes with an intelligence beyond his eleven years. As though he approved what he saw, Buck nodded. "I didn't really understand what was worrying her. What's a 'squeeze play?' "

Andrew frowned. The boy's words confirmed the information that Hennegan had uncovered. Andrew felt a sudden, strong grief for Christina, so near and yet so far from her dream, too far.

"Buck, I want you to take a message to your mother. Tell her I understand. Tell her I . . ." Andrew's voice died as he realized that he was putting the boy precisely in the position he had wanted to avoid. "Forget I said anything, Buck. I'll carry my own messages, if and when it's time. Until then, your mother will do all right. She's as strong as she is beautiful."

They did not speak of Christina again. It was as though they had a tacit realization of the nature of their days. They had created a world that was impervious to other people, other pressures, a world that could exist only if they did not speak Christina's name.

Buck met Andrew almost every day. They rode wherever curiosity and chance took them. They explored hills and mountains, canyons and silences that had changed little since Leander Buckles had ridden the same trails almost eighty years before.

But one day when Andrew met Buck, he saw that the boy was deeply unhappy. His eyes were pale, nearly opaque, much too old to be a child's eyes. Andrew looked at him and sensed that their serene world of land and horses, man and boy, had ended. Silently, Andrew handed Buck a tan Stetson that was a smaller replica of the one Lee had worn and the one Andrew now wore.

"Happy birthday," said Andrew.

"But—how did you know?"

"Spies," said Andrew, smiling crookedly. "Try it on."

Buck put the hat on his head with a smooth gesture that unconsciously imitated Andrew. "Perfect!" he said, smiling at last.

"That's good," said Andrew. "Hennegan's too old to look for another job. Come on, birthday boy, let's ride."

For a few hours the ride, the unexpected present and Andrew's deft conversation reconstructed the magic world where tomorrow never came. But Andrew knew, even as he smiled and laughed, that their world was as fragile as the shadows sliding deep within the boy's gray eyes. Andrew dismounted and waited for Buck to join him. They walked until finally, abruptly, Buck spoke, as though he could bear it no longer.

"Mom's so unhappy."

"Winning sometimes does that to people," said Andrew, stopping his horse and facing the boy.

"But she's not winning. She's losing. When I went in at bedtime she was crying. I've never seen her cry. I asked her what was wrong and she"— Buck swallowed suddenly—"she didn't seem to see me but she whispered 'I lost him and now I've lost the land.' She was crying and saying that over and over. I don't know if she even saw me. I—" he swallowed again. "I wanted to help but I couldn't."

Andrew put his hands on the boy's shoulders, comforting him wordlessly, wishing that he could slide back on time's spiral until Christina was sixteen and he could hold her, cry with her, and not have a lifetime of experiences separating them.

"I wish I could help her too," said Andrew simply.

"Who did she mean?" asked Buck, his voice muffled. "Who was the man she lost? My father?"

"I don't know," said Andrew, wanting to know as much as he wanted to hold Christina, sixteen again.

Buck's arms went around Andrew suddenly, holding him with a child's fierce, surprising strength. Unnoticed, Buck's hat tumbled to the ground.

"The land she lost," said Buck against Andrew's ribs. "Is it the ranch?"

"Yes."

"But—how? The men are her partners now. How could she lose?"

Andrew held Buck gently, wanting to tell the boy only those things he could understand. With a long sigh, Andrew began to speak slowly, trying to explain the ways of adults to a child.

"From the time you were born, your mother has

501

worked to control the Buckles Ranch. She felt that it was her right. Just as I felt it was mine."

Andrew's hands tightened unconsciously, thinking as always of the land, the golden empire that owned people while remaining free itself.

Andrew looked down into gray eyes almost as sad as his own.

"Christina waged a very smart, very tough war against me. And she won," said Andrew, trying to filter regret and anger out of his voice. "But she paid a very high price. Pyrrhic victory," whispered Andrew, looking over Buck's head into the past and future.

Buck stood unnaturally still, his head tipped back so that he could see Andrew's face. What he saw was not much different from the face that looked out of another of his mother's photographs, a faded picture of a boy on a horse. In front of him, protected in the circle of his arms, sat a tiny girl with hair the color of the sun.

The picture dissolved into Andrew speaking slowly as he held another child in his arms, wanting to protect this child as he had not been able to protect the other, knowing he could not.

"I was forced to sell the Buckles Ranch," Andrew said quietly. "Your mother's original plan was to buy the land herself, using what was left of her grandfather's legacy. The Crash hadn't left much, but—" Andrew stopped, realizing that the boy did not understand. "During the years your mother and I fought, the price of the ranch doubled, then tripled, then doubled again. She found that while she could force me to sell the ranch, she didn't have enough money to buy it herself."

"Was that why she needed partners?" asked Buck hesitantly, after it was clear that Andrew was not going to say any more.

"Yes. She promised what she already owned of the ranch to help pay for the part she wanted to buy. Her partners gave her cash for her promise."

Andrew looked down and saw that the boy did not understand.

502

"It's complicated, Buck, but the result is simple. Your mother's partners are corporations, companies. They bought the ranch, which was what she wanted. But there are international problems which are forcing her partners to sell off the land immediately, rather than hold it as she wanted to. The sale will make her one of the richest women in the world, but she won't have the land." Andrew shook his head. "That wasn't what your mother wanted. Nor did I . . ."

Buck closed his eyes, understanding more from the sorrow in Andrew's voice than from his words. Then Buck looked up again, sad and angry at the same time.

"Why couldn't the two of you get together?" demanded Buck.

Suddenly Andrew wanted to turn away, to mount his horse and ride off, never to look back, never again to hear the question he had so many times asked himself. He started to step back, but the child's arms were too tight, too strong, as unavoidable as tomorrow. Buck's unspoken plea was as potent and unreasoning as the sun, forcing light into areas left dark by chance and choice, unbearably bright, blinding.

Andrew saw, but could not answer. He could not touch the child and talk about rape and revenge, murder and hatred, the tangled history of Heer and Buckles and the land . . . and worst of all, about the sly weakness of a man called Jason Heer, Buck's father.

Buck stepped back, frightened by Andrew's white eyes. For a moment the boy wavered, blinded by tears and shame. Then he wiped away the tears as though they belonged to someone else. He looked up at the man who stood so close to him, so far away.

"You're leaving, aren't you?" said Buck, an adult certainty making his voice steady.

"Yes, it's time that we got back," responded Andrew, his voice as emotionless as the pale sky.

Buck shook his head. "That's not what I meant. The ranch is being sold tomorrow and you're leaving."

Andrew's eyes were very pale, but Buck did not look away. "Yes, I'm leaving."

"Aren't you even going to say good-bye to Mom?"

"Your mother," said Andrew coolly, "hasn't spoken to me for many years."

"She's afraid of you," said the boy softly.

The words sank into Andrew like thin knives, cutting him until he bled. Only Christina had ever been able to hurt him like that. And now her son.

Andrew bent down and picked up Buck's hat.

"Andrew?" asked Buck hesitantly.

Andrew looked down into the boy's eyes, older than they had been a moment ago, before he knew that adults could bleed.

"I'm—I'm sorry. I was just trying to—" The boy's eyes were wide, the color of rain. "I didn't mean to make it worse. It's just that she's so unhappy and you're un-happy—and I—I love both of you!" he finished defiantly.

Buck took his hat and yanked it into place, using the exact gesture that Andrew used. Andrew hesitated, then reached out until his palm lay along the boy's face, touching skin that was amazingly smooth and soft. Buck looked up, his gray eyes young and luminous, asking and needing. Andrew felt time turning again, uncoiling, and he was twelve once more, aching from the taunts of other children. He had mounted a horse and ridden blindly, looking for something that he could not find until Lee found him, held him, told him quietly that he was loved.

Andrew blinked and time curled around him again. He realized that he had never spoken of love to anyone but Lee, had said nothing through all the times he had held Christina, both of them too afraid to trust. He wondered if it was too late now, if it had always been too late for Lee's bastard. And he wondered if he had the courage to find out.

"I love you, Buck."

Andrew spoke so softly that the boy sensed more than heard the simple words. Buck smiled suddenly, beauti-fully, and then he turned away, almost shy.

504

"Then you won't be leaving?" asked Buck with a quick sideways glance.

"Not this instant," Andrew said, smiling in return. "There's time for me to show you one last place on the ranch."

Childlike, Buck ignored the implication that Andrew would leave later. The boy mounted eagerly, then turned toward Andrew with barely concealed impatience.

"Where are we going?"

"Just a few hills over," Andrew said, swinging easily onto his tall horse. "You can see almost all of the ranch from there. It's the highest coastal hill, the one that dawn touches first." Andrew turned his horse. "Your great-grandfather is buried there."

They rode in silence but for the chaparral whispering to itself and the dry wind. The dust-colored horse needed no guidance; it had been this way many times before. Buck looked around at grass and brush, sky and ocean, but most of all he looked at the man who rode beside him, as silent as a river flowing deep beneath the land.

Winter storms and summer sun had gradually returned the tiny graveyard to the land. Andrew had seen the process, had fought it, then had accepted it with a serene sense of rightness. Little was left now but the two names carved by Gil into an outcrop of native stone. Names, and a jacaranda tree planted by Andrew, sheltered from the ocean wind by the outcrop, tree and rock merging in a unity of opposites.

It was Andrew who first recognized the figure leaning with one hand on the jacaranda tree, turning at the sound of hoofbeats, and for an instant she was sixteen, light pouring through hair that was pale and thick, the color of his dreams.

Sunshine.

Buck looked up, sensing the change in Andrew, but Andrew saw only Christina, standing between jacaranda and stone, more beautiful than his memories. Instinctively Buck slowed, then stopped his horse.

Christina straightened, not knowing whether to walk or

505

run away. In the end she could do neither, trapped between jacaranda and stone, what she wanted and what she feared, past and present. When Andrew dismounted and began walking toward her, she saw the second horse, the second rider, her son waiting. Then she would have turned and run, but Andrew was too quick, too close. Christina leaned heavily against the jacaranda tree and closed her eyes, wishing she had lived one day less.

"Christina?" said Andrew, suddenly unsure. She looked fragile and worn, barely able to stand. Her clothes were dusty, stained, as though she had walked here without using the path. "Christina?"

Christina's hands came up to her face, hiding the tears that burned behind her eyelids, hearing her loss in the resonance of his voice, his gray eyes shadowed with concern.

"I'm sorry," said Christina, "I'm sorry. But don't take him away from me, please don't take him. I've lost Lee and you and the land. I've lost so much . . . I can't lose him too."

Andrew stood close enough to touch Christina, but he did not, afraid that if he touched her he would not let her go again.

"Christina," Andrew said quietly. "You're not making any sense."

Christina opened her eyes. The violet shadows and exhaustion made Andrew want to take her in his arms, but he did not, knowing how she could sink into him and he into her. He was afraid to risk the small peace he had found in the last weeks.

"You found out," Christina said raggedly, "and now you're going to take Buck away from me."

Andrew felt the skin on his neck move. Without thinking, he reached out and shook her.

"You're not making a damn bit of sense," he said roughly.

The shock of Andrew's touch went through both of them. Christina trembled between his hands, burning them. She closed her eyes, unable to meet his, remembering the time he had called her Jason's whore. The memory of that had strengthened her throughout the fight for the land, but now nothing was left but the humiliation of having loved a man who did not love her.

Christina's eyes opened, clear and violet, as empty as the sky. Andrew looked into them and read a defeat as great as his own.

"You've won," Christina said tonelessly. "You always win. You and Lee, both so strong. Aren't you strong enough to leave Buck for me?"

The simple anguish in Christina's question moved Andrew as nothing else could have. He knew too well how such defeat and humiliation and helplessness felt. He had never wanted her to know that feeling.

"Christina," Andrew said, touching her cheek gently. "I'm not trying to take your son away from you. I have no reason to. The land is gone. Nothing can change that."

"Then why?" said Christina blinking. Her eyes focused on Andrew and her hands gripped his shoulders with a strength that was almost painful. "Why have you spent so much time with him? Why have you showed him all of the ranch, our memories, canyons and eagles and mountains, the silence and the sky—everything Lee showed you and you showed me."

Andrew's lips twisted into what could have been a smile. "I never thought I'd say this about a Heer," said Andrew bitterly, "but I've spent a lot of time with Buck because he's damned good company."

Christina's eyes went blank with surprise as she heard the truth in Andrew's voice. She shook her head as though he had slapped her.

"Christina, I know you hate me, but please believe me. I don't want to take your son away from you." Andrew hesitated, then continued with an intensity in his soft voice that he could not conceal. "But I would like to . . . share him . . . once in a while. Could that be arranged?"

Christina kept shaking her head until tears and pale hair caught light in a tangled network of gold.

"Why?" Christina asked, as though Andrew had not answered. "I don't understand."

"I don't understand it either," said Andrew quietly, "but then, neither of us ever understood much about love, did we?"

"Are you saying that you love Buck?" asked Christina, her words slow, unbelieving. "Is that why you brought him to Lee's grave, and your mother's?"

"Yes . . . but I wasn't planning on telling him about Cira and Lee."

Christina said nothing for long moments, searching his eyes. "Tell him," she said quickly, recklessly. "A boy should know about his grandparents."

Andrew's eyes went blank with shock as he realized what Christina was telling him.

"His *grandparents!*" Andrew's fingers dug viciously into Christina's arms. "Haven't you had enough of hurting me? What kind of cruel game are you playing now?"

For the second time in her life, Christina felt Andrew's fury aimed solely at her. She set her jaw against his white eyes and the pain of his fingers digging into her arms.

"No game," Christina said through her teeth. "Just something we should have tried a long time ago. The truth, Andrew," she said bitterly. "The simple goddamned truth. I was wrong about the land. You were wrong about me. I'm not Jason's whore. Buck is your son."

"I don't believe you," whispered Andrew, knowing that what she said was true, afraid to believe in words that changed the past and the future. "You would have told me sooner."

"Why?" Christina laughed raggedly. "Would you have believed anything Jason's whore said? You were wrong, Andrew."

"And you made me pay by taking the ranch."

"Not just for me," Christina said, exhaustion thinning her voice. "It was for my son. Your son. Oh, Christ . . . what does it matter now? It's gone. I did what I believed right and I was wrong. Everything's gone."

Christina stood between Andrew's hard hands, crying

508

silently, her violet eyes staring through him to a past that she could not affect though it kept reaching out and tripping her. Andrew felt her sag subtly, saw defeat and exhaustion pulling her apart as he himself had been pulled apart. He did not know if he could help her or himself, but he did know that he could not stand and watch her wither between his hands.

"Don't cry," whispered Andrew, pulling her close. "Sunshine, don't cry anymore."

Andrew closed his eyes and whispered against Christina's hair until he sensed Buck approaching. Andrew looked, saw the boy watching him with Lee's eyes, his own eyes, the past curling toward him out of the future. Andrew bent his head, shutting out everything but Christina, sinking into her and she into him, holding onto her and hoping that this time tomorrow would not come.

If you liked the movie,
you'll love the book!

FRENCH POSTCARDS 14297-3 $2.25
by Norma Klein

An utterly charming story of mischief and romance in Paris, written with the same warm sensitivity that Norma Klein has brought to her other bestselling Fawcett novels IT'S OK IF YOU DON'T LOVE ME and LOVE IS ONE OF THE CHOICES.

THE IN-LAWS 14252-3 $1.95
by David Rogers

The hilarious tale of a prime crime and young love in search of a motel. From the Warner Brothers motion picture starring Peter Falk and Alan Arkin.

CAPRICORN ONE 14024-5 $1.75
by Ron Goulart

To all appearances the launching of Capricorn One, the first spaceship to Mars, seemed perfectly normal. But behind the scenes, a NASA director was warning the three astronauts that their spacecraft was faulty. For them, a special fate had been arranged. . . .

ICE CASTLES 14154-3 $1.95
by Leonore Fleischer

Alexis Winston was a beautiful young woman with a dream— to become a champion figure skater. She was also in love with Nick, her childhood sweetheart, who had some dreams of his own. . . . Some dreams are shattered. Some come true.